Nucky Mac

A. D. FITZGERALD

Rosewood Publications
County Limerick
Ireland

Cover photograph by Geraldine Daly

ISBN-13: 978 - 1460935316

For Mary

Be not afeard, the isle is full of noises, sounds and sweet airs that give delight and hurt not. Sometimes a thousand twangling instruments will hum about mine ears, and sometimes voices that, if I then had waked after a long sleep, will make me sleep again, and then, in dreaming, the clouds methought would open and show riches ready to drop upon me, that when I waked, I cried to dream again.

The Tempest
William Shakespeare

Chapter One

Edward Conway had decided to be as good as his word. Today, being the first day of May, he would leave his home in the fashionable suburb of Corbally and venture forth. Alone and on foot, he would strike out for a quarter of his native city that was as unknown and mysterious, it seemed to him, as the Amazon Basin itself.

He had come prepared, however. He wore his overcoat, his university scarf, his gloves, and his green wellingtons. The day, so far, had been quite warm and he did feel that his insulation was perhaps a little overdone but you could never tell with the weather. There might still be a cold snap, even in May, and it was better to be safe than sorry. In any case, his overcoat, with its numerous pockets, was ideal for the storage of essential travelling accessories, which included: map, compass, dictionary, a field guide to flora and fauna, binoculars, a pocket-knife, a pocket-camera, notebook and pencil, a bottle of Detox antiseptic, a bottle of Dopacof expectorant, plasters and salt tablets. Lastly, there was his umbrella, neatly furled and sharpened to a point. He would use it in its customary role of keeping the rain off, but, should it prove necessary, he would employ it as a defensive weapon to fend off would-be attackers.

The place had a name, as they say. Though exactly what was meant by having a 'name', he wasn't sure. It was a term his mother, his aunt, and others of their generation would use, and although obviously disparaging, it was not said without some reverence in the voice. At all events, he was told to keep well away, and being a dutiful son not wishing to upset his poor widowed mother, he had. It would suit his purpose on this occasion, however, to conclude that the less his mother knew of his enterprise the better. Though poor in the sympathy provoking sense of the word, his mother was not poor financially. While not exactly rolling in money, they were comfortably-off, being well provided for by the shrewd foresight of his father who died when Edward was but a babe in arms.

All his life he had felt he owed his father a great deal. The proximity of his father's death and his own birth seemed too much of a coincidence for him and, though assured many times that it was God's will, he could never quite shake off the suspicion that he was somehow responsible. Absence makes the heart grow fond, as the saying goes, but the absence of a man he never really knew, a ghost, a shadow, inextricably linked in his memory to God's will, such an absence is awe-inspiring. Yes, his heart had grown fond, his imagination and his mother's loving testimony had seen to that but there was much more in his heart.

'...make your father proud of you...' he could hear his mother say, her words filling his mind like a sacred mantra, '...you're your father's son, so do your best...'

And so the perfectionist was born. And just like all perfectionists it wasn't long before his best wasn't good enough. It never would be. The unbearable burden on his delicately sensitive soul would lead to an addiction to the proprietary cough medicine, Dopacof. His dependence on the sweet, fortified linctus was so great that he was unable to function if deprived for any length of time of the elixir's tender mercies. Eventually the strain proved too much, and so reality and fantasy, with the help of a malicious prankster, compromised on a mental breakdown. This would happen in his final year at university. That was six months ago.

He was returned home to recuperate. Home to River-view, Sycamore Avenue, Corbally, the semi-detached forge of his semi-detached and troubled psyche. A sad and reluctant dropout, he was left scrabbling about for the scattered jigsaw pieces of his sanity. But he was on the mend now and had managed to piece together most of his mind. There was enough of him there to return to his ambition of doing his best, not letting anyone down and making people proud of him.

Today was his first day outside the precincts of Corbally since his fall from grace. With the concerned permission of his mother he had sallied forth to take up the reins of life again. He walked with the light step of a man reprieved. He drank the cool, blessed breeze on his face and savoured its normality. He was delighting in life, in the simple things. In the sun that played peek-a-boo from behind the clouds. In the discarded yoghurt carton carelessly tossed from a passing car. In the paw prints of a roving dog set down forever in the cement of pavement repair. How wonderfully random it all seemed.

His walk stepped to a marching rhythm but he remained careful to avoid treading on any living thing that might cross his path. He had a kind regard for all of nature and the unnecessary loss of a hapless beetle or centipede or some other innocuous creature was to be regretted. This sanction he extended to the tiny plants that had somehow managed to creep through the cracks in the pavement. He marvelled at their pioneering tenacity. Such vitality had a right to a place in the sun.

The strain in his neck that was developing from looking down, prompted him to cast his inquiring admiration elsewhere. His neck muscles eased back in relief as he turned his attention to the old stone wall that accompanied the footpath as far as O'Dwyer Bridge. There was much to be admired in the wall. It sheltered lichens, mosses, dandelions, stonecrop, ivy and herb robert. It was home to spiders, slugs, snails, beetles, mice, shrews and more besides. The stones, set in their aging mortar, were a variety of shapes and sizes with flat and irregular surfaces. Nurtured by the very mortar that held it together, and tended to by the husbandry of sun, wind and rain, the wall was indeed a reservoir of life. With a gloved hand Conway patted its surface to acknowledge his approval and his fellowship.

In his pre-occupation he failed to acknowledge several passers-by who were on a nodding acquaintance with him. Each in turn had eyed him for a salute in vain and had gone on their way composing theories as to why their nods of recognition were not returned. These theories included the possibility that Conway hadn't seen them, that he was an odd bastard, that he must be blind, or was up to no good. The wall, ending abruptly at O'Dwyer Bridge, brought back to Conway the reason for his journey. He was, after all, a man with a mission. True, his journey was a diversion from homebred boredom, but it was a diversion with an ulterior purpose. The ulterior purpose of this journey would form the basis of a thesis entitled *Proximity and Inaccessibility*, and sub-titled, *the nearer things are, the less you know about them.*

It was a desperate, last-ditch effort to try and retrieve his interrupted academic ambitions. A thesis that would secure his university degree and thereby provide an unconditional pardon from his mother, and everyone else concerned, for having a temporary and very inconvenient lapse of sanity. A thesis that would investigate and survey, both physically and culturally, the unknown and the uncharted.

For hours, the night before, while May Eve bonfires blazed all over Limerick, he had pored over a map of the City and its environs, focusing his attention especially on the oblong blob of land that was King's Island. A sausage-shaped island, roughly one mile in length and a third of a mile in breadth, it was used as a thoroughfare, a dubious stepping-stone, between Corbally and the City. Here, the Shannon River slows and meanders as if having second thoughts about passing through the great City of Limerick. Indeed, one could imagine it to be divided in its intentions, as the river separates to form the offshoot Abbey River, a slender arm of water that cradles the Island's eastern bank. Again, if one allowed poetic licence to run amok, one might assume that the Abbey River was indeed the midwife to Mother Shannon and her alluvial babe, the Island.

After a short journey below Mathew Bridge, one of four connecting the Island to its hinterland, the Abbey rejoins the Shannon to complete a tidal, amniotic encirclement. The eastern side of the Island is mostly floodplain marshland and accommodates the fluctuating moods of the Abbey River somewhat like a sponge. The western side of the Island incorporates, among many other things, no less than two corporation housing estates that fringe the marshland. Conway paused at the thought. It wasn't too late, he told himself as he neared the brow of the bridge, he could still abandon this perilous quest and continue in a straight line along Athlunkard Street, which would take him to the relative safety of commercial enterprise in the City Centre. There, he could while away the hours, book-browsing in Eason's and O'Mahony's, or thumb through LPs in HMV and Clancy's, or even join the motley groups of stagnant pedestrians content with window shopping.

But he would have none of it. He would not yield to timidity. Seizing on his resolve and aided by a timely gust of wind that enveloped him at the corner of O'Dwyer Bridge and Athlunkard Boat Club, he propelled himself off to the right, off the well-travelled path of Athlunkard Street and down the one less travelled that might well make all the difference. The die was cast and his mind settled to the certainty that he was on his way. To the resolved mind all is easy. There would be no going back.

The path he travelled was dusty, its surface consisting of loose grit scattered over larger aggregate stones that had bedded down with the passage of time. It was a broad path with a grass and weed verge on either side, hemmed in by the perimeter walls of a house and garden to his left and the boat club to his right. The walls were topped with shards of glass to keep intruders out. Like daggers, as much as four or five inches long, they were bottle-green, bottle-brown, but mostly crystal clear. Turned towards the sky they refracted sunlight, what was there of it, into scattering hues. Conway was enchanted. 'Very Newtonian,' he informed himself, 'very Newtonian indeed...'

As he gazed upon the prismatic splendour, he became aware of a strange whistling coming from the canopy of a chestnut tree that had spread beyond the boundary wall of the boat club. He cocked an ear and listened. It *was* peculiar. Unlike any bird he had ever heard. Maybe it was a mimicking starling adding to its counterfeit repertoire. Or a blow-in from abroad, blown off course by the recent storms. Perhaps it was a sick bird in its death throes.

However, as he was soon to discover, it was none of these things. With first a faint rustling and then a sudden whoosh, leaves and twigs were sent flying everywhere. From nowhere, there appeared before him a grey-haired gentleman dressed in a green tweed suit. Hanging by his arms from a swaying branch, he seemed to be contemplating his wingtip brogues that hovered just feet above the ground.

Conway stood transfixed by the dangling spectacle. The man, his shirt and pullover riding up to expose a bleached potbelly and scarlet braces, fixed him with a stare. As leaves and twigs continued to fall around him, he spoke.

'And what, may I ask, are you looking at?'

'I...' Conway began before being interrupted.

'And who, may I ask, gave you permission to traipse about looking all inquisitive?'

'I didn't know I needed permission,' Conway protested timidly.

'Officially,' the man said, looking wisely downwards as he considered his words, 'you don't, but unofficially, well that's a different matter.'

'I don't understand...'

'Wait, wait,' the apparition said tetchily, 'give a man a chance. Let me get down from here first. No need to help.'

Conway, who had no intention of helping, watched as the low-hanging fruitcake let go of the branch.

Back on solid ground he resumed his normal height of five-foot-four or thereabouts. Despite his undoubted agility, an estate agent would have placed him in his upper sixties or lower seventies. A large head gave him the appearance of being top-heavy and his bush of grey hair retreated in a crescent of curls to the crown of his head to extend an already lofty forehead. Yet his face was kind, reminding Conway of an affable Karl Marx, without the beard. His eyes were blue and childlike with that tilt of destiny that comes from looking at horizons.

'There you are,' he announced, 'no bones broken.' Then, becoming all business-like, he went on, 'Now, down to brass tacks. What is it you want? And no shilly-shallying, mind, I haven't got all day.'

'Well, I don't want anything, as it happens,' Conway began, 'I was simply...'

But the old man cut across his words again. 'Come on now,' he said, as he dusted himself down, 'don't be backward in coming forward. You're not going to tell me that you're here for the good of your health, now are you?'

This time Conway was determined to finish a sentence. He took a shallow breath and quickly said, 'Well, in a way yes, but no matter. I'm doing a thesis, you see, and I...'

Again he was cut short. 'A thesis is it,' the old man exclaimed, 'ah yes, a thesis. Well now, don't tell me, let me guess. Would I be right in saying that this was a thesis concerning lamprey eels?'

Conway settled for the shortest answer.

'No,' he said briskly.

But as heedless as ever, the old man went on. 'Don't tell me. Let me guess. Is it about the misappropriation of beer kegs and their subsequent use as moorings for gandelows, angling cots and suchlike river craft?'

'No.'

'Does it concern unsynchronised and unofficial flushing of untreated and inappropriate effusions from sewage pipes at low tide?'

'No.'

'The relentless advance of the Giant Hogweed along our riverbanks?'

'No.'

'The relentless advance of Japanese Knotweed along our riverbanks?'

'No.'

'Mayflies?'

'No.'

'Magpies?'

'No.'

'Moorhens? Mallards? Cuckoo Spit?'

'No.'

'Sphagnum moss?'

'No.'

'The Summer Snowflake?'

'No.'

'I only mention it because, to my knowledge, it is only to be found naturalised in two places in these islands, the banks of the Shannon and the banks of the Thames, and thereby, I'm sure you'll agree, most worthy of a thesis. But it's not that?'

'No...' Conway repeated.

Narrowing his eyes, his inquisitor asked cautiously, 'It's not about me, is it?'

Conway shook his head. The old man translated the gesture. 'No, I didn't think so,' he said slowly, in words tinged with regret. But it was only a momentary lapse and he was soon off again.

'Let me see now, what could it be at all,' he began brightly but Conway was ready for him this time.

'It's about the King's Island...' Conway declared with a peevish resolve.

Not in the least diminished the old man was back again.

'The King's Island, did you say?' he asked in amazement, 'Island as in, *the* Island? This Island? In its entirety?'

Conway pursed his lips and nodded.

The old man went on, 'Well, that's a good one. I'd never have expected that now, I can tell you. Hows'ever. And what exactly had you in mind to put in this...thesis?'

'A physical and cultural study.' Conway replied, digging his umbrella into the gravel and leaning nonchalantly on it.

'Ah, I'm with you now,' the old man said, tapping an index finger on his right temple, 'and indeed you do have that predatory look about you. Hemingwayesque, I would say, without fear or favour. Well, you've come to the right man, I can tell you. Do you know what they say? Well, I'll tell you now. They say that if you want to know anything at all about the Island, or Limerick for that matter, all you have to do is ask Tom Madigan. That's what they say...'

'Perhaps I should consult him...' said Conway shrewdly.

The old man's eyes bulged with incredulity. 'But sure you're talking to him. Amn't I Tom Madigan...himself.'

'Oh, I didn't realize,' Conway said ruefully.

'There you are now...' the old man said, laughing, clearly enjoying his tactical superiority in the conversation.

'Well, I'm Edward Conway,' said Conway, proffering a hand to seal the exchange of names, 'pleased to meet you.'

'The same and likewise,' Tom Madigan replied, then said earnestly, 'no, I could be useful to you. I could give you concise, pocket versions of all the official and unofficial histories, past, present and future of Limerick, or indeed the Island.'

'History of the future?' Conway said doubtfully.

'It is easy, very easy,' Madigan began in reply, 'to give a history of the future. As every schoolboy knows, history repeats itself. Is that not so? History is made from very pliable materials, bad memory, quantum physics, wishful thinking and, sad to say, lies. Oh there is truth, some truth, but not too much, mind, or history will not repeat itself, and if history is to repeat itself, it follows that it must appear in the future.'

'But,' Conway meekly protested.

'But,' Madigan said, taking the word as if it was a mere conjunction, 'enough of that. What about this thesis? I can see you are a man who likes to get on with things. So let's get a move on. You can take notes if you like. Now, first things first...'

As Conway heaved an acquiescent sigh, the old man went on in a conspiratorial whisper.

'...always start from where you are. Like a sniper, always survey your immediate surroundings and then work your way out from there. This path you're on, incidentally, is called the Island Bank and continues as a raised embankment that skirts the river all the way around to the other side of the Island. Now, as we walk on, you'll see a broad vista opens up to your left here, showing off a skyline dominated by large religious objects...'

Like some proud impresario, Madigan extended an arm to present the scene and, raising his voice, he pointed and proclaimed, 'that's St Mary's Church, Catholic, and that's St Mary's Cathedral, Protestant. And that there, is St Mary's Convent, Catholic, and that is St Munchin's, Protestant, now disused. There is another St Munchin's Church, Catholic, that's not on the skyline. In fact it's not on the Island but just across the water, on the other side of Thomond Bridge in the Parish of St Munchin. Just out of eyeshot if you like...'

And so the onslaught continued. Tom Madigan, without interruption, displaying his encyclopaedic knowledge of the area while Conway, having removed his gloves, was taking notes and having his dodgy shorthand tested to the limit as he tried to take it all in.

'Down to your right, here,' Madigan continued, hardly stopping for breath, 'is the Abbey River, flowing quietly by its green banks. Ahead, this bridle-path, now beautifully tree-lined, seems to aim its destination at the sleepy Clare hills, way off over there to the north. And that, over there, is the pebbled-dashed Sarsfield Park. A housing estate of eighty houses or so, named in honour of that great Limerick hero, Patrick Sarsfield, who defended this city in the sieges of 1690 and 1691. The man who built them, they say, went broke shortly afterwards. After building the houses I mean, not after the sieges. That happened a long time before...'

Madigan stopped for a moment, lost in recollection, then carried on as before. 'And then, there's Stella Maris Park, the jewel in the crown. Named after the Blessed Virgin. The older of the schemes, built in the thirties, three hundred and sixty-five houses, one built for every day of the year, so they say. And do you see those old trees? There, in the gap between Sarsfield Park and Stella Maris Park, there with the low stone wall, well that's the old soldiers' graveyard. They'd be British soldiers stationed on the Island, ah years and years ago. Mostly Protestants and Presbyterians and what have you...'

Madigan stopped in his tracks and fell silent. Conway adjourned his note-taking to look up at the old man who was now gazing vacantly into the distance. He seemed to be preoccupied with some internal landscape that required his full attention. At last he spoke, his voice slow and deliberate, as if repeating the words of someone else.

'The Island is an ancient place, you see, shrouded in mystery. In ancient times it was known to the Celts as Inis Sibhtonn, or Sibhtonn's Island. Who he was, or what he was, we may never know. Many have come and claimed this patch of land. The Vikings settled here in around 812 AD. The Normans came and named it *King's Island* after their King John. It was he who granted Limerick its first charter in 1197...'

Suddenly, a bell rang out, striking the air with solemn tones. A snipe flew up from the marsh in alarm, just yards away, and zigzagged quickly out of sight.

'I must leave you now,' Madigan said, rousing himself, 'I have to go. Do you hear the death-bell? The funeral of a friend, don't you know...' He grimaced, put his hand inside his coat and began rubbing his left shoulder. 'You get to my age and they all start dropping away like flies. I've walked behind so many funeral cars these past few years that I'm in constant danger of carbon monoxide poisoning. Between that now, and the coffin-shoulder, they'll be the death of me. I've been so taken up with talking, time has caught me out. If you should ever need me, to further your research, don't hesitate to call. I'll be only too delighted to be of service. Here's my card.'

Getting a faint whiff of mothballs, Conway took the card and read: *Tom Madigan Esq., Lepidopterist, The Gables, Convent Walk, Limerick City, Ireland.*

'Butterflies?' said Conway, surprised and intrigued.

'Butterflies, and moths,' Madigan amended, 'Yes, I breed them. You must see my collection sometime, I'm sure you'll find it most interesting.'

'Thank you, I'm very much obliged...'

'Take care, my friend, and mind how you go,' said the old man, offering a farewell handshake. Then invoking an Irish blessing, he added, 'Slán agus beannacht leat.'

Conway watched him go. So sprightly, so full of vigour and so enthusiastic, it was difficult to believe he was off to a funeral or anything of the sort. Having gathered enough information for one day Conway put away his notebook. He had made good progress and was fortunate, he had to admit, to have encountered such a knowledgeable person in the shape of Tom Madigan.

Chapter Two

He was indeed pleased with the way things had gone, and as the sun saw fit to break through the clouds to endorse his feelings, he decided to leave the path and venture onto the marsh below. After scrambling down the steep bank, he negotiated, with some degree of difficulty, the narrow ditch that lay between. Taking in the new perspective of the low-lying terrain he caught sight of two figures trudging towards him, far off to his right.

From their hair colouring, a sandy blond, and similarity of features, the two were obviously brothers. The older one was perhaps sixteen, or thereabouts, the younger, much smaller and thinner, was some years behind. Conway judged him to be no more than ten years old. As they approached, the older one shouted.

'Hi, sham, did you see a pieball horse anywhere?'

'Ahmm, no...' Conway answered, not at all certain that the question was even addressed to him.

'Are you sure, sham? He came this way,' the younger one piped with accusation in his voice.

'No, sorry.' Conway said regretfully.

The older one, looking away to the distance, commented, 'You must be fucken blind, sham...'

'I beg your pardon,' Conway said, a little taken aback by the aggressive tone, 'I didn't quite hear...'

'Nahan, sham, forgerrit,' came the swift reply from the older one. Then turning to his brother he said, 'Mikey, did you bring the fucken halter?'

'I forgor it, but I gorra rope...' the waif-like Mikey replied, somewhat nervously.

'You fool,' his brother exploded, 'Jesus, Mary and Joesup, grant me fucken patience. I thought I told you to bring the fucken halter, didn't I?'

'Don't hit me now or I'll tell Nucky on you.' Mikey said, backing away as his brother advanced on him.

'You can tell Nucky all you fucken like,' said the older brother, 'think I'm afraid of Nucky? Gimme the fucken rope or I'll hang you with it. The ghoul of a horse is miles away by now. I thought you said you spancelled him?'

Mikey blurted out his explanation as he continued to back away. 'Nucky said not to, he wasn't gettin' anuff grass, he had a rope on him, he was tied to a rocker. Someone must have robbed the rope off him. He was on the rocker.'

This explanation seemed to appease his brother, to some degree, for he now diverted his threats to the 'someone' mentioned. 'If I ketch the fucker,' he said, eyeing Conway suspiciously, 'I'll dig the head off him...'

Conway, who was shifting about uneasily, found himself searching his conscience.

'No...' he assured himself, he definitely had nothing to do with the theft of a rope.

Spitting at the ground as if trying to rid himself of the venomous frustration he felt, the older brother snapped out an order. 'Come on, Mikey, we better get that dope of a horse. We havta go down the Dock Road, there's no fucken coal in the yard...'

Off they went, heading in the direction they had come from. Conway eyed their retreat with some relief and as he listened to their receding voices, as they carried themselves away, he found himself slipping into his customary analysis.

He noted the liberal use of expletives and the blasphemous invocations to the Almighty. All common enough language characteristics throughout Ireland. But there was something quite different about this dialect. It had a defiant tempo to it and a no-nonsense syntax that was very arresting. The use of facial expression seemed particularly interesting. The way the lips were mobilized in pronunciation, and the peculiarly aggressive body posture, too, seemed fundamental to the conveyance of words. It was a lean, direct dialect with very little fat, designed for utility by the parameters of necessity, and, though not readily understood, one could fill in the gaps in comprehension by the use of context rationalization.

As Conway was metaphorically kicking himself for not having brought a tape-recorder, he heard what sounded like a blood-curdling war cry.

'Hike! Hike! Hike!' It was the brothers. Back again like two bad pennies, their heads, just about visible above the vegetation, bobbing like mad as they ran frantically in his direction.

'You stupid fool, I told you to hold him...' he could hear the older one saying. Then, with the words, 'stop the horse, sham, stop the horse...' ringing in his ears, Conway turned to his left to behold a most terrifying sight.

There before his eyes, kicking up clods of earth like a muck spreader and making a beeline, straight for him, was a huge, muscular, wild-eyed piebald horse. The massive hoofs thumped the ground and Conway's heart, catching their rhythm, thumped in his chest. Like slow motion eternity the beast swelled before him as it bore down on him with nostrils flared and eyes wild with warning. Rooted to the spot and waiting for certain death, he closed his eyes and prayed a quick fervent prayer.

'Oh God, I am heartily sorry for all my sins...'

As he mumbled the words, his life flashed before him and he could see himself revealed for what he was and for what he had been: an uncommitted, theoretical communist cum socialist cum liberal cum utopian, a neo-Christian nice person leaning towards agnosticism, basically believing that people are basically good, that he himself was basically good, and God, if he did exist, and he wasn't sure he did, was basically good. It wasn't much of a life Conway had to admit as the ground rumbled and death thundered towards him.

Instinctively he tensed his muscles and held his breath as he waited for the moment of impact. This is it, he thought, what a stupid way to go. What would his mother think? His heart filled with remorse at the thought of causing her grief.

He could see her now, getting his supper ready. Setting a place for her one and only son. Indeed, her only child. A place that would never again be occupied. He thought of the sausages, eggs and black pudding that would be warming for him beneath the grill. A meal steeped in every animal fat imaginable, defying all medical condemnations. His weekly guilt-ridden treat in an otherwise vegetarian diet. They would find his young pulverized body, low in cholesterol, high in polyunsaturates and devoid of life.

As his mind pondered the consequences of his death, he felt a gentle breeze brush past him. He opened his eyes. To his amazement and relief the horse had vanished. So grateful was he to be alive, and so grateful and humbled was he by the Almighty's generous intervention in saving the life of a miserable, wavering agnostic, that he resolved, at that very moment, to bend himself to God's will and obey his each and every commandment.

'Grab the rope!' a voice commanded. Convinced that this was his first test of faith, Conway was determined not to be found wanting.

'Grab the rope!' the voice commanded again.

The rope, he saw, trailed past him like some determined and very direct snake sliding through the grass in pursuit of prey. He leapt on the rope, grabbing hold of it. It pulled rudely and hotly through his hands as if it were alive and he was just in danger of losing his grip when a knot presented itself. He held on to it for all his worth, determined not to let go. Like a crazy, committed rag-doll, he was dragged along the ground, careering through the mud and marsh foliage as if turning on a spit.

A compendium of emotions hustled for his attention, fear for his life, admiration and fear for the animal's brute strength, amazement at his own apparent lightness, and recklessness, and a guilt-laden resentment that God really does work in mysterious ways. All emotions gathered now in a rushing, tumbling kaleidoscope of mud, grass and sky and became as one. A twelve-letter, polysyllabic word with a scrabble value of twenty-two sprang to mind: *exhilaration...*

Yes, this is what that word must mean. There was no other feeling to describe it. Wasn't life extraordinary, he thought. Only moments before he had escaped death by a hair's breadth. Now, it seemed, he was trying to capture it even as it dragged him along. Suddenly, without warning, it all stopped and he found himself lying in several inches of black water that oozed from the spongy marsh as if in protest of his weight. Very Archimedean, thought Conway for the briefest of brief moments.

He was surprised to see he still had the rope in his hands. Surprised, also, that his arms were still attached to his shoulders. Several yards away, the horse snorted deeply at the end of the rope and shook his mane before settling to feed on a tussock of grass that took his fancy. Still clutching the rope, Conway got to his feet and pulled himself to the horse. His burning hands, smeared in mud and blood, trembled as he neared the animal. Indeed, his whole body trembled, not with fear but with nervous exhaustion and a dizzy excitement.

As he gently patted the horse's shoulder, the massive neck quivered and the great head came up to snort steam and roll a big chestnut eye back at him. Then, like a lamb, the head was lowered to resume his feeding.

Gasping for breath after all their running, the brothers finally appeared.

'Why didn't you let go the rope?' the older one managed to say between gasps.

Feeling very foolish, Conway replied, 'It was *you* who told me to grab the rope?'

'Yeah, and then I told you to let go, I didn't ask you to get fucken killed, did I?' the older brother said defensively.

'I'm all right...' said Conway, looking anything but. He was a sight to behold, destroyed from head to foot. His hair plastered to his head, and his face, all but for his eyes, obliterated by what looked like a mudpack.

'You don't look it,' the older brother said astutely, 'you're a lucky fucker anyway. Dead fucken lucky. You should have let go.'

'Yeah, he could have kicked your head in,' the younger brother chipped in, after finding his breath.

With a snarl on his lips, the older brother snapped, 'Who asked you?'

'I only said what you said,' replied the younger, recoiling into himself.

'Shut your gob,' his brother snapped again, 'and never mind what I said...'

Without warning, a cloak of shadow was cast over them as a cloud sped across the marsh. As quickly as it had come it was off again like some dark intention seeking refuge from the sunlight. While Conway reflected on how apocalyptic it all seemed, Mikey shouted with excitement and pointed in his direction.

'It's Nucky,' he said. 'It's Nucky, he's coming...'

Conway turned about-face to assess the cause of the commotion. Striding towards him, not twenty yards off, was a very determined and powerful-looking individual in T-shirt and jeans, and carrying in his right hand what looked like, and sounded like, a bridle. The face, strong and intelligent and as sallow as a kipper, was framed by a mass of black curls as black as ripe blackberries. The nearer he got the more powerful he appeared. His shoulders were outsize, as were his arms and hands. Everything about him seemed an exaggeration, yet there was a strange kind of harmony in all of it.

'Are you all right?' he asked, addressing Conway and sounding very cross.

'...I'm fine,' Conway said, looking into the dark, frowning eyes of the inquisitor, 'I think,' he added doubtfully, 'just a bit shook up.'

'Hi, Nucky,' the young Mikey chimed in.

'Hi, my arse,' came the short reply from Nucky, 'what the fuck are ye two up to. I thought I told ye to get the fucken horse hours ago?'

'We couldn't help it, Nucky,' the older brother explained, '...he ran off...someone must have took him off the rocker, we were lookin' everywhere...'

Not hearing, or pretending not to hear, Nucky contorted his lips as if to chew his words before releasing them.

'Do you know somethin', Bobsy,' he said, addressing the older brother, 'you're some tulip anyway. Do you ever do anything fucken right. Why didn't you bring the feed-bag? He'd have come to you when he saw it, instead of chasin' him all over the fucken place.'

Getting red in the face at the injustice of it all, Bobsy retaliated. 'He forgot the fucken feed-bag, and the fucken halter,' he shouted, pushing his younger brother to the ground to emphasize his outrage.

Nucky raised his right fist and put it on display an inch from Bobsy's nose, then, in an un-natural, calm voice, he said emphatically, 'Bobsy, do you see this, if you don't stop hittin' him, I'll fucken kill ya with it, ja hear me?'

Conway listened in amazement as Bobsy, apparently unaware that his life was about to be shortened, said defiantly, 'You're always pickin' on me. Am I a plum, am I?' Then, in reference to his brother Mikey, who had picked himself up none the worse for wear, and who was by now smiling broadly, he added, 'He gets away with everything...'

Lowering his fist Nucky warned, 'Lay another hand on him and you'll know all about it, mind. I'm tellin' you now. Pick on someone your own size.'

Sounding like something between automatic gunfire and

21

a nanny goat, and plainly infuriating Bobsy all the more, Mikey became afflicted by an uncontrollable and sniggering laughter. Uncontrollable that is, until Nucky shouted at him, at the top of his voice, to shut up.

'Now,' proclaimed Nucky, 'the two of ye, get the fuck home ouravit before I lose my patience.'

And so the brothers departed. Mikey running off ahead and giggling to himself and Bobsy sullenly bringing up the rear with murderous intent.

Picking up the bridle from where he dropped it, Nucky approached the horse, who, though at the centre of much controversy, had continued to browse to his heart's content, oblivious to everything going on around him.

'Up boy,' Nucky coaxed, grabbing the horse's mane with his free hand. Obligingly as you like, up came the great head and in one swift movement Nucky had the bridle on.

As Nucky busied himself with final adjustments, Conway, for the want of something to say as much as anything, commented, 'They're a right pair those two...'

Nucky spun around to face Conway. 'Whaddaya mean, sham?' he asked with an edge to his voice.

Feeling he might be on shaky ground, Conway faltered, 'I mean, ahhm...Mikey and, what's his name, Bobsy...'

'Whaddaboud um?' insisted Nucky.

Conway, now certain that he was on very shaky ground, decided it was time for tact, diplomacy and above all, self-preservation.

'I was just saying,' he began, as nonchalantly as he could, '...that...that they are...ah...um...'

'If I were you, sham,' Nucky said, mercifully interrupting Conway's tongue-tied gibberish, '...I'd take my advice and keep your mouth shut. Nobody says anything about my brothers, right?'

'Your, your, brothers?' Conway said, the mud-caked face cracking in disbelief.

Nucky's body language now took a turn for the worse. Visibly bristling, he asked, 'Worrofit?'

'I don't mean anything by it,' Conway was quick to point out, '...I'm just surprised that's all. I mean, you don't look like brothers...'

'Well, we are,' Nucky said, his jaw tightening, 'we're all Macs. Every one of us. Have you somethin' to say about that, sham?'

With all the sincerity he could muster, Conway said, 'I didn't mean to give offence.'

In what at first seemed to Conway as a contemptuous gesture, Nucky sniffed the air, then said, 'What the fuck is that smell?'

Conway had to inhale deeply through his nostrils before the penny dropped. 'Ah, Detox Antiseptic,' he pronounced at length. 'I had a bottle in my coat pocket. It must have broken...'

'You're bleedin', sham.' Nucky said matter-of-factly.

Conway looked down at his muddied and bloodstained trousers. 'Ah, it's just a scratch,' he said, 'lucky really, being cut by a bottle of antiseptic. At least it's a clean cut.' Then, as if a sudden panic had gripped him, he began searching frantically in his overcoat pockets. 'The Dopacof, the Dopacof,' he muttered anxiously to himself before finally laying his hand on it. With a sigh of relief and a shaky little laugh, he unscrewed the cap and put the bottle to his lips.

Nucky eyed him curiously. 'You feelin' all right, sham?' Conway, having imbibed the sweet elixir, remembered himself, forced a little cough, then by way of explanation said simply, 'cough bottle...'

'You sure you're all right, sham?' Nucky asked again.

'Yes, why?' Conway asked, screwing on the cap and slipping the bottle back in his pocket.

'Never mind,' Nucky shrugged, then, grasping the horse's mane with his left hand, he leapt onto its bare back as if his legs were made of springs. 'Right,' he said, when he had steadied the animal, 'hop up...'

'What? Me?' Conway asked cautiously, looking up at Nucky in disbelief.

Leaning forward and extending his arm, Nucky said, 'Grab my arm and hop up on the horse.'

'Ah, no thanks...' Conway declined, 'I think I'd be better off walking.'

'Don't be fucken stupid,' Nucky said politely, 'look at the state of you. You look on your last legs and you're manky with the dirt. Come on, I'll take you home.'

Perhaps it was the low sugar level in his blood, perhaps it was the numbing cold that was seeping through his bones, or the wisps of fog the marsh was now exhaling. Perhaps it was an enchantment of dusk. Perhaps it was a conspiracy of all these things. Whatever it was, it was enough to persuade Conway, against his better judgment, to accept Nucky's offer of transport.

'Put the toe of your left rusher on my foot,' Nucky said, and extending his left arm, he added, 'and grab hold of that.'

Rusher must translate as wellie, Conway was thinking to himself, as he followed the procedure Nucky had indicated. Using Nucky's curled foot as an impromptu stirrup, he was hauled onboard the horse with such surprising ease that he almost tipped over on the other side.

'Hold on tight.' Nucky advised.

Conway didn't need to be asked twice. With his eyes tightly shut he flung his arms around Nucky's waist and clung on like some terrified limpet.

'Not that fucken tight,' said Nucky, 'loosen up a bit.'

Conway loosened his grip a mere fraction. 'Sorry,' he said shakily, 'I've never been on a horse before.'

'I'd never have guessed,' said Nucky, gently spurring the horse's flanks with his muddy sneakers. Then making, what could only be described as loud clicking noises with his tongue, he addressed the horse with, 'prup boy, prup, prup...' The horse, who had remained rock-steady up until then, plucked his heavy feet from the mud and plodded off, creating great, squelching sounds as he went.

Every fibre in Conway's body tightened in response to the rocking, rolling motion of the horse's perambulation.

'I was on a donkey once,' he ventured, his eyes still firmly shut, 'when I was five, in Kilkee, on the beach.'

'Really,' said Nucky, not overly impressed.

Slowly but surely, Conway grew more accustomed to his predicament. As his premature rendition of rigor mortis began to thaw out, his grip began to loosen, his body began to relax, and his eyes began to open. What sights and what feelings were opened to him. *Intoxicating* was not a bad word to describe it, Conway thought. The world looks very different on horseback. One is elevated, not only physically, but emotionally and spiritually. The world's perspective is enlarged and horizons beckon.

Clearly relishing his new vantage point, Conway asked facetiously, 'And what is our mount called?'

'A horse,' said Nucky, giving a short answer.

'No,' Conway pressed, indifferent to the sarcasm, 'what is his name?'

'Gypsy,'

'Nice name,' Conway said, 'for a horse.'

As if to show he was in agreement, Gypsy snorted loudly and brushed Conway with a swish of his tail. This is the only way to travel, Conway thought, inhaling the potpourri of smells that assailed his olfactory sensibilities. Oh the sweet, heady smell of horse, of grass, of water mint, crushed freshly under-hoof.

On they plodded, heading towards the embankment and the boat club, avoiding on the way what Nucky described as 'the wobblin' or 'the shaky island'. Through inquiry, Conway divined that this was a reference to several ditches that dissected the marsh in various places. Thick mats of vegetation had knitted together to form a skin that covered the inky-black water of the ditches, disguising their presence. Though treacherous, and often fatal to anything as heavy as a horse, they could support the weight of a man, but, as Nucky had put it, it was like walking on a trampoline.

On reaching the boat club, Conway, peering over the wall from his perch, could see the pedestalled, painted statue of a forlorn oarsman. A raised arm held aloft an imaginary oar, the original having been requisitioned by some discerning vandal. Dressed in blue-and-red vest and long, old-fashioned trunks, and sporting black lacquered hair, he seemed to be looking longingly across the Abbey River towards the parish of St John and its cathedral spire. The tallest in Ireland by all accounts.

When they reached the turning for O'Dwyer Bridge, the street lights were on. Premature, pale and ineffectual, they seemed embarrassed by a sky determined to hold onto daylight for as long as possible. Nucky spurred Gypsy into a canter and out they went onto Athlunkard Street and clattered on over the bridge. Conway listened to horseshoes ringing on the toil-worn concrete, and couldn't help thinking how wonderfully 'Kavanaghesque' it all sounded. Allowing a metrical memory to play in his mind, he recited exquisitely to himself, '...footfalls tapping secrecies of stone...'

With the aid of the gradient, the canter was developing into bone-shaking proportions and Conway and Nucky, like two peas in a pod, were fairly bouncing off Gypsy's broad back. Despite their considerable speed, a line of traffic had formed behind them, waiting to pass. Very soon they were assailed by a cacophony of bleating horns.

Nucky's response was as diplomatic as ever. 'Ah, take your fucken time,' he shouted, over his shoulder, 'what's your hurry?'

The poignancy of the moment wasn't lost on Conway. There was something defiantly noble in this clash with twentieth-century technology. The old versus the new. The fashionably defunct versus the expedient. A single horse-power against so many. At that moment Conway found himself, both physically and morally, on the side of the underdog, or, in this case, the underhorse. With quixotic fervour he dismissed the bleating vehicles as being little more than motorized ego-buckets.

At last, and not before time, they turned off the main road and wheeled right into the sedate and quiet sanctuary of

Sycamore Avenue. Gypsy's speed had now dropped to a comfortable, leisurely stroll. Just as Conway was settling to the new tempo and beginning to enjoy thoughts of home, there came a sound, not unlike, he thought, the falling note of a saxophone.

As he cast his head about to catch the source, Nucky said, 'Good for you, Gypsy, better out than in...'

The realization, prompted by Nucky's congratulatory remark, that what he had mistaken for a tuneful note was nothing more than equine flatulence, brought a blush to Conway's face. It was as well, he thought, that his face was caked in mud. He was grateful for the camouflage it now afforded.

To make matters worse, Nucky, without any warning, suddenly burst into song, 'Oh the whistling Gypsy came over the hill,' he sang, at the top of his voice, 'down through the valley so shaaaaydeeee...' Conway listened, horrified at the thought of the social consequences that might follow such spontaneous ribaldry. Indeed, as Nucky continued like some overwrought operatic baritone, Conway could see that the twitching curtains were already in action.

'...he whistled and he sang till the green woods rang and he won the heart of a layaaaadeeee...'

Conway could take no more. 'You can drop me here,' he said, 'and thanks very much, I'm just at the end of the road.'

'Not at all, sham, stall on,' Nucky said, in a generous mood, 'may as well take you the rest of the way. We've come this far.'

'No really,' Conway protested, 'I'll be fine from here.'

Nucky was insistent. 'Shur, you're nearly there now,' he said, and proceeded with his singing, louder than ever, stopping only for a moment to give a royal salute to a bewildered resident who had come out to see what was going on.

'...ah di du ah di du daa day,' Nucky continued, 'ah di du ah di day dee, he whistled and he sang till the green woods rang and he won the heart of a layaaaadeeee...'

'I live here,' Conway said wearily, on reaching his house.

Mercifully, Nucky brought Gypsy, and his singing, to a halt. 'Here we are so,' he said, while Conway slid from the horse. As soon as his feet touched the ground, Conway felt his knees buckle beneath him and he was just on the point of collapse when Nucky, who was dismounted in a flash, caught him from behind.

'You're okay,' said Nucky reassuringly, hauling Conway onto the footpath and propping him up against the garden wall. Then, taking Gypsy by the halter, he proceeded to secure the animal by tying the reins to the garden gate.

At that moment, the door of 'Riverview' opened and out stepped the diminutive figure that was Mrs Conway. She stood aghast at the sight before her. 'Merciful hour!' she exclaimed, putting her hands to her round, horrified face, 'what in the name of God happened to you?'

'He's had a little accident, Missus,' Nucky explained, 'but he's all right now.'

'All right?' Mrs Conway cried in disbelief, running to her son. 'Will you look at the state of you! Edward! You look like someone dragged through a bush backwards.'

'Near anuff, Missus,' Nucky said helpfully.

'And who, may I ask, might you be, young man?' Mrs Conway inquired and pursed her lips.

Regaining his breath and some composure, Conway intervened. 'Mum,' he said, a plea for clemency in his voice, 'he brought me home...'

'Yes, I could see that very well, thank you very much,' she said to her son, fixing him with a wide-eyed stare.

'I think I'll make myself scarce,' said Nucky tactfully.

Mrs Conway, her emotions now aroused, turned on Nucky. 'And what is your horse doing tied to my gate?'

Nucky, looking over his shoulder at Gypsy, replied, 'You're in luck, Missus. I think he's droppin' a load.'

Conway, whose belief in the veracity of Murphy's Law was now unshakable, wished the ground would open and swallow him whole. Unbelievably, Gypsy had decided, there and then, at the most inopportune moment, to open his bowels and relieve himself of his intestinal burden.

Smiling broadly, Nucky said, as he untied the reins, 'I won't charge you for it, Missus, you can use it on the roses.' Then, using the garden wall as a mounting-block, Nucky leapt onto Gypsy's back, and was soon off down the road and going like the clappers.

'Well, I never!' Mrs Conway said, outraged. 'Edward, come in at once! At once, I say! Do you hear me? Of all the cheek...'

Feeling quite faint and with head bowed low, Conway entered his carpeted, centrally heated, lavender-polished home and waited for the inevitable onslaught.

His mother wasn't long in starting. 'What in the name of all that's holy,' she began, as soon as the front door was shut behind her, 'possessed you to go off like that without as much as a by-your-leave, without a word of warning and to nearly get yourself killed and then to turn up like this in that condition. What would your father say if he saw it? It's a blessed relief that he's not here to see this, that's all I can say. Putting the heart cross-ways in me like that. I didn't know what to think, and what if you had been killed? Did you think of that? I really don't know where you were got. Just look at the cut of you! What will the neighbours think, turning up like that at the front door, on a horse, like a Red Indian. I won't be able to show my face for a week with the mortification of it, so I won't. God grant me patience...'

'I'm sorry, Mum. It was just a little mishap...' Conway said feebly.

'I'm sorry...' his mother repeated back to him, 'Is that all you can say?'

'It's no big deal, Mum, really,' he muttered.

Putting on her most painfully patient face, his mother continued remorselessly, 'Is that what you think?' she asked, not expecting or waiting for an answer, 'you could have been killed. Just look at your clothes. They're ruined. They'll have to go in the bin.'

Conway, now taking refuge in his own silence, meekly submitted to the inevitable inspection.

'Right, it's off with them,' his mother commanded, 'and into the bath with you and then to bed.' Then putting a hand to his forehead, she said in alarm, 'My God, you're boiling! You have an awful temperature. I'll have to call the doctor and that's all there is to it.'

Then, as if she remembered something she had almost forgotten, his mother asked sternly, 'And who was that, that person, with that horse?'

'Nucky Mac,' Conway said, under his breath.

'Who?' his mother screeched and gave him a doubtful side glance.

'Nucky Mac, that's his name,' Conway explained wearily.

'What kind of a name is that? I ask you,' his mother said, in her haughtiest voice, 'well, I can tell you,' she went on, 'I don't like the sound of him, or the look of him. Not one bit.'

Chapter Three

Dr Patrick Dalton was a tall, robust-looking individual who had played senior rugby in his day. Years of having his head squeezed in scrums had all but rubbed out his features, so that his face looked as bland as a bespectacled moon. Dressed in an oatmeal suit, and sporting a tie that looked like a fillet of smoked haddock against his potato-cream shirt, he was, from his salt-and-pepper hair to the soles of his chestnut shoes, a sartorial ode to bad taste and food motifs. No doubt, Conway decided, the victim of a colour co-ordinating wife.

'Well, how's Edwooord?' Dr Dalton asked with strident geniality. His pronunciation of the name was disconcerting. There was an insinuation in the voice that suggested some disapproval with the name, or its owner. Or both. Whatever it was, coming from the mouth of Dr Dalton, the name *Edward* just didn't sound wholesome.

'He's not well at all, Doctor...' his mother said in a reverential whisper.

Scrutinizing Conway with the watery, glass-magnified eyes of a man who'd seen too much of life and its excesses, Dr Dalton said, in the tired voice of a cynic, 'Is that so?'

From the moment his mother had opened the front door, Conway knew by the pervasive, pungent, pine-woody aftershave that invaded his home, that Dr Dalton had arrived. It had travelled into the hall, up the stairs and under his bedroom door like some windy herald spreading the good news that a rare home visit was about to take place.

With the giant doctor now towering over him in the small confines of his bedroom, the smell was overwhelming. Dr Dalton interpreted Conway's choking response as 'a touch of asthma'. Indeed, he remarked, to Mrs Conway, on the near epidemic proportions the 'asthma problem' was reaching in recent times.

His mother, supporting the elbow of her right arm in the palm of her left, that crossed beneath her bosom, brought her right hand to her chin and, looking for all the world like a worried shot-putter, spoke in a confidential voice.

'Well, I'll tell you now, Doctor, he was always a bit chesty. It runs in the family. I remember my grandfather, God rest his soul, on my father's side, the Barratts always had trouble with their chests, emphysema he had, hadn't a minute's peace with it and he died a young man. Worked in the post office. And my own father, God rest his soul, he died a young man as well, he was troubled for years with a bad chest, worked in the civil service, so he did. Forty-seven when he died...'

And so on it went, his mother chronicling the colourful pathology of the family tree, a family tree, it seemed to Conway, that appeared to have had everything but Dutch elm disease. To his credit Dr Dalton gave a very good impression of someone who was listening. In truth, however, he had taken the opportunity to catnap while still on his feet and, in testimony to the great tradition of his profession, did so with his eyes wide open.

Finally, Mrs Conway brought things up to date and full circle by recounting the medical highs and lows of her only offspring. From nappy rash through teething trouble to measles, mumps and jaundice and a lot more besides, it was brought home to Conway that he had been a great deal of trouble to his dear mother and the medical profession.

Who is this woman? Conway thought, looking curiously at his mother. He had seen this same strange performance many times before. In the presence of doctors, priests, dentists, indeed anyone endowed with the titled authority of a profession, she would engage these people as if seeking some endorsement of her own worth.

His mother, the source of all his nourishment, all his strength, all his confidence, indeed his entire world and all that was familiar and safe, was transformed before his eyes into a babbling alien personality. As a child it had made him anxious and fearful. Now, all he ever felt was a puzzled embarrassment.

Sensing that Mrs Conway was on her way to a full stop, the good doctor roused himself from his catnap and said, garnishing his words with wise solemnity, 'Not to worry.' A safe enough pronouncement in any context. And, as if struggling to remember what it was he was actually referring to, he repeated the advice, 'Not to worry. Not to worry.'

With wide, thankful eyes, Mrs Conway smiled a consoled smile. 'Thank you, Doctor,' she said, seemingly awe-struck by the wisdom of the medical deity. With that, she retreated respectfully from the room and, with a meticulousness that bordered on the painful, she closed the door behind her, muttering something about fresh towels as she went.

After savouring a short silence, Dr Dalton suddenly became rather jovial and man-to-manly. Confidentially, he told Conway, that regarding the asthma epidemic, he laid the blame firmly at the door of central heating, carpets and soft furnishings, which, he informed Conway, were a breeding paradise for the house-dust mite, who, to quote Dr Dalton, '...is an ugly-looking bastard, mercifully microscopic, whose faeces, though even more microscopic, caused allergic reactions in susceptible people.' At this, he eyed Conway in a way that might suggest that susceptible people were not that highly thought of.

'These women,' the good doctor went on, 'they will insist on festooning every room in a house with all the gewgaws and falderals they can lay their hands on. A mite's delight, you might say. God be with linoleum and the open fire...'

At this, he sighed, and looked with nostalgic regret at the offending carpet beneath his chestnut shoes.

Lying prostrate in a lather of sweat, and impatience, Conway could take no more. Raising himself up on his elbows, he said feverishly, 'I think, to save time, Doctor, I may as well tell you what's wrong with me...'

Taken aback, Dr Dalton checked his balance and blinked. Then, as if to check his hearing, he said tentatively, 'Pardon?'

Still on elbows, Conway, with a no-bones-about-it tone in his voice, said simply, 'I have the ague.'

'The ague?' Dr Dalton echoed, nodding and smiling and looking over the rim of his glasses as if waiting for the punch line of a joke.

With the courageous, couldn't-care-less recklessness that illness often imparts to some people, Conway went on, undaunted. 'You should look at the section on malaria and marsh fever,' he said, pointing to bookshelves behind the good doctor. 'There, the third shelf, the blue book, the big one. That's it. I have the ague, pure and simple. It's in that, it's all there...'

In an effort to recapture and stabilize the doctor-patient relationship, Dr Dalton, gently and affably, pulled rank.

'Now where did you get your medical degree, son?'

'If I'm not mistaken,' Conway said boldly, and with slow emphasis, 'your medical fraternity asked Pasteur the same question.'

Dr Dalton laughed, somewhat defensively, as Conway flopped back on his pillows.

'All right,' he said, placing a cold shovel of a hand on Conway's forehead, 'well the symptoms are right enough, high temperature, bouts of shivering, you certainly have a fever. Tell you what, I'll make a bet with you. If it turns out that you have malaria or marsh fever, or the ague, as you like to call it, I'll hang up my stethoscope, give up medicine and take up golf.'

In Conway's fevered brain a retired doctor in plus-fours and flat cap was teeing up a small, white, dimpled ball.

Dr Dalton rummaged in his medical bag and fished out a stethoscope. Familiar with, and anticipating the procedure, Conway showed off his medical knowledge by undoing his pyjama top. As the ice-cold metal branded his mortal flesh, Conway inhaled sharply.

'Breathe deeply,' Dr Dalton advised.

Conway grudgingly complied. But as the examination proceeded, a strange feeling of redundancy came over him. Here he was, with a relative stranger listening to his heart and his lungs, while his crowning glory, his mind, the seat of reason, the great interpreter, abstracter and diagnostic tool, was completely ignored. His heart and lungs, which up until then were under his sole jurisdiction, were now speaking, as it were, with treacherous abandon to an outside agency.

With an, 'I won't tell you I told you so' smile on his face, Dr Dalton gave his verdict.

'Well, young man, your heart is sound,' said he, opening his mouth to yawn with tired satisfaction, 'your lungs are a little congested. But it's nothing to worry about, and that includes the ague. You mustn't fret yourself about exotic diseases. Something for your fever should do the trick...'

Smiling all the while, as Conway remained silently and utterly unconvinced, Dr Dalton snapped his bag shut and walked philosophically to the door. Holding the door open, and about to leave, he turned. 'You know, books are all very well but they don't tell the whole story. They never do. Try and get some sleep.'

With that he was gone. But not far. Through the ivory-coloured door of Conway's bedroom, muffled voices came from the landing. His mother must have waylaid the man with the golden stethoscope. At first he could not make out what was being said but then his mother raised the volume considerably to declaim on the reasons for her disquiet.

'...and they closed Barrington's Hospital,' he could hear her say, 'the Regional and John's are under a lot of pressure. Isn't it awful, beds in the corridors, people on trolleys, isn't it shocking, what do you think, Doctor? What's the country coming to at all. God bless us and save us all. I blame all these cutbacks so I do. What do you think, Doctor?'

Every now and then Dr Dalton would contribute a few murmured sounds but these were unintelligible to Conway. For some reason he found this extremely irritating. Why, he asked his tired mind, was he so annoyed? His tired mind, prodded by the intellectual challenge, staved off sleep a little longer and tried to answer. For one thing, his mother was a widow and by definition was vulnerable. Was that not so? His father's premature departure had left a vacuum and nature abhors a vacuum. Was that not so? But what nature fills it with sometimes, leaves a lot to be desired. Again he heard the doctor's muffled voice. Then he heard his mother laugh. A laugh altogether too young for her and her station in life. It was almost girlish. In his mind's eye the letters of the words 'coquette' and 'mother' merged and danced to the hooley sounds of her laughter. Conway felt the poison dart of jealousy infect the region of his heart. His sacrosanct mind warned him of the dangers of a purely emotional response, and, for one fleeting moment, he almost resented his logical reasoning.

His mind now fled such absurd thoughts as sleep rose and swelled within him. The room, no longer mindful of his presence, withdrew into shadows. But just as he was about to slip away, his mother's words dragged him rudely back. She was speaking in her best mother-weary voice.

'...I told him, but you can't be talking to him, he's very headstrong at times. Him and his books. I don't think he knows what he wants. Like his father before him, he's a bit of a dreamer...'

The doctor laughed. His mother laughed. The landing laughed. Then he thought he heard his mother say, 'He's not going to die, Doctor, is he?'

If Conway was disturbed by the question, he was startled by the answer. He was almost certain he heard the doctor say, rather too carelessly for his liking, 'What if he did, sure he'd be no great loss...'

Shrouded in a cold, shivering sweat, Conway, with white-knuckled hands, pulled the bedclothes to his chin and pondered Dr Dalton's death-knell words. What a wonderful bedside manner, he thought, before slowly slipping into unconsciousness.

Chapter Four

He had given up his thoughts and surrendered his head to the pillow. In a spiralling descent he went deeper and deeper into its fabric, slipping into a profound and tranquil sleep. For how long, he had no idea, but he did recall how wonderful it felt to cast off his body like some old and cumbersome overcoat. He felt buoyant now, curiously self-contained, and was enjoying floating about in the darkness.

Though he could not see a thing, he sensed he was high and somewhere near the ceiling. Brushing against the ceiling, he was amazed to find it gave way to him as if it had been made of candyfloss. Finding the experience both pleasant and intriguing, he repeated the performance, dunking himself into the delightfully accommodating ceiling again and again. Then he tried the walls and found them to be the same. As compliant as you like.

He remembered thinking that he should have thought this somewhat unusual and improper. But, like a wayward child who's having too much fun and deliberately forgets to remember, Conway decided to be irresponsible. To his surprise, he achieved this without creating a single particle of guilt in himself or his surroundings. Then, impulsively, a thought bubbled up from his enjoyment to suggest that he move farther afield. Maybe he should leave the room and explore outside. As he was about to plunge through the wall of his fancy, he was pleasantly overcome by a powerful and familiar aroma.

'What is that smell?' he asked, unleashing his thoughts to hunt the memory. It was all to no avail. For the life of him he could not remember. 'What is that smell?' he repeated impatiently to himself as he tried to winkle it out of his memory.

A voice, not his own, answered through the darkness.

'Lavender,' the voice said in a long whisper.

'That's it!' Conway exclaimed knowingly, 'Lavender,' he said, repeating the word lovingly, caressing the returned memory of it. Then it occurred to him that the word had been given by someone other than himself. Therefore, and it didn't take a genius to work it out, he concluded that he was not the only one in the room.

Curious, and genuinely unafraid, Conway asked, 'Who's there?'

After a short pause, the darkness answered in a man's voice. 'Do you not know me? Can you not see?'

'It's too dark.' Conway said, a little peeved by the illogical impertinence of the questions.

'You must not look with the eyes,' the voice from the darkness said patiently, 'you must look with the mind. Then you will see.'

Conway's mind, a consensus of nervous butterflies at the best of times, now reacted as it always did when faced with intellectual uncertainty. It panicked, then became dogmatic. The integrity of his sanity could be at stake after all. He must get a grip. He did not want to go that road again. Candyfloss walls and disembodied voices were all very well but enough was enough. It was all a dream, he told himself, that's all.

But the voice from the darkness, a voice not unlike a controlling hypnotist, spoke again. 'You are not dreaming,' it said with slow emphasis.

Conway decided to ignore it. He would soon be back to normal, he assured himself. Then, thinking again, he found himself slyly admitting that the voice did seem very real. But that's the way with some dreams, he again assured himself, they can be so real.

'Think me out,' the voice said, 'see with the mind's eye.'

'What absolute nonsense!' Conway said in a fit of pique, flinging his thoughts at the source of the directive.

Then it happened. As if ignited by his thoughts, an image burst into flame before him. Taken aback, Conway watched in amazement as the flame swelled to the size and shape of a coconut that glowed with the most beautiful purples and mauves he had ever seen. As the aroma of lavender bloomed all around him, Conway felt himself being cornered into some very uncomfortable conclusions.

'What's going on?' he asked in exasperated disbelief.

The flame flickered in response, glowing more brightly.

'Look down,' it said, in an encouragingly friendly voice.

Conway had no intention of responding but, despite his resolve, he found himself somehow compelled to look. And what he saw appalled him. There below him, illuminated by the purple light of the glowing flame, was none other than himself. Pale, prostrate and apparently dead.

He saw himself lying there with his sweat-matted hair, his sunken eyes shut forever, and his breathless mouth open like some poor flounder. The indignity of it all and what an ugly corpse he made. God, what would his mother think? As morbid self-pity was about to engulf him, the voice spoke again.

'You're not dead,' it said matter-of-factly, 'but you're not quite alive either, at least not in the sense you are thinking of, though you are probably more alive now than you are ever likely to be. Do you understand?'

'No,' Conway said with bewilderment.

The flame flickered in response. 'Good,' it said, rather too jovially for Conway's liking, 'the admission of ignorance is the beginning of wisdom. I should explain to explain. You are in, what you and your waking world would call a coma, brought on by an extremely unlikely series of events. First of all, that little rodeo act of yours today brought you into contact with a very rare, what you would call, a bacteria, which harboured, for want of a word, what you would call a virus, which has precipitated, I think that's the word you use, a very rare condition that mimics, for want of yet another word, your common or garden coma. You are not dead, you are merely displaced. You have fallen out the wrong side of sleep. Your very essence has somehow slipped through the boundary of infinite planes...'

'This is not real,' Conway told himself, 'this is not really happening, this is a figment of my imagination...'

The light flared in glorious purple. 'This is real, this is happening, this is no figment of your imagination,' it said, contradicting, verbatim, Conway's unspoken words.

Conway, peeved and intrigued, asked, 'How did you know I was thinking what I thought?'

'I knew you were going to ask that,' the Coconut said, without a trace of smugness, 'you see, on this plane there is no confinement. Your thoughts are free to wander where they will. I simply listened to your thoughts.'

'How is it that you can hear my thoughts, but I can't hear yours?' Conway asked.

'That's because you're not listening. You're too used to hearing your own thoughts.'

'Who are you?' Conway asked guardedly.

'I will tell you what I am,' the Coconut began, in a voice slowed by deliberation, 'but I would ask you not to ask my name.'

This threw Conway somewhat. On the face of it, it was a simple enough request but Conway found himself drawn to know a name. Any name.

Remembering his manners, and in the process of shelving his need of title, Conway noticed an eerie glow emanating from the waxy face of the 'corpse' he still scarcely believed was himself. He watched with slow amazement as three lotto-sized balls proceeded, one by one, to pop from the imbecilic, broad-vowel mouth.

One by one they floated luminously up; the first was a pepper-red; the second, a pepper-green; and the third, a carbon-copy blue.

'What are you lot doing here?' the Coconut asked angrily and flushed a furious bright purple.

'We're here to take your man for a spin,' Red Pepper said jauntily, as if this sort of thing was a very regular occurrence and the most normal thing in the world.

'Trip the light fantastic,' said Green Pepper.

'Tiptoe through the tulips,' said Carbon Copy.

Then, all three added, 'Show him the sights, know what we mean?'

The Coconut was outraged. 'You're not supposed to be here,' he insisted, 'it's against the rules.'

By now intrigued and rather flattered that these colourful balls-about-town types should show such an interest in him, Conway felt obliged to introduce himself. But before he could do so, the three uttered, in dismissive unison, 'We know who *you* are.'

Chastened, and offended, Conway timidly responded by asking who they might be. Putting himself between Conway and the three intruders, the Coconut warned, 'Have nothing to do with them, do not engage them in conversation. They are out of bounds.'

Completely ignoring the Coconut, Red Pepper said to Conway, with sly crypticality, 'We might be anyone.'

'Tom, Dick and Harry, maybe,' offered Green Pepper.

'Athos, Porthos and Aramis,' offered Carbon Copy.

Red Pepper, warming to the game, added his tuppence worth, 'Eeny, Meeny, Mynee, even,'

'What about Mo?' Conway asked and immediately felt foolish for he sensed that the question was rather silly, and worse still, would be regarded as such. But the lotto balls fielded it as if it was a perfectly sensible question. Indeed, they seemed pleased with it.

'Mo?' the three balls explained with sweet accord, 'now that would be our surname.'

With their voices separating, each of them rose high to the ceiling, and, in what can only be described as manic oscillation, they began to recite, with solemn incantation, an avalanche of identities.

'...we be the rule of three; beginning, middle and end; we be the three blind mice; three coins in a fountain; three steps to heaven; three sheets to the wind; hop, skip and jump; furies, fates and graces; the world, the flesh and you know who; we be three, we be three, we three loggerheads be; Grand Inspector Inquisitor Commander, Sublime Prince of the Royal Secret, Sovereign Grand Inspector General. All present and correct. That's who we be...'

Red Pepper descended and nestled in close to Conway.

'Now, the question is,' he said, with sinister suggestion in his voice and obviously referring to the Coconut, 'who is he?'

'Do not listen to him,' the Coconut warned, 'he means you no good.'

'Am I,' Red Pepper began, 'are we, the ones who will not identify ourselves?'

The other two rallied to their comrade's argument, 'Not us,' they cried, 'not us...'

'No, not us indeed.' Red Pepper continued, 'Isn't that right? We cannot tell you his name, rules you see, but we can spell it out for you.'

'We can indeed,' said Green Pepper.

'Indeed we can,' said Carbon Copy.

And so, one by one, in a countdown beat, the three lotto balls began to spell out the Coconut's name.

'G...'

'Do not listen to them,' the Coconut vehemently advised.

'I...'

'Close your mind to them,' he urged.

'L...'

'You can do it,' he coaxed.

'G...'

'Be strong,' he said firmly.

'U...'

'Be firm,' he said fiercely.

'L...'

Conway's mind, trained as it was, had begun to reel in the sounds to form a necklace of letters.

'Do not speak my name,' the Coconut commanded.

Despite the warning Conway began, through sheer force of habit, to form the letters into syllables.

'Say it, say it, say it,' chanted Red, Green and Blue.

'No, no, no,' the Coconut bawled.

Conway tried valiantly not to observe the word that was forming in his mind for fear he would release it. But he was unable to resist. A subtle and seductive reflex within him sprung the syllables free and they, disastrously, formed the word. He could not help but give it recognition and out it popped, as bright and brazen as a neon sign. GILGUL was the word and it danced and pranced about in shameless fashion, then scampered off on a lap of honour of the room, before finally disappearing through a wall. With the word out, the Coconut vanished but not before leaving the long, anguished cry of 'shithead...' ringing in Conway's ears.

Addressing himself to Conway, Red Pepper, with abject disgust in his voice, said, 'You killed him.'

'As sure as eggs is eggs,' came Green Pepper's solemn endorsement.

With emphatic disdain Carbon Copy got in on the act.

'Why, you careless bastard,' he said, giving the distinct impression he would have spoken through clenched teeth, had he had them.

'Slimy cut-throat,'

'Didn't stand a chance,'

Conway was in despair. 'What have I done?' he said with pathetic rhetoric.

'You pronounced him dead, that's what you've done,' said Red Pepper, mercilessly helpful.

'His name will live on, forever,' Green Pepper intoned panegyrically.

'But alas he is gone,' Carbon Copy sighed.

Citing extenuating circumstance, Conway said lamely, 'I didn't mean to do it, it just slipped out. I didn't mean to harm him...'

As Conway persisted in explaining himself, Red Pepper felt obligated to condemn.

'You just couldn't resist, could you?' he said accusingly, 'you just had to have his name, didn't you? Always one for the nomenclature, aren't we, Conway? For the dotted line and the pigeon-hole, Conway is your man. One for the file was it? What is it with you? You have to have a name for everything and everything just has to have a name. For office use only. For fuck's sake!'

'Bet he sticks pins in butterflies...' snorted Green Pepper.

'Bet he dots his t's and crosses his precious i's...' sneered Carbon Copy.

'Pathetic fucker!' came Red's summation.

Crushed and deflated, Conway went into slow descent. From the high and honoured position of the ceiling, down he sank until he came to rest on the traditionally patterned, wool-twist carpet his mother had bought in a massive stock-clearing sale.

Icarus in carpet slippers, he never felt so low. It wasn't long, however, before he was overhearing a conversation he was patently meant to overhear.

With a loudness that often accompanies magnanimous gestures, Red Pepper was heard to say, 'Perhaps we are being too harsh...'

'Overly harsh,' Green Pepper, even more loudly, agreed.

'Extremely unfair, I would suggest,' said Carbon Copy at the top of his voice.

'We'll not mention the purple thingamajig again,' Red Pepper advised, 'he's of no importance, he was an...'

'Awkward customer...' Green Pepper said, venomously finishing Red Pepper's words.

This description opened the floodgates. In a follow-the-leader fashion, Red, Green and Blue set out in search of a succinct, denigrating expression.

'Bloody oaf...'

'Confounded chancer...'

'Dithering oddball...'

'Egotistic numbskull...'

'Filching user...'

'Grumpy toad...'

Finally, Conway could take no more. He could not permit himself to sit idly by while the Coconut's name was being blackened, even if it was being done in a systematic and alphabetical way.

'I thought he was nice,' Conway said, raising his voice in protest.

'Nice?' considered Red Pepper, 'oh, he was that too.'

'A gentleman,' Green Pepper concurred.

'Nature's finest,' said Carbon Copy.

'Now you mustn't upset yourself,' Red Pepper advised Conway, 'after all, you're new to this craic.'

'But where is he gone to?' Conway asked with crest-fallen sadness.

'Gone to?' Red Pepper repeated, then said as casually as he could, 'oh, nowhere...'

'Nice place,' Green Pepper added.

'Sure, 'tis fecken utopia, boy...' Carbon Copy guffawed.

Red Pepper was there in a flash to soften the blow.

'Look, kid,' he said, 'these things happen, don't beat yourself up over it. The Coconut was just a minor orderly whose job it was to keep you confined to the bed. Not physically, you understand, but,' here Red Pepper hesitated, then said, 'psychically...'

'I cannot believe you used that word.' Carbon Copy said, his voice awash with outraged incredulity.

'What am I supposed to use?' Red Pepper protested, 'it is the nearest approximation I can find to his vocabulary. How am I supposed to make him understand if I don't use his own language? Appallingly inaccurate, as it is, it's the best we can do in the circumstances.'

'You could use Intrinsic,' suggested Green Pepper.

'That would be useless,' Red Pepper said dismissively, 'by the time he got the hang of it, it would be too late.'

'Too late for what?' Conway asked.

'Oh nothing,' said Red Pepper defensively.

'Oh nothing at all,' Green Pepper assured.

'Absolutely nothing at all, whatsoever.' Carbon Copy re-assured with far too much sincerity.

Conway, not wishing to give offence, sublimated a roused suspicion and changed the subject.

'What's this Intrinsic?' he tentatively inquired.

Clearing his throat, Red Pepper gladly explained,

'It is an old lingua franca, a common-currency language, something akin to your Esperanto, except that we use it, except that there's no grammar, words, colons, semi-colons, commas or full stops, or any other such scaffolding. Come to think of it, it's nothing remotely like your language...'

'It doesn't sound much of a language.' Conway remarked.

'Precisely, no sound at all,' Red Pepper disclosed rather proudly, 'it is the greatest language of all, for it allows perfect understanding.'

'Then why can't you teach me to use it?' Conway asked.

'Because of one simple fact,' Red Pepper began.

'Yes?' Conway asked expectantly.

'You're an idiot.'

Stung, Conway retorted, 'I'll have you know that I have a high IQ and I have been tested, you know. I'm an honorary member of Mensa.'

'Densa, more likely,' quipped Carbon Copy.

'A high IQ, yes,' Green Pepper explained, 'but alas, a very low intelligence.'

'A complete idiot,' Carbon Copy said in some mitigation.

'But an idiot nonetheless,' Red Pepper amended.

'You shouldn't really call him an idiot,' Green Pepper piped up, 'you should call him an eejit.'

'Yes,' Red Pepper agreed, 'this Anglo-Irish idiom is rather tricky. My dear Conway, which do you prefer to be called, idiot or eejit?'

Conway found himself seriously considering the choice set before him. *Idiot* definitely seemed the more correct. It did have a Greek heritage, (idiotes: private person, layman, ignorant person, idios: own, private). It had more syllables than the alternative 'eejit', always a good sign, and was widely recognised in the English-speaking world. It was profiled in Oxford, Cambridge and Webster, and defined by the medical profession as a precise technical term, (idiot n. person so deficient in mind as to be permanently incapable of rational conduct).

By contrast, the term *eejit* was coined in the Irish mists of the vernacular. It was softer, somehow, less offensive, less hurtful than its English cousin. Indeed, it was often used as a term of endearment. Though less correct, it was the more preferable. But Conway could not bring himself to endorse a word unsanctioned by the proper authorities. Not being listed, ostensibly the word did not exist. The Concise Oxford Dictionary was bible, and verbal informality was anathema. Conway, with no real choice, plumped for *idiot*.

'That's settled then,' Red Pepper said with satisfaction, 'you're an idiot.'

'I suppose so.' Conway grudgingly conceded.

'Now that that's out of the way,' Red Pepper said, in a voice that was becoming all conclusive, 'may I suggest we leave this place, hemmed in as it is by its own confinement, and venture forth, across O'Dwyer Bridge and beyond, to ahhm, whatever it is, we're seeking, as it were...'

Then, in a spellbinding voice, he added with imperious command, 'Gather in, gather one, gather all...'

Conway watched as the three balls went into orbit around each other, creating intricate patterns of light as they did so. Faster and faster they went until all the colours of the spectrum were carouselled around the room. It was the most beautiful sight he had ever seen. It was the colour-card of the universe revealed. He knew in an instant that his field of vision, up to that moment, had been nothing but a hair's breadth of perception in the infinite symphony of things. As he struggled with the implications of this revelation, the orbiting balls suddenly kicked into a higher gear. It was not unlike, Conway thought, looking on, the spin-cycle of a washing machine. As he watched, all three balls were lost in a blur of acceleration. Now they coalesced and became one, and as they became one, all colours were absorbed and became one. When the transformation was at an end, there before Conway, floated a brilliantly white sphere, the size of a billiard ball.

Now speaking with a conglomerate voice, the sphere loudly intoned, 'North, South, East and West, on a spinning compass, draw short straw and you shall know the way the wind will shunt us. Come cat, come bat, come weather-vane, we're stepping through the window-pane. Up on my coat-tails, boy! Time to be gone!'

Suddenly, in a howling gust of wind, the billiard ball headed towards the window. Conway found himself being sucked along in its turbulent wake. As he was dragged relentlessly towards the inevitable, he found himself looking back at his room with nostalgic regret. He looked forlornly at his books that covered the walls. They were the only real friends he had ever had, and as he gazed about the room for the last time, his eyes alighting here and there on all its paraphernalia, it seemed to him that all the trinkets, toys or useless ornaments were pathetic milestones in a life that never quite got going. He thought of his mother and how she would ever manage without him, and casting a cold eye on the pitiful sprawl of his corporeal remains, draped in candlewick, he doubted, sadly, he would ever make it back.

Chapter Five

A pot-bellied, mother-of-pearl moon was shining down on Nicholas Street as Garda Tim McInerney stood teetering on the kerb outside the perimeter wall of St Mary's Cathedral. He looked right, looked left, and looked right again before expertly crossing the road. All was quiet. Too quiet, he thought. He could hear no alarm of any description. He had been told to be on the lookout for resuscitated bonfires. Sent on a fool's errand. No doubt, the Sarge was having a good laugh back at the station.

Coming to a halt at the bookie office that stood opposite the Cathedral, he scanned the large white results sheets that were sellotaped to the window. It was all bad news from the red marker that ringed, with hindsight flourish, the places and prices of the day's racing. Catching enough of himself in the reflection of the window to prompt a preening reflex, he set his cap to rights at a rakish angle and tugged down on his tunic.

It was only the poor light, he assured himself, that gave him that gaunt and victimized look. He was handsome, it could not be denied. And he had the height. That surely was why the Sarge had it in for him. What else could it be?

Don't forget that at six-foot-two he was well over the minimum height for a Garda, whereas the Sarge barely made the minimum of five-foot-nine. It must be a constant strain on the nerves worrying all the time that he might lose height. Something the body tends to do with age, compaction of the vertebrae and all that, and the Sarge was getting a bit long in the tooth. Sure to be compacting. They would never throw him out, of course. But merely falling below the requisite height, to be a Garda under false pretences, must be a terrible strain. No, he suspected the Sarge was nothing but a sad little man. Literally. Jealousy is a terrible thing.

You know, he did not hate the Sarge but it's hard not to dislike someone who has it in for you. From the first day he arrived in Limerick, the Sarge had been down on him. Of course, Bean Garda Molloy flinging herself at him, the way she did, didn't make matters any easier. The Sarge was furious, gave out stink about fraternizing in the ranks. Called him a young puppy.

Now, if there was one thing he did not like, it was being called a young puppy. And he'd been called everything and anything under the sun, from a Blue Shirt bog-trotter to a West Brit gobshite.

That's another curious thing now, why is it that a Bean Garda is not required to be as tall as the men? Five-foot-five is all that's required of the women. It was discrimination right enough. And like all things today they had a name for it. Heightism, wasn't that the word? Sure, wasn't it the height of discrimination. He chuckled at his little joke. That's a good one, he must remember that.

He sauntered on at a stately Garda pace, his head periscoping the vicinity. Near Styx Snooker Emporium, two youths with shaven heads and dubious body language were hovering around, what appeared to be, a badly parked Toyota Starlet. Garda McInerney cast a wary eye over them. The model citizens were wearing combat-camouflage co-ordinates by Army Surplus and black, calf-hugging, leather-wrap-around boots by Dr Martin. He homed in.

'Goodnight to ye, lads,' he said, in a tone of voice that undermined any pleasantry.

They answered him with malignant scowls and slouched off like resentful scavengers ousted from a carcass.

'And where would ye be coming from, lads?' he inquired.

Without stopping, without turning, the smaller of the two, who had an 'earring' in his nose, answered with a sour defiance.

'Down the road.'

'And where would ye be going?'

'Up the road.'

'You're an absolute mine of information. Do you know that?' McInerney said, then, not wishing to lock horns with hormone-troubled youth, he added, 'Stay out of trouble.'

'Right,' said the smaller one, over his shoulder, 'we're just goin' into town.'

'Bollicks,' muttered his companion, only half-smothering his contempt with the back of his hand.

Garda McInerney watched after them until they turned left and out of sight by Devane's Pub. The wrong way for town and duly noted. Turning his attention once more to the aforementioned vehicle, he began his examination, checking tax and insurance discs. Was it badly parked, or abandoned?

As he searched for clues that might yield a definitive answer, a dog with no collar, and looking the worse for wear, came moseying along out of a side-lane. The dog, looking for all the world like a cross between a mop and a brillo pad, stopped at the rear wheel that was nearest the kerb, sniffed knowledgeably, then cocked a leg to sprinkle his blessing. He turned and gave McInerney one of those looks as if to say, 'check out the tread on that tyre' before he sidled off down the road. It's a well-known fact that the dogs in Limerick are working for the authorities.

McInerney began to think on dogs. What a wonderful system of communication they had all the same, using encoded messages, in urine, to communicate far and wide via our transport system. A dog has a piddle, say, in Dublin, and a few hours later the message is decoded by another dog in Limerick. Sort of hubcap telegraph.

Garda McInerney's theorising was put on hold when a butty, bow-legged, bull of a man in white shirt-sleeves came trotting towards him in a bit of a lather.

'Probable owner.' McInerney surmised.

The suspect was roughly five-foot-four, or thereabouts. Far too small to be a Garda. His button-stretching beer belly, Garda McInerney noted, did seem less an encumbrance than a vital part of the man's equilibrium, for he appeared to be lively enough on his feet. He also noted with interest how the man's belt buckle, which was near enough the size of a manhole cover, was rotated downwards so much so that it faced the suspect's brown suede shoes. A fine head of black hair he had too, slicked back aerodynamically with hair gel, giving the impression of an Elvis impersonator perpetually involved in wind-tunnel experiments.

'Is there anything wrong, Officer?' the man said, as he jangled a bunch of keys in his right hand.

'Are you the owner of this vehicle?'

Keys were jangled again. 'Yes.'

'Would you mind parking a little more parallel to the pavement?'

'Sorry, Officer. I didn't intend to stop so long. Just popped into the shop for fags. But there was this kid in front of me, no bigger than a footstool. Buyin' sweets he was and askin' for something the shop assistant, a young slip of a girl, had never heard of, and so she asked him was he sure he was askin' for the right thing and after much guessin' and strainin' to pick out what it was he was sayin', she finally decided that what he was askin' for was a Cough-No-More Bar. She had never heard of a Cough-No-More Bar. But I had, so I said so, but she assured me that in all her life she had never heard nor come across a Cough-No-More Bar. And when I thought about it, I knew she was right. They had them when I was a kid but that was donkey's years ago. So I asked the kid to choose whatever he wanted, never mind the cost, I'd pay for it. He then decides, doesn't he, to have something else that hasn't been on sale for donkey's years, Trigger Bars, Flash Bars and the like. Then he asks for a pennart of car'mels. Six for a penny! Six for a penny, says he! I mean, it's a long time since they were six for a penny...'

Inflating himself to a fit of pique, McInerney bristled and sniffed all at once.

'Have you been drinking, sir?' he asked in a voice and demeanour that said, 'I am not to be trifled with. Capisce?'

'I swear, Officer, not a drop, scout's honour,' came the fervent reply.

McInerney, grabbing the reins of his temper in an effort to regain his composure, said simply, 'Watch the parking.'

'Won't happen again, Officer.'

'Try and see that it doesn't. It's only inviting trouble sticking out like that.'

'Of course, Officer.'

'Keep it in mind for the future.'

'I will, Officer.'

'Goodnight to you now.'

'Goodnight.'

You do meet the strangest, McInerney was thinking, as he watched the man squeeze himself into the Toyota and then nearly shake the shit out of the car in his efforts to get the seat belt on. Eventually he pulled away from the kerb. Without indicating.

'Uuuhuu! Officer! Could I have a word?'

McInerney was still tut-tutting to himself when he turned to see he was being hailed by an elderly woman who was standing at the door of a terraced house nearby.

As he struggled to open the gate the old woman issued instructions. 'You'll have to give it a good push,' she said, '...it's a bit stiff, so it is.'

After gaining access, McInerney asked, 'What can I do for you, Mrs?'

'Mrs Connolly, Officer.'

'Mrs Connolly.'

'What I want to talk to you about now, Officer, is the trouble I'm having.'

Up close, McInerney could see that the woman was in her eighties. At least. Very frail with rheumy eyes. The lower lids, distended and sore looking, reminded him of fresh fish gills.

'My heart is broke from him,' she went on, 'ooh the noise. He'd a be kicken that fecken canny all day long...'

'Canny?'

'Yeah, you know? A canny? A fecken tin can!' she said, shaking with impatience.

'Like a Coke tin can?'

'Well, I don't know if it's Coke, or Pepsi or what the fecken hell it is, it could be Fanta for all I care. I jus' know I can't take any more of this bla'garden. I don't be well in myself. It's got to the stage now where I can't cope with it any longer. He has my melt broke so he has...'

'Who would we be talking about now?' McInerney said, pulling out his notebook.

'That little scourge, Tommy Nolan, of course. Sure the whole street knows who I'm talking about.'

'Did you have a word with him?'

'You can't talk to the child. He doesn't pay a blind bish a notice and he'd cheek you up to the balls of your eyes, so he would, that's what he would.'

'What age is he?'

'Six, if he's a day.'

McInerney tucked in his chin and popped his eyes. 'Six?'

'He's an ould man,' the old woman countered, 'born with his pension book in his hand.'

'Did you have a chat with his parents?'

Nearly swallowing her false teeth at the suggestion, the old woman let fly, 'Is it coddin' me you are? Sure jaysus, I'm wastin' my time talkin' to that woman, will you go way from me, and her husband's no better. I can't be runnin' down the hill every five minutes to complain the little fecker. I can hardly walk, never mind run. I'm crippled from the arthritis and me eyes don't be the best. I wouldn't know where I'd be, so I wouldn't...'

'Well, I'll have a word with his parents and we'll sort something out.'

'Something will have to be done, because I'm at my wit's end. I don't have an ounce of peace with the racket at times. It do be goin' on all day long. It's a holy terror, that's what it is, that I can't have a bish a peace this hour of my life.'

'We'll sort something out.'

'Well I hope so, Officer.'

'Leave it to me.'

'I will so. I don't want to be complainin' but I have no alternative. It's got that bad.'

'We'll take care of it.'

'Okay, Officer. Thank you.'

'Goodnight now.'

'Goodnight and the blessens a jaysus on you. Thank you so much. You're very kind.'

'Goodnight now.'

'Goodnight and god bless.'

'Goodnight...'

No point in seeing the little shagger now, McInerney decided, probably tucked up in bed asleep. Call tomorrow and sort it out. God, had it come to this, Garda Timothy McInerney, Templemore's finest, in pursuit of a six-year-old canny kicker.

Chapter Six

Slipping into one of those moods of thinking nothing in particular, McInerney was carried down the road on legs that were just happy to be moving. As they walked him past a darkened laneway to his right, a sudden blast of cold air brought him to his senses. And as it did so, he thought he caught the sound of whispering coming from the lane. He stopped, retraced his steps, and inclined his head to have a listen. Was it a moth that brushed past his ear? Was it a vagary of the wind? He listened, straining to discern the sounds.

Nothing.

But wait, what was that? There was something. Very faint, on the breeze. He checked his radio to see if there was something coming through but there was nothing from the barracks. Maybe frequency interference. He switched off his radio and listened.

Listen! Hear It?

It came again, on the wind, sighs, whispers and voices entreating.

'...the first of May is a very good day, something for the bonfire...'

Something told him to turn on his heel and skedaddle. But he never did like being scared by things he was afraid of. From early childhood he had always defied his fears. He had this inexplicably stupid compulsion not to run from things that any normal human being would run from. All the survival instincts that nature had given him seemed to be stuck in reverse.

Like when he was twelve years old, 'skinning' apples (stealing apples from an orchard without prior permission, a misdemeanour) with his pals. There was this bull in a field. Yes, you've guessed it, all ran but for the bould Macca, as he was known back then in his short-pants days. He was the only non-runner. The bull became totally confused, lucky for Macca, he just stopped in his tracks, turned away and pretended to be a cow, hoping nobody would notice. The lads had said afterwards that it must have been a cow, it acted so cow-like. But it was definitely a bull. Macca knew the difference between a bull and a cow. Sure wasn't he a farmer's son.

The lane called again, more insistent now. The words swirling about his ears, '...the first of May is a very good day, something for the bonfire...'

Footstep by footstep, McInerney echoed down the lane. It was narrow, so narrow in fact that his outstretched arms would have spanned the gap. He could touch both sides with room to spare. And it was tall as it was narrow, all the way up to a three-storey building for most of its length. It had the smell of a well-used and neglected urinal about it. The bouquet of stale piss was very near overpowering and the damp, weepy walls, covered as they were with moss and weeds, appeared to be pressing in on him with malice aforethought.

A rusted drainpipe, broken well short of its original length, trickled water just above his head. He looked up as he manoeuvred to avoid it and caught a spray of cold water full in the face. All of a sudden, he was enveloped in a maelstrom of wind and the disincarnate voices of children, as high-pitched screams and squeals of delight filled the whole laneway. It was as if they had been released from school, such was their euphoria. Though he could not see, he could hear and sense them all around him, running, jumping, shouting and laughing at the tops of their voices. Almost catatonic, his mind and body cast immobile, McInerney stood rooted to the spot. He was surrounded.

'Welcome to Bob's lane...' the choir of sundry voices announced. Then came a questions and answers game. Like singsong catechism, all shouted, all answered.

'Who made the world? Bob made the world. Who is Bob? Bob is our father in heaven, the creator and lord of all things...'

Then one dissenting voice, a little girl, lisping.

'No, he isn't.'

'Who is he so, smarty pants?'

She took a big breath and explained, 'Bob lived at the bottom of the lane in a white-washed cottage with a half-a-door that was red. Bob al'ays wore his striped pyjama top even in the middle of the day. Bob was very nice. Knew we was just kids. He al'ays said hallo and we said hallo back. And Bob al'ays had an army coat on his bed with brass buttons on. Al'ays the door was open 'cept when we was told Bob died. Dident know what died was, but we knew it was bad and Bob wasn't comin' back, not ever, ever...'

There came a dismissive reproach, 'We know all that...'

'Whygeeaskmeso?' the little girl snapped.

Devastating logic put an end to the squabble.

'That's why...'

Then they sang, all together they sang, without a care in the world, to the rattling accompaniment of tin cans.

'...the first of May is a very good day, something for the bonfire...'

McInerney listened as off they went up the lane, carrying their little song with them, their voices fading as they went.

'...the first of May is a very good day, something for the bonfire...'

Then they were gone. For a few moments he listened to that strange silence only children can leave in their wake. Without knowing how he had got there, McInerney found himself back at the entrance to the lane, silhouetted by an inquisitive moon. What was all that about? Was his mind playing tricks on him? Was he hallucinating? Losing his marbles? Had he even gone down the lane in the first place? He wasn't all that sure that he had. He had heard of the queer goings-on that can occur around May Eve. It was common knowledge where he came from. The bonfires were still glowing embers after all.

A little shimmy of a breeze brushed against his face. Then he heard a petulant voice in his head say, with slow emphasis, 'Get a grip, McInerney. Get a grip.'

He was fairly certain it was his own voice. It sounded like his own voice. It must be his own voice. He listened to what he thought his own voice was telling him. That he had a bit of a turn. That was all. That it could happen to a bishop. And what he needed now was the wholesome distraction of some honest-to-goodness normality. And he knew just the thing. He had seen the light.

He crossed the road to King John's Castle and climbed the steps that took him to the entrance, an entrance that was, for all intents and purposes, nothing more than an elaborate greenhouse. He had read about it in the local papers, the architects insisting that they were not going to pretend it was anything other than a modern addition to the thirteenth-century castle. What you see is what you get, sort of thing. Others felt it was out of character. A bit like welding a glass crate to a pyramid. Known by locals as 'the thing', it was already famous for growing yuccas and tomatoes.

A petite, and very pretty, young woman with short black hair, unlocked one of the large glass doors and, pulling it open, politely inquired.

'Is there something wrong, Garda?'

'Ah no, just saw the lights. Just curious to see what was going on.'

'Well, aren't you the conscientious one,' she said jovially, then after getting a good look at him, she added, 'you look as if you've seen a ghost, you're as white as a sheet.'

Not wishing to entertain the idea of ghosts, McInerney muttered sheepishly, 'Just a bit cold that's all,' then added, 'it's a bit late, isn't it? To be working?'

'Poetry reading...' she answered, rolling her eyes. Then smiling, she said, 'Would you like a cup of coffee? I was just about to make one for myself.'

'You know, I wouldn't say no.'

'Grand, come right in. You're more than welcome.'

'You the receptionist here?'

'That's me. Betty, Betty Winston.'

'Tim...' he said, then responding to her raised eyebrows he proceeded to give his full name before asking, 'Where's security?'

'Down at the Viking settlement having a fag. Tom loves his fag.'

'Viking settlement did you say?' To McInerney's ears it smacked of unlawful assembly.

'The excavations,' she explained, 'Viking excavations. We have our Vikings here in Limerick too, you know. They must have got lost, that's all I can say.'

'You know, you could do with more security here.'

'Sure amn't I safe anuff here with all the poets to protect me,' she said, laughing, 'what a bunch, god love them. Do you hear them spoutin' inside? I got anuff of it at school. Poetry, that's all I need...'

'I don't know, we can all do with a bit of culture. I write a bit of poetry myself.'

'You don't...'

'Oh yes. Nothing great mind. When I'm on the beat now, things adbe croppin' up in my head, you know. I'd be jottin' them down in my notebook. You know, little limericks like. Since I'm in the capital place for them, ha ha ha...'

She laughed politely at his terrible joke. 'I'd say you'd chance anything.'

Somewhat encouraged, he took out his notebook. 'Here's one for you now,' he said.

'You're a howl, I swear. You actually have them in your notebook.'

McInerney cleared his throat and began to recite:

There was a young woman called Dora
Who was a terrible snorer
Her husband distressed
Left in his vest
And now sleeps with the woman next doora...

Betty threw her head back and let go a squeal of laughter.

'You're a howl and no mistake,' she said, then laughed all the louder.

Flattered and enchanted by this uninhibited response, McInerney found himself looking at Betty Winston with new eyes. And now that he looked at her, wasn't she a lively little thing, right enough. With a little pixie face and not a hair out of place, and her eyes full of divilmint and her little ears so exquisitely sculptured and god, didn't she have lovely teeth, and a mouth on her with lips and lipstick just hangin' to be kissed, and her pencil skirt with the slit so high above the knee and...and...

And soon McInerney found himself trying to deal with a crisis of insubordination going on in his trousers. Although there was no official ruling regarding such an event, as far as he was aware, the right side of his brain suggested to him that it might be regarded as a tad unprofessional.

'Are you doing anything for the long weekend?' he asked, forcing out the words as casually as he could.

'No plans,' she answered, 'the weather isn't up to much.' Then giving him a knowing smile, she asked coyly, 'Why? Have you something in mind?'

'I might,' he said.

Just as things were hotting up between them. Just as the chemistry was beginning to simmer and the kettle on the points of boiling, there was an almighty bang as the door of the theatre crashed open and out tumbled two middle-aged gentlemen who were clamped on each other in a seriously unfriendly manner.

'Doggerel, doggerel, I say! And bad doggerel at that,' one cried out triumphantly.

'Doggerel is it?' said the other, flushing red with rage and giving him a puck in the mouth for his trouble.

Soon they were trading blows to beat the band, flailing away at each other like crazed, synchronised swimmers, as they rolled around the lobby. And spilling out into the lobby after them came a motley group that McInerney immediately profiled as 'arty types'. The corduroy and cable-knit brigade with neck scarves, feathered hats and medieval haircuts much in evidence. Like refugees from Oxfam they just stood gawking at the antics of the two on the floor.

'Do something, Officer!' someone shouted.

Garda McInerney reached for his radio. Then thought the better of it. What was he going to say! I need backup, the poets are running amok! The only 'backup' he'd get would be the Sarge's and that was for sure. He decided to handle the situation himself.

'Come on, break it up there,' he said, disentangling the two adversaries and pulling them apart, 'have you forgotten where you are?'

Like children acting the innocents they both protested, 'You're not going to arrest us just for having a difference of opinion? Surely?'

'Oh, a difference of opinion? Is that what you'd call it?' McInerney said in disbelief.

'Sure 'twas nothin' at all, just a bit of a skirmish,' said one.

'That's all,' said the other.

It seemed that Tweedledum and Tweedledee had now set aside their mutual animosity and found a common purpose. And all was going fine until a small, dumpling, polo-necked-jumper of a woman stepped forward. She had strikingly beautiful eyes, set in a strikingly beautiful face, and spoke in a strikingly beautiful voice.

'They're the best of friends, you know.'

This seemingly innocent endorsement was enough to re-ignite matters.

'No, we're not,' said Tweedledum, theatrically rolling his eyes and breathing fire.

'Most definitely not,' said Tweedledee, pulling a face of disgust at the thought.

And just to prove how each felt about the other they started trading insults. With one word borrowing another they were soon at loggerheads again, but this time they were joined by others who decided to get in on the act. Sides were taken. All hell broke loose.

Above the mayhem, McInerney heard the pleading voice of Betty Winston, 'Tim, what are you going to do?'

There was something about being specifically chosen by this woman. He was breathing the rarefied air of the elected, the elite, and the anointed. It was the way she said his name. It was said with that subtle intimacy that declares a personal bond. She was not just appealing to the uniform but the man behind the uniform. She had touched the protector within him. He knew, there and then, that this woman would one day be his wife and the great-grandmother of his great-grandchildren. Swelled with the authority vested in him, he reached for his radio. It was time for action. It was time for backup. It was time for the paddy wagon.

Chapter Seven

They had come to the Castle by way of the scenic route. The Orb, as the tricolour amalgam now preferred to be called, it having a more regal ring to it, thought it would be a nice idea to do the grand tour. Conway, with no real choice but to tag along, being bound as he was to the Orb as if by some invisible string, was, to his surprise, overwhelmed by the enchantment of it all. Doubts, fears and misgivings simply evaporated in the cooling breeze of the night. Over roof, road and railing they had flown, weaving their way high and low past a slalom of chimney pots, tool sheds, pergolas, gnomes and wheelie bins. Through gardens, front and back, they went in their mazy flight with no regard for bylaw or private property, setting dogs to barking and cats' eyes wide with indignant stares.

To his amazement, they flew right under the nose of Tommy Prendergast, an old schoolmate of Conway's, who walked blithely on, unaware of their presence. Even Mrs Hayes, an accomplished curtain twitcher who never missed a thing, missed them, though they passed within inches of her at a pelican crossing. This immunity from recognition even extended to Mr Power, a good observer and a highly-trained nosy parker, if ever there was one, he being a retired Tax

Inspector no less. It appeared they were invisible to all and sundry except dogs, cats and such 'lower' life forms. The exception that proved this rule was the gleeful recognition of a baby in a buggy who gurgled with delight as they past, much to the bemused mystification of the mother. Wind, she surmised, was the likely explanation.

Down the Corbally Road, they came upon a sight that grabbed Conway's attention. Stopped at traffic lights, with a long line of cars close behind, was a horse and cart. And who should the horse be, only Gypsy, and standing erect on the cart, as tall as his height would allow, was none other than Nucky, with reins in hand and a frown of determination on his face. Gypsy, standing nobly to attention, tinkled his harness with a shake of his head as Conway passed, as if to say, I know you from somewhere.

'Hike, boy! Hold up!' Nucky called out, thinking Gypsy might have it in mind to break the lights.

Sitting at the back of the cart, wedged between two bags of coal, was Mikey, with Conway's binoculars held to his eyes.

'You're miles away, Nucky...' said Mikey, observing the back of Nucky's head.

Nucky glanced over his shoulder. 'You have them the wrong way 'round, you shaggin' eejit.'

'Oh yeah...' said Mikey, not in the least bit offended or embarrassed, and proceeded to correct his error. 'Now I have it,' he said, as he adjusted the focus, 'all I can see now is your head, Nucky, it's fucken huge. You're right close now...'

'Close anuff to give you a box,' Nucky snapped, 'now put down the fucken things before you break them.'

'I won't, I'll be careful.'

'Did I tell you to put them down? You'll drop them in a minute and have them in pieces.'

'I won't...'

'All right, but break them and you're for it...' Nucky conceded as he shook the reins to let Gypsy know that the lights had changed.

'I won't break 'em at all...' Mikey assured.

'My binoculars...' Conway had lamented, as he watched them move off up the road, 'my beautiful Zeiss 10x50 coated optics. The thieving magpies!'

Through the stained-glass doors of O'Driscoll's Pub the Orb and Conway flew, doing a full circuit of the boisterously busy lounge, weaving in and out among the sober, the merry and the inebriated. Flying past the mirrored optics, Conway caught sight of what he immediately knew was his own reflection. A custard-coloured ball! Of all things! Why did he have to be that colour, of all colours? It symbolized so many things that were negative. Yellow for sickness, cowardice, heresy and treason. To name but some!

Before he had time to further indulge his disappointment he was whisked past an aristocracy of intoxication. Past the Hennesseys, the Powers, the Jamesons, the Smirnoffs, the Cinzanos (Rosso and Bianco), the Dubonnets, the Gilbeys and all the rest. Some purveyors of, some very special, some very superior, some old, some old and pale, some sweet, and some dry. Established since whenever.

Totally unnoticed by the patronizing throng, they slipped out the back door and out into the night. Out on past the tree-lined railway tracks they zoomed, before meeting the marsh and the Sally Grove that marked the curve of the Island. Away from the counterfeit light of the suburbs the night sky blossomed into a glittering extravaganza of stars that sparkled like low diamonds overhead.

As capricious as a summer breeze, the Orb decided to 'ruffle a few feathers' and hitch a ride on the back of a hapless heron that made its way along the river. Conway was enraptured. It was as if he had stepped into one of those magical, moonlit paintings from a children's storybook. No longer observer, no longer outsider, he had become part of it all, part of the magic. There was a strange and intoxicating sense of initiation in the air that left him with the conviction he was on the threshold of something very special. In honour of his inaugural flight it seemed all things primordial were beginning to stir. Vague intimations vibrated in all he saw. In the swans treading water to become airborne, in the cormorant perched on an angling cot, holding its wings out to dry, in the blossoming rings of rising salmon, in the thrumming of the snipe across the sky. And down among the reeds, swaying in truculent currents, he could, with heightened perception, sense the river below as if it were his own bloodstream. To his eyes, all appeared peculiarly new and mystical. He was consumed with signs and symbols, and commonplace miracles. He swooned in awe of creation.

With head tucked back in its shoulders and legs trailing, the heron, with slow, powerful wing beats, took them over the Salmon Weir and on towards Thomond Bridge. In a response to a half-hearted attempt at harassment by a pair of black-headed gulls, the heron hitched itself higher into the air and seemed to be headed straight for the moon before finally deciding that the threat had passed.

Beyond the bridge, below the dimming stars, there before them stood the City. Like some great ocean liner decked in carnival lights, it seemed uncertain of its port of call. Limerick, the new Jerusalem-on-Sea. He never saw, nor thought it so beautiful, a hazy watercolour, an impressionist's dream, that might at any moment weigh anchor and sail off down the estuary and out into the broad Atlantic.

At Curragower Falls the waters broke in low murmuring and sluiced over moss-covered rock, churning up white fluorescence in an ancient quarrel for right of way. There, at the water's edge, a stone's throw from the Castle, the heron decided to set down at one of its old haunts. Leaving the bird to fish in its statuesque and solitary way, the Orb and Conway skimmed across the short stretch of water.

As luck would have it, they had arrived at the Castle just in time to witness the ignominious departure of the poets. Perched high in the battlements, they watched the scenes below with bemused detachment as the Gardai herded their unwilling charges into the waiting police vans. A crowd had gathered to gawk and to jeer, and curious heads in passing cars, slowing to a crawl, craned to see what was going on. Some youths, full of bravado and intent on more physical interaction, started pushing and shoving one another with no particular aim in mind. Like random bidding at an auction, the catcalls and jibes came thick and fast as the wits tried to top each other.

'Why are you arresting them, Officer?'

'Drunk in charge of iambic pentameter?'

'Assault with a deadly sonnet?'

'Reciting an elegy in a built-up area?'

'Shower of spanners!'

With masterful indifference, the Orb turned from the scene below and beckoned Conway to follow. And so they withdrew deep within the Castle, away from the street and the commotion. Through dark and narrow passageways they went before finally reaching the open walkway of a curtain wall that fronted the river. Illuminated by the moon, the spires of St Mary's Cathedral were plainly seen. Its ancient, half-muffled bells rang the changes, rousing the memory of stone. Conway was dreamily admiring the red valerian and pellitory-of-the-wall that sprouted high on the tower above his head. So heroic, he thought, to conquer these sheer walls and to blossom forth against impossible odds, though pellitory-of-the-wall, he had to admit, wasn't exactly a star when it came to flowering. Still, it had a simple charm.

'Conway!' He heard his name spat at him with such vehemence it sent him spinning.

'In the name of St Peter's cat,' the Orb said impatiently, 'do I have your attention?'

'Sorry, yes,' said Conway sheepishly, spinning slowly to a standstill.

'Good! Now to the purpose of coming here to this medieval pile of masonry. What we would like, Conway, is for you to run a little errand for us. We want you to retrieve something, and, as soon as that's done, you can go about your own business. Now, do you happen to see the shadow remains of a tenement building?'

Conway looked about him and saw nothing that fitted the description.

'Concentrate,' the Orb counselled.

He did as he was told. And, sure enough, there before his very eyes, as if knitting itself from the shadows, the form of a tall and gaunt building ghosted into view.

'In nineteen fifteen,' the Orb continued, 'on the third floor of that building that once stood within these Castle grounds, an event took place that was to have far-reaching consequences. On the stroke of midnight, on the twenty-fifth day of January, during a howling storm, the worst in living memory, a child came into the world. No ordinary child, no, but a very special child, to say the least, for Mrs Bridie O'Sullivan, Birdie to all who knew her, had given birth to her seventh son, the likes of which had never been seen before. In fact, a seventh son, of a seventh son, of a seventh son, of a seventh son, of a seventh son, of a seventh son, of a seventh son. A very rare event, indeed, as you can imagine, a seventh son raised to the power of two. This tiny scrap of life held, by all accounts, the key to the answer...'

'The answer to what?' Conway asked.

'The answer to the question,'

'And what is that?' Conway inquired, intrigued.

'The whereabouts of a string of pearls.'

'That's the question?'

'That is the question.'

'I see,' said Conway, not at all sure he did but deciding to let it go.

The Orb responded with rhetorical irony.

'Well, aren't we the devastating loss to Mensa,' said he, before going on in a familiar, conversational tone, 'he was a normal enough child in his infant days. Laugh at a penny bun, he would, and cry at the drop of a hat. Spent his days like any child, babbling, chuckling, squealing and screaming, and generally making no sense at all. For most of the day he'd be lying on the flat of his back, sucking his toes and staring up at the ceiling. Then one day, out of the blue, up he stands in his Moses basket and utters his first word, 'Dada'. This was the earliest indication of his latent powers, recalling as it did the international movement in art and literature that flourished between nineteen fifteen and nineteen twenty, a revolutionary movement that set out to overturn convention and shock the self-satisfied equilibrium of the status quo. You may have heard of them?'

'Yes, I have, as a matter of fact,' said Conway proudly.

'Well,' the Orb continued, 'the fact of the matter is that, at the tender age of two, we had another milestone in his development when he announced rather precociously to his mother, 'I'm brilliant, amn't I, Mam?' To which his doting mother tenderly replied, 'You are, love...'

After a significant pause the Orb proceeded.

'All went well, until, at the rebellious age of four, in the merry month of May, of a Sunday, disaster was to befall him. Slipping the surveillance of his older siblings, *and* a guardian angel who was too busy playing hopscotch, what did the little fecker do only march off after some other kids that were there, and off down to the Water Passage with him. Throwing stones they were and didn't he have to be doing what they were doing. Copying the others he was, climbing the river wall to throw stones. But whatever way he went, didn't he fall, and wasn't it just as well the tide was out. He cracked his skull on the rocks below and did a right job of his head.

For hours they struggled at Barrington's to save his life, fair play to them now, they did their best, but it was all to no avail and didn't they send for the priest in the end. But the divil a bit of good it did him and in the heel of the hunt wasn't he given up for dead. But, when all seemed lost, a most extraordinary thing happened. Of all things, didn't a ball of lightning come flying through the window and strike the metal bed on which the lad was lying and, miraculously, he regained life.

He lay unconscious for three days, however. The prayers that were offered up for that child is nobody's business.

Anyway, when he finally came to, he woke with a bandaged head and a considerable headache. Like a little Sikh, he was, with an outsized turban. He had survived, but he was never the same child again. Something was lost. Something very precious. It is the *answer* we speak of. The secret of secrets. It was no more. It was gone forever.'

The Orb fell silent for a moment, purely for dramatic effect, then said shrewdly, 'Or so we were led to believe. There have been rumblings down the years, rumours, you know, straws in the wind, that might suggest all was not lost. Now we have reason to believe that it is still accessible and that our time is at hand. It is your destiny, Conway, to seek the answer, to find this child, now an old man, and retrieve for us that precious knowledge that is still, we believe, locked deep within his mind. It is a great prize, for it is surely the Rosetta stone of all mysteries.'

'Why me?' Conway bleated, 'I mean, why can't you do it?'

'Can't, there are rules, you see, you alone are in a unique position to do this. The only disembodied entity to carry out this job. You are the right man, in the right place, at the right time. Cometh the hour, cometh the man.'

'Where is he?' Conway asked.

'In sanctuary, somewhere. That is all we can say because that is all we know.'

'I'm not sure I can help you,' Conway said doubtfully.

'Well, we have news for you,' the Orb said, becoming dogmatically emphatic, 'it is the only way you'll ever make it back home. Do this for us and we guarantee your safe return. Otherwise, your goose is cooked and your poor mother can start making funeral arrangements.'

At the thought of his mother Conway relented.

'But I wouldn't know where to begin.'

'Just follow your nose and you'll find your way. Think of it as a sort of treasure hunt. If all fails you could try praying to St Clare with lighted candle. Ask for three favours, one business and two impossible. Pray, whether you believe or not, and publish on the ninth day...'

Now hovering before Conway with intent, the Orb coolly announced, 'We must take our leave of you for a while. We have to split and be elsewhere as time is moving on. But remember, you haven't got forever. You have only as long as Yokam's water lasts...'

And so saying, the Orb, like a whiz-bang firework, shot straight up and into the night sky. Higher and higher it went before silently exploding into red, green and blue streamers that fell away in different directions. As Conway watched them fizzle out and disappear in the darkness, a strange feeling of desolation fell upon him. It was as if an umbilical cord had been severed. The feeling surprised him, after all he hadn't asked for their company, nor was he too keen on their weird ways, but now that they were gone he had to admit that he missed them. Alone and at a loss, he pondered his next move. Yokam's water? What the hell was that? It was all nonsense of course, he told himself. It all seemed so real and yet it was all so preposterous. He was getting used to this sort of thing. Nothing should surprise him.

Chapter Eight

Turning his attention to the river, Conway observed some pipistrelle bats flittering about a dance of mayflies that coiled above the reeds. Below Curragower, on the far side of the falls, a lone fisherman stood knee deep in water and cast a gossamer line in the tide. As dark clouds ghosted by in mercurial silence to engulf the moon, a shroud of mist rose slowly from the river and then began, by some unearthly conveyance, to creep towards the castle walls. Onwards and upwards it came, relentlessly laying siege, until finally it surmounted the battlements to spill its malignant vapours. Unnerved, and chilled to the bone, despite his disembodied state, Conway looked on in horror as an apparition began to form before his eyes.

A floating, ethereal, hologramatic kind of thing it was, and as it took shape, Conway began to see the figure of a man in battledress, with goatee beard and long hair in the style of a Cavalier. So close now, he could see details of its lace collar, and the rivets that bound the metal plates of armour together.

With deathly-pale face and eyes full of foreboding, it beckoned to Conway as if pleading to be heard, and in death-knell words from beyond the grave, it spoke.

When eye of day deserts the sky
And crescent moon comes with the tide
To cast its net for mortal dreams
It's time for sleep, it's time for schemes
Some, alone, deceit compose
Remain awake while others doze
And like the moth whose realm is night
Some deeds, though dark, require some light

On nights like these you may see
A ghostly anniversary
From Thomond Bridge with seven arches
On nights like these, an army marches
Listen careful and you may hear
Their footfalls echo far and near
Sounds of arms and fearful cries
Red blood runs cold, the wind it sighs

Yet of their struggle what remains
But tarnished stone and tarnished name
For like the salmon, ghosts return
That we their sons might live and learn
As waters on the rocks must break
The dead repeat their past mistake
And on and on with kindred foe
They fight and fight for evermore

The brooding Castle marks the hour
By Angelus and Curragower
An aged sentry, still it stands
To watch toward Thomond and the Strand
The jackdaw in its towers won't nest
Within those walls there is no rest
By day, to tourist it plays host
By night, to shadow, phantom, ghost...

Suddenly there came a sharp, rhythmic sound. Conway, looking to his right to where the slow handclap was coming from, heard a dark, phlegm-thickened voice cry out.

'Bravo! Bravo!'

With a howling gust of wind the spectre vanished and the mist retreated, slipping away like some dutiful footman in search of its master.

Conway, startled, as if woken from a dream, called out fearfully. 'Who's there?'

From the shadow of an alcove the voice said, 'There he goes, exit stage left, pursued by his conscience. Poor old Ireton, he captures Limerick only for Limerick to capture him. Died of the plague, you know, in Nicholas Street, embalmed and shipped back to England and buried as a hero at Westminster Abbey. Only to be dug up again, years later, along with his father-in-law, Ollie Cromwell, when Charles II was restored to the throne. Strung up, he was, before they mutilated his mummified carcass. And his head, along with the heads of all the other traitors, was impaled and put on display in London. But you can't embalm the soul. His soul remains here and his ghost is doomed to mope about the Castle. Forever. Looks too cavalier for a Roundhead, if you ask me. Not a bad poet though. For a Sassenach. You know, Conway, it's a funny thing about poets, the longer they're dead the better they seem to get.'

It was difficult to describe the stench that emanated from this shadowy figure, but a mixture of putrid, decaying flesh with a soupçon of vomit, diarrhoea and damp, musky mould would be a fair approximation.

As if sensing that Conway had caught a whiff, the voice said ingratiatingly, 'I smells a bit, but you get used to it,' then it asked, '...know who I am?' But, as Conway must have appeared bewildered, it proceeded to introduce itself.

'They call me Blackpot. Born from the egg of night and had no father, born in a nettle patch and nourished on the blood of criminals. Blackpot is my nickname. A soubriquet, don't you know, one of many. Stupid ghoul of a word, don't you think? Soubriquet! French of course. Literally, it means a tap under the chin. But I suppose you knew that anyway, you know so much. I'd love to give whoever's responsible for importing that word a tap under the chin. A puck in the gob I'd give him. Blackpot is my name. But I have so many...'

Am mangy dog
Am squeaky wheel
Am winter butter
Am summer fly
Am fleabite
Am hangnail
Am non-runner
Am blinky neon
Am uneven ground
Am stye in eye
Am fallen arch
Am stubbed toe
Am fuse blown
Am dinged tin
Am broken teabag
Am oil slicks
Am sleek eels
Am milk spills
Am raw deals
Am runny egg
Am dry rot
Am slipshod
Am slapdash
Am acid rain
I smoulder
Am legion...

Noticing Conway's revulsion and instinct to withdraw, the creature felt obliged to acknowledge the aversion.

'The festival of light it ain't, but don't you go gettin' me confused with what's-his-name. Different parish altogether. He'd be related to a cousin of mine, used to live near the Dispensary. Sure, that man don't be well in himself. Awful shook lookin' lately. He don't be up to the mark. All this diabolical craic, you know, wore him out. He's gone off. It's not easy havin' to be diabolical all the time.'

Just then, as if to show it was still on duty, the moon hoved into view, illuminating part of the alcove. Conway was dismayed by what he saw. Blackpot appeared to be half man, half tree, charred and blackened, with two large tawny eyes.

'Too much light! Too much light!' the creature groaned as it retreated deeper into shadow. Then, in a mocking voice that sent shivers through Conway, it said, 'It's all so very somethingesque, isn't it, Conway? You have to ask yourself the right question, do you take the wrong road for the right reasons, or the right road for the wrong reasons?'

There was a long pause, a deep sigh and a sad little laugh before it spoke again.

'God said, let there be light, and the ESB said, let them pay for it,' then it added hoarsely, 'before you go and leave me to the darkness, I have something for you...'

From out of the shadows it proffered a black and gnarled hand that held, what appeared to be, a note.

Chapter Nine

Everything about them was shifty. There was an intensity in their behaviour that suggested a contrived front. No doubt about it, they were a strange pair. Communicating mostly by winks, nods and nudges, they occasionally lapsed into a kind of mumbled dialogue. Words were ushered to the side of the mouth before being covertly discharged into hand, sleeve, shoulder or chest, while the eyes, intent on disowning what was being said, wandered aimlessly.

'He'll fucken know,'

'He won't, he won't, he's a tulip. Go on, for the craic and fill 'em up, will you, he's not there at all...'

'Are you sure he's gone out?'

'He is, I tell you,'

'He might be only out the back havin' a piss,'

'He's not, I tell you. He's gone up the road to Casey's to get a few cartons of fags,'

'How ju know?'

'He told me while you were out havin' a piss. You're one windy bastard, you know dah, Miko.'

'You're so fucken smart, Willy, why don't you do it?'

'Ah come on will you, get the fucken drink,'

'What about his nibs?' said Miko, nodding over at the only other customer in the place. Under a glass showcase, containing the tatty remains of a fox in close pursuit of a rather pathetic-looking partridge, an old man sat nursing a pint of Guinness.

'Don't mind him, he's as blind as a bat, he can't see a fucken thing.'

'Okay, gimme your glass, and watch the fucken door...'

Miko, standing up on the brass footrest of the bar, leaned across the counter and with the dexterity of a lemur helped himself to two pints from the Heineken tap.

In the semi-circle at the baulk end of a pool table, among the beer stains and cigarette ash, a yellow ball of agitation, who had been ruefully monitoring this queer carry on, now began to ask himself some searching questions. Was he in the right place? Had he got it wrong? What was it that note had said?

Take the cure from Dr Ink
Take it as you may
Your port of call is The Two Door Inn
That's Tudor a.k.a.

He had come to the Tudor Inn, a ramshackle and down-at-heel public house at the corner of Convent Street and Nicholas Street, in the hope that he might be re-united with his taskmasters. He had intended re-negotiating his position. Explain that he really wasn't up to carrying out the quest they had set him. Throw himself at their mercy. If needs be, quote the 'quality of mercy' speech from the Merchant of Venice. Anything to get back home.

His hopes had been raised, somewhat, when he spotted what he thought was none other than the Orb itself. Of course it had all been a mistake, hadn't it. The 'Orb' turning out to be nothing more than a common species of cue ball of the pool variety, kept for its own safety in a half-pint glass behind the bar. It seemed they had a tendency to 'walk', as it were, when not in play. It was a mystery to Conway why anyone would steal a cue ball.

'Sound man, Miko, I never doubted ya, boy.'

Conway watched as Miko returned to his table and set down two foaming pints in front of his accomplice. The piracy of pool balls was no longer a mystery.

'Fair fucken play to ya, Miko, boy,' said Willy, rubbing his hands together in anticipation.

The front door of the pub creaked open and a tall, gangly man with advanced receding hair, and a luxuriant moustache the size of a scrubbing brush, entered. With a great loping stride he sauntered across the threadbare carpet that marked the well-worn path between door and bar, validating Euclid's assertion that the shortest distance between two pints was indeed a straight line.

'Here's the dopey fuck now, say nahan,' Willy whispered into his pint. 'Act the fool. Be wide.'

'Everything all right, lads?' the returned barman inquired cheerfully, then did a double-take on seeing the miraculously replenished pints. With a frown of resignation, he said no more but went about his business, unwrapping cartons of cigarettes from their cellophane and stacking them in neat columns.

Willy elbowed Miko.

'Wait now, watch this,' he whispered mischievously, then called out, 'John, John...'

'Yeah?' said John, who was now down behind the bar, clinking and rearranging bottles.

'There's somethin' dodgy about this pint,'

'Yeah, I thought so myself,' said John warily.

'He fucken knows,' said Miko, getting agitated, 'I tell ya he fucken knows...'

'Hould your whist, will ya?' Willy hissed.

'You'll draw him on us,' Miko protested.

Regardless, Willy raised his voice in disgust.

'There's an awful taste off it,' he declared.

Elbowed rudely for support, Miko added lamely, 'Yeah, mine's the same, fucken awful.'

'That's funny now,' said John, still busy down behind the

bar, 'I cleaned the pipes only yesterday.'

'Ah, that's it so. It must be the cleaning fluid,' said Willy, unable to disguise his delight at being given a foothold for his spurious complaint.

'Dah fucken stuff would killya,' Miko chipped in, sensing victory.

'Well, nobody else is complaining,' said John defensively, popping his head over the counter.

'I don't see a lot of people in here, do you?' said Willy, then referring to the old man, he went on, 'except that poor amadán at the end of the bar and he doesn't know where the fuck he is...'

'It's always slack of a Wednesday,' said John matter-of-factly.

'It's like a fucken graveyard,' said Miko.

'Well, John, what am I goin' to do with this pint? I can't drink it,' Willy said with a plea in his voice.

'Jaysus, you've made a fair fist of it all the same. There isn't half a finger left in it,'

'Look, are you goin' to fill me out a dacent pint or are you not?' snapped Willy, giving an excellent impression of one mortally offended.

'Jaysus, John, mine's the same,' cried Miko, 'there's an awful taste off it. I hope I don't get the trots from it,'

John had heard enough. 'All right, all right,' he said, 'what do you want?'

'Give me a Carling. Is the Carling awright?'

'Yeah,'

'Gimme a Carling so,'

'You miraswell gimme one, too,' Miko added rapidly, not wishing to be left out of the settlement.

On receiving two free pints of Carling in compensation for their distress, Willy, after thanking John for being so understanding, turned triumphantly to Miko and said with a satisfied sneer, 'I told you he was a stupid fuck.'

After taking a swig from his glass and noisily wiping his mouth with the sleeve of his jacket, Willy took a crumpled photograph from his breast pocket and stuck it in front of Miko's face.

'Take a looka dah phosha. What ju think a dah?'

'Dah your dog?'

'Yeah, now that's what I call a dog, a bull tarrier, great fucken dog, sham, great fucken tack,'

'They're not as good as the pit bull, there's some dog for you, sham, they wouldn't bate them,'

'They fucken would,'

'They would, in my eye,'

'Not in your eye now at all, sham,'

'Well, I'm tellin' you they wouldn't,'

'And I'm tellin' you they would,'

'You can tell me all you like, but you're fucken wrong...'

If Conway didn't know differently he would have sworn he was listening to a Punch and Judy show. On it went.

'What the fuck do you know about dogs anyway?'

'I know anuff,'

'I'll tell you what you know, fuck all.'

'I know more than you anyway...'

This verbal ping pong came to an abrupt end when the front door of the bar swung open and, lo and behold, who should enter only someone Conway instantly recognised. In donkey jacket and jeans and carrying what appeared to be a cast iron fire-surround slung over his shoulder, it was the same someone who that very day had carried him home, on horseback, to his outraged mother.

'Here's Nucky now,' Miko said, 'we'll ask Nucky. Now we'll see who's right.'

'I'll betchu anything he'll say the bull tarrier is better.'

'We'll see now, we'll ask him. Nucky, com'ere a minute,'

'What?' replied Nucky wearily, distracted with finding a suitable spot to set down his burden.

'Is the pit bull better than the bull tarrier?' Miko asked.

'None of them are any good,' said Nucky conclusively, still looking for somewhere to offload the surround.

'For fightin' now, Nucky, which is the best?'

Finally, in exasperation, Nucky propped the fire-surround against the bar. 'I told you, none of them are any fucken good,' he said, wiping his hands on his jacket, 'they're no good for huntin' or the bad weather. The best dog you could have is the Cocker or a Jack Russell or a Labrador...'

'But for the fightin' now, Nucky, if you wanted a dog for fightin' only.'

'Listen,' Nucky said, with a grimace, 'if you want to carry your balls on a lead that's up to you but I don't agree with this fightin' craic at all. If you want to fight, do it yourself. Don't be havin' a misfortunate dog doin' it for you.'

Miko blinked, began mobilizing a belligerent posture and said, 'There's no need to get sour over it...'

'Who's gettin' sour?' Nucky challenged with a smile.

'I was only askin' a question,'

'Well, I gave you your answer.'

'You did an' all,'

'So?'

'So nahan. Like I said, I was only askin', that's all.'

'What have you got for me, Nucky?' John the barman interrupted pleasantly, as if nothing was going on.

Nucky turned his back on the retreating Miko and said, as casually as you like, 'The fire-surround, John, I was tellin' you about. It's in good condition. A bit of a clean and it's as good as new.'

'Don't want them new, Nucky,' John said, laughing, 'the older the better, it's what the tourists want, they get very sentimental about the past, you know. Did we agree a price?'

Nucky scratched his head and winced.

'Ah, give me forty and we'll call it quits...'

'Fair enough, if you come across any more, let me know.'

'Right so,'

'And any brass stuff, Nucky,' the barman went on, 'you know, like lanterns, that sort of thing, anything that's olde-worlde. I tried the antiques shops but you know what they're like, they'd rob you, and then I don't want to be paying too much for something that could go missing. What's not nailed down, know what I mean, they're going around with claw hammers these days. Will you have a drink?'

'I'll have a Cidona,' Nucky said, and glancing over at the old man, he added, 'and give Tom a drink as well.'

Back in his seat, the smouldering Miko took a swig of his Carling, and said dourly, 'I'll do him some day.'

'You would, in your dreams,' said Willy.

'Is that so?' Miko said defiantly.

'In your dreams,' Willy repeated.

'Not in my dreams at all, sham.'

'Nucky is one tough nut,' Willy said, shaking his head to emphasize the point.

'I'm not frightened of him at all...'

'Dah wouldn't save ya.'

Miko threw a scowl at Nucky's back. 'Look at him,' he said, 'thinks he's a hard man.'

'Ah, he's hard awright. It's all the coal he be liftin'. Shur, didn't he bate the daylights out of Jimmy Mullins for hittin' one of the brothers, and Jimmy Mullins is as hard as nails...'

'Jimmy Mullins wouldn't bate Kashy Barry,' Miko said with a dismissive contempt.

'Is it fucken jokin', you are,' Willy said, swinging around to face Miko, 'Jimmy Mullins was an all-Ireland boxer in the fucken army.'

'He was in his eye.'

'He fucken was an' all,'

'Anyway, I did a bit of boxin' myself, and karatee.'

'You fucken never did karatee.'

'I fucken did,'

'I suppose you've a black belt in Irish dancing, as well.'

'No, sham, for your information, I did a lot of judo...'

'Will you go 'way from me. You're some plum for talkin' crap, you know dah?'

'I'm not talkin' crap at all.'

'Prove it so.'

'How ju mean?'

'You wouldn't claim Nucky, would you?'

'I have no reason to claim Nucky.'

'You said a minute ago you had.'

'Dah don't mean I'm afraid of him...'

'No, you're just scared, that's all. You're all talk.'

'I'd take Nucky any day,' Miko insisted.

Willy laughed. 'With all your karatee, boxin' and judo he'd be no trouble at all to you. He wouldn't stand a chance.'

'Very smart, aren't you? I suppose you'd hold my coat?'

'I'd even call an ambulance for you.'

'I'll show you,' said Miko. Getting to his feet, he shouted over at Nucky, 'Hey, Nucky, any chance of a pint?'

'Do you think I'm made of money,' Nucky said, turning around and giving Miko a quizzical look.

'Ah you always have a few bob,'

'And you don't?'

'Ah go on, Nucky, give us an oul' pint,'

'Would you politely fuck off,' Nucky said jovially.

'You're sly, anyway. You must have got a few bob from the insurance dah time,'

'What time?'

'When the father died.'

Nucky put his two hands on the counter and lowered his head. Then, taking a deep breath, he raised his head again. His face like thunder, he lowered his voice to a rumbling growl.

'Let me tell you somethin', Miko, and get it through that thick skull of yours, if you ever mention my father to me in that way again, you'll get a pint all right, maybe more than a pint, you'll be drinkin' your own fucken blood. Is that clear?'

'Don't be threatnen me. I'm not frightened of you at all.' said Miko, visibly shaken.

'Miko, I'm in no mood for you now. I came in here for a bit a business and a quiet drink, okay, but if you want to start trouble, I'll give you trouble. I swear I won't be responsible for what I'll do to you and do you see that gobshite with you, I'll put him into hospital as sure as I'm standin' here.'

'I did nahan, Nucky,' Willy protested.

'No, of course you didn't, you're innocent out. You know what, Willy? You should be a fucken promoter. You're very good at settin' fights for people. You just love to see people gettin' a baten, don't you? But I'm tellin' you, Willy, you're barkin' up the wrong tree with me. Mind yourself now.'

Willy, shifting uneasily in his seat, blurted out, 'I don't want any trouble, Nucky,'

'I didn't think so. Take your friend here and fuck away ouravit before I lose my patience with you.'

'Come on, Miko, let's go.'

'I haven't finished my pint,' Miko said, going for his glass.

'Leave it, for fuck's sake, we'll go up the road.'

Chapter Ten

When Nucky left, Conway felt obliged to follow. There was nothing to be gained, he was convinced, in remaining where he was. And despite his disenchantment with the unsavoury altercation that had taken place, and some reluctance to be anywhere near him, he was of the opinion that Nucky might be of use in finding a solution to his problem. After all, the chance convergence of their paths had somehow led to the weird predicament he now found himself in. All things considered, and with nothing else to go on, Nucky did seem the best bet.

But things were to get weirder still for Conway, for as he followed Nucky out the door of the Tudor Inn, a most extraordinary thing happened. Instead of returning to the night, as expected, he found himself inexplicably in broad daylight. There was no sign of Nucky anywhere. It was as if he had vanished into thin air and, more peculiarly, so had everything else that was familiar. The Tudor Inn was no more, where it had stood, only moments before, there now stood in its place a decrepit building, its thatched roof a dilapidated, scraggly affair teetering on the brink of collapse.

Bewildered though he was, Conway struggled manfully to get his bearings. Marshalling his thoughts into a makeshift council of inquiry, it did not take him long to decide that things were not as they should have been. If he was not in a dream, and he felt certain he was not, then there was only one explanation to it all. He had entered another time, another world. He had somehow found his way into the past.

The evidence was all around him, vibrant, organic and irrefutable. The main road that swept up in a curve from Thomond Bridge was now a mere dirt road, inhabited with people dressed in the most antiquated fashion, reminding Conway of those quaint figures he'd seen in old prints of Limerick. The Castle was still there but not as before, looking decidedly shabby and rundown with sections of its walls in disrepair. Its demeanour was somewhat menacing, its towers rearing with gloomy disdain above the street, a street that was now a good deal lower than it had been, criss-crossed with wheel ruts and pitted with holes.

Stones, some quite sizeable, were strewn about the road. Footpaths, laid haphazardly with flagstones and patches of cobblestone, were narrow and uneven and trailed along the base of buildings like an afterthought. Thomond Bridge was unrecognizable, no longer the picture-postcard bridge he knew but a sad-looking pile of stones with an odd little building imposed upon its entrance.

Conway was inclined to the view that he had wandered onto the set of some period film in the making. But this was all too real to be contrived. It could not be dispelled by a concentration of will. He tried but it would not shift. Like some fatalist locked in a carnival ride, he sensed a conviction growing within him that it was futile to resist. He would have to see it through. In any case, he consoled himself that it was an opportunity of a lifetime, and wouldn't any student of history, worthy of the name, jump at the chance to be where he was right now? Although a detour from his purpose, it seemed he had no other choice but to take advantage of this temporal slippage. The past was now an open book and he should embrace it. These were his people, after all, this was where he came from. Deciding to explore, he journeyed up the road, surrounded on all sides by people who were long since dead. A ghost among ghosts, he moved among them as if they were contemporaries.

Presently, a woman's voice declared in pleasant, tour-guide mode,

'...the year is 1798 and we are standing on the main thoroughfare of The King's Island, at this time called Great Street...'

Conway looked about for the source of the voice but could see nothing. The voice from nowhere spoke again.

'...the scene is one of neglect with many buildings in a rundown state...it is a time of rebellion in Ireland...'

A donkey and cart, piled high with animal hides, trundled its way up the middle of the road. The driver, an undersized and wizened individual, wearing a wide-brimmed hat and moss-green waistcoat, sat cross-legged holding the reins. A clay pipe fastened in his mouth, he seemed asleep as he passed with his noxious cargo, oblivious to the stream of stench he was leaving in his wake.

There was a mouldering atmosphere to the place, stone and brick buildings, some two, three and four storeys high, encroached upon the road from all angles, threatening to engulf it. Indeed the whole street for as far as he could see, was lined, for the most part, with these tenement structures that seemed to lean against each other for support. Like a row of dominoes, they gave the impression that if one should fall then all would fall. Occasionally, a more robust building of stone did appear, adding to the overall sense of improvised planning, but these, too, bore the stamp of dereliction. Windowpanes, where they survived, were often cracked, or covered with papers, and doors, where they existed, hung precariously on their hinges.

So bad were these dwellings that one could not imagine they were inhabited, but nothing could be further from the truth. They overflowed with people, housing several families at once. They hung out of windows and doorways, or peered from murky stairwells. Women cooking, cleaning, or hanging out washing or nursing babies or gossiping, while barefoot children, who seemed to be everywhere, ran about in play.

Cheek by jowl with these domestic scenes were men plying their various trades or hawking their wares. Tinsmith, blacksmith, weaver, cooper, candle-maker - the place was a hive of activity where home life and industry mixed together in a boisterous confusion. Commingling with the noise, odours of every variety added to the assault of the senses. From out of every doorway, window or laneway, a musty stink of dubious origins vied for supremacy with stewed bacon and cabbage and the malted grains of brewery and bakery. The compromised signature floated on the air as a heady concoction, enveloping the whole street.

An enthralled voyeur, Conway meandered along, soaking up the atmosphere as he went. Down a laneway to his left, an old woman wielding a sally switch was shouting her disapproval and invoking all manner of oaths as she chased a large sow and her piglets from an open drain. Across the road, outside a quaint tavern with the name of *King's Head* emblazoned above it, old men sat around wooden barrels smoking pipes and trading stories.

Farther on, a dilapidated old shop was doing a brisk business. So brisk, in fact, that piles of its merchandise were left outside on the flagstone pavement to be picked over by poverty-stricken customers.

Men and women, young and old, patiently rummaged through mounds of clothes and shoes that had passed down the generations more than once too often. In a doorway, close by, a young man in a soldier's tunic was singing to himself and his dog. At first glance, the lower half of his body appeared to be hidden down a manhole, until Conway realised that the misfortunate man had no legs and had to haul himself about on mittened hands. The dog, a scrawny wire-haired terrier, barked at Conway with one defiant eye.

'What ails you, a stór?' his master chided, then turning in Conway's direction, and seeming at first to be aware of the intruder's presence, said softly, as he affectionately ruffled the dog's ears, 'what ails you, 'tis but the wind, 'tis aisy rile you. Too long in harness you are and you wantin' to be chasin' rats, rats, rats...'

Retreating from the frantic yelps and yaps of the canine Cyclops, Conway moved on up the road where he came upon a shop that looked, for all the world, like a museum of natural history. It displayed every dead specimen imaginable in its grimy shop windows and on rickety stalls placed outside. Geese, duck, woodcock, snipe, skins of stoat, hare and rabbit, and what looked like an otter to Conway's eyes, were offered. A plump, rosy-cheeked woman wearing a blue apron dress and white cloth bonnet kept flies at bay with swipes of a goose wing.

In a doorway, an elderly man wearing a red neckerchief and a top hat crumpled like a concertina, sat playing the uilleann pipes. He beat time with bulbous, hobnailed boots, and sounded a good deal like someone who was strangling an asthmatic cat. Impish children, who looked as if they had never seen soap or water, or a comb, had gathered around him, dancing about and gleefully clapping their hands.

But soon their dancing stopped when out of a laneway came three very black and very peevish-looking cows. They bounded along ahead of the drover, a low-sized man with pockmarked face and dressed in shabby frockcoat and hat. He was waving high a blackthorn stick and calling to a scrawny sheepdog who seemed mystified as to what to do next. To Conway, there was something very familiar about the livestock. Then it occurred to him that they were not unlike the Kerry cows he had seen in Muckross, in Killarney, an ancient breed of cattle adorned with long, gracefully up-curving horns. The children's squealing and scattering in all directions brought the wrath of a mother down on the drover's head. With hands on hips and hair like a flaming bush, the wild-eyed woman screamed at the poor man, who, doing the gentlemanly thing, kept his composure by ignoring her. No sooner had they come and the cows and the drover and his dog were gone, disappearing down a laneway on the other side of the road. As the sun beat down, flies buzzed above the fresher deposits of dung that lay scattered about, forsaking older cowpats that were curling at the edges as they dried to the consistency of papier-mâché.

Drifting from the scene, Conway approached a more affluent section of Great Street. Splendid buildings, some three and four storeys, and in excellent upkeep, occupied both sides of the street. Many had the bell-shape roof so characteristic of Dutch gables. Here, as if in keeping with the improving architecture, the people looked to be far more prosperous than previously seen. An ornate carriage of huge proportions, and drawn by four well-groomed horses, was setting down passengers who were dressed in all the finery one would expect of a Strauss Ball. Top hats and dress-coats, bonnets, bustles, white gloves and parasols were the order of the day.

The upbeat tone of the tour guide cut in:

'...to our right we see the old corn Exchange, a fine stone building, it is supported by seven stone columns in the Tuscan order, housing a market and municipal offices within. It is the meeting place of the old Limerick Corporation. It was here that a low limestone pillar known as the Nail was housed. It was on this pedestal that debts were discharged, hence the expression, to pay on the nail...'

Conway looked at the 'old' Exchange, now in pristine condition, and marvelled at its six graceful arches and its six substantial windows. He had known it only as a filled-in portico, a remnant that served as a perimeter wall to the Cathedral. Now it stood a three-dimensional, magnificent building in its own right.

People milled about in twos and threes, some leaning against columns to rest up, or chat, or to smoke. Accents, home-grown and foreign, carried on the air and Conway distinctly heard both Spanish and French being spoken. A knot of soldiers, dressed in vibrant-red waistcoats with fancy epaulettes and high braided hats, sauntered about, chattering boisterously. Apart from their polished boots, and spurs that jangled with every step, and their burnished sabre hilts that hung in scabbards by their sides, they would not have looked amiss in an American marching band on St Patrick's Day.

'Now that *is* odd...' thought Conway. From where he stood, Athlunkard Street should be on his left, but no such street existed. Instead, an unbroken line of houses barred the way. And opposite, on the other side of the road, two Dutch-gabled houses stood where the boundary wall of the Cathedral should be. Indeed, the houses concerned infringed upon Bridge Street, narrowing it considerably.

As Conway puzzled it out, a breeze with the brisk scent of the river on it began to blow his way.

'...as we turn right and down the hill and into Bridge Street, at this time called Quay Lane, we see, on our right, the ancient cathedral of St Mary's, founded in 1168 by Donal Mór O' Brien, King of Thomond. It contains some fine, pre-Elizabethan carvings that are unique in Ireland...'

Down past the old City Courthouse, which now looked remarkably fresh, an elderly woman, her weathered face enclosed in a black shawl, sat by wicker baskets filled with crab apples, pears and bunches of heather. Now and then she would cry out in words unfathomable to Conway. A donkey and cart carrying a battered milk churn gave way to the coach and four that had, just minutes before, delivered up its illustrious patrons at the Exchange. It drove on by, its massive wheels spewing up a choking, nonchalant dust. On Conway flew, past rows of shops that sold everything from a needle to an anchor. Rope, lace, leather goods, furniture, lanterns, ploughs, sacks of meal, geese, chickens, pigs, and barrels of fish that stank to high heaven.

On reaching the quay, where the Potato Market should have been, there was now a magnificent sight. There before him, like a dream, a three-masted tall ship lay at anchor. He could see crewmen clambering over her rigging, while others on deck busied themselves with the loading and off-loading of cargo. On the quayside, all classes of people mingled and moved about and the noise of low commerce filled the air. Goods of all sorts were being shipped in all manner of carts that came and went in all directions. Supervising merchants stood about watching as drivers dealt with fractious animals, or shouted orders to workmen as they heaped sack upon sack or stacked wooden barrels in neat pyramids.

'...we now come to the bridge known as the New Bridge, a three-arched structure that spans the Abbey River, built in 1761...'

Conway turned his attention to the bridge in question and, to his surprise, it did seem a pretty decent forerunner of Mathew Bridge, which would replace it. But the bridge had another surprise in store, a surprise that would cause such academic considerations to evaporate. There, hanging from its ornate lampposts, on either side of the bridge, were the mummified remains of two bodies. Both knock-kneed and shoeless, and with their hands tied behind their backs, they faced each other on their impromptu gallows as if partners in some grotesque dance. The breeze coming off the river set the macabre pair to rotate slowly, turning them one way and then the other, as the ropes wound and unwound.

The gruesome sight stopped Conway in his tracks. He had no wish to continue but soon his resolve gave way to a strange and morbid fascination. Not knowing why, he felt a troubled, yet compelling need to cross the bridge. As he neared the terrible scene, he could see where the ropes had cut deeply into the blackened flesh. The necks, twisted and deformed, caused the heads to hang at an unnatural angle and rest almost horizontally on their shoulders. As Conway was about to pass between the two, the rope to his left creaked eerily, turning one of the corpses about. He looked up in horror to be confronted by a dreadfully disfigured face. Eyeless sockets fixed him with a black stare and through teeth, bared in a lipless, hideous grin, the corpse began to speak.

'God bless you for a fine gentleman, sor, and was it captivated by the allure of the past you were? And haven't you the anguish of nostalgia upon you, ah the good old days 'tis sure anuff. Beggin' your pardon, sor, but you find us fairly indisposed. They hung us, sor. Put our necks in a halter they did and didn't we dance a fine jig, meself and

me brother there. And isn't it the two finesht hangin' participles we make. And sure wasn't it a fine treaty we had and I'm thinkin' maybe they'll build a monument to it one day. For 'tis true that the English are so civilised in their dealings. What was the tarms of the treaty, brother? He has a fine head for recitations, so he has. Let the fine gentleman hear you recite the tarms of the Treaty of Limerick...'

In much the same sorry state, the other, a wisp of fair hair still adhering to its ravaged skull, turned slowly to face Conway and began to recite.

'...it is hereby decreed, that the Roman Catholicks of this Kingdom shall enjoy such Privileges in the Exercise of their Religion as are consistent with the Laws of Ireland; or as they did enjoy in the Reign of King Charles the Second; and Their Majesties will endeavour to secure the said Roman Catholicks such further security in that particular, as may preserve them from any disturbance upon the account of their said Religion...'

The sombre bells of the Cathedral broke upon the air and the bridge fell silent under a reverberating curfew. Looking back across the bridge, Conway was beset with feelings he could not understand. And as he grieved in his heart for the ill-fated pair, and all that remained of their humanity, the sky darkened over, it began to drizzle and the gruesome scene dissolved in a veil of rain.

It was night again and Conway found himself back, if not in the present, at least in modernity. Never would he have imagined that he could take such delight in seeing anything as mundane as traffic lights. But he was thrilled, thrilled at seeing telephone poles, electricity poles, thrilled to see a car turning left into Patrick Street and delighting in the winking orange of its indicator. He took in modern landmarks with new eyes, good-old-modern Mathew Bridge, it gladdened his heart, and the Customs House, the Granary and Cahill May Roberts Ltd, all appeared to him as reassuring endorsements of the present.

He felt like a man liberated. He was Orpheus returned from the underworld and, it seemed, he had got out of hell. As he congratulated himself on his return, it occurred to him that he was still in limbo. The job was only half done and he was only out on bail. Where did he go from here? As if in answer to his question, the pleasant voice of the tour guide whispered:

In the shadow of the tower
Where peregrines do prey
Seek you the wild goose
And he will show the way

'Here we go again,' Conway sighed, then began accessing his memory for definition. He recalled a commotion a while back about a pair of peregrine falcons that had nested in the tower of St John's Cathedral. It was all over the local papers. The peregrine is a relatively rare bird of prey, its natural habitat being mostly cliffs and mountains but, it seems, it has a liking for the gothic.

In level flight it can reach speeds of up to eighty miles per hour but is fastest in a stoop, diving like a Stuka bomber with speeds of up to two hundred miles per hour. Invariably, it kills its prey in the air. He had looked it up at the time in his Field Guide to Birds of Britain and Europe. The pigeon racing club was, very naturally, concerned about the loss of its pigeons. So it must be St John's Cathedral. But the 'wild goose' had him stumped. Still, St John's was a start. At least he had that.

Taking a left onto Bank Place and Charlotte Quay, Conway headed towards Baal's Bridge where the traffic-lights continued their cyclic change for non-existent traffic. It had to be late, thought Conway, for the roads seemed deserted except for the occasional taxi. Turning right at Baal's Bridge, he passed two drunks who were holding each other up, and singing *Please Release Me*, as they staggered across the road.

Clouds, like blue-black ink, were piling up against the cathedral spire. St John's was resplendent in floodlights, which served both security and aesthetics, bathing the neo-gothic cathedral and its verdigris roof in a comforting orange glow and casting out shadows where undesirables might lurk.

Moving along Cathedral Place, trailing a perimeter wall topped with spiked railings, he came to a halt near a stand of old trees. Taking stock of his situation and at a loss as to what to do next, Conway hung about waiting for inspiration.

Presently there came a sound which he ignored, thinking it was the wind in the trees overhead.

'...psssst, psssst...' It came again, more insistent now, until finally it could not be ignored.

'...pssssst, pssssst, for God's sake, pssssssst...'

Conway turned towards the voice but there wasn't a soul to be seen, nothing but the bronze statue of Sarsfield, depicted in manly pose, the frozen epitome of leadership pointing the way with outstretched arm and sword drawn. As he was about to concede that his imagination was playing tricks on him, the statue let go a deep sigh and said with utter weariness,

'God give me strength, where were you got?'

Taken aback, Conway could only stand in amazed silence.

'Well? Nothing to say? I don't know why I bother. I really don't. Look at the get up of me, and the state they have me in, standing like some gaum and me sword in me right hand, which is the wrong hand. I'm a ciotóg, always have been, damned awkward I can tell you. And as for you, you should have been here ages ago, what kept you?'

'The *wild goose* bit threw me,' said Conway sheepishly.

'Wild Goose? C'est moi!' Sarsfield shrieked in disbelief.

Of course, Conway thought, The Wild Geese, a name given to Irish Jacobites, those soldiers who left for France and Europe after the Treaty of Limerick.

Feeling very foolish, he explained, 'Didn't dawn on me that it was the singular referring to the plural.'

'Come again? Oh never mind, talk about a wild goose chase!' Sarsfield grumbled, shaking his head. Then, having recovered somewhat from his fit of pique, he added more amiably, 'Mind if I sit down?'

Conway watched in respectful silence as the great man manoeuvred himself, with some ceremony, into a sitting position. Finally settled upon his pedestal, with his cavalier boots dangling feet from the ground, he set his long mane of curls to rights with a nonchalant pass of his hand and said, rather prissily, through sensuously mobile lips,

'Correct me if I'm wrong, Mr Conway, but there's a rumour going about that you have the key of the street and that you're on the trail of one Stephen O'Sullivan. They say you are looking for a piece of his mind, no less. Something's in the air, something's astir. But my guess is you are aware of all that. And, in point of fact, you're not too far from your destination. Quite near in fact...'

Here Sarsfield, casting several obvious and exaggerated glances in the direction of Mulgrave Street, said in a low confidential tone, '...follow me eyes, follow me eyes...'

Sensing Conway's stupidity, Sarsfield decided to spell it out for him. 'I speak of St Jude's. On the Via Dolorosa, Mulgrave Street to you, perhaps the most singular street in the realm, for it contains a prison, a lunatic asylum and a cemetery. All in a row. You will find your man, O'Sullivan, holed up in the last bastion of sanity in Limerick, orbiting the outer regions of reality. I speak, of course, of the loony bin, the mad house, the funny farm...'

'The psychiatric hospital?' Conway said incredulously.

Sarsfield was dismayed, aghast and appalled.

'That is uncalled for, sir,' he said, becoming highly indignant, 'there is no need for such nefarious appellations. It is unworthy of a gentleman, sir. It is unworthy of you, Mr Conway! Unworthy!'

Chapter Eleven

Finding himself before the wrought-iron gates of St Jude's, Conway was pleasantly surprised to discover that it was not in the least intimidating. A majestic limestone building, it presented a concave facade to the world. Its centre section, and main entrance, was crowned with a clock tower, while two wings, curving out on either side, created in Conway's mind the comforting image of a mother's outstretched arms ready to sweep up her troubled children and gather them to her bosom. It appeared an embellishment of the moon. Unreal. Unworldly.

From where he stood he could see, off to his left, a solitary light in a window, shining like a beacon. Slipping through the bars he headed towards it for no other reason than it seemed a singularity worthy of his attention. He followed the winding, rose-scented path right to the base of the building. Tracking the silvered meanderings of a snail, he climbed the wall and entered through a gap at the base of the sash window.

man, in pyjamas, sat hunched over a bedside by an articulated lamp. He was well into ith the long-faced profile of a patrician. a top, open at the front, showed ribs and collarbones. A garland of white hair encircled his balding head and white, bushy eyebrows twitched above a gaunt, wax-like hand that wrote line after line in a foolscap folder.

As a spiralling moth cast shadows upon the page, the scent of ink and the scratch of pen on paper began to have a hypnotic effect on Conway. It drew him on, and in, and down the fountain pen to the dividing nib. Into copperplate writing he went, tracing the ink as it soaked into cellulose. Immersed in manuscript and a maelstrom of thoughts, he began to read.

By description they circumscribe, by prescription they define. All is numbered down, all is taxidermy and, by and by, no mysteries remain. The miracle of flight is mere mathematical. Flying ships like giant birds there are, and though a marvel to my eyes, it provokes not astonishment. Clouds in crystals do conjure spirits and ghosts do speak and move. By strange contrivance is moonlight made from fruit that are like milk-white pears, and by fingers summoned. How, I cannot tell, but, as I have observed, the walls do intercede, for they seem the very touchstone of light. I can scarcely believe what my eyes have seen, and all manner of things that move and by no beast harnessed, and most servile are they.

Yet am I cast down, for I have seen the future and have no wish for it, for in that place, Adam has eaten of the forbidden fruit, but it is bitter and clouds the mind. All is known and dies by the knowing, for in this age, science takes the soul of things and so the mind is filled with poisons, for where there's knowledge without wonder all magic dies. All is stale, the very stars are itemized...

Here, Conway disengaged, allowing the pen to continue on its merry way. The man did appear to be a philosopher of sorts but the archaic language, he had to admit, did not seem promising. For whatever reason, Conway decided to delve further into the foolscap folder, finally hitting upon an essay with the peculiar title of *Man, Myth and Mayhem* and pleased to see the style was now more modern.

Deeply rooted in the psyche there seems to be the notion that God will always provide. Prudence and planning are often regarded, therefore, as too scientific, almost like cheating. Religion is all pervasive and evident, even to the most casual of observers. The day is punctuated by calls to prayer and devotion by the solemn peal of bells on national television and radio. If you don't happen to be within earshot of these marvels of modern technology then you will surely be alerted by more traditional means. The ringing of bells is everywhere. There is no escape. This 'ringing in the ears' is a constant hazard in our society and is overwhelmingly Catholic. Indeed, one could be forgiven for thinking the country was a theocracy, rather than a democracy, for although it has no official links with the state, the Catholic Church is very instrumental in shaping public policy. It has dominated the educational system from the foundation of the state, particularly at first and second levels, the most formative years of an individual's development. It has shaped and indoctrinated the policy makers and those affected by the policy makers.

The Irish psyche has been greatly influenced by this powerful, dogmatic religion, which inculcates temporal neglect by the over-emphasis in its teachings of redemption and eternal salvation. The biblical admonitions that 'the poor are always with us' or 'this is not a lasting city' are drummed home from early childhood. Irish eyes have been focused too much on the hereafter rather than the here and now, to the detriment of the economy, among other things. The pursuit of excellence is regarded with suspicion. Pride, after all, is a deadly sin.

True intellectual autonomy is difficult to achieve in any hierarchical society. In a society where the moral capital is the Vatican, it is even more difficult. The Church's relationship with the scientific world has been a stormy one down through the centuries. Religious doctrine has never sat easy with empirical, scientific reasoning. Society has suffered greatly from this conflict. The educational system, dominated for so long by the Church, has often failed to be the educational system it purported to be. Too often it was used as a vehicle of indoctrination.

Inquiring minds were discouraged from inquiring too much and internationally respected scientific theory was often ignored or, indeed, dismissed. There has been suppression, by neglect, of any knowledge likely to upset Catholic moral teaching. The result of these practices has been the creation of, in the minds of many, the belief that scientific reasoning is like opening Pandora's Box. To think rationally is dangerous. An affront to God. The conclusion of this line of 'thought' is that the psyche of its victims becomes a fugue of superstition, myth and blind faith. The link between cause and effect becomes tenuous and is *easily dislodged. In such an environment, self-determination can become illusory. The conviction that one is not, nor is meant to be, in charge of one's own destiny often leads to fatalism. Needless to say, personal development and ultimately national development is going to suffer as a consequence.*

Could these heretical and iconoclastic thoughts possibly be the man's own? Or were they dictated by some mental aberration? Conway was unsure. It seemed peculiar for an old man to harbour such convictions. In Conway's mind old age was associated with old beliefs, and rebellion was the preserve of the young. Despite his prejudice, he began to allow for the possibility that the old man was not deranged. After all, genius has no age bar and is always considered deviant. And maybe, just maybe, he had stumbled upon the man who knew the answer to the question of the missing pearls. He dug deeper, scanning page after page after page before alighting on a blunt declaration.

The Equalization of Libido

The unrestrained sex drive of the male is directly, and indirectly, responsible for the vast majority of misery in the world. The rutting season is always with us, it seems. We accept this because it is natural. It is nature's way, but nature does not always know what is best. What is natural is not always desirable, or good. So many things that occur in nature are abominable. Evolution has played a trick on us, left us with a behavioural mechanism that is inappropriate and out of date. It should be abundantly clear that something is very wrong.

I propose that men become more like women, this is to be achieved by chemical intervention. The objective is to chemically subdue the male sex drive to sensible levels. We can no longer ignore a world made miserable because of a primeval itch. The solution to many of society's ills is the equalization of libido. For the sake of sanity, men should be more in touch with their feminine side, as indeed should women.

Ironically, some women may well object to this cultural shift. They may consider they have too much to lose. For one thing, the male, not so driven by his sex drive, will not be so easily manipulated. Men are slaves to their sexuality, and women have exploited this fact for centuries. They have always used this sexual advantage and many would wish to keep sex as a power base, a trump card, that can be played in trade-off. Women have always worn the mantle of sexual martyrdom but it is not the fault of men. It is not simply a case of men being evil and women being hormonal. Men are the burdened victims of a long heritage imposed by nature. They carry a liability between their legs. Women's argument is not with men, it is with nature.

The resistance to the use of chemical subjugation of chemically driven mayhem is rather hypocritical. After all, the male sex drive is chemically driven. We scoff at the prospect of chemical intervention, yet our lives are awash with chemical interventions. Powerful mind-altering drugs, such as alcohol, are freely available with, or without, prescription. We have to acknowledge the profound effect our sexuality has on our lives and take steps to alleviate what nature has done to us. We must free ourselves from the tyranny of hormones. We have to accept that the human body is out of date with our expectations, it is primitive and needs assistance. It is flawed, stuck in an evolutionary backwater that is no longer relevant. The problem lies within us, but we have the means to solve the problem. We owe it to ourselves and future generations to become better than we are. We can stop being victims of our past...

Beginning to feel uncomfortable with the subject matter, Conway decided to break off from what appeared to be the effusions of an unbalanced intellect. If these essays were written by the same hand, they were not of the same mind. But Conway had not given up hope entirely. So what, if O'Sullivan was schizophrenic, if indeed this was O'Sullivan, it did not mean to say that he could not make sense sometimes. Even a stopped clock is right twice a day.

Any doubts, however, were to be dispelled by the next instalment, a gem called *The Mechanics of Corporal Punishment and the various Techniques of Avoidance:*

The Retractor

The recipient's hand is repeatedly retracted so as to avoid the strap, thus necessitating restraint to be applied. Holding the fingertips of the offending hand is not to be recommended as it is somewhat restricting and, indeed, one runs the risk of hitting oneself in the process. A firm grip of the pupil's wrist is the recommended procedure to restrain the wayward hand. This has the added advantage of helping one to retain balance and, at the same time, affords a fluid swing, essential in imparting an accurate and forceful strike.

The Elevator

Here the miscreant raises his hand in an effort to escape retribution, rising incrementally so as to stay one step ahead of the strap. This could be particularly embarrassing, especially if the pupil happens to be taller than the teacher. I have heard of a teacher so frustrated with this ploy that he resorted to standing on the seat of a desk in order to administer punishment. Again, a firm grip on the wrist is the only sure way of defeating the elevator.

The Descender

This culprit takes the opposite tack and will, if not wrist-restrained, begin lowering the target palm so as to cushion the blow or, indeed, avoid it altogether. This devious ploy can be quite hazardous for the administrator of punishment as he could well find himself missing completely and striking into fresh air, resulting in an unwanted follow-through that may well lead to a loss of balance and the possibility of falling over. Apart from the obvious risk of physical injury, the sniggering guffaws this will often elicit from onlooking pupils can seriously undermine the authority and respect due to a teacher. The psychological damage of been made to look ridiculous should not be underestimated.

The Twister

This is perhaps one of the more difficult traits to deal with, as the culprit holds his hand aloft, much in the manner of a waiter holding a tray. He pivots and twists, often incorporating a kind of flamenco dance into his routine, ending up, quite often, with his back to the teacher. Again, a firm grip of the wrist is essential, but allied with this, a few well-placed pokes to the ribcage will often have the desired effect of unfurling the offending contortionist.

These, then, are the archetypes, but many individuals will employ combinations of these techniques. For example, the retractor may elevate or descend, the elevator may descend or retract. And so on. Now some words on stalling techniques.

Stalling Techniques

Where the culprit, on receiving his just punishment, will remove the object hand to safety, hiding it behind his back or tucking it away in his armpit. Though thankfully rare, the culprit will sometimes take the direct route of avoidance and run about the classroom causing great uproar and a wholly embarrassing spectacle. In such cases the teacher is advised not to give chase but let the culprit calm down and come to his senses.

Psychological Ploys of Avoidance

Offenders will enact facial contortions in an effort to elicit pity and bring about the cessation of punishment. Low and shameful tactics are often employed such as tearful protestations, submissive body postures and various cries of pain, such as whimpering and yelping, are not unknown. All should be ignored, be firm and resolute, increasing the number of slaps will soon cure the miscreant and bring home to him that his ploys are worthless and will only prolong the agony.

The Stoic

I now come to perhaps the most disturbing and sinister type of recipient, the stoic. On the face of it, his compliance and co-operation does seem welcome. A boy who takes his punishment like a man is always to be welcomed, but the stoic is a different proposition altogether, he is the bête noir of the classroom and a destructive influence. He takes his punishment, he does not complain but he does not truly accept it. He stands as proud as a peacock and does not flinch, and in his eyes there is the sin of defiance. Why, he seems to dare you to hurt him. How to deal with such spiteful disregard? It is most perplexing, as no amount of punishment seems to effect a cure, indeed, he seems to thrive on it. There are no easy solutions to this intractable problem and the offender needs to be watched closely. It is my fervent wish that all such deviants should be banished from school entirely, but, as we do not live in an ideal world, this is not always practicable...

The chattering alarm call of a magpie brought Conway to his senses. He had to concede that his 'philosopher' was not playing with the full complement of marbles. It was time to leave this research cul-de-sac. Rising up through the pages, he found the old man asleep and snoring, his ancient head and encircling arms resting on the makeshift desk. His pen, laid neatly in the groove of an ornate inkstand, was engraved with an inscription that read: *To Martin Tubridy on the Occasion of His Retirement.* It endorsed Conway's intuition that this was not the man he was looking for. Sunlight, flooding in on a breath of fresh air, began to fill the room and the drone of morning traffic outside the hospital walls gave him the impetus to be gone. He would now do what he should have done at the outset. He would check the register.

Chapter Twelve

Conway was flummoxed, bamboozled and stumped. He had gone through the hospital files and systematically examined every filing cabinet he could find. All to no avail. There wasn't a Stephen O'Sullivan or a Steven Sullivan, patient or staff member, that remotely fitted the age profile. Not restricting himself to O's and S's, he had gone through the entire alphabet just in case a file had been misplaced. He even tried *Ó Súileabháin*, to cover the possibility that the man he sought was an Irish Language enthusiast. Had he been misdirected? Sarsfield seemed so sure and so sincere. Maybe it was all a joke, maybe it *was* a wild goose chase.

As Conway emerged dejected and discouraged from the filing cabinet, Dr Phillip Mathews closed the door of his office. For the third time he had been disturbed. The signing of this, the signing of that, and now his secretary inquiring if it might be possible for him to decide on his holidays. Whatever next? he thought, closing his eyes in defiance of the possibilities. But no sooner had he returned to his chair when someone, ever so timidly, was knocking again.

Muttering to himself, he sprang to the door, swung it open and wheezed, 'Yessss?'

'It's me...Terry...you remember...' the startled interloper explained, '...you had asked me to...'

The troubled eyes, the haunted face and the moustache were instantly recognizable to Dr Mathews.

'Oh, please do come in, Terry,' he said, indicating a chair with the pages in his hand, '...have a seat, I've just been going over your file.'

Terry took the chair offered to him and sat opposite Dr Mathews who had removed his glasses to massage his eyelids. In his late forties and dressed like a high-street salesman, Dr Mathews was a dapper, handsome man with greying hair swept back from a high forehead. Slipping his glasses on again and setting them to rights, he leaned back in his chair, swivelled a bit, then picked up a see-through plastic ruler from his desk.

'Now, Terry,' he said, in a faint Welsh accent that was both informal and re-assuring, 'I would like you to tell me, if you could, when you first began to have,' here he paused, then tapping the file on his desk with the ruler, he added, '...these problems.'

Still sitting on the edge of his chair, Terry rolled his eyes in a gesture of impatience. Then, as if stating what he thought was blindingly obvious, he said pointedly, 'It was the day that dog came into our lives...'

He was about to continue when an agitated fly began head-butting a windowpane in a frantic effort to escape the room. Terry's hands drummed a tattoo on his knees, and his gaze, on a sigh of exasperation, floated to the ceiling.

Dr Mathews smiled an indulgent smile and got up from his desk. 'Excuse me a moment, Terry,' he said, stepping around his chair and going to one of two large recessed windows in the room. With a rumbling whoosh he lifted the window. Plaintive birdsong and the soft hum of distant traffic came in on a draught of cool air that pounced at the opening.

'Out, Beelzebub!' he commanded. The fly made good its escape and Dr Mathews resumed his seat.

'Could you describe,' he began, in a casual manner, 'what happened that day,' then added encouragingly, '...in your own words.'

Terry didn't need a second prompt. He was off, speaking ten to the dozen. Something about a dog he had rescued that was exhibiting super-canine powers and exacting retribution on anyone who so much as looked crooked at its master. It was as if a damn had burst. Feeling at a loose end, Conway, who had been browsing through the framed accreditations that lined the walls, decided he would stay and sit out the interview. Who knows, he might learn something. Clues to O'Sullivan's whereabouts might well present themselves. He would have to remain vigilant. What else was there to do. As he listened to the torrent coming from the patient, he regarded himself not so much as an eavesdropper, but as a sort of co-opted research assistant. He had often fancied himself as a psychologist, or psychiatrist, and prided himself on knowing the difference. Having had a breakdown of sorts himself, he felt, almost, like an associate member of the profession. He profiled the subject.

Well-dressed, middle-class, thirties, over-shaved, the skin still angry, a strange, minimalist moustache confined to the edge of the lip. Clinical signs: eyes on the side of the head with paranoia, anxious, possibly neurotic disposition, rapid speech pattern would suggest racing thoughts, a tendency to be overly inclusive...

The patient continued and continued.

'...it was uncanny how well that dog recovered. Almost overnight. He showed exceptional intelligence, right from the beginning. Seemed to predict my thoughts, anticipate my wishes. I mean, we never had to house-train him or anything like that. It wasn't long, however, before I began to get suspicious...'

'Suspicious?' Dr Mathews queried.

Terry, seemingly irritated at the interruption, gave Dr Mathews a sullen look before continuing.

'...it was little things, at first. For instance, the time we were visiting the mother-in-law's. The local priest had just

110

been to bless the house, the mother-in-law goes in for that sort of thing. Anyway, *Jeepers*, that's what we called him, it was my wife Terri's idea. She's a Terri, too. With an i. Anyway, the dog had no sooner got his nose inside the door when he starts peeing like a garden sprinkler. Totally out of character. Then more serious, more sinister things started to happen and I really began to get worried...'

And so it continued, the patient recounting tales of woe and worry that were solely attributed to the arrival of the dog. Finally, becoming very emphatic, Terry unflinchingly declared, 'Do you know what I believe? I believe that Jeepers is none other than the Jackal-headed Egyptian god, Anubis, the Guardian of Cemeteries, who conducts souls to the underworld to be judged by Osiris. I have researched this. Anubis would assist by weighing the hearts of those who had passed over...'

Here Terry paused to see if Dr Mathews was suitably impressed. Taking advantage of the opportunity, the doctor slipped in a question.

'Did you speak to anyone about this?'

'Well, yes, I did mention it to my wife but she seems to think it's all my imagination. It's all pure coincidence, that's what she keeps saying. And I spoke to Father O'Byrne about it, as well. I'm not religious, you understand, but I was desperate. I know it sounds crazy now, but I was hoping that maybe he could perform an exorcism, or something.'

'What happened?'

'He laughed. Assured me that there was some rational explanation for the whole thing. Coincidences happen all the time, he said. Said I was jumping to conclusions. I needn't tell you that really got to me. Having to sit there and listen while someone, who is evidently steeped in superstition, tells me it's all in my head. I felt a right fool, I can tell you. After twenty-two years in the wilderness, I return to the fold for spiritual solace, and who do I find? Father Scientific, full of logical reasoning. My god, when I think of it! That really knocked me back on my heels...'

Like a traffic policeman with upraised palm, Dr Mathews halted the tirade.

'I hope,' he said, 'you don't misinterpret my intentions for asking, but are you on medication?'

'Medication?' Terry asked.

'Yes, tranquillizers, for instance?' Dr Mathews ventured.

'Well, yes,' Terry said, coughing lightly, '...I take *Roche 5*, actually, twice a day, for my nerves, and *Xanax* for anxiety. It's been a trying time. I can assure you though, that I have all my faculties.'

'Any other medication?' Dr Mathews pressed.

'Well, yes, I'm on sleeping tablets, *Dalmane*. And there's the tablets for the breathing as well. I'm asthmatic you see...'

'Smoke?'

'Ah, yes,' Terry said, shifting uneasily in his chair.

'Many?'

'Forty to fifty...'

'A day?'

'A day.'

'Drink?'

'Socially,' Terry conceded, with a shrug.

'Socially?' Dr Mathews said, repeating the word like a man who was about to go hunting for a dictionary. Then, in a consoling voice, he added, 'you know, Terry, an under-stimulated mind can sometimes create an environment that appears more interesting and more rewarding. Fantasy can be very captivating, even to the extent that it will intrude on reality. It can become a kind of reality in itself if you give it too much leeway...'

Visibly bristling, Terry interrupted, 'I know what you're thinking,' he began defensively, 'you're thinking that I've stepped into the happiest kingdom of them all. A fantasy land, induced by drugs and boredom. But you're wrong. I want to believe that the world, my life, is bound by logic and rationality, and not by jiggery-pokery, or spiritualism, or whatever. But, in the light of events, all my rationalist posturing seems to be an illusion. I want my illusions. I don't want to believe in a world that's run by elves, or pixies, or weegie boards, or malicious dogs for that matter. I want a quiet life...'

In normal circumstances, Conway would have thought Terry was as daft as a brush but the experience of his own condition tempered his judgement. In fact, in a strange way, he envied Terry's exotic delusions. His own had been quite ordinary by comparison, but it could not be denied that *weird* did seem pretty normal to him right now.

'I am sure this is all in your mind,' Dr Mathews said, responding with professional calm, 'you must try to keep busy, and I would advise that you get rid of that dog of yours. He does seem to be the focus of your discontent and though the dog is an innocent party in all of this, I think it would be wise to find a new home for...Jeepers.'

Before Terry could raise an objection, Dr Mathews asked, 'How is your relationship with your wife?'

'I needn't tell you, Doctor,' he began defensively, 'how disappointed I am to hear you talk like that. My relationship with my wife has nothing to do with it. I'm not crazy, you know...'

Terry stopped, took in what he thought was a doubtful look on Dr Mathews' face and said with a heavy heart, 'You don't believe me, do you...about Jeepers...being Anubis...and all that?'

Dr Mathews raised his eyebrows in consideration, then gathering them in again, calmly spoke.

'Let's just say, Terry, that I don't believe you've taken out a franchise in divine retribution. I will say this, you need help and we're here to help you. We are all prone to mental difficulties at times, depending on our circumstances. Put under enough stress, no one is immune.'

Biting his upper lip and nodding his head as if he had decided to agree with his thoughts, Terry said cautiously,

'Sometimes things seem normal, sometimes I'm out on a limb, not knowing if it's madness or evil I'm dealing with. It's like I'm Dr Jekyll, one minute, and Mr Hyde, the next.'

'As regards being mad, you most definitely are not,' Dr Mathews began earnestly, 'I can assure you, Terry, the fact that you have doubts is a good sign. You've been through a rough patch, that's true, but with proper diet, proper rest and a positive outlook you'll be as right as rain. What I would suggest is that we change your medication for a start. And some psychotherapy might be in order. And as regards evil, Terry, we live in enlightened times, not the Dark Ages. In our profession we're not inclined to believe in evil. We would look upon Mr Hyde as someone with a personality problem. Nothing that Immac, Prozac, a good tailor and a first-class orthodontist couldn't cure...'

Terry smiled. A vague, ghost of a smile, but a smile nonetheless.

Chapter Thirteen

High in the outer branches, among the cherry blossoms, a thrush was singing a vigorous, joyful aria. Looking through the dappling foliage that danced in the bright May sunshine, Conway could just about make out the mottled plumage, when a sudden, rasping sound set the songster off in a flutter of wings. Presently, like some presiding spirit, a wraith of smoke curled up through the branches.

Below him he could see two men seated on a wooden bench. One had a construction worker's yellow hat perched on his head and wore a black duffle coat. The other, who wore spectacles, and whose hair was in rampant recession, drew heavily on a cigarette and exhaled the smoke with relish. He was wearing a pinstripe jacket, open-necked shirt and green corduroy trousers. This eclectic ensemble was finished off with red socks and white trainers. He had nicked himself shaving. The minute spots of blood on tissue paper, stuck all over his face, reminded Conway of those relics of saints he'd seen his mother with from time to time.

'What's with the hat?' the Pinstripe asked, blowing smoke in the direction of his companion.

The Hard Hat turned, smiled and nodded, but did not answer. A white plastic flex, hanging from his ear, trailed to a transistor radio that he held in his lap.

'You can't be too careful,' Pinstripe said, carrying on regardless, 'I was reading in the paper about the strange things that do be falling from the sky, cows sinking trawlers, and blue ice, you know, someone flushes a toilet on a 747 and it falls as a lump of ice and your troubles are over. No, can't be too careful. Work in the building, did you?'

No response from the Hard Hat.

'Worked in the building myself. Worked all over, tough game the building. Oh, I've been everything, civil servant, salesman, line painter, decorator, barman, locksmith, vault keeper, worked in factories all over, even did a spell as a gravedigger. I'd say that's what started me on the drink...'

Taking a hefty pull on his cigarette and pushing his spectacles off his nose, he continued in a conversational vein while Hard Hat remained noncommittal.

'...went across the road for fags the other day, and on the way back didn't some loose change drop out of my pocket, there I was down on my hands and knees trying to pick it up, when this shagger in a car starts hooting and hooting, then starts shoutin' would I mind gettin' off the road and out of his way, did I think he had nothin' better to do than be waitin' around while I was acting the bollicks.'

He shook his head, turned to Hard Hat, who was smiling obliviously, and added indignantly, 'Oh, I gave him his lemon. Do you know what I said to him? I said, I'm not acting the bollicks at all, says I to him. Then I looked him straight in the eyes and I said, I'm a child of the universe, no less than the streets and the cars, I have a right to be here. And do you know what he says to me? Get out of the fuckin' way, says he, you four-eyed, fuckin' eejit. Isn't that lovely, ha, isn't that just choice?'

Again he drew on his cigarette until the tip glowed like a brazier. 'Is that what they're teaching them these days?' he went on, his words tumbling out of smoke.

'I tell you, there's people goin' today who have no respect for anything. There's some mad bastards out there and no mistake.'

Then, jabbing the air with his cigarette and nodding his head in the direction of the street, he said, 'Out there, that's where the lunatics are, not in here, on the outside. That's what the walls are for. To keep the fuckers out...'

He fell silent, his words giving way to the drone of traffic and the rustling of leaves.

'Fecken new money,' he said at length, holding a penny in the palm of his hand for Hard Hat's consideration, 'take a look at the new penny,' he went on, shaking his hand for emphasis, 'look at the size of it, I ask you, look at that, I mean all these Celtic designs and squiggly bits with birds looking up their you-know-whats is all very fine, from the Book of Kells and all that, and a fine bit of craftsmanship it is too, but I mean it's so fecken small. It was the same with the ha'penny and they had to get rid of that, it was worth nothing in the end and you couldn't see it, it was so small. At least with the old money, you knew you had something in your pockets.'

He sniffed appreciatively at his own words. Then, in a nostalgic tone, continued with coin of the realm.

'Remember the old penny? The Irish one now, not the English one, the one with the big chicken on it, remember? The pingin, isn't that what it was called? Now, there was a coin. And remember the ten bob note, they replaced that with the fifty pence piece, so they did, and the half crown with the horse, that was some coin, and the florin, with the leaping salmon. And the shilling, aah, the good old shilling, do you remember what was on that? A bull, that's right, and then there was the tanner, the old sixpence that is, with the greyhound. And the thrupenny bit, of course. That was the rabbit, or was it a hare? Ah sure,' he added dismissively, 'money is worth nothing today...'

Looking past the copper beech trees that screened the hospital entrance, Pinstripe could see an assembly of people outside the main gates. Cameras clicking. Japanese tourists. He waved to them. They waved politely back.

'Conas atá tú,' he called out, with hand cupped to his mouth, then giving a thumbs up sign, he shouted, 'slán agus beannacht, maith fear, maith fear...'

After flicking some ash from his trousers, he turned to Hard Hat and said, 'Don't you just love tourists. Over here for the craic, no doubt. God, I hate that word *craic*. It's so full of shamroguery and paddy-wackery shite and all for the benefit of tourists. When you hear how friendly we Irish are, and how wonderful Ireland is, you think to yourself, jaysus, I must go visit there sometime. Bring back a stick of rock.'

With an air of disclosure in his voice, he added, 'Never could take to the Irish language. Too many bad memories of it at school, don't you know. Brother Quirk, thumpin' the blackboard to stress a grammatical nicety, while his voice boomed out the message that we must be thick for him to be repeatin' himself so many times. I can see him now, standing there before us, his big red face shaking with anger and his eyes filling with tears as they scanned, with utter contempt, the forty-odd turnip heads in front of him. Then, in a wild frenzy, he would rub out the board and the chalk dust would fly all over the place. I remember how I used to focus my mind away from that demented and deranged figure in black, and gaze upon the chalk particles that were caught in the sunlight streaming through the big windows. And, as they floated around the classroom, I'd be thinking of all the millions of tiny little creatures, fossilized all those millions and millions of years ago, that went into making the 'cailc' and I'd be thinking to myself how weird and wonderful life was all the same.'

Curling up his lips and blowing some half-decent smoke rings, he said, as he admired his fleeting creations, 'We didn't have Irish in the home. It wasn't the language our parents or grandparents spoke, and yet we were expected to take to it like ducks to water. And when we didn't, we were made to feel like little shoneen traitors, or just plain stupid. Made to feel like we were foreigners in our own country, we were. Because we weren't fluent speakers, or wearing báiníns or coming to school in currachs, we weren't quite Irish. Know what I mean? What a great way to teach a language. The English bate it out of us, and what do our own do? They bate it back in. Jaysus, do we have to copy the English in everything! They killed any love we might have had for the language, our own did. Done it a great disservice, they did. Bilingual Man speak with forked tongue! Still, I suppose, like German, it's a great language for getting up phlegm...'

He paused, closed his eyes on the ensuing silence, then asked casually, 'Do you remember the bun and milk? The stubby little bottle of milk, a half-pint I guess it was, and a currant bun, for children who were in need of nourishment. Supplied to the school by the state. It was means-tested, meaning that only those who were thought to be in need, for instance, those whose fathers weren't working or on low income, would get it. The system divided the class into those who were made to feel like charity cases and those who were made to feel excluded. We often looked on with our gobs open and our tummies rumbling as the self-conscious bun-and-milkers had their little meal. It was an unfair and lousy thing to do to children, to segregate them like that. Because, from what I remember, everyone was in need of the bun and milk. Every child could have done with it. What a country, I ask you, by making little of some, they made little of us all.'

He fell silent for a moment, then spluttering smoke as he laughed aloud, he said with a smile, 'I remember the day of the Great Bun and Milk Fiasco. It was the day everyone got the bun and milk, due to some administration cock-up. We all partook, we were all one, no second-class citizens. No, we were a nation once again. One up on those lousy gobshites who are always warning about the dangers of giving anything away for free. You know the type, the *no such thing as a free lunch* brigade. They would put a tax on breast-feeding if they could. Do you know what I'm going to tell you? Being poor wasn't all that bad, it was bad enough, mind, but being laughed at for being poor, that was the real killer. That was intolerable. Ah, mustn't be bitter...'

Removing the cellophane and the silver foil from another packet of cigarettes, he offered them to Hard Hat who smiled, frowned, shook his head, and smiled again. Pinstripe took a box of matches from his pocket and shook them like maracas. He had a distant, lost look about him as he lit his cigarette.

'What are you here for?' He inquired of his companion.

There was no response from Hard Hat.

'Well, that's a man's own business. I'm here because of the drink, myself. Drying out. A martyr to the drink. A black concoction that I cannot name due to advertising restrictions but, suffice to say, it has a foreign accent. You might ask why I drink. I've asked myself a thousand times. The convivial atmosphere of the pub, the company, the banter, the clink of glass on glass, shimmering delights and shining trinkets. My brains were swamped with alcohol. Pickled with it I was. They say Bacchus has drowned more men than Neptune, and it's true. The first for thirst, the second for nourishment, the third for pleasure, and the fourth for madness. If you could only stop at two, or three, and leave it at that...'

He sighed, pursed his lips, then leaning forward with elbows on knees, continued with his thoughts.

'I suppose I'm not right in the head. Could be the lead soldiers I used to chew as a kid. Or the DDT my mother used to douse the bedclothes with. Oh, if she found a flea she'd be raging. Mad she'd be. Getting into bed was like climbing into a box of talcum powder. We'd kick up a right dust storm. We'd be like ghosts from the powder, or you'd think we worked in a flour mill. Used to catch me chest too, no wonder I'm asthmatic.'

Coming briskly up the path towards them, a middle-aged woman, well-dressed, well-groomed and with a face plastered in make-up, gave them a royal salute.

'Good afternoon, lovely day!' she said, ever so loudly, as if she thought they might be hard of hearing. As she breezed past them on a drift of perfume, Pinstripe winked in Hard Hat's direction.

'You can always tell a visitor to St Jude's,' he said, 'spot them a mile off. Tripping over themselves in their efforts to look *oh so normal* and sane. The purposeful walk, the clenched jaw, eyes gazing straight ahead. As if to say, I'm not a patient. I'm only visiting. I'm here on business. I have people to meet and bins to put out...'

Communing once again with his cigarette, he closed his eyes to reflect in silence before picking up another train of thought.

'But the drink doesn't help, only makes things worse. No, that's the thing about fags,' he said, glancing at the cigarette cupped in his hand, 'you never have to say, the next day, *sorry about last night, I had one fag too many*. Know what I mean?'

Rolling the cigarette between thumb and forefinger, he continued, 'Know what I think, it's all psychological. I have this theory about fags, it's a primitive thing going back to the cavemen gathered around the campfire. There's something very comforting about the glow of a fag, it's like your own personal campfire, especially on a cold morning. There's something very alive about it. Every time I strike a match I feel like what's-his-name, Prometheus. There's nothing like a box of matches.'

A few feet away, two tortoiseshell butterflies, intent on a territorial dispute, went cartwheeling by. Pinstripe put an imaginary gun to his shoulder and took aim.

'For you I will kill a butterfly,' he said, then with the target in his sight, he improvised the sound of gunshots with a feeble and improbable, 'poiffff, poifff...'

After pausing to fill his lungs with smoke, he went on.

'Do you know what gets on my goat? People always saying they knew exactly where they were when President Kennedy died. I can't remember where I was when that happened but, strangely enough, I know exactly where I was when Oswald got shot. Isn't that odd now? And people saying things like, 'wrote me', isn't that annoying? Why can't people say, 'wrote *to* me'. And people saying, 'it behoves me'. My Uncle Pat was a terror for it. He was always behovin' this and behovin' that. He'd be behovin' all over the place. He would say things like, 'it behoves everyone here to behave themselves'. I suppose he liked the sound of it. Roll over behovin' there's a whole lotta hovin' goin' on.'

He laughed, then struck a match to light up again. It flared, illuminating his face. After a few puffs, he shook the match out and sighed with smoke.

'Of course, myself and the wife have gone our separate ways. Once the kids were all grown up, we just looked at each other and thought, who the hell have I been living with all these years. Just couldn't get on. Too many irreconcilable differences. She was a woman, and I was a man. You know yourself now. I couldn't begin to tell you. And little things, like she'd say, 'eczema', while I'd say, 'eczeema', she'd say, 'Hiroshima', and I'd say, 'Hirosheema'. There's probably a name for it, something like, Variable Stress Syndrome, or VSS for short, I suppose.'

After a quick check on Hard Hat's attentive presence he felt safe to proceed with yet another disclosure.

'I used to manage a public house for my Uncle Pat, out the Tipperary road. It wasn't a strong house, sorry to say, it having the unfortunate bad luck of being in the wrong location, sited as it was on a grand, straight bit of road where you could put the boot to the floor and get up a bit of speed. Cars used always bomb past the place, shaking it to its foundations. So, being a great man for coming up with solutions, didn't I hit upon the idea of changing the name. So, when the uncle was out of the way, I decided to do a bit of sign writing. Did I tell you I was a sign writer? Anyway, didn't I change the name to *Stopyekuntz*. Well, he wasn't a bit pleased, I can tell you. There were complaints, you see. I needn't tell you what he said to me. Packed my suitcase, he did. It behoves you to get the fuck out of here, says he, in no uncertain terms, and get yourself sorted out. So here I am, courtesy of Uncle Pat.'

Prompted by a sudden urgency, Pinstripe then stood to attention and announced, 'Jaysus, I have to make a slash.' Heading towards the shrubbery, he disappeared into the rhododendrons. Before very long, Conway heard the telltale sloshing sounds and groans of satisfaction as the steaming incense rose with the words, '...ooohhh...there is nothing like ...the exquisite release...of pent-up piss...'

Chapter Fourteen

There was something very odd about the magpies, Conway thought. They were behaving in a most peculiar way, hanging upside down from a branch, as they were, more reminiscent of birds of paradise in courtship display than the impish, no-nonsense birds in dinner jackets he knew so well. Pirates of woods and suburbia, common thieves of eggs and amulets, the magpies were now making soft and conciliatory noises. Their attention seemed focused on an open window, just yards from their magnolia perch and its graceful downward facing flowers.

At the window, Conway could see a middle-aged man reach out a hand and drop a fistful of capsules onto the grass verge. He slipped in through the open window to investigate. Inside, the owner of the hand turned out to be a dead ringer for George C. Scott, as he appeared in the title role of *Patton, Lust for Glory*. Without the uniform of course. Instead, he wore an immaculately white shirt that contrasted with, and showed to advantage, his sallow complexion. This billowing shirt was tucked inside the belt of his baggy, plaited trousers. The belt, buckled as it was just below his ribcage, gave the impression of all legs and very little torso. His hair was closely cropped and badger grey.

Oddly enough, *Patton* was one of Conway's favourite films, which puzzled him greatly because he had always regarded himself, emotionally, as a bit of a coward and, intellectually, as a pacifist.

Standing behind the 'patient', for he indeed seemed to have all the attributes of one, was Dr Mathews, his usual dapper self, and with him another more obvious member of the profession who stood with an upright, self-assured bias, clipboard in hand and stethoscope thongs springing from the pocket of his white coat.

'Do you see that?' the patient asked, with a strident eccentricity in his speech of stressing certain words to the level of a shout, 'that's what your drugs do to the birds and I only gave them a few grains and look at the misfortunes, away with the fairies they are...'

'You simply cannot go around conducting your own medical trials,' Dr Mathews quietly admonished, 'particularly on unsuspecting subjects. And I would strongly advise you to continue with your medication.'

'Look at them, with their eyes out on stalks and you want me to take that stuff?'

'It wasn't prescribed for them, now was it? You're not a bird.' Dr Mathews paused for a moment to allow his words to sink in, then added with the certainty of a scientist, 'You don't have a bird's brain.'

At this, the patient threw back his head and laughed convulsively, displaying a mouthful of teeth that, Conway decided, were all too white and perfectly even to be his own. When he had recovered, somewhat, he said, wiping a tear from his eye, 'Well, I have been called a bird brain on more than one occasion.'

He laughed again. Then fell silent. There was something fierce, yet vulnerable about the man. His large aristocratic nose tilted defiantly over a clenched jaw. Conway noted the disconcerting tendency to sway, ever so slightly, from side to side when standing still, which wasn't often for the man was a ball of nervous energy.

Eyeballing Dr Mathews, the patient spoke candidly.

'I saw you yesterday, Dr Mathews, as you swept down the long corridor with Dr Whatshisname and Dr Whatshername struggling to keep up with you. And that blasted painter, Jackson Pollack himself, with his four-inch brush and his overalls and he slapping paint on those chunky radiators that look like clenched fists. You know the ones. And he was crooning that Sinatra song, *start spreading the news, I'm leaving today*. I wish to God he would! The bubblehead has been here forever. But you pulled up as you drew level with the Pollock, and the others almost crashing into you. Oil paint, says you, peering over your glasses. Well, he gave you a look as if it was a trick question. Do we have to have oil paint, says you, can we not have something less toxic. We've always used gloss, says he, easier to keep clean. There is a water-based gloss, isn't there, says you. Yeah but, says he, and you says, people have enough problems in here without us trying to poison them as well. You'd have to take that up with the Health Board, says he. I will indeed, says you, and in the meantime, no oil paint, is that clear, and you turned on your heel and down the corridor with you and the other two tagging along behind and not a word between them. And you says, over your shoulder, it does exactly what it says on the tin. It poisons you...'

Dr Mathews smiled in response, then asked, 'How goes the world, Thomas?'

'You, Dr Mathews,' the patient went on, intent on his own train of thought, 'you have a nice voice. The kind of voice that is most reassuring, the kind that says everything will turn out fine. You wear the cologne of confidence. I like that in a man. Now you,' he added, turning towards Dr Mathews' companion and pointing a forefinger and thumb in his direction, 'you make me nervous.'

'This is Dr Peters,' Dr Mathews explained, 'a colleague of mine. He's doing research as part of our training scheme in postgraduate psychiatry.'

'Pleased to meet you,' said Dr Peters with a vague grin.

'Writing a book, are we?' Thomas the Patient asked, with more than a whiff of disapproval.

Dr Malcolm Peters stood tall and overly erect with a worried, earnest look about him. He forced an indulgent smile. 'Not quite...' he said, blinking.

Before he had time to elaborate, Thomas cut in.

'That's all the world needs, another book,' he said, with a dismissive shrug of his eyebrows, 'the trouble with people today is they have nothing to say, but say it anyway. The mind too often thinks the way it feels and it only takes something like indigestion to cloud that thinking. In other words, our motives are suspect. Language drives thought and that's just plain wrong. It should be the other way around...'

He stopped abruptly, laughed an impish laugh, then after a stabilizing little cough, he went on, '...I'm rambling again. I have these periods of lucidity, you see, when I just can't resist pontificating,' then he added, with a curt nod of the head, 'mind you, the thing is, I do make a lot of sense to myself at times. Now that's scary...'

With his eyes darting about knowingly, he edged closer to Dr Mathews to ensure confidentiality, and lowering his voice to a mere whisper, he said, speaking out the side of his mouth, 'Do you ever feel we're just characters in a novel? Do you? Have you noticed the improbable situations, the coincidences,' then, eyeing Dr Peters, he added, 'the badly drawn characters with no real depth to them, the sketchy thoughts, the orphaned words and floundering sentences. And alliteration running amok,' he continued, 'always a sure sign. Literary devices strewn here, there and everywhere. I mean, *listen* to me. Everything on the tip of the tongue, so witty and so contrived. I tell you, it does seem like we're living in detached paragraphs and high-rise chapters. This whole columnar edifice is one big illusion. Stands to reason.'

Wheeling away from Dr Mathews and loudly changing the subject, evidently as a diversionary tactic, he inquired, at the top of his voice, '...ever play conkers?'

Dr Mathews considered the question for a moment, then

said doubtfully, 'Conkers? This time of year?'

Thomas promptly produced from his bedside locker a plastic bag that was bursting at the seams with conkers. Conway recognised the Dunne's Stores shopping bag. Green with gold lettering. St Bernard. The brand of quality. Better value. Beats them all.

'Last year's harvest,' Thomas said, pleased as punch. 'I've holed them, and strung them with hairy twine, and hardened them off with my secret recipe. Tough as nails, they are. Bet you'd love to know what my secret recipe is?'

Dr Mathews tried to look intrigued.

'Sorry, can't say,' Thomas explained, 'wouldn't be a secret if I told you. Now would it?'

'Can't argue with that,' Dr Mathews said cheerfully, then added, 'it's a while since I played, but I'll have a go.'

'That's the spirit,' Thomas urged, 'now all that remains is for you to choose your weapon, but I warn you, I have the first shot.'

Dr Mathews selected his conker and, rather lamely, held it up as a target.

'Higher, higher. Hold it up like a man,' shouted Thomas, then taking his own in hand, he placed it behind the V of his forefinger and middle finger. Pulling the string as taut as he could he took careful aim and with a preparatory, rocking motion he let fly, scoring a direct hit that sent Dr Mathews' conker into a loop the loop.

'Ho-ho!' Thomas cried out triumphantly, 'right on the kisser. Now your turn.'

Dr Mathews, under the tutelage of his patient, spread his legs for balance, kept his eye on the conker, and, using the arc of his swing to gain momentum, missed completely.

'Take another go,' Thomas said magnanimously. This, Dr Mathews did and scored a direct hit.

With a somewhat worried look on his face, Thomas inspected his conker. 'Jaysus, you gave it a right smack, so you did,' he confided, then with a groan of relief, added, 'but no damage, no damage.'

On they went, each taking turns and exchanging blows, until Dr Mathews missed his target once more and managed to spectacularly entangle both strings and conkers.

Thomas was in like the proverbial Flynn.

'Tangles three shots,' says he, 'Limerick rules, of course. I get three free shots because you tangled up the conkers.'

'That doesn't seem fair.' Dr Mathews protested weakly.

'Well that's life, Doctor. It's never fair. Now take your punishment like a man, I see cracks appearing...'

Dr Mathews did as he was told and held up his conker like a sacrificial offering.

'...always go for the sweet spot,' Thomas was advising himself, '...and hit downwards.'

On the second shot the conker disintegrated and went scattering and skittering over the tiled floor.

Thomas was jubilant.

'Bang goes your conker, along with your ego,' he said, laughing, 'you know,' he went on, 'they used to feed conkers to horses when they'd get sick, hence the name *horse chestnut*. Though I believe they do more harm than good. Or maybe the name comes from the distinctive horseshoe shape left on twigs after the leaves have fallen. Who knows? And *conker*, that comes, I think, from the word *conquer*. Though there are some who believe that *conker* is from the French *conque*, a sea shell, since the game was originally played with sea shells. It's hard to know what to believe, but it's all fun and games until someone loses an eye, right?'

'Right,' said Dr Mathews, somewhat mystified, wrinkling his forehead and peering over his spectacles.

Dr Peters sniffed, then said, 'We used to bake them and soak them in vinegar,' then he added, in response to the bewildered looks from the other two, 'you know, to harden them...the conkers...'

'Would you like to have a go, Dr Peters?' Thomas asked out of politeness.

'No, thank you, no,' Dr Peters said hastily. After forcing a half-smile, he began biting his upper lip.

Thomas withdrew to his bed, and, having stashed his conkers under the pillows, sat with his face stuck behind a book curiously titled *It's Far From Umbilical Cords I Was Born.*

'How would you describe yourself?' Dr Mathews asked of his patient.

'Myself, is it? Well now, let's see,' Thomas responded, closing the book and laying it aside, 'I suppose I'm apolitical, amoral, agnostic and, to keep the alliteration going, some might say I was an asshole.' He gave Dr Mathews a knowing wink, then with a resigned look in his eyes, began reciting a rhyme from his childhood, 'If I were an apple and grew on a tree, I think I'd fall down to a nice boy like me...'

Dr Peters stopped biting his upper lip, cleared his throat, then asked rather bluntly, 'Why do you think you're here?'

Thomas was on his feet again.

'I am given to understand,' he said, sniffing defensively, 'that I have an inferiority complex.' Tightening his jaw, and reddening a little, he went on in a voice of protest, 'If I have an inferiority complex, who gave it to me? That's what I'd like to know. Who gave it to me? I overcompensate I know. Hence the arrogance. But, if forced to make a choice, a superiority complex is infinitely superior to an inferiority complex. Don't you think?'

He paused just long enough to monitor their response, then ploughed on. 'And you guys, you're just a sigh away from depression yourselves, a foxtrot away from insanity, that's what you are. Highest rate of suicides, along with dentists and lemmings, if I'm not mistaken. Read it in one of the papers, *The Limerick Hysterical*, I think it was, or was it *The National Outrage*, I forget which. The memory isn't what it used to be...'

Dr Mathews intervened with a question. 'Did you say you were agnostic?'

'Agnostic?' The word seemed like a talisman to Thomas. 'Ah yes, agnosticism,' he said, weighing its precious syllables as he went for a stroll around his bed. Then bringing the palms of his hands together, and pressing his thumbs to his lips, he summoned up the authoritative voice of a lecturer, '...a most demeaned, disregarded and underrated vision of reality. It is the ultimate honesty. To be able to say, *I do not know*, and not be burned at the stake for it. Look it up in a dictionary. Hardly gets a mention. And why? Because people are afraid to admit they don't know. It goes back to our schooldays, to the classroom, where humiliation was the punishment for not knowing something. If every schoolboy knew what every schoolboy is supposed to know, there'd be no need for teachers. Now would there?' With defiant eyes and some finger-wagging, he added solemnly, 'Blessed are the confidently incorrect for they not only fool themselves but others as well.'

He was smiling now and nodding to himself, pleased with his witticism. He decided to continue, set up another one.

'I tend to ramble on and over-elaborate. You may have noticed. Nothing wrong with that. It's a well-known fact, and a popular lie, that brevity is the soul of wit. But wit, my friends, if the truth be known, wit is the runt of wisdom...'

Suddenly, a look of doubt clouded his features and, as if dealing with some mental intrusion, he said wryly, 'They tell you that life in the past was nasty, brutish and short. Now? Now it's just long, boring and neurotic...'

'By the way,' he added with a cheery nonchalance, 'I've written some papers on claustrophobia. Perhaps you might care to read them sometime. Tell me what you think...'

The open window, caught by a sudden gust of wind, swung to a near closed position. Thomas, catching sight of his own reflection, launched a verbal assault upon it.

'You again, you son of a sea cook,' he bellowed, his eyes wide and wild, '...delusional, am I? Well, let me tell you, I'm a student of the guessing game myself. While you lecture me with your pet theories on human behaviour, I'm indulging your obsessions in the hope that I might break through that citadel skull of yours and get you to listen! Doctor! Because you are as bloody well confused as I am. Difference is, *you* make a living from it, and good luck to you...'

At the behest of a breeze, the window flew open. His reflection gone, Thomas stood bewildered and disorientated. Clearly distressed, he flopped down on an armchair by the window. After a long exhalation he began to breathe deeply, calmer now as the anger drained from his face.

'Listen,' he said, closing his eyes, '...it's gone very quiet. Like the grave. You could hear a pin drop if it wasn't for the tinnitus.' With eyes peering shrewdly through his eyebrows, he asked, 'want to know why I'm here? Well, I'll tell you,' he added with a solemn dignity, '...it's because of the Jews. You see, I look Jewish. Whatever that means. So I've been told, time and time again...'

Turning to show his profile and pointing to his nose, he went on, '...see this, a bridge too far. Now, it could be Greek, could be French, even Arab or, indeed, Roman, but no one says I look French, Greek, or Arab, or Italian. No. You look Jewish! That's what they say. Was I offended? No! I've always admired the Jews, but it dawns on me that it's not meant as a compliment. What is it with people and the Jews? Will you tell me that? So, I'm here, because of the Jews. The constant sniping, the sly digs, the overt and hidden prejudice, has, over the years, brought me to nervous exhaustion. The older I get, the more Jewish I seem to others, it appears. I'm not Jewish, but I may as well be. And, by the way, I'm not circumcised either.' Here, he stood up and went in search of his zipper, 'Wanna see?'

'That won't be necessary!' Dr Peters quickly intervened.

Dr Mathews merely smiled and coughed politely.

Thomas settled back in the armchair and began to hum some nondescript tune. He stopped, screwed up his eyes and focused in on a memory.

'...an incident happened to me one night, oh years ago, in London of all places, this drunken lout, for the want of a better name, a complete and utter stranger, started raving at me. He was shouting at the top of his lungs, 'Jewish bastard', among other things. This went on and on. I stood there speechless. And my so-called friends seemed to take great delight in my discomfort. Do you know what it feels like to have such vile hatred spewed at you? It's a very depressing and ugly feeling...'

He paused for a moment, rubbing his knees with the palms of his hands, then, with a snort of contempt he continued, '...but I always suspected those jokers anyway. Friends, how are you! You know the type, buys everything German, the washing machine is Siemens, the car is a Volkswagen, the food blender Krupps, shaves with Braun and hums Erika. Always going on about German efficiency. If there's one thing I've learned from life, it's that people are not to be trusted. The things I could tell you...'

He stopped, a bemused expression on his face, then he added with a cheerless grin, 'So here I am. Out of harm's way, here because of anti-Semitism. Jesus, they even have a special name for it, like it's institutionalized.' Flapping a hand to wave away some mental irritation, he added tetchily, 'And moneylending? Don't get me started. Of course, there are no Christian moneylenders. That's what they'd have you believe. But most of the banks are owned, and run, not by Jews, but by so-called Christians. Usury *is* the capitalist way. It's been that way for a very long time now.'

He laughed, then shaking his head in disbelief, rose from his chair to begin walking back and forth. 'Marvellous...' he went on, '...I'm here because of the Jews. I don't even have the privilege of being what I'm accused of. I don't even have the benefit of being Jewish!'

He stopped up for a moment, displaying his teeth and grimacing as if he felt some dart of pain.

'You know what's wrong with the Jews? I think it's possible to be too talented. That's what wrong with the Jews. Have you seen the list? They are a most talented people. That's their crime!' Locking onto some other notion that troubled him, he said, 'I wonder was Einstein a German Jew or a Jewish German. Do you know that we don't have the faintest idea what his last words were? He spoke his dying words in German, but the nurse attending him didn't speak

German. Died in the land of the free, Princeton, New Jersey. Probably the greatest genius that ever lived and we don't know his final words.'

After enduring a brief silence, he added abruptly, '...but hey, I meander. I'm a paranoid schizophrenic, remember? Don't listen to me! I have ceased to be myself and have become a definition. I've been explained away. But I'll tell you something, and it's this, there are no adults in this world, just grown-up kids. That's all we are. I do apologise for any inappropriate language I may have used, but one should be wary of toxic politeness and not allow decorum dictate to reason. It seems that logic peppered with expletives is less desirable than polite insanity. That's the way of it, I suppose, but the more I see of people, I can tell you, the more I like Emperor Penguins. Now, gentlemen, if you will excuse me, I have to get back to my research.'

And so saying, he undid his laces, slipped off his shoes and placed them neatly by his bedside locker. Then, still fully-clothed, he climbed into bed and disappeared beneath a pile of blankets. Dr Mathews, Dr Peters, and Conway, took the hint.

Chapter Fifteen

A prisoner of not knowing where to go, or what to do, Conway was moved along on a stream of happenstance. Eventually he found himself in what could only have been the TV communal room. Mounted on metal brackets, and sitting precariously halfway up a wall, was a massive and very loud television that demanded attention.

Patients, some in dressing gowns and slippers, some in civilian dress, sat before the goggle-box in a flotilla of armchairs and sofas that looked as if they had been gleaned from a Dutch auction by Salvador Dali. Conway had never seen such a diverse collection in one place before. Different colours, different styles, frilled, patterned and plain. From newish and highly-sprung, to battered, old and comfortable. A crazy mix-and-match to accommodate all tastes.

Getting up from an armchair that was forefront in the viewing stakes, a wiry, red-haired gentleman in tracksuit and runners turned to face the sedentary spectators. Clambering onto the armchair, he placed a leg on each arm and stood upright with arms outstretched. Ignoring the chorus of protest and complaint that his blatant obstruction of the television provoked, he roared, his electric-blue eyes wide with intensity, 'Any news? Any news? Loads of news! Loads of news! All day long, on the hour, every hour, nothing but news, news, news. Disasters, disasters and more disasters. It's so depressing. We're not cut out for all this global village shite, you know. It's all a con. There's no respite. We're forever worried and in a state of agitation. If it's not some fuckin' disaster in Addis Ababa, it's El Salvador or Baghdad or Borris-in-Ossory or Timbukfuckin'too...'

Agonised cries of frustration went up.

'Will you give over will you...we can't hear the shaggin' news with you...it's an absolute disgrace...so it is...'

Impervious to appeals, the offending demagogue pointed a tobacco-stained finger at the television and shouted at full volume, 'here's how the world will end, not with a bang, but with a newsflash!'

Moving with the agility of a gymnast, he snatched the remote control from a sensible-looking gentleman who was wrapped in a candy-striped dressing gown, with matching slippers. The man, apparently a trustee of sorts and keeper of the remote control, cracked open his grizzled beard and yelled with blustering outrage.

'Nurse! Nurse! Toomey's run off with the flicker again.'

King of the remote control, Toomey held sway.

'Time to switch channels,' he said wilfully, then turning his back on the television he placed his head and the remote between his legs and began flicking through the channels.

As if performing some bizarre form of interpretive dance, he began to try out new permutations of channel-surfing, shooting from under his arm like a gunslinger, arching his back like a matador and crying out olé, olé, olé, and, with the remote hand curled around the back of his head, stamping his feet like a demented flamenco dancer.

The channels churned, and electric guitars screamed in a drawn-out climax of sales pitch.

...the car for all seasons and all reasons, the Nova...

A bouncy, self-assured female voice-over boldly sold,

...a one way, dri-weave top sheet for that extra absorbency...

An insipid jingle for washing-up liquid,

...for glass that sparkles without smears...

Low, didactic tones insinuating dreadful consequences of missing something vitally important and up-to-the-minute,

...we return to our report on that update of the situation in...

Then, macabre music, worthy of a Hitchcock film,

...the assassin bug injects its victim with deadly venom, and then sucks out the liquidized innards...

A voice of disgust bawled in protest.

'For god's sakes, will you turn over to something else, I'm just after me shaggin' dinner. Do you want me to bring it up again...'

It got Toomey's attention. Whetted his appetite. He now lowered the sound to inaudible and shouted with a rhetorical air, 'Isn't nature wonderful?' Then, as his features collapsed into a frown, he added contemptuously, 'what's so fucking wonderful about nature, anyway? That's what I want to know. We're stuck in a food chain where miracles eat miracles. What a fucking system! Do you know that children today, by the time they are seven, see more kills than a lion or tiger will ever see in their entire lives. That cannot be good for children. It is so lopsided. Always around teatime. Notice that? It's all murder and mayhem and cannibalism and infanticide and sex, but because it's *a nature programme,* it's okay. It's okay to take reality and soup it up to ludicrous proportions and show it to kids. And the watershed? What happened to the watershed?'

Suddenly, from out of nowhere, three burly men in white jackets, accompanied by the sensible-looking man with the grizzled beard, swooped on Toomey, grabbing hold of him. The remote control was twisted from his hand and he was forcibly carried off, still wanting to know what happened to the watershed. To the opening strains of Coronation Street's signature tune, the TV room was soon becalmed. Conway, retreating from the caterwauling dirge, followed the rolling maul of Toomey and his would-be subduers down the corridor.

Going on the premise that you don't need a sense of direction when you have no idea of where you're going, Conway wandered aimlessly through a labyrinth of rooms, stairways, lofts, basements and passageways. In a dusty old storeroom, he came upon a life-size statue of St George. It was a realistic and vivid portrayal of the armour-clad saint upon his wild-eyed, nostril-flaring stead, and beneath them, run through with a lance, was a snarling, demonic dragon. This moment of drama, frozen in white marble, had an unsettling effect on Conway. He couldn't help but feel for the defeated dragon.

Why was it in the storeroom? And what did it represent? Christianity expunging heresy? Good triumphing over evil? Reason eclipsing ignorance? Or was it simply a case of St George snuffing out a species on the brink of extinction?

Conway was put in mind of an inventory he had once undertaken. He had counted every religious image and article in his home. There was the holy water font by the hall door. Many's the time his mother drenched him with its contents as he left the house, to keep him safe from all harm.

In his bedroom alone, there resided the Child of Prague, St Martin, St Therese, a tapestry of the Last Supper, a statue of St Anthony that glowed in the dark, the Holy Family, and, last but not least, St Christopher who had become a bit of a favourite with Conway ever since the unfortunate saint was demoted by the Church for being more myth than man. Though he thought of himself as an incurable sceptic, he had always found something very moving about St Christopher carrying the infant Jesus across a stream on his shoulders. Indeed, he had often cried bitter tears, in the privacy of his own bed, because of the emotions that this simple depiction had aroused in him.

On passing an alcove in a corridor, he couldn't help but notice the outline of a figure. It was not unlike those curious shadows that are left after nuclear blasts. Where a statue once stood, all that remained was a faint image. It was as if the paint's covering power was not sufficient to blot out the hallowed or the divine. The image had somehow become ingrained in time and space. Then a peculiar thing happened. Conway began to see the previous tenants of the corridors. A vast congregation of statuary loomed out of nowhere and floated on the air like diaphanous transparencies. It seemed that all the statues in Ireland had wandered into view. It was a dizzying spectacle that Conway didn't much care for.

Another episode of temporal slippage, he assured himself knowingly. It would soon pass. He wondered if, in all of Limerick, or indeed the entire island of Ireland, there were no statues to Pasteur, Lister, Jenner, Curie, Fleming, Koch, Mendel or Röntgen, or any such benefactors of humanity. After all, many owed their very existence to these great people. But we do not openly honour them. Why? For a brief moment, Conway had in his mind's eye the image of an Ireland where the likes of Pasteur might well take his place alongside DeValera, Collins, Pearse, Kennedy and the Sacred Heart. A light burning brightly below his portrait, for good measure. The image could not be sustained, however, it having a half-life not dissimilar to a snowball's chance in a microwave oven.

Scattering his thoughts, words, wrapped in reverberating indignation, floated down the corridor.

...I know what I know and I know what I'm talking about...

Drawn by the power of suggestion, he headed towards the source and was soon on the scent. By some involuntary trick of teleportation he found himself in a bright and airy room 'seated' on one of five blue chairs that formed a crescent. To his left, sat the source of the shouting, a man wearing a polo-necked jumper and sporting a goatee beard. To his right, who else but his old friend Tubridy, his arms folded, his legs crossed and sitting as shtum as an Easter Island statue. Next to Tubridy sat a thickset man wearing sports jacket and flat cap. Farther on, making up the end of the crescent, was an anorexically thin young girl whose face was half-hidden behind a screen of lank fair hair. Conway himself, it seemed, had taken occupancy of an empty chair.

At the focal point of this crescent of stackable chairs sat one Dr Clair Brill. It said so on the nametag that was clipped to the breast pocket of her white coat. She was young, fresh-faced, most likely in her twenties, with raven hair tied back in a ponytail. Behind her, were large windows that led to a patio area. Conway could see a small group of patients outside, sitting around easels, and involved in what he assumed was 'therapeutic painting'.

Backlit by the sunshine that streamed into the room, Dr Brill tilted her head, causing her ponytail to fall upon her shoulder.

'Remember the ground rules? We promised, didn't we?' she said, her voice soft and measured as if she was reading a list of ingredients for a cake. 'We must respect each other's point of view, no matter how we feel about it. That was our agreement. Go on, Father...sorry...John.'

The man with the goatee beard, to Conway's left, grew quite agitated. Twitching about in his chair, he said, rather tersely, 'I am no longer a priest. In my case, once a lapsed Catholic, always a lapsed Catholic.'

'Of course,' Dr Brill said, momentarily closing her eyes on her faux pas, '...please do go on.'

John, the priest formerly known as Father, sulked for a moment, then regaining what little composure he had, said wearily, 'I know what I know and I know what I'm talking about...'

'So you keep saying...' the man in the flat cap sniped, tucking in his chin and eyeing the object of his censure from under the peak of the cap.

'Well, I've said it again, haven't I?'

'Ahh you go too deeply into things,' the Flat Cap said dismissively, turning up his nose and twisting his mouth into an expression of disdain.

'Spoken like the true and shallow person you are...' John countered, then, without a trace of repentance, he went on in a defiant voice, 'the Bishop said to me, quoting someone or other, that he wished he was as certain of anything as I appeared to be of everything. But he's a fine one to talk. He let me down badly on the Tridentine Mass. My argument, all along, was that the language that glorifies God should not be the same as the language that sells guns or hamburgers. Latin might well be dead for some, but it is safe and incorruptible, not the language of advertising or grimy commerce. Without Latin the mystery is gone, and mystery is important. I would venture to say that it is essential...'

Surprised that he still held the floor unchallenged, he decided to expound.

'I think you could call me the definitive lapsed Catholic. With all our prayers and our supernatural, priestly powers and turning the bread and wine into the body and blood of God, made man, we can't make the Holy Communion host gluten free. Or so the bishops, in their divine wisdom, have decided. I'm a coeliac. Do you know what that means? It means I'm allergic to God! For heaven's sake! Well, that did it for me. That, on top of everything else. The constant round of baptisms, weddings and funerals. The whole damn ceremonial carnival. I just had enough of the rituals. I could take no more...'

'What about your flock? Your parishioners?' his ever-willing antagonist asked accusingly, 'did you think of them?'

'Oh the laity, is it?' John asked, grimacing in disgust, 'don't talk to me about that lot, with their à la carte religion and their lip service to church teaching and the Gospels. And their dreadful video cameras. Even funerals are turned into a spectacle. Nothing is sacred. Recording coffins being lowered into the ground? Is there no decorum? They use the sacraments as an excuse for a party. Spending money hand over fist, mostly over the bar, while half the world starves. And tanning salons for children? So they can look good in Communion white? Aren't we missing something here?'

'You had a crisis of faith?' Dr Brill intoned, as if it were both question and statement of fact.

Getting red in the face, John said vehemently, 'To no longer believe in something I consider not to be true, is not a crisis of faith. I haven't lost my faith, I have gained insight. I decided not to live under the shadow of religion. I decided to be free of it. And take the word Oberammergau, or Medjugorje, while I'm on the subject. Do you know why they're such a hit with the pilgrims? I'll tell you, it's as much to do with their exotic syllables and the difficulty in their pronunciation as for the Passion play or their spiritual value. And everyone in Limerick says, *Lourdes*, when it should be pronounced, *Lourde*. They always pronounce the damned 's'. It's French, so it is. It's supposed to be silent. It really is so irritating...'

In a great huff of indignation, Flat Cap interjected.

'Well, excuse meeee. We know not what we dooo. Do weeee?' He swung his left leg over his right, which had the effect of turning him away from Conway, and the source of his annoyance, and towards the rest of the group where he could bask in their approval of his contempt.

'You promised...' Dr Brill admonished.

'Sorry, but he'd try the patience of a saint, that fella would. Even St Francis of Assisi, himself, would throw the head, so he would...'

'May I continue? May I?' John said, fiercely eyeing his detractor, '...I had this road to Damascus experience. You could call it an epiphany if you're so inclined. It was during concelebrated mass, I remember. I suddenly realised that Catholics and Protestants are lapsed Christians, and that Christians, god bless their troubled souls, are but lapsed rationalists. Though it hadn't been used for years, I went straight to the pulpit. You should have heard me. For too long, I told them, our intelligence has been limited by the circumference of our collars. We've become the Church of the Holy Profit Margin, and the Church of the Divine Divvy, with indexed-linked salvation.'

Standing now, with arms extended, he began to chant like some crazed evangelist.

'...again he gave thanks and praise, took the wine, gave it to his disciples and said, this is my blood, the blood of the new and everlasting controversy. Call it transubstantiation. That should be yet another reason for centuries of bloody conflict. That should cause a difference of opinion that will keep the death squads and the undertakers busy for a few millennia. Good enough for an inquisition or two. Do this in memory of me. Blessed are you, Almighty God. Response: I am not convinced of this. All light and holiness comes from you, Almighty Father. Response: I am not convinced of this...'

Exhausted from his theatrics, John resumed his seat, and while the others sat in stunned silence, he began rocking back and forth in an agitated manner.

'What time is it?' he asked at length.

'It's...' Dr Brill said, glancing at her watch, 'two-fifteen.'

'I make it two-sixteen,' whispered the girl at the end.

'Mine's stopped,' said Flat Cap.

Even Tubridy, who hadn't opened his mouth up to then, chipped in with the time, 'Actually, it's two-nineteen,'

'Thank you for your diligence in keeping me informed of the correct time,' Dr Brill said wearily, allowing herself just a smidgen of human frailty. Then, turning to John, she said, 'why do you need to know the time?'

'Well, you see, I become infallible at three,' he explained, 'I have decided that at three o'clock, everything I say, on matters both temporal and spiritual, will be infallible. I will become all-knowing and inspired. I become, how shall I put it, infallibly infallible?'

Clenching his fists, Flat Cap cautioned, 'You shouldn't be sarcastic, you haven't the build for it...'

'Do you know your problem?' John asked, then quickly supplied the answer, 'you're a consummate ignoramus...'

'I suppose you're going to educate me, are you?' Flat Cap said, puffing himself into a tizzy.

John didn't need an invitation. 'As recently as 1870, Pope Pius IX decides, doesn't he, to become infallible. Just like that. The question is, was the Pope and the Vatican Council of Cardinals speaking infallibly when they decided that the

Pope was to be infallible? I mean, let's face it, never has an organisation been proved to be so wrong, so many times, and still insists that it is infallible. Galileo, for some reason, comes to mind.'

'Without religion, where would we be? Answer me that?' Flat Cap countered, 'we'd be nothing but barbarians, that's what we'd be.'

Turning on his adversary, John derisively said, 'As far as I'm concerned, religion is for old women, philosophy is for men...' Then, remembering himself, he quickly added, 'saving your presence, of course, ladies...'

'Such downright blasphemy!' Flat Cap uttered with utter disgust, 'and you a man of the cloth...'

'Blasphemy?' John said, repeating the word in a voice near to hysterical, 'the closest you can get to insulting God, is to say that God can be insulted. God is greater than any religion. Religion does not glorify God, it diminishes God. You cannot encapsulate God in a box, or a book, or a building. When it comes to God, there is always some zealot who's willing to take offence and commit the most heinous crimes on behalf of God. All-powerful, all-knowing, God is big enough to take belittling. He's God for god's sake!'

'Try not to shout,' Dr Brill said, then added, 'at least not so loudly.'

'I'm sorry,' intoned John, going on with a grumbling emphasis in his voice, 'the Church may need defending, religion may need defending, but God does not!'

'The Church has survived thousands of years and who are you to come along and belittle it?' Flat Cap protested, and snorted contemptuously.

'The Church has been around a long time, that's true,' John said indulgently, 'it has stood the test of time. It's survived the centuries. Well, so has chickenpox. Longevity is no proof of validity.'

Getting up to get down on his knees, he went on, 'Now pray with me, for when an atheist prays, God will surely listen...' Making the sign of the cross, he chanted with mock decorum, 'in the name of the capsule, the tablet and the holy linctus, amen...'

'That will do...' Dr Brill instructed, and John, left in no doubt that he had gone too far, sheepishly resumed his seat. Turning her attention to the waif-like girl, who had remained quiet and unresponsive throughout, she asked, 'Charlotte, have you anything to contribute?'

Shy and reserved, the young girl swept her hair from her face only for it to fall across it again.

'I have...' she began haltingly, 'I have my proverbs...'

'Would you like to share them with us?' Dr Brill coaxed, nodding at the slim volume Charlotte held in her lap.

In counterpoint to all that had gone before, Charlotte's voice was soft and low, like the sighing of the wind after a storm. It was captivating, beguiling.

The moon does not heed the barking of dogs
The noblest vengeance is to forgive
The way to be safe is to never feel secure
They'd see faults if their eyes were out

'Words to live by, words to live by, a nod's as good as a wink to a blind ass...' said Flat Cap enthusiastically, giving his adversary a knowing stare.

'Shsssh. Let her finish...' John pleaded.

'Just one more,' Charlotte said timidly,
When you can tread on nine daises at once, Spring has come

Then she added, with concern in her voice, 'I don't like treading on the daises, they're such sweet flowers, but it's difficult not to, there are so many...'

Dr Brill hesitated, searching for words, 'I think we can all agree that that was most interesting, and informative.'

Thick and fast came the enthusiastic acclamations from the others. Conway begged to differ. He was as wise and as lost as ever.

Chapter Sixteen

It is a strange but a peculiarly regular phenomenon that just when you've convinced yourself it is pointless to continue, something turns up. Like in a game of hide-and-seek where the seeker becomes tired and the search seems fruitless, out pops the head of a grinning, self-satisfied playmate. Like the word, *Yokam*. Conway heard it in passing and it stopped him in his tracks.

A young, matronly nurse spoke distinctly into the ear of an elderly man in a wheelchair. Affectionately squeezing his shoulder, she had said, 'Mr Navilluso? Stephen? Your friend, Yokam, is here to see you.'

There was not a flicker of response from the old man. He sat perfectly still, leaning slightly to his right, his hands resting limply on the tartan rug that covered his legs. His eyes, wide open, stared from a mask-like face as if in a trance.

'Remember,' she said, addressing the visitor, 'he can still hear everything you're saying. So talk away to him.' Then, wrapping her light blue cardigan around herself with folded arms, she added, smiling, 'I'll see you on your way out, Yokam.'

'Thanks, Miss,' Yokam said, nodding respectfully.

Conway was more than a little annoyed with himself. Mr Navilluso, how are you! He had come across the name in his trawl of the records, and though unusual, it had sounded plausibly Greek to him. Not one Stephen O'Sullivan to be found. Not one! Not if O'Sullivan is spelled backwards! It was a humbling blow to one who fancied himself at word puzzles and conundrums. It was humiliating. But if Conway found this demonstration of his own fallibility distressing, the next revelation gave him grounds for greater concern.

'You're nearly out of water, I see, Stephen...' Yokam said, 'I went to get more, only to find that the well has dried up, whether 'tis the drainage schemes, or the weather, or what, but there's nary a drop left.' Nodding at the old Lucozade bottle that served as a recycled vessel, he added, 'you have the last of it there...'

Like some dreadful omission suddenly remembered, the Orb's leaden words of warning came back to Conway.

Remember, you haven't got forever. You have only as long as Yokam's water lasts

Conway looked at the half-empty bottle on Navilluso's bedside locker and cringed.

Dressed conservatively in a slate-grey jacket, white shirt, navy-blue tie and wine, V-necked pullover, Yokam had the look of a man who was wearing his Sunday best. He reminded Conway of a maths teacher he once had. A man of the old school. He seemed polite and had a kindly face.

'I'll be retiring soon, Stephen, did I tell you?' Yokam said, then added, 'I'm to be pensioned off. Anyway sure, I'm not up to the shunting anymore. The shoulder hasn't been right since the knock I took that time.'

Yokam was small in stature but broad in shoulder. His big hands, tanned and calloused, showed he was no stranger to hard work.

'They're all telling me to put in a claim. But I never claimed in my life and I'm not going to start now. You'd have no luck for it, so you wouldn't. I'll have me pension and we'll soldier on. Hard to believe I started in the railway all those years ago. Forty-three years I've worked there. Hard to believe. Joined straight after we were demobbed, do you remember? Ah, Stephen, how the time flies...' he added wistfully, thumbing the NUR service badge that was pinned on the lapel of his coat jacket.

'I can't stay long, Stephen, herself isn't well. I promised her I'd go into town to spare her the journey, she's not able to get around like she used to. I haven't been home yet. I just popped in to say hello.'

He got up to leave, his cap held loosely in his hands. 'Well, old friend, I'd better be getting along, I suppose.'

Conway watched as Yokam paused as if waiting for the faintest acknowledgment of his presence, or reaction to his imminent departure. There was none. O'Sullivan sat in his wheelchair, rigid and immobile, as if nothing had happened. Yokam, tears welling in his eyes, placed his cap on his head and, gathering up a canvas shopping bag, made his way to the door.

Well, Conway had his man. There he was before him. The elusive Mr O'Sullivan. The man who held the key to the whereabouts of the elusive pearls. And, more importantly, the key to Conway's freedom. But the man was catatonic. How was he going to get through to this man? It appeared hopeless. A lost cause. He had come all this way for nothing. He was trapped, doomed, it seemed, to remain in this limbo for god knows how long. Perhaps forever. Moving closer to consider his options, Conway went eyeball to eyeball with O'Sullivan. He could hear the man's breathing, low and regular. He noted the dilated pupils of the walnut-brown eyes. Perhaps there was something in a name after all, for the Gaelic for *O'Sullivan* is *Ó Súileabháin* and means 'dark-eyed'.

Suddenly, as if caught on the event horizon of a black hole, Conway found himself tumbling into O'Sullivan's left eye. Through the transparent cornea he went, through the aqueous humour of the anterior chamber and on past the pigmented iris, through the dilated pupil, through the fine focusing lens and on into the vitreous humour of the posterior chamber. Swept along on waves of light that washed against the retina and the optic nerve fibres, where, through the miracle of photochemical process, he travelled as an electrical nerve impulse, down the optic nerve, curving in to the crossroad of the optic chiasma and crossing over to the right hemisphere and onto the lateral geniculate body, before transferring to the visual cortex and ending up in the occipital lobe, just above the cerebellum.

All this seemed like a long time to Conway but in reality it was pretty much instantaneous. He had followed the miraculous route from the optic nerve to the brain, but felt none the worse for wear. It was a textbook journey to the enchanted loom. Conway was now residing inside a maze, a labyrinth, majestically set in amethyst. The human brain, three pounds of mystical complexity, probably the most precious and most complex structure in the universe.

All about him was Terra Incognita. He was down amongst the neurons. Nerve cells, like a forest of enchanted golden trees, spread their branching filaments. He travelled along on a relay system of stepping stones and branching complexities. He showered in the ion exchange of the synapses and was infused with the molecules of memory. Conway's conscience soon raised a flag of disapproval. His presence was an intrusion. He was taking liberties and had no right to be there. But his conscience was soon to be appeased.

Floating up before him, like a hologram, there appeared a face. Not the frozen face of a catatonic, but the animated face of a man in his prime.

'Welcome to my world, I've been expecting you,' it said in a composed, re-assuring way. Conway must have appeared dumbfounded for the face loomed ever nearer and asked expectantly, 'Is there something you wish to know?'

Like a child let loose in a sweet shop, and overwhelmed by this Aladdin's cave of possibilities, Conway sidelined the purpose of his visit. He could not pass up the opportunity of asking, what he considered to be, important and pertinent questions. But where to begin? For starters, he decided to ask the one question that has baffled philosophers, and taxi drivers, since time immemorial.

'What is the purpose of life?'

Without the proverbial batting of an eyelid, O'Sullivan said, not so simply, 'The question is, must everything have a purpose? Can a thing just be? Or just not be? Must our binary brains snip infinities with the simple scissors of logic? Must we try and cut the universe down to size, to the lowest common denominator, to our level?'

Conway was pretty sure it was a rhetorical question and took a chance on not providing an answer.

'You are matter dreaming,' O'Sullivan went on, his voice sounding like axiomatic certainty, 'there is nothing unjust to the inanimate. The inanimate cannot be condemned. It does not agonise. It has no need of redemption. The desire for redemption is within the animate. Man, his mind, his soul, or whatever he wishes to call his cerebral chemical reactions, is a distillation of matter, not its true essence.

Consciousness is a poor glimpse of things. Our minds confuse us. The journey of matter through the evolutionary process has led to this. We think that thinking is everything, but this is just an illusion. A little knowledge is a dangerous thing and that makes man a very dangerous species. Messing about with atoms to see how the universe began might well be a way of finding out how it will end. As you must know by now, being highly intelligent allows you to do incredibly stupid things. Just because you name something does not imply you know it, or understand it. The universe is already aware of itself, it does not need our approval or explanation. The truth is this, death does not exist. All atoms have intrinsic life. Anything that occupies a space is alive. It exists. Our 'death' is simply the end of consciousness and the return to the natural inanimate state. We are matter made flesh...'

Confused, yet intrigued, Conway posed a question.

'How do you know all this?'

'The fall was responsible for my awakening. It isn't that something was lost. Something was gained. I was born again to see things I should never have seen. To know things I should never have known. I was once like you, free and easy in my ignorance. I remember when I was a child, before the use of reason, I longed for a voice to tell the world but my fears took hold and my thoughts remained hidden.

I never spoke of what I knew, but succumbed to the intimidations of custom and prejudice. And when, at last, I was ready to speak, I could not. My words were garbled on their journey from heart to mouth. I wandered in here one day babbling nonsense. A voluntary patient seeking help and sanctuary. The cat was out of the bag, the genie was out of the bottle, but it's of little consequence when no one listens, or understands. It seemed I was as doomed as Cassandra, doomed to tell the truth but never to be believed. And so silence descended...'

Other voices now intruded on their dialogue. A cabal of callous, malevolent whisperings enveloped them. Muffled and confused they remained until one in particular spun away from the others, and sighing like the rise and fall of dying winds, it mocked and menaced.

'...remember the hiss of oxygen, unearthly in the night, on the threshold of death, on the threshold of life. Traitor! We saw the way things were going, after your fall from the Strand Wall. You were no good to begin with. You were pitched too high. You are neither here nor there. Neither this, nor that. A between kind of thing. A dividing line between nothing and nothing. You'll never be any good. You'll never amount to anything...'

'Ignore the voices,' O'Sullivan advised, 'as I have done for many years. They come and go.'

'Who are they? What are they?' Conway asked, a little unnerved by the episode.

'They are of no consequence. Pay no heed, they have gone now...'

Indeed they had. But Conway was curiously troubled. The intrusion had left him feeling somewhat lighter and he sensed something had been taken from him. Incredibly, he had forgotten what he had come for. Some pickpocket had stolen his question. Conway, at a loss as to what to do next, decided to ask the first question that entered his head. Anything, to kick-start the process. Anything, to re-establish his unique relationship with O'Sullivan.

'What were Einstein's last words?'

'Wie spät ist es?' O'Sullivan answered.

Conway's smattering of German came under the heading of 'most commonly used phrases'. But it was enough.

'What time is it?' Conway translated. The great man was simply asking the time. How prosaic. And yet how apt. Einstein had always been fascinated by the fourth dimension. Maybe he had a date with destiny.

As Conway continued to be intrigued, the hologram shimmered and O'Sullivan said, with urgency in his voice,

'A timely reminder. My time is short. If my mind can hold together long enough, I will endeavour to finish this task. Before my thoughts are put to sleep forever, perhaps I may leave behind something more durable than a headstone. You have come for the secret? The pearls?'

'Yes,' Conway said, mightily relieved that someone had their wits about them.

'Do you know what a numerical palindrome is?' asked O'Sullivan.

Conway ruminated for a moment then came up with a definition: A mathematical peculiarity whereby a number is reversed, and is then added to itself, until one arrives at a number that reads the same from left to right, and from right to left.

'Yes,' said Conway, 'I know of it.'

'Then let us begin. I am, you will not be surprised to know, a seventh son, of a seventh son, of a seventh son, of a seventh son, of a seventh son, of a seventh son, of a seventh son. A most unlikely chain of events, but true. That's seven times removed. That's seven raised to the power of two, or seven squared. So, we multiply seven by seven...'

Reacting to Conway's uncertainty, O'Sullivan continued obligingly, '...here, I'll do the figures for you.'

And so he did and they were projected thus, as if on a screen:

$$7 \times 7 = \begin{array}{r} 49 \\ \underline{94} \\ 143 \\ \underline{341} \\ 484 \end{array}$$

'Now, divide evangelically,' O'Sullivan said.

'Evangelically?'

'Divide by four,' he directed, 'what do you get?'

'121'

'That is your answer. Those are the pearls.'

'That's it? That's all?' Conway said in disbelief, 'the pearls are a string of numbers, three numbers, that hold the secret of the universe?'

'Yes, these are the Pearls of Wisdom.'

Conway was perplexed. 'What does it mean?'

O'Sullivan was sympathetic. 'Don't worry yourself about it. We are dealing here with the geometry of the invisible and the dark light. Your taskmasters will understand. I return the secret, so the secret can remain a secret.'

'But...'

Conway's protests were dismissed, 'Beware of wisdom, Edward, it loosens your grip on life...'

The eyes of the hologram closed and the image began to disintegrate. All that remained was a warning voice, 'Go now, the red tide comes, my walls have been breached. Go. We are finished. Go. Après moi le déluge...'

As Conway remained to ask himself the question, *whatever did he mean,* a busy, rumbling noise grew nearer and nearer, and louder and louder, until a thunderous roar swept down upon him. He soon realised he was caught in the middle of a cerebral haemorrhage. As he fled the advancing torrent of blood, he decided it best to leave the same way he had come. On exiting O'Sullivan's left eye, he was confronted by the revolving spokes of an upturned wheelchair and O'Sullivan's body sprawled helplessly on the floor. Somehow, the alarm had been sounded and medical staff had rushed to the scene.

In the commotion of this full-scale medical emergency, the Lucozade bottle containing Yokam's water was upset. It tottered and teetered before tipping over, and, as Conway watched in horror, it began to roll slowly towards the edge of the locker. Then, tumbling off, it shattered into smithereens on the tiled floor.

Chapter Seventeen

Moonlit clouds, like tarnished silver, dappled the night sky when Conway finally reached the hospital entrance. Try as he might, he found himself unable to leave the hospital grounds. He tried to exit through the gates but could not do so. He tried going over the wall but could not do so. Again and again he tried, but to no avail. It was as if some electromagnetic force barred the way.

Before he could work himself into anything bordering real panic, he was receiving visitors. Like will-o'-the-wisps they frolicked into view. There they were, Red Pepper, Green Pepper and Carbon Copy Blue. The 'Orb' brothers were back. But, whether by choice or by some necessity, they remained outside the gates. Business, it seemed, would have to be conducted through the bars.

Carbon Copy spoke.

'As Chairman, it falls to me to inform you that there are certain procedures to all these proceedings. We'll have to have a MAGEE. That is, a Meeting that is Annual, General, Extraordinary and Emergency. Simultaneously, concurrently, and at the same time. It is right and fitting.'

'Oh, Carbon Copy is a stickler for correctitude, don't you know,' disclosed Red Pepper.

'Letchu away with noshan, dah falla woodent,' Green Pepper concurred.

Carbon Copy spoke again.

'Riddle me this,' says he, 'what's got two m's, two t's and two e's, and you can drive a golf ball of the end of it for good measure, making sure of course to avoid the Bolshevik in the process?'

Conway, in no mood for guessing games, said, with some impatience, 'I don't know, tell me.'

'Why, a committee, of course,' they all answered in that, 'gawd, you're very stupid', sort of way. Then they began their usual litany of incontinence, speaking in fluent balderdash, blarney and baloney.

'I propose to support the proposal proposed.'

'I second that through the chair.'

'Proposed and seconded. We have a quorum of three. I now call this meeting open. Can we have the Minutes of the last meeting?'

'I deem them inadmissible, for the very good reason that if we recognise the Minutes, of the last meeting, it gives credence to the outlandish claim, that this meeting, we are now conducting, is not, in fact, the last meeting, which, we all know, very well, is indeed, not only the last, but, the very last meeting, we shall ever have the privilege of conducting...'

'A tad too many tadpoles, Comrade Commandant, but let's skip all that, shall we, and move on to the Treasurer's report?'

'As Treasurer, I have to inform the committee that this year's expenditure was nil, while this year's income was, by some extraordinary coincidence, also nil. And, although we haven't got two brass farthings to rub together, we have, nevertheless, broke even in a bankrupt sort of way.'

'Moving along. Any other business?'

'As Secretary, I have to inform the committee, that the only other business is that there is no other business.'

'I propose we call this meeting to a close. All those in favour, say *aye*.'

'Aye...'

'Eye...'

'I...'

'This meeting is now closed.'

Now that all 'formalities' had been disposed of, Carbon Copy finally saw fit to reward Conway's patience by getting down to brass tacks.

'Mr Conway, you have something for us? The pearls?'

Conway gave them the palindrome with all its weird particulars. This seemed to please them no end. Comments, expressive, jubilant and congratulatory, flew in all directions.

'So that's it!'

'So simple!'

'So beautiful!'

'So obvious!'

'So devious!'

'How did it not occur to us?'

'Why hadn't someone thought of it before?'

'The things we can do with it!'

'The limitless possibilities!'

'Can you imagine if this fell into the wrong hands?'

'You know what we gotta do?'

'Bury it...'

'Deep...'

'Very deep...'

'Where no one will ever find it...'

Carbon Copy then turned to Conway and said, in a voice dripping with convivial appreciation, 'Since you've been so co-operative, and accommodating, and so good, we have decided you might like to know something that concerns you. What of your secrets, Conway? Do you know you hold a secret you are unaware of? Of course you don't. How could you? Many are cold but few are frozen, and the perfectionist, by definition, is invariably unhappy, though never perfectly so. But that's only by the way. What I'm trying to say is, you are not who you assume yourself to be. Your name, by rights, ought not to be Edward, but Nicholas.

You are an accident of administration. Not malicious, you understand, not even intentional. Just an accident shaped by carelessness. A long day, a tired nurse, tags get mixed, bundles get switched, that's all it takes. You'd be surprised how often this sort of thing happens. There's people all over Limerick who are not who they think they are, for 'tis a wise child that knows its father. An old but a true saying. Baby Conway becomes Baby McNamara in a versa vice kind of way. Nucky is a thoroughbred mongrel and you, you're a mongrel thoroughbred. You are both changelings of a sort...'

Then, as if he had been a native of New Orleans, he drawled, '...you is Nucky, and Nucky is you.'

Bewildered, Conway asked, 'Whatever do you mean?'

'Oh you of little feet, Conway. Don't you know?' Red Pepper commented, 'All men are created equal, then they are born.'

'Be it nature, be it nurture, you is the stuff that dice is made of, child,' Green Pepper said, seemingly infected by the New Orleans drawl as well, 'you is the child of chance and circumstance.'

It was guffaws all round. Then, without further ado, they floated off into the night sky and disappeared into thin air.

'Wait, wait,' Conway shouted after them, '...how do I get out of here? How do I get back home?'

But they never answered. Like an ice pick through his heart, Conway suffered the cold and callous realisation that he had been duped. And he did not like it one bit. It began to rain and with the rain came doubts, misgivings and fears. But before desolation had time to fatally descend and settle upon him, he heard a voice he immediately recognised. The voice of a controlling hypnotist. It was none other than the Purple Coconut and was Conway glad to see him.

'Left you in the lurch, I see. You never hear from them unless they want something. They'll never change.'

'But I thought, you were...' Conway wavered, unable to verbalise the unpalatable.

'Yes, so did I,' said the Purple Coconut, his voice full of reproach, 'had to change my name by deed poll, which took the best part of a very long time, let me tell you. You've led me a merry dance, young man. The things I've had to do to get here. I told you, you could not trust them. But would you listen? No! They cannot be trusted. And if they've told you anything, or done you any favours, it isn't for your own good, believe me.' Relenting, somewhat, he added more amiably, 'now, it's time we got you home.'

'How?' Conway dared to venture.

'Just watch me,' the Purple Coconut said boldly, as if he regarded Conway's question as a challenge. In a spellbinding voice, he declared, 'I am the dative and the ablative, the threshold and divide...'

Now he began to vibrate, changing form, from oval to circular, hollowing out until a perfect purple doughnut, as round as Giotto's O, hovered before him. It was a gateway. And it beckoned.

Conway was overjoyed, like a child reprieved from a hospital bed, who sees its mother bringing clothes and hears those wonderful words, 'you're going home.'

Chapter Eighteen

The first thing he saw, on opening his eyes, was the silver Miraculous Medal his mother had pinned to the pillow. His first earthbound thought was, *bladder full, sphincter holding.* He was back in his body and, by all appearances, back in his bed. He scanned the topography of the candlewick bedspread, and, spreading his legs wide like a pair of scissors, moved them about under the bedclothes just to prove to himself that he really was himself again.

With the emerging awareness of a newborn, he lifted his hands to his eyes for inspection and examined every minute detail, every whorl and swirl of fingerprint, every crease and fold of his palms. Like an explorer surveying a new wonder he looked at his arms, scrutinizing the forest of tawny hairs that sprouted from his pores. How strange, how foreign it all seemed. He *was* this impossibly complex universe. He *was* this heavy empire, this world of heartbeat, this fortress of feeling, this framework of articulation, this ordinance of boundary, this vessel of miracles. At once familiar, yet alien. At once domesticated, yet feral.

The seduction of the ordinary and mundane gradually mopped up these eccentric thoughts, however, and as he glanced about his room he was glad to see his books, ranked and filed, waiting for him. He acknowledged old friends. Compendiums, dictionaries, encyclopaedias and anthologies. The full-colour poster of the solar system and the nebulous Milky Way. Planet Earth, no bigger than a marble, the Moon, no bigger than a pea, dwarfed between the Sun and Jupiter.

He gazed upon his beloved Dopacof, standing sentinel on his bedside locker, with its attendant sticky rings and silver spoon. The mottling bananas, the consumer-friendly oranges, aka mandarins, and the tease of green and purple grapes with suspiciously bare sprigs, all in a Waterford Crystal bowl. And, of course, that official stamp of infirmity, more illustrative than any laboratory slide, the obligatory Lucozade. He was luxuriating in how good it felt to be back when he heard the reverberating voice of a high-ranking, adult male. Standing in the diffused light of the window, Dr Dalton, who apparently had been in the room all the while, was droning on in monologue.

'...you know, if I had my time over again, I don't think I'd be a doctor. It can be a thankless job at times. The hardest part of all, is seeing people die and that is the contradiction. I can't win as a doctor because the very thing I'm trying to prevent, is unpreventable. Sometimes I feel as if I'm to blame for the existence of death. Silly isn't it? People die and I feel guilty. About something that is inevitable, natural and all part of the contract of life. There is no cure. With our stethoscopes we listen to the heartbeat, not of life, but of death. We are as temporary as mayflies, except that mayflies don't agonize. They just get on with it. But, it could be that the moment is the thing, the moment is all that matters. Who knows Who'd want to live forever, anyway. I mean, that's the genius of death, it's a cure for life...'

Had Dr Dalton lost his mind completely? And if not, it seemed to Conway most unprofessional for any doctor to admit he did not know everything. And though he had more than suspected this to be the case, it was a shock to the system to hear it openly declared. He never would have imagined that the big man could harbour such profound thoughts. No doubt, he had been talking in his sleep. And, no doubt, his fevered and wretched outpourings had set the good doctor to morbid thinking.

Dr Dalton wheeled away from the window.

'Back in the land of the living, I see,' he said jovially, as if his strange monologue had been nothing but a comment on the likelihood of rain. 'Your poor mother,' he went on, plucking a grape from its twig and popping it in his mouth, 'was convinced you had passed away. She asked me to drop by and have a look at you, and now that I have, I can see you are in no danger.'

As he watched the doctor leaving the room with his little bag of tricks, he thought how drawn and frail he looked. The man was grey in the face, his shoulders slumped, and he looked altogether too human. Conway felt within him a surge of goodwill and sympathy for the big man, and before he had time to censor the emotion, it was out.

'Thanks, Doctor,' he said hoarsely, his mouth as dry as unbuttered toast.

Suppressing an appreciative smile, Dr Dalton nodded and closed the door behind him.

Not long afterwards, Mrs Conway appeared, popping her head around the door to ask, almost accusingly, 'Well, how are you feeling?'

'Fine. How long have I been asleep?' Conway said dozily.

'Asleep! Is that what you call it,' his mother said, tucking the bedclothes under the mattress so tightly he could hardly move in the bed.

'Is it coddin' me you are,' she went on, plainly distraught, 'you were out for the count. You were so low I could hardly find a pulse. I had no choice but to send for the doctor. I felt certain he was going to shift you off to hospital. The poor man must think I'm an awful nuisance. You've upset the whole house, that's what you have. For heaven's sake don't be doing that again, putting the heart crossways in us. Gave us all such a fright, that's what you did...'

Roaming the bookshelves for some distraction, his eyes alighted momentarily on a pair of field glasses, then did a double take.

'My binoculars!' he exclaimed, in a cracked voice.

'That person,' his mother said, fluffing up his pillows, 'that young Mac, whatever his name is, came to the door yesterday to return them, said you must have lost them down the leeks, which I was given to understand was a field of some sort, couldn't understand half of what he was saying to me...'

Conway was dumbfounded. Was it not odd that the return of the binoculars should echo the pattern of his dreams? Had he not seen Nucky and Mikey at the traffic lights? Could it be that they had been on their way to Sycamore Avenue? Not wishing to entertain the notion, he dismissed it as coincidence, though he could not dismiss so easily the twinge of guilt he felt for thinking the worst of the Macs, and calling them thieving magpies, even if it was in a dream. And as for out-of-body experiences, he continued to convince himself that it was all a dream, a particularly vivid one, yes, but a dream pure and simple.

What else could it be? It was time to rationalise. He hadn't left the room. He had been rummaging about in his own head. That was all. Written, directed and produced by his own fears and anxieties, and filmed on location in the rubbish tip of his subconscious. Just as well that junkyard was, for the most part, censored. Hell must be living in the subconscious. He could think of nothing worse.

In the days that followed, a procession of people came to his sickbed. From what he gathered, there had been a family get-together. Uncle Eugene and Uncle Darragh, along with Aunt Ursula, had a meet to consider their nephew's future. Through family networking, various jobs were in the offing. These were to be considered if he was not to return to university. Like a sultan giving audience to state advisers he listened with moribund equanimity.

Uncle Darragh, who, for as long as Conway had known him, had never sat down. Anywhere. It was always, 'can't stay long, just popped in, a flying visit.' Always wearing that absurd fishing hat of his. His way of telling the world of the consummate ease with which he played the legal osprey.

He paced the floor, back and forth, as if fishing a stretch of river, constantly jingling the loose change in his pockets and spewing out stock phrases to beat the band.

'...time to pull yourself together, young man, pull your socks up, time to do your business or get off the pot, your mother is worrying herself to a thread over you, she has asked me to have a word. There's a job there for you, just say the word, give me the nod, more than happy to have you aboard, but no slacking mind, won't be tolerated...'

Then he went on to wax lyrical on the benefits of being a solicitor, a job for life, he said, and if he had a mind to be one he would be *only delighted* to give him a start at his office. Or he could be a barrister, 'they're the boys who make the big bucks.'

Then, there was Uncle Eugene, an accountant and senior partner with Conway, Oldham and Neville Investments Plc., who wore bi-focal glasses that were forever slipping down his nose. Most of his day, it seemed, was taken up with nudging them back into place with the tip of his index finger. A jowl-proud man, Uncle Eugene had almost been Mayor of Limerick on several occasions, and certainly would have been but for 'the back-stabbing and double-dealing of so-called political partners.' For some reason he had an intense dislike 'for all those avid socialists who had taken up the wineglass to become affable socialites.'

'In the old days,' he said, 'you knew who the enemy was. Now, you couldn't tell who the fuck you were dealing with.' He apologised for the language.

'Don't tell your mother. You know how she gets.'

He had come to give a bit of advice, which he said could be summed up in three words, 'trust no one'. It should be the family motto. In Latin, of course. Conway was left with the distorted image of the family crest: *two fingers rampant, with nails showing.*

Then came Aunt Ursula, as thin as a rake and as brittle as bone china, who prefaced every criticism with, 'I don't want to be criticizing now, but...' He was a good lad, she told him, with a tendency to feel sorry for himself. He needed to be more practical and not have his head stuck in the clouds. 'Your mother, she's very concerned. It hasn't been easy for her all these years. When I think of your poor father, God rest his soul...' After that she couldn't finish a sentence, her words trailing off in blubbering tears or sniffed back to the safety of a wistful and weepy silence.

On the third day of consciousness, there came a visit from Fr Mulally, a chubby little priest, who, in answer to Conway's disclosure that he was a non-believer, laughed and said, as he shoved the Communion wafer into Conway's gob, 'Ah shure, God will take no notice of that.' He went on to tell of Doubting Thomas, and what a poor excuse for a Christian he was. Then, nearly drowning Conway with holy water, he began to speak of the great debt owed to Conway's guardian angel and insisted on reciting the invocation:

Angel of God, my guardian dear
To whom God's love commits me here
Ever this day be at my side
To light and guard, to rule and guide, amen...

Sensing the heresy of disbelief in Conway's half-hearted mutterings, Fr Mulally went on to illustrate, for the benefit of his misguided soul, the reality of angels.

'Angels are very real, and no less real for those who mock their existence, which is a good thing for the likes of you, my boy. There is a hierarchy of the angels consisting of nine orders contained within three circles. You have the first circle in which we have,' here, on emphatic, chubby fingers, he began to count them off, '...the Seraphim, the Cherubim, and, of course, the Thrones. In the second circle, we have the Dominions, the Virtues and the Powers, and in the third circle we have the Principalities, the Archangels, and last but not least, the Angels themselves. All mighty and powerful fellows, I can tell you, and it's as well not to get on the wrong side of them.'

With an admonishing look in his eyes, he went on in a bible-quoting voice, '...who art thou that repliest against God? Shall the thing formed say to him that formed it, why hast thou made me thus? Hath not the potter power over the clay, of the same lump, to make one vessel unto honour and another unto dishonour?'

Then, without warning, he inflated his lungs to their full capacity, and, with eyes bright with evangelical zeal, sang out in a resolute, operatic voice.

Faith of our fathers, living still
In spite of dungeon, fire and sword
O how our hearts beat high with joy
Whene'er we hear that glorious Word
Faith of our fathers, holy faith
We will be true to thee till death
We will be true to thee till death...

Holding on to 'death' for as long as his lungs would allow, he ended with a flourish, thrusting his arms high in the air as if acknowledging an invisible choir of angels. With a final dash of holy water, aimed directly at Conway, he backed out of the room.

'Keep the faith, boy,' he whispered in a cajoling manner, as he closed the door, '...shure 'tis all we have.'

To Conway, who had always regarded positive, utterly convinced people as mentally suspect, Fr Mulally was not the exception that proved the rule.

Chapter Nineteen

The marsh was ablaze with yellow flag. What a beautiful, bright flower it was, thought Conway, and so underrated. He consulted his Field Guide to Flora and Fauna.

'...Iris pseudacorus. Native to Britain and Ireland. It is used medicinally, leaves and roots poisonous to livestock. Grows to three feet in height with sword-like leaves. Iris, goddess of the rainbow. Flowers June-August. Pollinated by bumble bees. Probable inspiration for the Fleur-de-Lys, the heraldic emblem of the Kings of France...'

Feeling as cosseted and as pot-bound as his mother's geraniums and having listened to all the advice he could take, enough to last several lifetimes, he had felt in need of a change. He had made a full recovery despite the attentions of his mother who continued to treat him as an invalid. He was reproached for sitting in draughts. His mother had a dread of draughts, believing them responsible for every illness known to man. Though his home was as draught-proof as a hermetically sealed jar, his mother, with the conscientious vigilance of a paranoid Rottweiler, was ever-watchful. If he wasn't careful he would have a relapse, and he was reminded of what happened the last time. The dreaded relapse has always had a mythical status in Irish medical folklore and is feared the length and breadth of the country.

Not quite knowing why, he had decided to return to the Island. The day was overcast with heavy clouds and the wind fairly strong. Prepared, as always, and weighed down with provisions, he made slow but steady progress as he faced into a stiff, south-westerly breeze. He had brought his brolly, and though useless in high winds, it still had a fine point to it and might yet serve a defensive role.

He found the riverbank deserted. Not a soul to be seen. The hour and the weather helped to keep it so. The tide was high, brimming the riverbank. Like a busy housewife in a temper of spring-cleaning, the wind at his back swept all before it. Watching some crows being buffeted by the winds, he was reminded of those curious birds he had seen on his mother's Willow pattern tea service that look as if they're being shot out of the sky. His mother was very proud of her tea set, 'a genuine eighteen-century antique'.

It was four weeks since his last visit and what a difference those weeks made. Though it was an unseasonable Sunday morning for June, nature's handiwork was there for all to see. The trees that fringed the river were mostly of the willow variety. Many showed signs of pollarding and with renewed growth sent long shoots arrowing skyward. Ruffled by the breeze, white willows showed the silvered undersides of their slender leaves. He noted that the leaves of osiers and pussy willows had caught up with their catkins which are always first to bloom.

The swarthy bark and green foliage of the alders were well represented, competing for river frontage with dense phalanxes of reed and bulrush. Delightful clusters of marsh marigold were in bloom, their buttercup flowers contrasting with the dark green of their heart-shaped leaves. On the slope of the embankment, stands of rosebay willowherb and purple loosestrife stood shoulder to shoulder with beds of stinging nettle, while fragrant blossoms of meadowsweet and hawthorn scented the air. Less conspicuous plants, too, like plantain, burdock, dandelion, pineapple weed, speedwell and ragged robin, contributed to the burgeoning display.

Along the pathway itself, like a guard of honour, were trees of good age and variety. Oak, chestnut, sycamore, lime, beech, ash and poplar were on display. Most impressive were the chestnut trees, flaunting their showy candles of white and yellow blossom. Carved into the bark of some, were initials, dates and hearts, proclaiming undying love down the years.

Deciding to take some photographs with his pocket camera, he adjusted for clouds and opted for a wide-angle lens. Disturbed by the whine of the motorized wind-on, a coot broke from the cover of the reeds and scootered across the water's surface to the far bank.

Off to his right in the far distance was Keeper Hill. Unveiled by shifting cloud it stood out of the landscape like a pop-up mountain. Nearer, to the north, the backdrop of the misty Clare Hills appeared like a sleeping giant. As the embankment veered westward the trees gave way to a grassy clearing that ran to the river's edge. Ahead, the Shannon flowed broad and majestic. He had arrived at the source of the Abbey River. An elbow of the main river, it slipped away to follow its own brief course as far as Mathew Bridge. The Shannon continued on its way, intent on the last leg of its journey, seemingly unaware of the desertion. Here the winds gusted fitfully, or ran at speed as if chasing some invisible quarry. He could see their traces, like brushed velvet, on the river's surface.

Now but a stone's throw from Stella Maris Park, the marsh began to peter out and give way to a grassy meadow where horses of all shapes and sizes congregated. Piebald, skewbald, bay, grey, brown and chestnut, some with foals who ran about in stop-start fashion, testing their legs and generally showing off. Conway watched in fascination as a foal trotted along on tiptoe. Then suddenly, with a swish of its feather-duster tail, it would sprint a short distance away before looking back for approval from its mother who seemed to be preoccupied with her grazing. As Conway approached along the embankment the mare lifted her head, and, pricking forward her ears, studied him as he passed, all the while munching the grass she had in her mouth.

He followed the curve of the bank and found himself facing into the wind. Here, boats nodded at their moorings, and snow-white swans browsed at the water's edge. One hissed as he drew near, puffing up its wings in a threatening posture. Across the river, the massive landfill dump in Longpavement rose like the stepped terraces of a vineyard. On his left, a large concrete structure loomed up before him. He hazarded a guess that it was a ball court of some sort. Handball most likely. It was not unlike a giant cold frame. The broad, plain surface was too much temptation for some and graffiti was the inevitable result. Some adventurous soul had managed to display his literacy in the most improbable of places. In the angle of the highest point of the structure, impossible to get to without a ladder, was the enigmatic proclamation, *Gilgul woz here*.

Now, that rang a bell for Conway. Where had he come across that before? He sensed he should have known but somehow couldn't quite place it. His efforts to remember were further undermined by a prattling playback in his head of Uncle Darragh's voice. His uncle blamed all graffiti on the sinister development of free education.

'...teach the shaggers the three r's and what do they do, only deface private and public property with their asinine daubings...'

He thought no more of it. Raising his binoculars to his eyes he casually panned upriver before halting at the sight of the grey railway bridge that spanned the Shannon. Indeed, if he was not mistaken, it was called the Shannon Bridge. One of two Shannon Bridges within the city boundaries. Was it an oversight by the namers? Had they forgotten its existence when they christened the second one? As he scrutinized the meccano-like construction and its latticed functional design, he caught the sound of soft and regular clicking to his left. Turning to investigate he could see, farther up the bank, a youngster of about ten years old reeling in a fishing line. Conway watched awhile before making his presence known.

'Any luck?'

'What, sham?' the youngster yelled back, giving him only a cursory glance as he continued to reel in his line.

Wearing pullover, jeans, wellies and a baseball cap, the young lad appeared to Conway to be slightly underdressed for the great outdoors. Still, he did seem impervious to the elements.

'Any luck with the fishing?' Conway shouted again as he approached.

'I cot a perch, I did...' the youngster said proudly and, laying down his rod, lifted the trophy fish by its tail for Conway to see.

It was a perch, sure enough. Unmistakable in its tiger stripes and bright, orange-red fins. And not a whole lot bigger than a sardine.

'Are you having it for dinner?' Conway said in jest.

'Naahh, sham, they're no good for eatin', they're full a bones. I'll bring it home to the cat. If I cot a trout, now, that'd be diffrent. I'd eat a trout all right, or a salmon, or a fluke, or a brame. I gor a pull there a while ago. I think it was a trout or it could've been a brame.'

'A bream?' Conway inquired, with more than a hint of correction in his voice.

'Yeah, a *brame*,' said the youngster, stressing the word to leave no doubt as to who had the correct pronunciation.

Picking up his rod again, he said, as he eyed the bobbing float, '...there's another pull there now...' then, expressing his disappointment at a false alarm, added, '...naaahh, it's just the fecken weeds...'

He began reeling in line, causing the fluorescent red-and-black float to skip along the water like an epileptic stick insect. Grabbing hold of the line he checked the bait, and, satisfied that it was okay, brought the rod back over his right shoulder with a sweeping motion to cast the line a good distance out into the river.

'What bait are you using?'

'Worums,' the youngster said, letting out line as he spoke, 'blue skulls, they're the best, sham...'

That word 'sham' again. As Conway was entertaining the thought that it was, most probably, a local salutation of some kind, he was asked a very direct question by the youngster.

'How much did you pay for them glasses, sham?' he said, referring to the binoculars that hung about Conway's neck.

'These? I'm not sure, they were bought a long time ago.'

'I'd say they cost a packet.'

'Yes, I suppose so...'

This exchange concerning the binoculars had put him in mind of Nucky, and it occurred to him that he should, at least, express his gratitude for their safe return.

'You wouldn't happen to know Nucky Mac, would you?' he inquired hopefully.

'Of course I do. Everybody knows Nucky. I pal around with his brother Mikey, we're in the same class at school. He lives over by Our Lady's shrine.'

Seeing the blank expression on Conway's face, he became more expansive, 'Go along the bank, past the weir, right down to the swimmin' baths, past the football field. You'll see the shrine. You can't miss it. He lives just up the road from that. Ask anyone, sham, they'll tell you where he lives...'

He found the weir, a lofty, rectilinear structure that stepped across the river on concrete buttresses from the Island to the opposite bank at Kileely. Topped with iron railings, it had the look of a vessel that had run aground. Neither bridge nor boat but a means of trapping salmon, its grilled gates, save for a few, were open and lifted clear of the river. In these days of depleted stocks the salmon were given a free run. A large branch of a tree, carried down by floodwater, had wedged itself firmly at the base of a gate.

Seven cormorants went flying by. It was unusual to see so many in flight together. He was reminded of Yeats and his swans at Coole. This was the Gothic version, he thought, smiling to himself. Cormorants were endearing, if ungainly. Flight always seems a struggle to them, not like seagulls or crows who seem to delight in the challenge of the winds. He remembered how he once saw a crow drop a crust of bread from its beak in mid-flight, descend and catch it before it fell to earth. The crow had repeated this stunt so many times, it was obvious it was playing. There was more to crows than meets the eye.

Along the bank came a middle-aged man accompanied by a jaunty, bright-eyed terrier. The man, with walking stick in one hand, and cap anchored to his head with the other, managed to give a royal salute. The dog, its ears flapping in the wind, was far more circumspect and tiptoed around Conway, giving him a wide berth.

The landmark of the abandoned swimming baths was easy to identify. Over a low wall he could see two platforms, their rusting moorings still intact. It was obviously designed for diving boards that had long since gone. He could hear the lapping of windblown waves against the large concrete steps that led down to the water's edge. To his left was the football pitch, fringed by low tubular railing. Well rotavated by studs, the goalmouth area was bare and grassless. Two donkeys and a portly Shetland pony, who was in need of a haircut, had somehow managed to gain entry. Their rumps to the wind, they grazed contentedly on the longer grass out by the corner flag.

The road up ahead signalled the end of the embankment. There before him was the shrine, elaborate and well-kept, with an impressive garden surrounded by ornate railings. A paved pathway led to the statue of Our Lady of Mercy. Garbed in blue and white, she stood in reflective pose with outstretched arms, spreading wide her mantle to protect the faithful who gathered beneath.

Chapter Twenty

A man on a bicycle, his chin almost touching the handlebar, was struggling against the wind. Wobbling to a standstill, he decided he was fighting a losing battle and dismounted. Conway took the opportunity to ask for directions. After catching his breath, the man had said, in words pummelled by the wind, '...up around the corner, past the redbrick houses, by the Water Passage, he has a coal yard there, you can't miss it...'

In the narrow confines of the street, the wind had eased. It was a picturesque avenue with neat terraced houses on either side. Doors, as if on parade, showed all shades of the spectrum, and flowers of every hue tumbled out of window boxes in a cheerful assembly. Strolling on, he came upon a high and impressive stone wall that swept away to his left. It was, very likely, the perimeter wall of St Mary's Convent, inside of which, if his research was correct, lay the remains of an old Dominican priory dating back to 1227.

And that quaint, untidy heap ahead of him, with its ivy-clad walls and clutter of chimney pots, that must be the Villiers Alms Houses. And the narrow lane close by, gloomy with high railings and overhanging trees, the Water Passage, perhaps?

The redbrick houses to his right gave way to a row of compact and cosy looking cottages. One in particular, at the very end of the row, caught his eye. It was fronted by a neat little garden with box hedging and went by the name of *Iona*, which was branded onto a wooden plaque fastened to the cottage wall.

Adjoined to this was a large gate made of corrugated iron sheets covered over with pitch. On an oblong board the size of a coffee table was painted, in white irregular letters, the words *Coal and Blocks*. The flame logo of Calor Kosangas lent a more official endorsement.

Conway could hear sounds of sweeping coming from within. Cautiously, he tapped on the gate with his umbrella. The sweeping stopped and soon he heard the approach of heavy footsteps. After some screeching and squealing, a bolt eventually slid back. When the gate opened, there before Conway stood Nucky himself, as large as life with a yard brush in his hand.

'Hi,' said Conway sheepishly.

Nucky narrowed his eyes and fixed him with a stern look.

As Conway shuffled about awkwardly, not knowing what to say next, Nucky's eyes widened with recollection and his face eased into a broad smile.

'Well jaysus,' he said, 'if it isn't the man himself. What brings you round these parts?'

'I was in the area. Just thought I'd drop by, to thank you for the binoculars.'

'Ah, think nothan of it,' Nucky said, scratching his head with the brush handle.

'No, they belonged to my father. He used to go to the races a lot.'

'Fond of the gee-gees was he? Bad game. Those bookies are on to a good thing. In a ten-horse race they'll have nine horses runnin' for them and you'll only have the one. Shur, you can't win. Give me pitch-and-toss, any time.' Then, remembering himself, Nucky said, 'Come in, come in, you look pinched with the cowld.'

'Aaahm, I shouldn't really, just wanted to say thanks. I can see you're busy.'

'Can't you come in, can't you,' Nucky insisted, grabbing Conway by the shoulder, 'come in for a mugga tea anyway, can't you?'

Without much choice in the matter, Conway had found himself accepting the invitation. As soon as he had got inside the gates, he was accosted by a large dog of uncertain breed.

'Give over, Bowser!' Nucky growled, 'he'd bark at the Pope himself, so he would.'

'What breed is he?' Conway asked, somewhat nervously.

'Breed?' said Nucky, laughing, 'as my father would have said, he's a cross between an Upsetter and a Disappointer, that's what he is. Gettin' on a bit and gettin' fat.' Then, as if to save the dog's feelings, he added, 'good dog though, aren't you, Bowser?'

Now that Conway had a good look at him, he could see that Bowser was indeed an old dog, greying at the muzzle and rather overweight.

The yard was much bigger than one would have imagined from the outside. Though mostly concrete, much of its surface was still cobblestoned. The back of the enclosure was demarcated by an old stone wall from which sprouted red valerian. Patched here and there with brickwork, it was sectioned off into several bays that were piled high with coal, blocks and turf. To the right of this, running along an adjacent wall, were several stables. Framed in a half-door was Gypsy's massive head. He pricked his ears forward and gave out a low, rattling whinny on seeing Conway. Next door, also framed in a half-door, was an off-white, dozy-looking pony. Farther along, there was the unladen coal cart, its shafts resting on the ground. Next to that, a horsebox and next to that again, an old jaunting car in a state of disrepair. Having only one wheel, it was tilted sideways onto a sack of turf that served as a prop.

'This way...' said Nucky, opening a decorative wrought iron gate that led under a rose-covered archway and on past beds of roses, chrysanthemums and delphiniums. In a bird cage, hanging just below the eaves, a yellow canary flitted from perch to perch piping melancholy notes. Below this cage was a rabbit hutch where two skewbald rabbits sat nonchalantly on their haunches, their noses twitching as if deep in conversation with each other.

Whistling some lively tune, Nucky pressed down on the thumb latch of a green battened door and pushed it open, then motioned Conway to enter.

'The dirt before the brush, and age before beauty,' Nucky said spryly.

Inside, in what appeared to be the kitchen, Conway was immersed in the smells of breakfast. The fried aroma of bacon, eggs and onion hung about the room with toast and brewed tea. Net curtains, veiling a sash window, hampered the light of the overcast day as the warm glow of a coal fire threw soft shadows. The table, covered in oilcloth, had been cleared except for an island of staples, where milk, sugar and butter rubbed shoulders with the condiments of salt, pepper, mustard and tomato ketchup.

'Grab a chair,' said Nucky, then asked, 'will you have a bite to eat?'

'No, I've had breakfast, thanks.'

'Have a mugga tea anyway, and a bite to toast.'

'I will so, thanks...' Conway genially conceded.

As he adjusted to the gloom of the kitchen, his eyes picked out the profile of a cat that was lying indolently upon a cottage chair and eyeing him with disapproval. From under the table came a low, resonating growl that made Conway's heart skip a beat. On a command from Nucky of '...down, Rex,' a tiny Jack Russell terrier emerged from his hideout, wagging his docked tail and sniffing at Conway, as if to say, 'no hard feelings, only doing my job'. The cat, of course, continued to stare with ill-mannered impudence.

Conway scratched the dog's head and looked about the room. It was like a time capsule. Nothing was new. From the spartan linoleum beneath his feet, with its fading pattern of

Greco-Roman tiles, to the ornate wallpaper and timeworn furniture, everything seemed bedded down, as if things had been as they had always been. Conway noted, with interest, the old-fashioned Bakelite light switch and two-pin electric socket that ran halfway down the wall. Old pictures, some quite large and heavy framed, leaned from walls on stout cord that hung from a picture rail that ran the room a yard or so from the ceiling. The pictures were mostly pastoral scenes and landscapes.

Over the cast iron fireplace, slightly water-stained, was a colour print of a Red Setter sitting proudly beside a basket of wayward, clambering pups. On the mantelpiece itself, two large ornaments of rust-red King Charles Spaniels sat staring at each other over a carriage clock in the ultimate game of 'who blinks first'. From an alcove by the chimney breast, emphasized in the gloom, the red glow of a devotional light shone beneath a picture of the Sacred Heart.

There was a faint whiff of carbolic soap as Nucky washed his hands at the sink, an old white porcelain affair, complete with robust brass taps, one of which dribbled slightly. A wooden draining board, covered with a jumble of plates, bowls, mugs, cups, saucers and cutlery, gave evidence of recent breakfasts.

After drying his hands on a towel that was draped on a line overhead, Nucky held a large copper kettle under a tap and half-filled it with water. Placing the kettle on a white enamel stove, he struck a match and lit the gas ring which whuffed into life, its jets flaming blue and yellow.

'Take your coat off and make yourself at home, hang it on the door there.' Nucky said, nodding at the three nails that were driven into the back door and on which several coats already hung.

'Ah no, I'm grand.' Conway said, and in an effort to show how relaxed he could be, he leaned an elbow on the table. Looking for something to say, his gaze fell on the country scenes that covered the oilcloth. A vibrant, colourful medley of pheasants, grouse, gun dogs, fishing and fox-hunting stretched from one end of the table to the other. The fox was at his elbow.

'The unspeakable in pursuit of the uneatable,' Conway said in a portentous voice, 'actually,' he went on, 'I've read somewhere that the fox is, in fact, edible. Apparently it's quite tasty...'

'I don't think I'd fancy eatin' a fox, somehow...' Nucky said, throwing two slices of bread on the grill pan and sliding it back into place.

'Ever eaten a hedgehog?' he asked, then said, in answer to Conway's headshake, 'I have. I got a taste of one from some Gypsies once. It's a delicacy with them, you know. What they do is, first, they plaster the hedgehog with mud, spines and all, then they stick it in a hole in the ground and cook it, when it's done then, the mud is cracked open and removed along with the spines. Tastes a bit like pork. Fucken lovely. Great tack...'

Conway was sorry he ever brought up the subject of exotic dishes. The image of the poor hedgehog encased in mud was hard to take, and, in an effort to change the topic of conversation, he said, referring to the sideboard cabinet on his right, 'that's a nice piece of furniture...'

'Ah that?' Nucky said, as he lit the grill, 'that's as old as the hills.'

It was a solid, ornate item, decked with medals, cups and trophies, representing an index of sporting achievement in boxing, hurling, rowing, rugby, soccer, swimming and table tennis. Evidence of its age showed in one corner of its polished mirror where flecks of silver had been lost. Several framed black-and-white photographs of rugby teams and rowing crews were scattered about its surface. And set apart, taking pride of place, was, he surmised, the smiling portrait of Mr and Mrs Mac on their wedding day.

With the unmistakable sound of shuffling slippers, Mrs Mac made her entrance. She looked at Conway, twirled a pink curler in her hair and said, as casually as you like, 'Hello!'

'This is the man I was tellin' you about, Mam, the fella that Gypsy dragged through the leeks.'

Mrs Mac was a plump woman with a round, pleasant face. The rolled-up sleeves of her cardigan showed strong forearms and dimpled elbows.

'Nucky was telling me all about it,' she said, as if she had known Conway forever. Her voice was warm and fresh and her words came in a stream of unselfconscious fluency.

'You were lucky you weren't kilt, God preserve us from all harm,' she added, crossing herself, 'I heard you weren't well in yourself after it, but you're over it now, thank God.'

'I am, thanks,' said Conway.

'You remind me of someone,' she went on, putting a forefinger to her pursed lips and scrutinizing Conway, 'can't put my finger on it. I feel I know you from somewhere. You're nothing to the Conways in the Abbey? No?'

'I don't think so, as far as I know.'

Then, as if surprised by the oversight, Mrs Mac swiftly said, 'Nucky, give the young fella a bite to eat.'

'He's already eaten, Mam.'

'Well, give him a cuppa tea and some toast, at least!'

'The kettle is on,' Nucky said, 'so's the toast...'

Just then, young Mikey sauntered in, and, without a word, headed for the newly opened sliced pan that Nucky had left on a low dresser.

'What do *you* want?' Mrs Mac asked.

'Just came in for a cush a bread,'

'I thought you had a match?'

'It was called off. The pitch was waterlogged.' Mikey said, coming to the table and buttering himself a slice of bread.

Mrs Mac threw her eyes to heaven, shook her curlered head and sighed.

'Look at him, smathering the butter all over the table,' then responding to Mikey's mocking face, she added, 'if the wind changes you'll have that face for good, mind.'

Mikey appeared unperturbed by such a consequence.

'Go 'way, you article you.' Mrs Mac warned.

As soon as Mikey had disappeared there was a pounding down the stairs. Bobsy entered the kitchen and, without looking left or right, went to take his jacket from the back of the door.

'You came down that stairs like a herd of elephants,' Mrs Mac scolded, 'and where, may I ask, are you going?'

'Out,' came the prickly reply.

'I hope you're not up to your old tricks again.'

'I warn't doin' nahan,' said Bobsy, resentfully.

'Well, don't think I don't know what you're up to. If it's a thing I ketch you smoking, mind, I'll have your life, do you hear me?'

Bobsy threw Conway a surly look.

'Hello,' said Conway, and got a scowl for his trouble.

'Pay no attention to him,' said Mrs Mac after Bobsy had gone, 'he doesn't have a word for the priest these days. Can't get an ounce of good out of him lately, whatever's gotten into him. Trying to best me at every hands turn, that's what he is. Those cigarettes are a disgustin' habit. I can't abide them. A waste of fecken money, they are. God forgive me for swearin' and I only after confession yesterday.'

She turned on Nucky and said, in an exasperated voice, '...can't you keep the place tidy, can't you,' then, taking hold of a brush that stood in a corner by the stove, she began sweeping the floor, 'don't be leavin' your rushers there. Put them in the cubby or leave them out the back, why can't you. He thinks nothing of bringin' people in and the place do be in a mess. You couldn't keep the place clean with them, shur you couldn't...'

With a perplexed frown on her face she suddenly asked, 'Where's Mary Rose?'

'She's gone with Tubbs to the shops.'

'I want to have a word with her when she comes in,' Leaving the kitchen, she added as she went, 'I must go off and get ready...'

She had no sooner gone when the back door opened and in, on a blast of cold air, came a toddler no more than four or five years old. He stormed into the room but on seeing Conway became very shy and gravitated to Nucky's side. Forgetting the chocolate bar he held down by his side, he looked at Conway from under his eyebrows.

'Aaah, Tubbs, well if it isn't the man of the moment,' Nucky said, laughing.

Tubbs looked lost in a coat that was miles too big for him. As were his trousers that were turned up at the legs. His mop of layered fair hair, his large blue eyes and smidge of a nose, gave him the look of a little Viking.

'He's gone all shy,' said Nucky, wrapping him in his arms and tousling his hair.

When Mary Rose entered, Tubbs ran to her. Slipping off the child's coat, and barely giving Conway a second glance, she asked Nucky, 'Who's your friend?'

As Nucky was about to introduce his new guest, Conway obligingly intervened, deciding to speak for himself.

'Edward Conway...' he said, beaming.

'Eat your chocolate before it melts on ya,' Mary Rose said to the child, as if Conway had never spoken.

'...pleased to meet you,' he ventured politely.

There was still no response. She turned to Nucky and asked, 'Where's Mam?'

'Upstairs, gettin' ready for mass.'

On hearing this, Tubbs headed for the stairs.

As Conway gazed on Mary Rose, some wild sentiment broke loose in his heart. She was exquisite. Her straw-blonde hair casually, yet perfectly, framing a face that was, to him, beauty incarnate. Her blue eyes, set above high cheekbones, were almond-shaped and had a strange quality of innocent and savante. Her mouth was elegantly sculptured, with lips arrested just short of petulance.

She stood there in her black bicycle shorts, her legs slim, tanned and athletic. Leaning on one hip, she tilted her head sideways and smiled as her hair tumbled to her shoulder. It was as if she knew the disorder she was causing in Conway's head. He blushed. She laughed. The effect upon him was shattering. Conway was a mess. He had been in the company of such women before and had always been uncomfortable. But this wasn't 'uncomfortable'. This was torture. She was different, somehow, a force of nature. To his amazement, things surfaced within him as if in homage to this vision. Things he never knew existed. It was unfair, he thought, that anyone should have such a hold over another human being, least of all him.

She didn't seem human but a superlative being that had branched off on another evolutionary plane. If she had asked him to kiss her feet, right there and then, he just might not be able to resist. Was this what love at first sight meant? Conway stared, his pupils dilated so much, his eyes must have appeared like glazed saucers.

Her expression transformed to a frown, still she was beautiful. Her mouth fell open and there was a moment's hesitation as she waited for words to arrive at their assembly point. Her lips mobilised and flung the tardy words in his direction. Conway's instinct was to duck.

'Are you feeling all right, are ya?'

'Yes.'

'Well, what are you gawpin' at me for, as if I had two fecken heads?'

Conway was stunned, 'I do apologise. I assure you, I didn't realise I was doing such a thing...'

'Are you trying to be smart, or something?'

'Whatever do you mean?'

'Talkin' like an eejit for a start,' she said with a disdainful laugh, 'you talk like Little Lord Fauntleroy.'

Conway was devastated.

She looked at him with downcast eyes. Then, standing as tall as possible, with her nose in the air, she turned on her heel and with a haughty swish of her hair left the room.

'Mary Rose, Mary Rose,' Nucky called after her in mild outrage, 'tut, tut, tut, don't forget your manners, Edward is a guest in our home.' He was putting on an act, of course, and clearly enjoying the situation.

'Mary Rose is very bright, you know. Bright as a button, she got loads of honours in her Leaving. Up in the School o' Commerce now she is, doin' a business course, a deeploma or somethin' like that...'

Before Conway had time to recover, *she* was back again.

'Edward? I haven't seen you around here before. Where you from, Eddie?'

'Corbally,' Conway ventured.

Again ignoring his answer, she asked Nucky, 'where's the clippers for Molly?'

'Up in Nelly's room behind the wallpaper, where ju think they are?'

'Very funny,' she said, making a face at her brother.

Nucky relented, 'They're in the cubbyhole.'

'Did you sharpen them for her?'

'Of course I did!'

Again she was gone, followed by Tubbs, apparently in search of the 'clippers'.

Nucky had a broad smile on his face as he poured out Conway's tea. 'She's somethin' else, isn't she?' he said, then added, 'she likes you.'

Utterly unconvinced, Conway said, 'She *likes* me?'

'Oh, she likes you all right,' Nucky assured him, 'never seen her react that badly to anyone. She has an awful mouth on her, but she usually has to know you really well for her to lay into you like that,' then he added, with reconsideration, 'well, she either hates your guts or she really likes you.'

Conway didn't know how to react to these diametrically opposed possibilities.

'There's your toast,' said Nucky, throwing the bread onto a plate and pushing it towards Conway, 'dig in, plenty of butter there.'

'Thanks,' said Conway, still shell-shocked.

'By jaysus,' Nucky went on, laughing, 'it's a brave man who'd take her on. But there's no rose without a thorn, isn't that what they say. And by jaysus, she can be one thorny rose, and no mistake.'

184

'Give over swearin' and takin' the Lord's name in vain,' Mrs Mac said, as she entered the kitchen followed by Mary Rose and Tubbs, 'I won't have that kind of language in this house.'

Mrs Mac had dollied herself up, somewhat, and was now transformed into quite a handsome woman. Carrying her handbag in the crook of her arm, she tied her headscarf and tucked in her hair. Then, placing her handbag on the table, she turned to Mary Rose, and still making adjustments to her scarf, she said, her eyes wide and questioning, 'did I tell you to hang out the washing?'

'I did!' said Mary Rose, putting a hand on her hip.

'Well, would you ever do it right, were you sparing the pegs were you, the first gust of wind and they'll be over the fecken wall...'

'Well, they haven't blown off yet, have they?' Mary Rose answered with some defiance.

'Don't give me cheek,' Mrs Mac huffed, 'it's a wonder they're not all over the scheme with the wind that's there. And what in the name a'gawd are you doing in that get-up?'

'They're all the style, Mam.'

'Style, is that what you call it? In the name a'gawd, the backside adbe frozen off ya in them things. It adbe more in your line to wear something decent for a change and the day that's in it.'

'What's wrong with them?' Mary Rose asked, throwing her eyes to heaven.

'What's wrong with them? Is it mad you are? God grant me patience. Young ones today, I swear to god...'

'Ah give over, Mam, you're like a broken record, you're always giving out.'

Undeterred, Mrs Mac went on speaking her mind.

'...and don't be feeding that child so much sweets,' she said, looking at Tubbs who was still chewing, 'he's always stuffin' his face with rubbish. He won't be able to eat his dinner, wait and see. No wonder he's gone so finicky with his food.'

185

'A bar of chocolate, Mam? That's all it was.'

Ignoring Mary Rose's plea bargaining, Mrs Mac added, 'Make sure you make mass today. And that goes for you too, Nucky.'

'Yes, Mam,' said Nucky, sounding like a good and dutiful son, '...I'll get the one o'clock mass in Parteen.'

Glancing up at the clock on the mantelpiece, Mrs Mac exclaimed, 'Motheragawd! Look at the time! Plucking her bag from the table, she said hurriedly, 'I'll have to rush or I'll be late for mass myself. With a nod in Conway's direction, she added, 'sorry I have to rush out on you...'

After Mrs Mac closed the door behind her, Mary Rose rounded on Tubbs, 'Will you stop messing,' she said to the child, who was fiddling with Conway's binoculars.

Conway sipped his tea and said, in a placating tone of voice, 'It's okay, he's only looking at them.'

Nucky added, 'Leave him alone, he's only a child.'

Mary Rose begged to differ, 'A child? An ould man you mean.'

Tubbs retreated to where the cat was sitting and took up position behind the chair. He poked the cat with a stubby little finger and said, 'ketch a mouse, Shibs...' The cat, a grey tabby, rolled over on its back and flapped a lazy paw. Tubbs withdrew his finger and giggled. Then, looking through the bars of the chair, he whispered to Conway, 'Are you a snob?'

'Pardon?'

'Are you a snob?' the child repeated.

'I don't think so, why do you ask?'

'...cos Mikey said you were a snob...from Corbally.'

'Did he now? Well, I am from Corbally,'

'Tubbs,' Mary Rose scolded, 'will you leave the young fella alone and stop tormenting him?'

The child bided his time, then in a wide-mouthed whisper that showed all his milk teeth, he said to Conway, 'Where's Corbally?'

'Well,' said Conway indulgently, 'you go out the road from here and over O'Dwyer Bridge...'

Tubbs screwed up his face and thought for a while, then eyed Conway doubtfully before asking, 'Why is it made of wire?'

Conway looked puzzled for a moment, then laughed.

'No,' he explained, 'it's not a wire bridge. It's called O' Dwyer Bridge after Bishop O'Dwyer,'

'Did he...did he...make it all by himself?'

Mary Rose roared at Tubbs, 'Will you stop pestering him with questions.'

'Did you feed the rabbits?' Nucky asked diplomatically.

Tubbs thought a moment, then ran off, saying, 'I'll feed um now...'

'Wait for me,' said Mary Rose, and as she strolled after him she called out, 'who's the best boy in the world?'

'I am,' came the confident refrain.

Nucky stretched his arms above his head and yawned.

'Jaysus,' he said, 'that was a grand mugga tea,' then added, 'will you have another one?'

'No, thanks.'

'More toast?'

'No thanks, Nucky, I think I'd better be getting home.'

Outside in the yard they found Mary Rose feeding the rabbits and Tubbs crouched down on his haunches chanting, '...shady muddy, shady muddy, stick out your horens...'

'What's he saying?' Conway asked.

'Go away you, Bowser,' Tubbs said to the old dog who'd come over to investigate.

'Oh, he's just talkin' to the snail,' Nucky explained, 'that's what we call snails around here, shady muddies. Jaysus, you'd swear you were from another country. What do ye call 'em?'

Before Conway could draw breath to answer, Mary Rose loudly suggested, 'Escargots...' and sniggered into a lettuce leaf.

'Snails,' Conway said lamely, shifting the ballast of his overcoat. Then, changing the subject, he asked casually, nodding in the direction of the stables, 'what's the pony called?'

'Mikey's horse?' Nucky said, throwing back his shoulders and heading towards the animal in question, 'her name is Shamrock,' then he added, laughing, 'Sham, for short...'

On hearing its name, the pony snorted and nodded its head. Becoming meticulous, Conway asked, 'How tall would she be now?'

'Ah, she's near anuff turteen hands high,' Nucky said, his tongue rummaging in his teeth as if trying to dislodge something, 'mixture of all kinds but a lot of Connemara. A pony can't be more than fourteen and a half hands high. A hand is four inches and you measure from the withers...just between the shoulder blades there...' Nucky rambled on knowledgeably, placing a hand on the spot referred to, 'a fine little pony, picked her up at Ballinasloe for a song. Bit of a stargazer she was, and the owner wanted rid of her.'

Seeing the mystified look on Conway's face, he went on to explain, 'the head adbe held flat and she'd be lookin' at the stars. Uncomfortable in the mouth that's all she was. Couldn't take the bit. It was all wrong for the misfortune. Now she's as good as gold, aren't you, girl,' he said, rubbing the pony's muzzle. Then spotting something amiss, he added crossly as he checked the pony's mane, '...I'm wastin' my time talkin' to that fecken gom of a young fella. A right hames he's made of it, I told him to get the hag-knots out, and what does he do but leave them in a bigger mess than he found them...'

Absent-mindedly, Conway traced a forefinger over the horseshoe that was nailed above the stable door.

'What height would Gypsy be?'

'There's a breed of a Shire and a Cob in Gypsy,' said Nucky, still fussing with the pony's mane, 'he'd be close to seventeen hands high.'

With a purposeful stride he went to the third stable, opened its doors and disappeared inside. Conway followed and found himself in a murky storeroom of odds and ends. Horse collars, harnesses, tackle and tools of all kinds, hung along the walls and out of roof beams. On the floor lay coils of old rope, gas cylinders, peat briquettes, planks of wood, corrugated iron sheets, and a lopsided wheelbarrow that had seen better days. Nucky was lost in the gloom, searching for something or other and making quite a racket.

'They look interesting,' said Conway, spotting some old books that lay in a corner, illuminated by the light from the doorway.

Nucky emerged from the darkness empty-handed.

'Well, shaggit anyway,' he swore, 'if the ground opened and swallowed it, I can't find it. I'll have to leave it...'

'Encyclopaedia Britannica?' Conway was saying, as he thumbed nosily through one of the books.

'Guess where I got them?' Nucky said, distracted from his frustration of not finding what he was looking for. In answer to Conway's arched eyebrows, he said, '...the dump in Longpavement...in that cardboard box they were. Seven books in all. Numbers four, five, six, seven, eight, nine, and ten. The first three are missing, and so are the last twenty. So I was told. Bit mouldy, but there's a fair amount a readin' in them...'

Conway considered the volume in his hands in a new light. 'You're not afraid of catching something, are you?' he said rather squeamishly. Then, fearing that his words might give offence, he added, with some enthusiasm, 'interesting places...dumps.'

'Didn't think they'd be your cuppa tea now,' Nucky said.

'From what I've read,' Conway went on, 'they're excellent places to find exotic botanical specimens. Apparently.'

'Jaysus,' said Nucky, throwing back his head, 'you're a right one for the jawbreakers, aren't you, you must have swallowed a dictionary. Could you repeat that in English?'

'Unusual flowers? Plants?' Conway offered.

'Never would have thought that now...'

'You see,' Conway went on to explain, 'with all the foreign stuff we import, it's not unknown for pips of lemons, oranges, kiwi fruit, and the like, to germinate. And then there's birdseed, people clean out cages,' said Conway,

189

nodding up at the canary, who was now celebrating with song the sun's reappearance from a scrummage of clouds, 'and throw the waste in their bins, the seeds germinate in the rich, warm soil of the dump. It's like a giant compost heap. You'd never know what you might find.'

'I could take you out there someday, if you like,' Nucky suggested.

'Would you mind?'

'Ah shur not at all,' said Nucky generously, 'how about next week, sometime? Saturday maybe, and we'll head out. Call to the house. You know where I live...'

Suddenly, doubts swarmed in Conway's head. What had he let himself in for? Had he lost his senses? He wavered, in a quandary as to whether he should accept Nucky's offer or not. The thought of seeing Mary Rose again, however, just about clinched it.

'Right so, I will. It might be interesting to see what goes on there.'

Chapter Twenty-one

Mary Rose was at the kitchen sink doing the washing-up. Shaking her head, and backside, from side to side, she was singing at the top of her voice an up-tempo rendition of an advertising jingle.

'...hands that do dishes...can feel soft as your face...with mild green...Fairy Liquid...'

In a low, funereal voice that made her jump, Conway said, 'Hello...'

'Jeezus!' she exclaimed, 'you put the heart crossways in me...sneaking up like that...so you did...'

'Sorry, I didn't mean to startle you,' he said, then handing her a single red rose, he added awkwardly, 'for you...'

Mary Rose wiped the suds from her hands with the tea towel and slung it over her left shoulder. Taking the rose from Conway she held the blossom to her nose.

'Hmmm, it's so lovely,' she said, closing her eyes and momentarily captivated by its scent. Regaining possession of herself, she added, suspicion flaring in her eyes, 'Are you for real? A rose? Are you mocking me? Nucky put you up to this, didn't he? It's a joke, isn't it?'

'No, it's, it's, not a joke, Mary Rose, I, I, I...' Conway mumbled, slipping into a hopeless stammer.

Flapping the rose about impatiently in her hand, Mary Rose barked, 'What?'

Conway began again, hitching up his coat and going down on one knee, 'I have never felt this way about anyone before, if you could find it in your, in your heart, to look with favour...'

A look of horror commandeered her eyes. Plucking the tea towel from her shoulder she threw it in his face.

'Will you get up off your knees you shaggin' eejit, don't let my mother catch you. There's no need to be carrying on like that, like some Mills and Boon gobshite, I'm not a bit impressed. Anyway, what makes you think I'd go out with the likes of you...'

Conway squirmed and felt the burn of embarrassment on his face. The g-forces his poor heart endured, in his mouth one minute, and in his boots the next. He wanted to turn and run but he was rooted to the spot. His mind went blank. His body went numb. All that seemed to be working was a trembling hand, still in the act of proffering a small velvet box.

'What's that?' she asked, frowning.

Devastated, dying, Conway said, 'Oh, I ah...forgot these, these were for you, a gift...I'm sorry, I've made a complete fo-, fo-, fool of myself...'

Mary Rose took the presentation box and flipped it open.

'Earrings...' she said dispassionately, 'with a note,' she added disparagingly. Then, as Conway flushed as red as beetroot, she unfolded the piece of paper and, taking on a ludicrously posh voice, she read:

Floribunda and Hybrid Tea
May do for some
But not for me
Give me a Rose
Wild and free
Give me a Rose
As sweet as thee

'Floribunda and Hybrid Tea are types of roses,' Conway explained, rather stupidly.

'I know, I know,' Mary Rose snapped, 'I'm not a fool. Do you think you're the only one who knows anything? I've done botany at school, you know, and, for your information, I have nearly all Dr Hessayon's books...'

Glancing towards the window, she said pointedly, 'What the feck do you think those things growing out there are? Pissybeds?'

Conway could say nothing right, it seemed. In his case silence was indeed golden and the less said, the better. Mary Rose leaned against the sink, her face softening to a sad smile.

'No one ever wrote me a poem before,' she said, turning down the corners of her mouth. 'It's not bad,' she drawled, 'write it yourself?'

Unaware that he was slowly mangling the towel with his hands, Conway nodded.

'Give me that before you have it in shreds,' Mary Rose said, taking the towel from him, then added more genially, '...I'll put on the kettle. Will you have a cup of tea? Do, have a cup of tea...'

With her back to him, she lifted the kettle to check it had enough water and replaced it on the stove.

'Okay,' she said, as she lit the gas ring, 'you can take me to the pictures on Friday night, if you like. There's a good one on.'

Conway was speechless. He could not believe his ears. What Mary Rose was saying, could, quite reasonably, be construed as a definitive, affirmative yes. Three little letters that in a syllable had turned his world upside down and the right way round. Yes! She said yes, yes, yes, yes, yes. The world was yes. Weak with elation, Conway staggered to a chair. He was about to slump onto it when Mary Rose let go a scream.

'Mind the fecken cat!'

Conway froze, arresting his descent just in time.

'Move, Shibs,' Mary Rose commanded, flicking the tea towel in the cat's direction. The cat jumped swiftly from the chair, turned about slowly and gave her a reproachful look. Offended, and not in the least bit impressed, it disdainfully slipped away.

'Fecken cat,' said Mary Rose, 'do you think she'd sit in the one place, no, musical fecken chairs she'd be playing...'

As Conway contemplated the subtraction of a cat's life, and the awful consequences of having claws embedded in his tender flesh, Nucky's voice boomed from the yard.

'Come on, Conway, are we goin' to the dump or aren't we? Time's a movin' on...'

Moments later he was standing at the doorway, carrying a smiling Tubbs on his shoulders. Stooping at the threshold, he directed Tubbs to duck his head, which the child duly did, laying his head flat against Nucky's dark locks and clasping his forehead.

'Have a cup of tea before you go, can't you?' said Mary Rose cheerfully.

'Jaysus, what's gettin' into you, are you feelin' all right?'

Responding to the withering look he got in reply, Nucky said, 'Ah shur, and why not, 'tisn't every day you see a blue moon,' and winking at Conway, he added, 'I'll have some toast and a rasher and an egg maybe, and a tomasha as well if it's goin'...'

'Don't push your luck...' Mary Rose said darkly, then calling Tubbs aside, she whispered in his ear. Whatever was said, it had Tubbs giggling and whispering back.

'There's a powerful lot of whisperin' goin' on...' Nucky pronounced gravely, 'someone's up to no good.'

Before very long, Tubbs was approaching Nucky and holding aloft an egg perched upon a blue china egg cup. Like a diminutive priest carrying a monstrance at Benediction, he moved slowly and with the utmost care.

'Nucky, do you want a egg? Here's a egg for you.'

'For me! Oh, a lovely egg, and in its very own egg cup an' all. Thanks, Tubbs, you're always lookin' out for me. I love an egg, I do, especially a big brown egg. Are you sure you don't want it for yourself?'

'No, you can have it,' said Tubbs, giggling mischievously.

'All to myself,' said Nucky, taking the egg and placing it ceremoniously on the table before him, 'well, aren't you the generous soul. Let me get my spoon. I can't wait to taste this lovely egg. With a bit a salt now, it'll be only grand...'

Nucky raised his spoon with hopeful deliberation, then tapped the top of the egg which instantly collapsed and crumbled to pieces. Tubbs was in a fit of giggles, his stubby little fingers covering his mouth. Mary Rose heaved with stifled laughter as Nucky feigned surprise, disappointment and horror.

'Oh no! My egg! What's happened to my egg!' he wailed, then grabbing Tubbs, who was now hysterical with giggles, he turned him upside down. 'D'ya see you, you rogue, you gangster. You made a feck of me, so you did.'

'I fooled ya,' said the inverted Tubbs.

'You did an' all. That egg was a dud.'

As Tubbs squealed with laughter, Nucky asked, 'Will I put you down the sink? Will I?'

'Don't, don't,' Tubbs shrieked, 'I was only joken. I won't do it again.'

'Promise?'

'I promise.'

Looking to Conway, Nucky said, 'He's a great man for the promises, you know. That's the umpteenth time he's done it to me. Down the sink with him, that's what I say. What do you think, Conway?'

'No, no, please. I promise,' Tubbs pleaded, going red in the face with the blood rushing to his head.

'Cross your toes and hope to die?'

'I promise,' Tubbs shouted, then, appealing directly to Conway, he added, 'don't let him put me down the sink.'

Smiling shrewdly, Conway said, 'I think we'll let him go this time. What do you think?'

'Right so,' said Nucky, 'but next time it's down the sink

with him,' then, turning Tubbs the right way up and setting him down on his feet, he added, 'it's a good job for you that Conway is here to save ya.'

'I fooled ya, didn't I?' Tubbs said triumphantly.

'You did, boy, you fooled me entirely so you did. You're a right clever dick and a ball hopper and no mistake...'

'He'd be nothin' to you if he wasn't,' said Mary Rose, in great form, 'he takes after you, that's what he does.'

Then in a bald disclosure only a child could countenance, Tubbs announced, 'Mary Rose told me to do it.'

'You big fibber,' Mary Rose said with mock outrage, 'I'll have your life for telling lies...'

'Will I kill her for you? Will I?' asked Nucky.

'Do,' Tubbs said, without a second thought.

'Traitor!' Mary Rose shouted, then looking at Conway she said, laughing, 'he'd hang you, he would.'

Bridled, blinkered, and with a shining brass on his forehead, Gypsy was chomping at the bit and eager to go. Nucky took the reins in hand and hopped up on the cart. Standing fast, with his legs spread for balance, he began making clicking sounds with his tongue as he shook the reins.

'G'wan, boy,' he coaxed, adding more of the clicking sounds as he did so. Conway, sitting on a bundle of coal sacks, took a swig from his Dopacof bottle and discreetly slipped it back in his overcoat pocket.

There was a creaking of leather and a soft jangling of breeching chains as Gypsy leaned into his collar and harness and took the strain. His proud head bowed, he lifted his huge feathered feet and plodded off through the open gate. With a slight tug of the reins and quiet command, Nucky turned Gypsy and the cart left towards the Marian Shrine and Stella Maris Park.

'Make sure you clean out the stables,' Nucky shouted to Mikey, who was munching on an apple in one hand and shutting the gate with the other, 'do you hear me?'

Mikey took another bite of the apple and blithely nodded.

When the gate had shut behind them, Nucky turned to Conway and said, 'Just a few bags to deliver first, then we'll head to the dump.'

'Grand, fine,' Conway said rather shakily, pulling his legs up under him to resume a petrified pose that was not unlike the bronze statue of the Little Mermaid of Copenhagen. Except for the overcoat, neck scarf and wellies, of course.

As they trundled along the road they drew some strange looks. Conway, the pale-faced new kid on the block, must have appeared somewhat conspicuous and out of place, overdressed as he was for a fine June day in his journeyman overcoat that was stuffed with the usual provisions of the 'just in case' variety. At least, on this occasion, he had dispensed with the umbrella and the binoculars. Nucky, by comparison, was in casual gear of T-shirt and jeans, his only concession to his workload being a leather waistcoat and a sturdy pair of boots.

Before long Conway found himself lulled into relaxation by the clip-clop rhythms of Gypsy's hooves. The slow but sure metronome of purpose and direction had a mesmeric effect on him. The dull bell-ring of iron on stone, the jingle of the harness, the creak and groan of the cart, cast their spell. If only he could be like Gypsy, he thought, as he leaned back against the recycled Net Nitrate fertilizer bags that were filled with blocks. If only he had purpose and direction.

He watched with fascination the little cloud-puffs of coal dust that plumed between the wooden slats when the cart jarred on a rough patch of road. He inhaled the musk-tang smell of horse and leather and the incense sap of freshly chopped wood. Reaching back, he pulled a wedge from a bag and sniffed the pungent, clean aroma of resin that oozed from the raised blisters of pine bark.

'Where do you get the wood from?'

'Ah, here and there,' said Nucky breezily, 'out the country mostly, the forestry crowd, Cappanty Woods. Fallen trees. Loads of them still around with the storms we had.'

Then he added, 'mind that sticky stuff, don't get it on your clothes, it's a fucker to get off.'

'They make turpentine from the resin, you know, the sticky stuff,' Conway commented.

'Paint thinners? Really?' Nucky said, genuinely surprised.

As Conway began to expound on some other gem of knowledge, there came the sounds of impish laughing from the rear. Both Conway and Nucky turned to find two kids, no more than seven or eight years old, hanging onto the back of the cart, their puny hands gripping its raised edge.

'Fuck away from the cart or I'll split ye open,' Nucky snarled, picking up a lump of coal.

To Conway's amazement, one said defiantly, 'You would in your arse, Nucky...'

'Do you want me to be tellin' your father on you? If I go after you, I'll give you such a fong up in the arse you won't be able to sit for a week...'

This last threat seemed to do the trick. They let go, made faces and rude gestures in token defiance, then ran off.

'Cheeky little fuckers,' Nucky muttered under his breath, then sitting down on the cart, his legs dangling over the side, he added, 'you have to get cross with them or before you know it, they'd be sixteen of them swingin' out of the fucken thing.'

'Why do they do it?'

Nucky threw Conway a curious look. 'They do it for the fun of it, for the jant, you know kids now. Used to do the same thing meself when I was a kid.'

'I never did.'

'No?' queried Nucky, twitching his eyebrows, 'Jaysus, you must have been a right little altar boy.'

'I was. I was an altar boy.'

Nucky threw his eyes to heaven, then said, in mitigation, 'Dangerous fucken thing to be doin', though,'

'Being an altar boy?'

'Nooo...' said Nucky, rolling his eyes and exhaling his exasperation, '...hangin' out of the fucken cart, what do you think! They could end up with a bag o' coal landin' on top of 'em. Or be hit by a fucken car...'

They passed a gaggle of children. Young girls, dressed in all the colours of Benetton, played hopscotch, their playing area outlined in chalk on the footpath. A pot-bellied toddler stood impatiently waiting and wanting a 'go'. Fobbed off with, 'in a minute', 'it's not your turn yet', or 'you're too small', the whingeing protest soon turned to the threat of, '...I'm tellin' Mama you won't let me play'.

Boys, disdaining *girls'* games, climbed walls and jumped over gates from pillar to pillar. A concerned mother roared from a garden fence, 'get down off that wall, I don't want to have to tell ye again', then casually she resumed her chat with her next-door neighbour. A chubby-faced baby in her arms sucked on a soother, then spat it out, and with eyes wide with wonder, pointed in the direction of the cart with a tiny forefinger and lisped, 'hossy, hossy'.

Up ahead, some older girls had requisitioned the entire width of the road with their skipping-rope. And, with a precision and skill that was an eternal mystery to boys, they took turns skipping in and out of the looping parabola under the compulsion and enchantment of rhyme.

...there's somebody under the bed, I don't know who it is, I feel very nervous, so I call Mary in, Mary lights the candle, there's no one there, with mi-ee-oo-aaddio we all run away...

As the cart approached, up went the cries.

'Here's Gypsy, let down the rope, let down the rope...'

It was salutations all the way.

'Hi, Gypsy! Hi, Nucky!'

As if acknowledging the hosannas, Gypsy began smartly nodding his head. No sooner had the cartwheels rolled over the rope when a woman, slim, fair and fortyish, in blue V-necked cardigan and hairnet, called out from a doorway.

'Nucky, come're I want you,' she said, grandly flicking ash from a cigarette she held in her right hand. 'I'll have two coal off you,' she shouted loudly to overcome the sudden blast of a radio that emerged from the doorway behind her.

'How much are you chargin' for the blocks?'

'If you have to ask, Mrs Mooney, you can't afford them,' Nucky answered, laughing.

'Very fecken funny,' she said, pulling a face, 'you're full of your fun, aren't you?'

Nucky laughed all the more, then said, '...a pound a bag. How many to do want? I can give you two...'

'Gimme the two so, and how's your mother?'

'Ah, she's grand, Mrs Mooney.'

'Tell her I was askin' for her, won't you. Shur, I'll see her at bingo, anyway.'

Grabbing hold of a bag of coal, Nucky lifted it as if it had been a bag of cushions, and carried it, on his back, up the path and through the front door. Having no side entrance, he had to go through the house. From where he was stationed, Conway could hear Mrs Mooney's voice coming loudly from within. 'Mind my walls! And turn off that fecken radio, you!'

Emerging from the gloom of the hallway with a deflated sack, Nucky was followed by a minuscule Jack Russell terrier who protested most vehemently at the outrageous intrusion. Mrs Mooney turned on the demented creature.

'Will you give over your yappin' will you, you shaggin' eejit of a dog. He wouldn't bark to save his life if someone was tryin' to rob the fecken place,' she began telling Nucky, who, ignoring the dog completely, just grinned indulgently. 'There wouldn't be a peep out of him,' she went on, 'he'd be gone missing, he would. Same with the postman. The man's nerves do be at him over him.' She turned on the dog again and in a breath said, 'Sharrupwillya. It's a wonder I get any shaggin' post withcha...'

As Nucky continued with the bags, Conway was left in charge of the cart. Though it was closer to the truth to say that Gypsy was left in charge of Conway. There was one disquieting moment when Gypsy began to move ever so slightly forward. Thinking that the horse was about to run away with him, Conway panicked and nearly lost his life.

'Hold it! Don't move! Stop! Don't go! Wait!' He tried all the commands, but to no avail. Then, remembering Nucky's code, he shouted, 'Hike, Gypsy! Hike!'

The horse tossed his head and rattled his bridle, then settled. He turned to give Conway an indifferent look, shook his great bulk and sent a shudder down the shafts and through the cart to launch a cloud of coal dust into the air.

'How much do I owe you?' asked Mrs Mooney when Nucky had finished the delivery.

'Ah, you can settle up with me the next time, shur.'

'Okay so, shur I'll see you again,' then she added, 'oh, before I forget, Nucky, would you ever do me one favour. Would you ever take that old washin' machine away with you? It's an awful fecken nuisance it is, it's in the way of everything, an eyesore that's what it is. It's out in the back. And I have no one to take it away for me.'

Unbeknown to her, a barefoot child, in nappy and vest, negotiated the doorstep and waddled down the path behind her and was about to proceed blithely past and out the gate when Mrs Mooney let go a scream.

'Merciful Jesus!' she yelled, grabbing hold of the child, 'you'll be the death of me, stay away from that horse,' then, to no one in particular, she added, 'ja see him, I'll murder him in a minute, he's al'ays runnin' after horses. The first chance he gets and he's off. You'd need eyes in the back of your pole, so you would. Get in that gate you little scourge or I'll have your life.'

Twirling the child about face, she shouted in the path.

'Ann Marie! Ann Marie!'

A dishevelled and bored-looking girl with long raven hair appeared in the doorway and, apparently with great effort, said, 'Whaah?'

'Are you gone deaf, are you?' Mrs Mooney asked, 'did I distinctly tell you to mind that child?'

Ignoring her mother completely, the teenager held out her arms and called the child to her.

'Come on, Petey, there's a cartoon on...'

Mrs Mooney drew heavily on her cigarette and sighed a world-weary sigh. '…I'm eatin' the fecken fags with them,' Then regaining her composure, now that the crisis had passed, she said to Nucky, 'Will you do that for me so?'

'I will a course.'

'Blessans a gawd on you.'

When Nucky re-emerged, he was carrying an old twin-tub washing machine in his arms. He hoisted it up onto the lip of the cart where Conway hauled it aboard. Nucky turned to Mrs Mooney, 'do you want rid of those old iron sheets?'

'Would you ever, Nucky, I didn't want to be askin' you, I mean, you have anuff to be doin' now.'

'Ah, no bother at all,' said Nucky, on his way in the path.

Again he re-emerged from the house, this time carrying corrugated sheets that were rusting and full of holes.

'Jaysus, they're all moth-aten,' Mrs Mooney commented, 'I'll be glad to see the back of them.'

'It's some moth now, that can ate iron, Mrs Mooney,' Nucky said, bursting into laughter.

She answered him with a wry smile, 'Ah go 'way, you're al'ays makin' a feck of me, you are.'

After stopping off at several houses along the way, Nucky's face soon blackened until he began to look like a commando out on manoeuvres.

'Want a hand?' Conway asked, feeling somewhat guilty and redundant.

'No,' said Nucky, 'you'll destroy your clothes, don't want you manky with the dirt when you're goin' to the dump, now do we?' Then having second thoughts, he relented, 'Right so,' he said, 'you can bring the bags to the edge of the cart for me.' On seeing Conway breaking into a sweat as he struggled with a bag of coal, he added, 'leave the coal, just bring the blocks to the edge.'

Finished with the final delivery, Nucky flung the empty bags onto the cart, turned to a reluctant youngster who was left in charge of taking the delivery, and said, 'Tell your mother, Jamesie, I'll drop the other two down tonight, along with the tank a gas.'

'Sound, Nucky, sound,' said the youngster, glad that his onerous task was at an end and he was free to join his waiting companions now that he was no longer tied to the house. Nucky wheeled the cart around and headed back the road. With the lighter load they were soon picking up speed and the pneumatic wheels began to whirr. Going past the football pitch, a posse of horses began to whinny and neigh but Gypsy carried on regardless. After all, he had a job of work to do.

Veering to the right at the Shrine, they travelled on past the defunct swimming baths and along the strand road, known to Conway, the map-reader, as Verdant Place. On the left was the Water Passage, an old lane-way that ran between Nucky's house and the riverfront. The broad sweep of the Shannon lay before them, fresh and breezy, on its way to the coast.

Looking to his left, Conway could see old St Munchin's Church, with its square pinnacled tower rising above the walled churchyard. At the junction of Thomond Bridge and Castle Street there was a curious-looking building of ancient design, with battlements and arrow slits, yet it retained a suspiciously pristine condition.

'What is that building?' Conway asked, 'It looks like a toll house or something.'

'Oh that?' said Nucky, 'my father used to say that the man who built that was a right pain, James Pain. Get it? James Pain?'

Conway forced a nod and a smile.

'It's known as Pain's Folly,' Nucky continued, 'in fact, the same man did Thomond Bridge as well. My father would be tellin' me all this when I was a kid and out on the road with him, helpin' him like...'

Across the road, the great bulk of King John's Castle towered over them. Its brooding presence stirred in Conway faint echoes of the weird visions he had encountered during his illness. Even the breeze from the river seemed filled with strange familiarities but, try as he might, he could only call to mind vague reflections of his dream experience. He was too much in the real world now and too much in the sun, it seemed, for them to have any hold on him. After waiting for a gap in the traffic to present itself, they turned right onto Thomond Bridge.

'Here's one for you now,' said Nucky, 'my father used to ask me this one. How many towns would you think there are in Limerick City?'

Conway thought for a moment before saying, 'Well, let's see, there's the Irishtown...'

'Right.'

'And there's English Town,' then wrinkling his forehead, he added, with an element of doubt, '...two?'

'No, there's three,' said Nucky, very pleased with himself, 'what about Newtown Pery?'

'Ah, yes, of course,' Conway conceded, 'I forgot about Newtown Pery.'

'It's a good one, isn't it?' said Nucky, 'A city havin' three towns in it...' His voice trailed off, then after some reflection he spoke again, '...you've heard of Drunken Thady and the Bishop's Lady? Written by the Bard of Thomond, Michael Hogan? Well, she used to live in the Bishop's Palace, back the road there, in Church Street. Her ghost is supposed to haunt this bridge here, Thomond Bridge. Well, the story goes that early one Christmas mornin', along came the bould Thady, drunk as a lord, on his way home from a night on the town. And who should he run inta, only your one, the ghost, and didn't she ketch him and fling him over the bridge and inta the freezing water below. Well, Thady survived but he never touched a drop after that. He was a real character. Died at the grand old age of ninety-seven, so they say. Just goes to show you...'

Without so much as a warning, Conway broke into verse.

At half-past one the town was silent,
Except a row raised in the Island

Where Thady, foe to sober thinking,
With comrade boys sat gaily drinking!
A table with a pack of cards
Stood in the midst of four blackguards,
Who, with the bumper-draught elated,
Dashed down their trumps, and swore, and cheated!

'Fair fucken play to you,' Nucky approved with a nod of his head, 'you've got it off pat. Though, I'd have the one criticism now,' he added, 'and that would be *chayted...*'

Conway looked very puzzled.

'We'd say *chayted*, instead of cheated,' Nucky explained.

Conway's eyes lit up with sudden insight, 'That's the way it would have been pronounced, sure enough. You can tell, because it rhymes with elated. Like in that poem by Pope...'

As Nucky took on a look of utter bafflement, Conway broke into verse once more.

Here thou, great Anna! whom three realms obey,
Dost sometimes counsel take, and sometimes tea.

'We know,' Conway went on enthusiastically, 'that they pronounced tea as *tay* because it rhymes with obey.'

'My grandmother, she would always say *tay*,' Nucky said casually, 'we still say it that way sometimes, if the mood takes us. Funny isn't it? Sometimes we even call it cha,'

'Cha, that's what the Chinese call it,' said Conway, 'it's Chinese for tea.'

'Well, you learn somethin' new every day,' Nucky said, laughing, 'there I was talkin' Chinese all the time and I didn't even know it.'

As they headed over Thomond Bridge they could see from their vantage point the immense splendour of the Castle, the Cathedrals, the County Courthouse and the City Centre where the river doglegged towards Sarsfield Bridge. Curragower was submerged in the tide. Fishing boats were moored off the Strand and a trail of mute swans, mirrored in the river, appeared like visitors from a fairy tale. The sky, a Marian blue, seemed a vast and high ocean where wisps of cloud appeared like distant breakers.

At the far end of the Bridge, they faced St Munchin's Church, Catholic, a neat and solid structure with doors wide open for service. Directly to their left, perched on its stepped pedestal, stood the celebrated Treaty Stone on which the infamous Treaty of Limerick was allegedly signed. For years, apparently, it had been used as a humble mounting-block for climbing aboard horses, until someone decided it should be elevated to a more prominent position. The pedestal bore the city coat of arms and the legend, *urbs atiqua fuit studiisque asperima belli*. Latin, of course, from Virgil's epic poem, the Aeneid, recounting the birth of Rome. It translated, rather stiltedly, *an ancient city studied in the arts of war*.

Referring to the ancient monument, Conway said, 'It's changed shape down the years. You know, with souvenir hunters. One particular individual even had cufflinks made from bits cut from it.'

Disbelieving, Nucky said, 'You're kiddin' me?'

'It's true. That was a while ago, back in eighteen-ninety-eight. They're above in the museum.'

'Jaysus,' said Nucky, 'you know, some people would steal the winkers off a nightmare,' then he added, 'and they were thinkin' of movin' it, you know, the Treaty Stone, down to the Courthouse. What will they come up with next? I don't know why they don't put wheels on it altogether and be done with it. They could wheel it where they want then. Shaggin' eejits, they can't leave nothin' alone...'

Turning off to the right at The Treaty Bar, they eased down a slope and onto a quieter road that fronted the river. Heading north now, they could look across at King's Island on the opposite bank and the route they had followed. Approaching the Thomond side of Thomond Weir, they took a sharp left onto New Road before veering north again.

Even this far afield, Nucky was known, getting salutes from anyone and everyone. It would have been easy for Conway to be a little envious of such popularity but he was too happy in himself for that. And he had good reason to be happy. For the first time, in a long time, he was beginning to feel accepted and, dare he even think it, normal. He was on a journey of discovery, it seemed, part of something special. And he had a date with the most beautiful girl in the world.

Filling the silence, Nucky became conversational.

'...heard a story, a while back, from a man at a fair. He was tellin' me this fella was havin' trouble with his horse, the horse wouldn't budge for him and your man lost the head completely. I'll sort him out, sez he, I'll show him who's boss. So, down he jumps from the trap, anyway, gathers up a pile of straw and sticks it under the horse and sets it alight. Well, it got the horse movin' awright, but jaysus, didn't the horse move just far anuff forward to have the trap right over the fire. Up it went in flames and your man hoppin' and leppin'. Oh, he showed him who was boss sure anuff. Serves the stupid bastard right...'

'Was the horse all right?' Conway asked, concerned.

'Oh, the horse was grand,' said Nucky, 'couldn't say the same for your man, though,' he laughed, then added, 'here, take the reins.'

Conway gave him a doubtful look.

'G'wan, you'll be awright. Shur, Gypsy knows the way. Relax, don't be nervous and if you are, pretend you're not. Fear travels down the reins, that's what they say...'

With nervous elation, Conway gingerly took the reins and was surprised to see that Gypsy just sauntered along as normal, seemingly unperturbed by the change of command. Placing a hand on Conway's shoulder, Nucky hauled himself up and went back to the washing machine with a screwdriver in hand. He turned it over and after a short tussle removed a rubber tube from the machine's innards.

'Perfect condition, not perished at all,' he said, holding the tube aloft, 'do you know how much they charge to replace this?'

Conway chanced a quick look behind before fixing his eyes on the road ahead.

'...five quid to buy,' Nucky went on, '...and twenty quid to have a technishan replace it for you. More even. The fuckers ad rob you, they would,' then he added, as he came forward and sat down again, 'there's a lot of stuff that can be salvaged, even down to the screws and washers. Make do and mend, as my father would say.'

Leaving Conway holding the reins, Nucky said, as he tightened the screw of a jubilee clip, 'My father was in the merchant navy, travelled the world, in his younger days. He told me a story that happened during the prohibition. In the States, it was. There was a lot of illegal booze, moonshine, you know, some of it very dodgy stuff, so they'd take a sample to the chemist to make sure it was safe to drink. Didn't the sample come back with a note that said, *your horse has diabetes.* The father used to kill himself laughin' over that.'

Nucky fell silent for a moment, seemingly preoccupied with the job in hand, then asked, 'What does your father do?'

'He used to work in the Post Office,' said Conway, 'he died when I was a child.'

'Sorry to hear that,' Nucky said, still fiddling with the jubilee clip, 'mine died a while back. Heart attack. A martyr to the fags, he was,' then he added wryly, 'Sweet Afton...'

Coming to the turnoff for Longpavement, Nucky took over the reins once more. It wasn't a busy junction and traffic was fairly light. As they negotiated the turn, Nucky commented sourly, 'They drive like lunatics here. They're always bombin' up and down this road.'

Chapter Twenty-two

'You'd be amazed,' said Nucky, with a bewildered look on his face, 'what people throw away. I mean, look at this,' he added, holding a plank of wood under Conway's chin, 'mahogany, you'd pay through the nose for that in a shop or a timber yard and yet, someone just fucked it away.'

He glanced about him, then pulled another piece from a pile of rubble. 'Look at this,' he said with emphasis, 'can you believe that someone actually threw this away.'

Conway was as wise as a pig looking into a bottle.

'What is it?' he asked.

'A fine piece of teak,' Nucky disclosed, running a hand along the surface to wipe the dust away, 'you can tell by the grain and colour. Long and even, reddish-brown, see?'

Nucky slung the wood aside and clapped the dust from his hands. 'I'll pick it up on the way back,' he said casually, then added, as he walked on ahead, 'long before this recyclin' craic, I've been comin' up here pickin' up stuff and sellin' it back to the kind of people who threw it out in the first place. Old bedsteads, picture frames, ornaments, bits and pieces. I found a gold pocket watch once, though I'd say it wasn't thrown out, now. Well, not on purpose anyway.'

They had left Gypsy, with the reward of a bag of oats, in the shade of a gnarled old hawthorn. Leaving the edge of the dump, they walked deeper into the alien landscape. All about them lay mounds and mounds of rubbish. A multicoloured collage of bottles, cans, cabbage leaves, cartons, tomatoes, newspapers, rags, magazines, plastics, cardboard, banana skins, and a heap more besides. Household names, famous and familiar, were tossed into this crazy consumer salad with huge chunks of masonry, rubble and wooden spars. Chef, Parazone, Kelloggs, Domestos, Cadbury, Fairy Liquid, Bird's Eye, Harpic, Coca Cola. They were all there, at the end of the line, with their logos and their advertising slogans, full of super value, variety and choice.

The smell of the dump was distinctive. A damp, musty overripeness that hung in the air and, like an obsequious cat, more than willing to impart its scent to anything it rubbed shoulders with. That the reek of this immense burial ground, this great catabolism, from wide and multifarious sources, could be reduced to one homogeneous pong came as a surprise to Conway.

And there was something else. A faint something or other that didn't quite register with him, at first. Conway, who had good reason to mistrust anything beyond his five senses, put it down to his susceptible nature. But, just as it was about to be disregarded as beyond the dictionary, the air grew heavy with it and the mysterious something implied an identity. Despite his conviction that he was, once again, entertaining nonsense, he allowed the suggestion to take hold and for a moment, just for a moment, a feeling of stale bereavement held sway. Then, in a breath, it was gone.

As they plodded on they could see, away down to the left, the discarded cookers, fridges, and washing machines that they themselves had so recently added to. Like higgledy-piggledy panzer divisions, the white goods were headed towards the river, invading marshland that was blossoming with Yellow Flag. Some way off to their right were the flashing lights of the dumper trucks and the canary-yellow bulldozers. Like boorish monsters, the massive bulldozers fumed blue-black smoke from their vertical exhaust pipes and began pushing flat the mounds of newly deposited rubbish. Raucous crows and seagulls hung like scavenging confetti above the chaotic scene.

Leaving the foothills they began to climb the terraced slopes, the angle of ascent so steep at times that it required the use of all fours. On one of his many stops to catch his breath, Conway came across something of interest.

'You're not going to believe this,' he said, as he examined a clump of foliage that splurged out of the rubble.

'What is it?' Nucky shouted back to him.

'It's aahmm,' Conway began, as he thumbed through his reference book for confirmation, 'it's solanum tuberosum...'

'What?'

'A potato plant,'

'Spuds?' Nucky laughed, 'Jaysus, if this keeps up, we'll be able to tell the Dutch to stuff theirs...'

Up and up they went, terrace after terrace, until they finally reached the summit plateau. The panoramic view they had gained of the surrounding landscape was figuratively and literally breathtaking.

Flushed in the face, and panting like an asthmatic bull, Conway took the weight off his feet and parked himself on a conveniently nearby stone.

Shielding his eyes to take in the scene, Nucky remarked, 'Why the fuck you insist on wearin' that overcoat on a day like today, I do not know.'

Conway smiled a self-righteous smile. For his part, he thought Nucky ill-prepared for any exploration. Nucky had failed to grasp the fact that the overcoat was not so much an overcoat but a holdall and repository, a silk-lined filing cabinet with pockets and sleeves. Nevertheless, he undid several buttons as a compromise and flapped the open coat to create cooling draughts. Having regained his breath, he got to his feet and went to join Nucky at the edge of the summit.

Elevated on decades and decades of buried landfill, they surveyed all before them. Beyond the willows and alders that shimmered in the heat at the edge of the river, they could see in the far distance the majesty of Keeper Hill, capped with snow-white clouds and, spread out before it, the glinting, glorious meander of the Shannon. Closer to home, they could see the Island and the Abbey River with its green banks and clustered sally groves. They picked out landmarks. The handball alley, the Island Bank, the Salmon Weir Bank, or, as Nucky described it, the 'Samway Bank'. And then there was Shannon Bridge, which Nucky insisted on calling the Red Bridge, even when Conway pointed out the obvious fact that it was not red, but grey. As Conway was anxiously inclined to believe that either he, or Nucky, had a serious case of colour blindness, he was enlightened.

'We've always called it the Red Bridge,' Nucky said, 'just because they go and paint it a different colour, doesn't mean we have to call it a different name, now do we.' Then to confuse things even more, he added, 'sometimes we call it the Metal Bridge, and sometimes we call it the Railway Bridge.'

The confounded bridge, Conway concluded, had more names than a Spaniard.

Contrasting the natural beauty that encircled the mess of his immediate surroundings, Conway was not in the least impressed. The dump went right down to the river and toxic chemicals could well leach into the water. Plastic bags and aeroboard, scattered by the four winds, were netted by the trees in what seemed a pathetic and poignant effort to stop the defacement. Overhead, gulls, having had their fill of nouvelle cuisine, winged their way to the nearest reservoir where they would bathe in, and possibly contaminate, municipal water supplies.

Yet, even here, it seemed nature could not stand idly by. Groundsel, shepherd's purse, willowherb, dock, nettle and ragwort were already staking their claim. At his feet, clinging to a ragwort that would be the food source of its poisonous offspring, the day-flying cinnabar moth flaunted its black and scarlet finery. On dark, scimitar wings swifts criss-crossed overhead, scything the air with their screams.

As if catching Conway's thoughts, Nucky commented.

'The dump is too near the river. Too near the Island. It's been closin' down for years,' he said, 'choked you'd be at times from the smoke and the smell when it catches fire or there's a bad fog. And the people in Moyross are plagued with it. Whatever way the wind is blowin', but that's the Corpo all out, takes them forever to do anything.'

'We get it in Corbally, sometimes.' Conway said casually.

Nucky sniffed, then replied, 'Well, in that case, something might be done about it.' Then, with a sweep of his head he scanned the ground that fell away to their left, and said with satisfaction, 'Ah, there's the lads.'

Shielding his eyes, Conway squinted in the direction of Nucky's gaze. All he could see was a trail of smoke, the length of a football field away, rising up from behind piles of earth that dotted the landscape like Native American tepees.

'Where?' Conway whispered doubtfully to himself.

'Come on,' Nucky said, setting off down the slope.

Conway followed sheepishly and they descended to lower ground, terrace after terrace, until they were eventually on the same level as the 'tepees'. This new viewpoint incited Conway into switching metaphorical similes. The piles of earth now looked like so many dormant volcanoes. All, that is, except one, which seemed to puff smoke like a miniature Etna. It was towards this, Nucky had set his compass.

As they traversed the caterpillar tracks that scarred the moonscape through which they moved, Nucky confirmed Conway's assumption that the massive cones of earth were heaps of infill soil laid by for the burial of rubbish. Rounding one of these heaps, they came upon a motley group of individuals, four in number, ranged around a fire that was busily consuming a wooden pallet. Conway's presumptions ran riot and he immediately summed up the foursome as shady, seedy and unsavoury.

Like keepers of some dark and private knowledge that gave them immunity, they gave the disconcerting impression that though they may have been hiding out, they were not in the least surprised, or concerned, at being found.

They could well have been waiting for Godot, Conway thought facetiously, and went on to struggle nervously with classification. Was the word *Beckettesque*? Or *Beckettsian*? Or even *Beckettian*? He wasn't sure. As they approached, a pair of dogs, a Rottweiler and a Jack Russell, sprang forward to investigate. So determined were they to outdo each other, with the doggedness of their barking and the acrobatics of their posturing, that they failed to recognise Nucky for who he was. Nucky set them straight with a soothing command.

'Down, Butch...down, Sundance...'

As if mortified by their error, they begged his pardon by fussing around him like wolves greeting a pack leader. After a cursory sniffing of Conway, they waddled back contentedly to the fire where they hit the deck and laid dutiful heads on dutiful paws.

'Hi, Nucky, how's she cuttin', all right?'

The salutation came from a brawny-looking individual with cropped hair and a sad-to-serious face. Dressed in a grey, hooded sweatshirt, tracksuit bottoms and trainers, he sat hunched forward on a plastic crate, his trailing left hand massaging the head of the Rottweiler that dozed at his feet. Though small in stature, he did have the well-developed musculature of a bodybuilder. His nose, taking up more room on his face than was originally intended by nature, had obviously been broken and reshaped. A trim moustache redressed the loss of symmetry to some extent. Conway also noted the scarring about the eyebrows and was left to conclude that these embellishments may well have been the result of confrontations inside, and outside, the ring.

'Not too bad, Seánie, not too bad,' Nucky's answer was familiar and casual. Then, nodding to the other three, he acknowledged them in turn, 'Donie, Jack, Bilbo...'

They responded with nods and affirmations of his name.

'Who's your man?' said Seánie, casting a disapproving look in Conway's direction.

'Ah, he's all right, he's with me.'

'I thought he was a Corpo official,' said the suspicious Seánie.

'No, he's sound.' Nucky assured him.

More genially, Donie, a fine-featured man with a high, sun-burnished forehead and scruffy beard, held aloft what appeared to be a large bottle of cider and said, in a voice embroidered with civility, 'Fancy a drop of Scrumpy Jack?'

There was a kind of dowdy grandeur about the man that set him apart from the others. For one thing, he wore a shirt and tie, and a check jacket, even if the tie was a grubby item that seemed to be hanging on for dear life and the shirt, having popped most of its buttons, had seen better days. The jacket, which he had either outgrown or was never intended for him in the first place, was well on its way to threadbare. Baggy corduroy trousers and muddied slip-on shoes completed this strange, out-of-place and down-at-heel look.

'I won't, Donie,' said Nucky.

Donie smiled, then holding the bottle up to Conway, he eyed him for a response.

'Ah, no thanks,' said Conway, when he finally realised he was the subject of Donie's questioning gaze.

There was no offence taken. Indeed, the refusal seemed to meet with approval.

'Bilbo, throw on another pallet will you,' said Seánie to a tall, gangly youth with a prominent Adam's apple. He was kitted out in a Liverpool football jersey, jeans and sneakers. His hair, except for a bleached mohican crest, was closely cropped like Seánie's and mapped out in scar tissue all the knocks, nicks and cuts he had so far accrued in his young life. His right eyebrow was pierced with a bar and stud, and his neck, just below his left ear, was tattooed with a spider's web. With a cigarette butt dangling from his mouth, Bilbo slouched his way to the stockpile of pallets and, grabbing hold of one, dragged it to the fire where he manoeuvred it gingerly into the flames.

'Find anything worthwhile, Seánie?' Nucky asked.

'A Singer sewing machine thing. Any good to ya?'

Seánie spoke in that careless, slack-jawed manner that endeavoured to imply he wasn't much bothered if it was or not. Nucky went to have a look at the item in question. It was one of those old ornate stands, with baroque flourishes typical of a bygone age. After turning it over for inspection, Nucky said cautiously, 'How much you lookin' for?'

'Tenner.'

'Done.'

As this transaction was being finalised with the exchange of money, Jack, a hoary-looking individual, who could have been in his fifties or his sixties or even older, and who appeared to be sitting on an old toilet cistern, slapped his thighs and got to his feet. Painfully thin, his face frosted with week-old stubble and framed by a shock of grey hair, he had the appearance of someone recently shipwrecked. A ball of cotton filling sprouted like candyfloss from the elbow of his anorak. He stood for a moment in a state of downcast hesitancy as if contemplating his black wellies that were turned down like a fisherman's. Then, all of a sudden, he stomped purposefully in Conway's direction with a look on his face that fell somewhere between a grin and a grimace. Conway was more than a little alarmed at his approach but, not wishing to lose face, he held his ground.

At close quarters he could see the man was missing most of his teeth. The teeth that did remain were yellow and not in good shape, the only thing holding them in place, it seemed, were the deposits of plaque that were plainly visible. Now eyeball to eyeball, so close that Conway could see the red, threadlike veins on his nose, words poured out on a breath from hell with a high-pitched loudness that suggested deafness or insanity, or both.

'Whatjuthink of Limerick's chances this year? I can't see them batin' Clare. Nor Cork. Or Tipp, for that matter. They haven't the players. They're a spent team, over the hill they are. Whatjuthink? Whatjuthink? They'd want to be givin' the young lads a chance...'

Conway, who regarded sport in general as one gap in his knowledge he had never regretted and whose acquaintance with Ireland's national game of hurling was, to say the least, minimal, was at a loss for words. The man could have been talking about basket weaving, for all he knew, but feeling pretty certain that this wasn't a time to display his ignorance on the matter, he remarked carefully, 'I would have to agree with you there.'

'Do you play yourself?'

Blinking at the cul-de-sac expression on Conway's face, Jack turned his line of inquiry into broad pronouncements, 'Best game in the world, hurlin', fastest ball game in the world. Can't count ice hockey, they don't play with a ball, so they don't...'

Nucky laughed. 'Will you let the man alone, Jack, you'll have his nerves at him in a minute.'

'Right, right, right,' said Jack, hopping about on his spindly legs and flapping his hands as if trying to put out the flames of conversation. Then, as if he had been struck through with a stupendous thought, he stood bolt upright and said, his eyes wild and staring, 'oh, I have sumten to show you, Nucky, do you see what I'm sittin' on?' Pointing to the old toilet cistern he so recently vacated, he continued with pride, 'Do you see that? Read that there now, ha, made by Royal Staunton of London. Eeestablished in 1885 by appointment to her Majesty the Queen! The Queen, Nucky! The Queen! The Queen! The Queen! Watchu think o' that, ha! Watchu think?'

'Nice piece, Jack,' said Nucky, 'I might have a use for it.'

'I was thinkin' maybe...' Jack began, throwing Nucky a judicious look and rubbing his grizzled chin, 'I was thinkin' twenty.'

'You were thinkin' twenty?' said Nucky, sticking out his lower lip in consideration and nodding doubtfully.

'Twenty,' Jack affirmed.

'I'll give you the ten,'

Jack clapped his hands together, did a little dance on his spindly legs and let go a yelp of delight.

'Sound man, Nucky, ten it is, ten it is...'

In a voice rounded with the cadence of someone who enjoys the pronunciation of words, Donie, who now seemed blissfully inebriated, said, directing his gaze at Conway, 'And where do you hail from, yourself?'

'Corbally,' said Conway, still in a queasy state of recovery from Jack's onslaught.

'Corbally? A most salubrious place if I may say so,' Donie said, then popping his cigarette in his mouth to facilitate a handshake, he extended his hand. After the exchange of names and pleasantries, Donie puffed some smoke and gathered his thoughts.

'I'm from *the* Parish, myself,' he said, stressing the word *the* with a solemn curtsy of the head, 'born and raised in Nicholas Street and proud of the fact, you can be sure of it. Most assuredly. But of course, I must concede that one is still regarded as a blow-in of sorts, after all, my family did not arrive on the Island until some years after the Siege of Limerick. Only three hundred years ago. Heritage is most important, I'm sure you'll agree.'

Indicating his surroundings with a grandiose sweep of the cider bottle, he went on, 'Welcome to this most salubrious place, Edward. Welcome to the New Colossus.' Now, with arms held aloft, cider bottle in one and cigarette in the other, he enunciated in a portentous voice:

'Give me your threadbare tyres, your jaded pallets
Your empties, your nonreturnables
The worn-out mattresses
The wretched refuse of your teeming shore
Send these, the polythene and polystyrene
Tempest-tossed to me
I lift my methane lamp
Beside the gaping hole...'

'Jaysus, you're an awful man, Donie, and no mistake,' said Nucky, shaking his head and smiling.

The others chuckled, chortled and snorted.

'He's a fucken beaut,' said Seánie.

There was laughter, merriment and glee.

Donie closed his eyes for a moment, then he smiled indulgently. 'You'll have to forgive my colleagues, Edward, they're not ones for morbid whimsy or poetic licence.'

'The fucken off-licence, you mean...' said Bilbo loudly, '...that'd be more in your line.'

An imperious, stately smile played across Donie's face as he ignored the jibe with good humour.

'Pull up a stool and make yourself at home,' he said to Conway, indicating the plastic crates that were strewn about the place along with boxes and boxes of shredded paper and tangled heaps of what looked like electrical cabling. Conway chose a crate for himself and settled down beside Nucky who was already sitting.

Reaching to his left, Donie grabbed a fistful of shredded paper from a cardboard box and held it out to Conway.

'Do you keep greyhounds?' said he, '...great stuff for bedding, as good as straw any day...'

'I don't, I'm afraid,' said Conway, almost wishing he had owned a greyhound, if only to oblige Donie's generosity.

'No? And there's bubble wrap there, a great man to keep out the cold and keep the mind occupied. I knew a man, once, who used to say the Rosary with it. He did. He'd keep track of the Hail Marys with the bubbles. Burst a bubble for the Our Father and the Gloria. He would. That's the truth. He'd do the Joyful Mysteries of a Monday, the Sorrowful Mysteries of a Tuesday and the Glorious Mysteries of a Wednesday. Then back he'd go to the Joyful Mysteries on the Thursday and repeat the whole thing again...'

'Will you fuck away ouravit, Donie,' said Seánie, laughing.

With a look of long-suffering patience, Donie intoned solemnly, 'He is stripped of his garments, he is nailed to the cross, he gives up the ghost...'

Once more he turned his attention to the cardboard box. And, after some rummaging, he came up with a handful of official-looking documents.

'What have we got here, then?' he said, taking a pair of spectacles from his breast pocket, 'let's have a look.'

It was patently obvious that the tortoiseshell prescription glasses, which were now wedged on his face, had not been prescribed for him. The frame was altogether too small and the arms barely reached his ears.

'Gives a new meaning to the expression, *not a shred of evidence*,' he said, eyeing the boxes scattered about, 'and plenty of it,' he added with a laugh that brought on a hacking cough. 'Excuse me,' he said politely, after he had recovered somewhat, and took a swig of cider before continuing, 'you can tell a lot about people from their rubbish. This letter here is marked private and confidential.'

With grimy hands he held the letter at arm's length, then brought it forward again until he was satisfied that he had found an acceptable focus. After a little introductory cough he began to read in a suitably formal voice:

Dear Miss Fortune,

We are pleased to state that the Deed of Assignment from Mr Michael Tobin to your good self has now been stamped and registered in the Registry of Deeds. We enclose for your attention a photostat copy of the said Deed of Assignment which as you can see has been stamped and registered in the Registry of Deeds.

We have placed the title documentation to your dwelling house in our strongroom for safekeeping. If you have any questions or queries in relation to the matter please do not hesitate to telephone us.

In the meantime we wish to thank you for your instructions herein and if we can be of further assistance to you please do not hesitate to contact us.

Yours faithfully,

Myrtle Foley

Foley, Osborne and Bowen

Donie, lifting the glasses from his eyes, said, squinting, 'Her signature looks remarkably like the mark of Zorro.'

'Those fuckers are so full of crap,' said Bilbo, hunching forward and tetchily flicking ash from his cigarette.

After some paper shuffling, Donie went on, 'Listen to this...'

This is the last Will and Testament of me, Agatha Fortune, of Thomas Street, in the City of Limerick.

I hereby revoke all former Wills, Codicils and other testamentary dispositions heretofore at any time made by me.

I appoint my sister Patricia, and my niece, Philomena Carmody, to be the Executors and Trustees of this my Will.

Subject to the payment thereout of my just debts, funeral, and testamentary expenses, I give, devise, and bequeath all my property real and personal of every description which I may die possessed of or entitled to in the following manner:

I devise and bequeath unto Sister Bernadette and Sister Maria of St Luke's Hospital, the sum of £100.00 each. If however, Sister Maria predeceases me, I give, devise and bequeath the sum of £200.00 to Sister Bernadette, for her own use absolutely.

I devise and bequeath the sum of £100.00 to the Parish Priest of St Luke's Church for masses for the repose of my soul.

I devise and bequeath the residue of my Estate both real and personal of every description which I may die possessed of or entitled to, to my sister Patricia, for her own use absolutely. If however, the said Patricia predeceases me, I devise and bequeath the residue of my estate both real and personal of every description which I may die possessed of or entitled to, to my niece Philomena, for her own use absolutely.

In witness whereof I have hereunto set my hand this 5th day of September 1984.

Agatha Fortune

Signed published and declared by the above named Testatrix as and for her last Will and Testament in the presence of us both present at the same time, who in her presence and in the presence of each other and at her request have hereunto signed our names as attesting witnesses...

Seánie, Jack and Bilbo let their feelings be known.

'They're always spoutin' that fucken legal shite,'

'Those solicitors are so full of fucken bullshit,'

'Shower of fucken ghouls...'

Donie took another swig of cider and wiped his beard with his sleeve before continuing hoarsely.

'Whereas,' said Donie.

'Oh jaysus no, there's more of it,' said Seánie.

'Whereas,' Donie continued:

By Indenture of Lease, hereinafter called the Lease, dated the 9th day of February, 1984 between Robert Edmund O'Rourke and Mrs Sarah McNab of the one part and Daniel O'Sullivan of the other part, all that the premises described in the Schedule hereto, hereinafter called 'the Scheduled Property' were demised to the said Daniel O'Sullivan for a term of 500 years from the 25th day of March, 1884 subject to the yearly rent of eight pounds, thereby reserved and subject also to the covenants on the part of the Lessee and conditions by and in the Lease contained.

By divers means, assurances, and acts in the law and ultimately by Deed of Assent dated the 11th day of May, 1984 between Noel Thomson of the one part and of Robert Thomson the other part, the property described in Schedule hereto became vested in the said Noel Thomson to be held the residues then unexpired of the term of 500 years under Lease, herein called 'the Lease' dated the 13th day of February, 1884 and made Robert Edmund O'Rourke of the one part and Daniel O'Sullivan of the other part subject to the yearly rent of eight pounds thereby reserved to the covenants on the part of the lessees and conditions by and in the Lease contained.

The Donor is desirous of making provision for his son the said Robert Thomson and has also agreed to the Assignment herein in the manner hereinafter appearing.

Now this indenture witnesseth that in consideration of the natural love and affection which the Donor bears for his son the Donee...

'Would that be you now, Donie?' interrupted Bilbo.

'No,' said Donie, with patient consideration, 'it refers to something entirely different, I can assure you. It's a technical term that defines someone as being on the receiving end of getting something.'

Bilbo looked as wise as ever and threw his eyes to heaven as Donie proceeded: *The Donor as beneficial owner hereby grants and assigns unto the Donee all the Scheduled Property, to hold the same unto and to the use of the Donee, for all the residue yet unexpired of the term of years granted by the Lease subject to the payment of the yearly rent thereby reserved, and subject also to the covenants on the part of the Lessee and conditions by and in the Lease contained...*

'They're givin' everything to Donie,' Nucky laughed.

'He's one jammy bastard, that's all I'll say,' said Seánie, joining in.

'A load of codswallop, that's what it is,' said Jack sourly and spat his contempt into the fire.

'I would have to sssay,' said Donie, his speech beginning to slur, 'quite categorically, mind you, that I wholeheartedly concur with your analysis. Solishitors speak English as a foreign language.' Here he punctuated his sentence with a burp, then added, '...suitable only for the fire.'

Developing a nervous tick and blinking furiously, Bilbo queried, 'Hould on a minute, it might be important stuff.'

As if conscious of some indiscretion, Donie fidgeted with his tie as he gathered in his thoughts and, with a wobble of his head, he advised, 'I can ashhhure you, that they are of no great importance. It is my experience that being left anything in a will is an open invitation to have people pelt shit at you. Pardon my French.'

'They're only all phoshacopies shur, not worth a fuck,' said Seánie forcefully.

'Not worth a hat of crabs,' added Jack.

Without further ado, Donie flung the documents into the fire. Sparks rose like fireflies from the burning embers. The incense from the burning wood became all the stronger with the sudden resurgence of flames.

Donie dipped his hand into the cardboard box once more and pulled out a small dog-eared booklet with string attached. 'Now look at this, a blast from the past. Pun intended. The Irish answer to a nuclear holocaust, a little book you can hang on a nail in case of an emergency. Issued after of the Cuban Missile Crisis. I remember this...'

Survival in a Nuclear War
Advice on Protection in the Home and on the Farm

He paused for a moment and sighed, then went on with some disquiet in his voice. 'I was just a kid at the time. We could see on the cover that planet Earth was sprinkled with red dust, like German measles, representing the invissible menace of radiation. The awful truth written in blood red.'

Here he handed the book over to Conway who began flicking through its pages. On page forty-two, he came upon the instruction:

If you are out in the open turn your back to the flash.

Below this advice was the graphic drawing of a man turning his head away from the nuclear flash. And on the page opposite was a prostrate schoolboy, with schoolbag on his back, having thrown himself to the ground as advised.

Throw yourself down in a direction away from the explosion.

Conway returned to the introduction and read silently.

I would urge you to read this booklet carefully. It could be the means of saving your life and the lives of your loved ones. If you are a farmer, it could also help you to protect your livelihood, and the nation's food supply. You will see that there are some things you could be doing now to help yourself and your family to survive in a nuclear war. Ní hé lá na gaoithe lá na scolb!

The risk of nuclear war, which has caused the Government to issue this booklet specially for householders, may remain for many years. So keep the booklet carefully. Hang it, or place it, where you can easily find it in an emergency. It could mean the difference between life and death for you and your family.

When he had finished, Conway returned the booklet to Donie, who commented, 'Insane isn't it? *Ní hé lá na gaoithe lá na scolb*, I love that, don't you? Nice and cosy. I can tell you it was one of the most sinister, macaburrra books I have ever read. Forget Bram Stoker or Edgar Allen Poe, or Stephen King. That book scared the living daylights out of us, so it did. That was the Cuban Crisis, and a crisis it was, and I'm not talking about running out of rum or cigars.' He took another swig of Scrumpy Jack to calm his nerves.

With a gormless expression on his face, Bilbo asked, 'What does that mean, knee hay...whatever the fuck?'

Delighted to be called upon to elucidate, Donie obliged.

'Loosely translated, it means you shouldn't fix the roof on a windy day. And I have to admit that such homespun wissdom does not sit well with Armageddon.'

Shuffling through some more documents he had found, Donie stopped and said, unsmiling, as he perused a page he had just unfolded:

Death Certificate issued in pursuance of Births and Deaths Registration Acts 1863 to 1972. Certified Cause of Death and Duration of Illness: Myocardial Infarction...

'What the fuck is that?' asked Seánie.

'A broken heart...' Donie answered wistfully. Then after a modest silence, and a swig of cider, he continued, 'On a lighter note,' he said, almost jovially, 'here's something from the funeral undertakers...'

Dear Sir/Madam
Please find enclosed our itemized bill for services rendered.
Panelled coffin with casket mounting and ornaments as selected.
Lined with swansdown.
Engraved nameplate.
Motor hearse from funeral home to St John's church.
Motor hearse from church to Mount St Lawrence cemetery.
Blue habit.
Disbursements. The following items have been paid on your behalf.
Opening of grave in Mount St Lawrence.
Tip grave diggers.
Church and clergy offering St John's.
Church clerk.
Four cars. (two removal and two burial)
Six family wreaths.
Two obituary notices. (Independent and Leader)
Funeral Account   £580
Disbursements   £411.50
Total Account   £991.50

Setting his spectacles back on the bridge of his nose, Donie rubbed his chin and wryly intoned, 'Ask not for whom the bill tolls, it tolls for thee.'

'Jaysus,' said Seánie, 'that poor misfortune was a jolly soul, nothing but wills, dead certs, solicitors and fucken cemeteries...'

'Are they still plantin' people in the new berrin' ground?' Jack inquired and was totally ignored. His question going unanswered, he began talking to himself, '...they're usin' JCBs to dig them now. They wouldn't be bothered with a shovel no more...'

'Can anyone here tell me,' Donie began, gathering his features into an inscrutable expression, 'why undertakers are the most dependable people in the world?'

He waited for a response, then smiled at the blank faces that greeted his question.

'Because,' said he, pausing for the punch line, 'they're the lasht people to let you down!'

Accompanied by the outbursts of amusement from the others, Donie laughed unashamedly at his own joke. Even Conway, forgetting himself, was doubled up in a fit of the giggles.

'Ha ha, that's a good one,' said Jack, slapping his thighs.

'The last people to let you down, jaysus, that's a good one,' said Seánie, wiping the tears from his eyes.

When the laughing finally subsided, Seánie, turned to Bilbo and said, 'May as well throw on the flex there.'

Bilbo rose slowly from his seat and slouched over to the tangled mess of wires and cabling that were piled in a heap near the pallets. After struggling for some time to disentangle the jumble of wires, he let go a string of swear words before finally conceding defeat.

'Gimme a hand willu,' he shouted over his shoulder.

'Ah for fuck's sake,' said Seánie, 'can't you do anything, bring the whole fucken lot over.'

'Is it jokin' me you are? It's too fucken heavy...' Bilbo protested loudly.

'Ah for fuck's sake,' said Seánie, rising smartly from his crate. After surveying the problem, he said impatiently, 'here, you grab that side there and I'll take this side.'

Together they carried the tangled mass over to the fire and heaved the lot into the flames. Before long the acrid smell of burning plastic rose from the smoking pile.

Conway followed Nucky as he got up from his seat and moved in an anticlockwise direction to sidestep the coil of smoke. Now upwind of the awful choking fumes, Conway quietly inquired of Nucky, 'What are they doing?'

'Burnin' plastic off the copper,' Nucky explained, 'they sell it for scrap, you'd get a fair good price for it.'

As Conway was deciding whether or not it might seem impertinent to suggest the use of wire strippers, instead of the unpleasant and unhealthy method now being employed, Jack let go a shriek of alarm.

'Rats! Rats! Rats! Fucken rats as big as fucken banbhs...'

Conway and Nucky turned just in time to see Jack throw a stick at a rat that was scurrying away from the cardboard boxes. Roused from their sleep, Butch and Sundance sprang to life.

'Rats! Rats! Rats!' Jack informed them.

'Go get them, boys,' urged Seánie.

'Rats! Rats! Rats!' Bilbo reminded them.

The dogs went berserk, whining and whimpering and growling themselves into a frenzy, but, not really knowing what was expected of them, since the rat had long gone, they began frantically digging holes all over the place.

'The dump do be crawlin' with 'em...' Jack pronounced.

'You'd get the plague from them fuckers,' said Bilbo.

Unable to stop himself, Conway had to comment, 'That's rather doubtful, you're unlikely to find black rats here.'

Bilbo narrowed his eyes and said fiercely, 'But they are black, I seen 'em shur...'

'You can't always go by the colouring,' said Conway, 'because some brown rats can be almost black and some black rats can be brown.'

'Thanks a lot, sham, I'm just confused now,' said Bilbo with a smirk and a roll of his eyes.

'The man knows what he's talking about,' said Donie, 'he knows what's what.'

Encouraged by this vote of confidence, Conway decided to give more particulars about the rodents in question.

'It was the black rat, rattus rattus, or ship rat, that carried the bubonic plague, or the Black Death, as it was called, or I should say carried the flea that carried the bug that carried the plague. They arrived here in Ireland around the time of the Crusades, in the thirteenth century, whereas the brown rat only arrived as recently as the eighteenth century, and more or less took over from the black rat. The brown rat, rattus norvegicus, is bigger and more aggressive than the black rat and is better able to tolerate cold weather, being originally from Russia, whereas the black rat is from the Mediterranean. You'll only find black rats in dock areas, busy seaports, like Cork and Dublin...'

Seeing that his words were being met with stony silence, Conway stopped abruptly. He sensed his pronouncements weren't all that well-received. His audience stood in a semi-circle of amazement and stared at him as if he had come from another planet.

Donie came to his rescue. 'There's none in Limerick?'

'Not to my knowledge,' Conway said awkwardly, 'as far as I am aware, no.'

'Jaysus, that's a good one, and I thought we had all kinds of rats in Limerick,' Jack said, laughing.

'There's fucken plenty of the two-legged ones, that's for sure,' said Seánie.

'Can you get an'thing from them?' Bilbo asked, '...you know, like a disease?'

Conway hesitated, then said, 'Well, you could get Weil's disease. It can be fatal...'

'But could you die from it?' Bilbo said, without blinking.

Seánie erupted. 'If it's fatal, it can kill you, and if it can kill you, you can die from it...for fuck's sake...'

'I know, I know,' Bilbo shouted defensively, 'I was only askin', that's all...'

'Would that be the water rat, now?' Jack asked, looking shrewdly at Conway.

'Well, I suppose so, they are very good swimmers, though the water vole is often referred to as a water rat.'

'Howja know all this, sham?' inquired Bilbo.

'Research. I aahm, read it in a book.'

'Cripes,' said Jack, 'but you're a mine of information so you are and no mistake...'

'A handy man to have around.' Donie acknowledged.

With a grave look on his face, Jack turned to the others and said glumly, 'I tell ye, lads, ye'd need to be takin' fistfuls of antibioshics hangin' around this place, so ye would. Do ye know what I'm goin' to tell ye...'

But before Jack had time to tell anyone anything, his words were interrupted by the blast of a hooter way off to their right. Down below them, Conway could see a tipper truck trundling along with a new consignment of rubbish.

'Another load,' said Bilbo matter-of-factly, heading in the direction of the truck along with Seánie.

'Seek and ye shall find,' urged Donie, following in their footsteps.

The hooter sounded again. It was obviously a signal. A prearranged tip-off.

'Are you comin', Nucky?'

'Not today, Jack, I've got to get back.'

'See ye around so,' said Jack, then calling after the others, he shouted, 'stall on will ye...'

'Will you come on, you slowcoach,' Seánie shouted back.

Conway watched as the four, shepherded by Butch and Sundance, scampered down the slope towards the truck that was already tipping its load. They descended on it before the bulldozers had a chance to lay it flat and cover it with a layer of earth.

'Who are those people?' Conway asked, as Nucky picked up the sewing machine stand.

'Pickers,' said Nucky, 'except Donie, of course. Comin' here for donkey's years. Pickers' rights they have. The Corpo are tryin' to put a stop to them.'

'And Donie?'

'Ah, Donie's a harmless oul' soul. He was a teacher, once. Took to the drink when his wife died.' He gave Conway a questioning look, then added, 'Do you think you can manage to carry this stand?'

'Sure,' Conway said, without hesitation.

'Good,' said Nucky, 'I'll take the cistern. It's a bit on the heavy side. We'd better get goin' before the horse comes lookin' for us.'

Chapter Twenty-three

Conway had the feeling that their presence was not wholly unexpected. For one thing, the door of number fifty-two had opened even before Mary Rose had laid a hand on the knocker. With the door held wide, a fine figure of a woman, perhaps in her late forties or early fifties, stood before them. Dressed in slacks, candy-striped blouse and blue canvas deck shoes, she had a tanned and breezy look about her, like someone who had just stepped ashore from a yacht. Her hair, chestnut brown, was tied in a bun. She was all smiles.

'Come in, love,' she said, beaming at Mary Rose, 'and who's this?' Her voice was loud, declamatory and undeniably welcoming. 'So this is the boy you were telling us about,' she added, giving Mary Rose a knowing look. Then, turning to Conway, she stated warmly, as she offered her hand, 'You must be Edward.'

'Pleased to meet you,' Conway muttered, as he shuffled forward into the hallway to take the graceful and petite hand in his own dead-fish, sweaty palm.

'Call me Molly,'

'Molly,' Conway repeated awkwardly, aware that he was being scrutinized by the most beautiful brown eyes he had ever seen.

'Come in, come in,' Molly coaxed, then added, with a mischievous loudness, 'she's been dying to have us meet you and to show you off.'

'Molly!' wheezed Mary Rose disapprovingly.

Her aunt responded with a gleeful chuckle, turned on her heel and then, as if she had altogether lost her senses, threw back her head and let go a squeal of delight.

'Oh she's mortified,' she shouted, her words convulsing with laughter.

Drawing a calming breath through her flared nostrils, Mary Rose twisted her mouth into an indignant pout and rolled her eyes. Then, seeing the self-satisfied smile on Conway's face, she flashed a censorious glance at him. But he continued to smile. The revelation that he was, in her eyes, worthy of being 'shown off', pleased him no end. He remembered the priming he had got from Mary Rose.

'Oh you'll just love Molly,' she had said, 'everybody does. She's lovely.'

For his own part, Conway could not help but note the similarities between Mary Rose and her aunt. Though they did not look so much alike, there was the same vibrancy and candid irreverence. He had taken an instant shine to this middle-aged woman and her seemingly abrupt, impolite and forthright manner. There was no pretence about her. She seemed strong and confident enough to be just who she was. And her laugh, though frayed around the edges, was so full of life. This was powerful medicine to someone who was, it had to be said, mostly apologetic about his own existence.

Leading the way, Molly walked on ahead in a curiously quaint, flat-footed manner, holding her feet splayed like a ballet dancer. Conway caught the scent of her perfume. It was subtle, delicate and restrained. Everything she was not. He found the contradictions endearing.

'Don't be shy, don't be shy,' Molly cajoled as she stood at the doorway and ushered Conway into the sitting room. It was a warm welcome, indeed too warm, for as he stepped over the threshold he was met with a blast of heat from a roaring fire. In the haze of first impressions, it seemed to occupy the room like a caged and ill-tempered animal.

'What filum did ye go to see?' asked Molly.

'War of the Roses,' said Mary Rose.

'A war filum?'

'No, kind of a comedy. Michael Douglas, you know, the fella from the Streets of San Francisco...'

'Kirk Douglas's son?'

'Him. And the fella out of Taxi was in it, the fella who used to play the grouchy boss, Danny De Vito.'

'Oh, Danny De Vitro,' said Molly knowingly, 'oh I like him. He's good.'

'And Kathleen Turner,'

'I don't know her now at all,'

'Ah you do, Molly,' Mary Rose assured her, 'the blonde one. She was in a few things.'

Molly put a forefinger to her chin and considered, 'I can't place her. Was she in that Moonlighting thing with Bruce Willis?'

'Ah no, you're thinking of someone else altogether,' said Mary Rose, then conceded, '...you know her all right.'

'Was it any good?'

'A howl, Molly. Wasn't it, Edward?'

Somewhat startled that he should be consulted, Conway said, 'Yes, it was good...very good...'

'Well, I'm glad ye enjoyed it anyway,' said Molly, smiling, then addressing Conway she instructed, 'sit down there now and make yourself comfortable. Let me take your coat and hang it up in the hall.'

Gladly divesting himself of his overcoat, he mumbled his thanks and handed it over.

'Mother a'gawd,' said Molly as she took hold of the coat, 'what have you in the pockets? Rocks?'

'Odds and ends,' said Conway shyly.

'It weighs a fecken ton,' Molly exclaimed, and added, laughing on her way to the door, 'I hope the hook doesn't come away from the fecken wall.'

Both Mary Rose and Conway chose to forego the two armchairs that flanked either side of the red brick fireplace and sat as far back from the oppressive heat as they possibly could. Their preferred choice was an emerald three-seater couch near the window. The emerald refuge was decked with white crochet cushions and lace antimacassar. This last item, with its strikingly exotic name, happened to be of interest to Conway. A dictionary gem.

antimacassar n a covering for chair backs, etc to protect them from being soiled (orig from macassar oil or other grease in the hair) or for ornament.

It had, he felt, a noteworthy etymology. A living fossil of a word whose imperially serious, polysyllabic gravity was at odds with its lightweight and outdated purpose.

Molly inquired, 'How's your mother?'

'She's grand,' Mary Rose answered matter-of-factly.

'And all the lads?'

'Grand.'

'You're a mine of information. Do you know that?' said Molly with an exasperated look, 'everything is grand, grand, grand with you.'

Mary Rose hummed a laugh, then asked, 'How's Maisie?'

Making a face, Molly said, 'There's a fear of her. She'll be getting up now in a minute. She heard you coming in the gate. I have to have the fire high for her. I'm roasted from it. You'd nearly have to sit out in the fecken hall with the heat. She's always complainin' with the cold. She has very thin blood, she keeps tellin' me. If you ask me, she has no fecken blood at all.'

Suddenly going wide-eyed, Molly went on, 'Come out to the kitchen, you can talk to me while I'm puttin' on the kettle.' She turned to Conway, smiling, and sweetly said, 'Excuse us now a minute, Edward.'

The two disappeared into an adjoining room, and after a whispered, 'close the door' from Molly, the door was pushed gently shut. There was talk, some whispering, some laughing, then more whispering.

Left to his own devices, and the laboured tick of the clock on the mantelpiece, Conway occupied himself with a distracted inspection of his surroundings.

The sitting room was cosy and cluttered, the left side of the chimney breast was occupied by a low dresser festooned with photographs and ornaments. Above the dresser was a three-dimensional picture of Jesus holding aloft a lantern and knocking, or about to knock, on someone's door. The resulting hologram was rather eerie and strangely beautiful. To the left of this was hung the handsome Pope Pius X, looking very pious indeed. To the right, hung the fatherly and careworn Pope John XXIII. On the other side of the chimney breast were stationed a table and four chairs. On the wall above these was a gilded picture of the Sacred Heart and beside it the year's calendar that came courtesy of St Anthony's Pools. The haloed patron, St Anthony himself, knelt above the days of the month, seemingly in devout contemplation of a cobweb situated in the far corner of the ceiling. In the corner, below the cobweb, stood a wooden clotheshorse draped with laundry. There was no television to be seen.

The fire's obstreperous roar had now diminished to a low, burring murmur. It glubbed and piped and blew little smoke signals and seemed quite cheerful in itself. And still giving out too much heat for Conway's liking. Overhead the fireplace was a picture of a moorland scene with mountains, misty in the distance. An old man was gathering turf while a basket-laden donkey stood patiently by. His eyes drifting to the far window, Conway peered through net curtains into twilight and the dimming outline of trees and shrubbery.

Settling back on the couch, he rested his head on the antimacassar and looked at the ceiling. The pearl white bulb that peeked below the fringed lightshade reflected a curved and minuscule window. After tracing a delta of hairline cracks from the ceiling rose to the wall behind him, he noticed an ornate mirror circled with golden leaves. On either side of the mirror there was an assortment of framed photographs. His curiosity getting the better of him, he got to his feet to have a closer look. One in particular caught his attention, a First Communion portrait of an angelic looking Mary Rose. Unmistakable. A studied pose with prayer book and rosary beads in hand, made all the more poignant by her artless smile and wide-eyed innocence. It made him smile. It touched his heart.

There she was, in black and white, on the verge of the use of reason. And, as he stared in wonder at her, a curious alchemy of emotion swept through him and he thought how strange it was that she had lived a life separate from his own. As children they must have passed each other many times, but had grown up unaware of each other's existence. He grieved at not knowing her sooner. And yet, somehow, he had a haunting conviction that he had always known her. It was their destiny to meet. To be together. Catching sight of his face in the mirror, its convex glass ridiculing his features and distorting the room behind him, he felt a twinge of resentment towards providence that things, profound and elemental, were being kept from him. Tantalisingly close, but always just out of reach.

The door of the kitchen opened and Mary Rose popped her head around it to cheerfully ask, '...how many sugars?' then quickly added, reacting to Conway's puzzled response, '...in your tea?'

'Ahhm, two please. Thanks.'

'Ask him do he like it weak or strong,' Molly called loudly from the kitchen, as if shouting to someone who was across the road and not just a few feet away.

Still hanging out of the door, Mary Rose just smiled and relayed the message, 'Weak or strong?'

Conway blinked before deciding to say, 'Ahhm, medium please. Thanks.'

Mary Rose relayed the compromise to Molly, who then responded with the loud inquiry, 'Do he like much milk?'

Deadpan, Mary Rose repeated the words that were still ringing in her ears. The role of ludicrous go-between and

Conway's 'ahhm, medium please, thanks' was just too much for her and she fell into a fit of giggling.

'What are you skittin' at?' Molly chided.

Still giggling, Mary Rose managed to say, 'Nothing...'

'I know,' said Molly, 'I'm shoutin' like a fecken eejit, that's what I am. Look, I'll let the young fella sort out his own tea, isn't it true for me, there's nobody can do it like your own self.'

After what sounded like conspiratorial whispering, Molly and Mary Rose re-entered the sitting room with a loud and busy self-possession.

'...you can take your eyes off them,' Molly was saying to Mary Rose, 'them apple tarts are for your mother. G'wan, lay the table, let you.'

'I don't want them at all, I was only teasin' you,' Mary Rose was saying as she carried in a tray laden with all the paraphernalia of high tea, 'the marble cake will do me fine,' she added primly, as she set down the tray and began to decant its cargo of milk, sugar, cups, saucers, knives, spoons, and side plates of cake and biscuits. 'Is this the tea service from the china cabinet?'

'Yes, it is,' Molly answered, 'nothan but the finest, fine bone china for our guests.'

Sweeping her blonde hair behind her ear with her fingers, Mary Rose said light-heartedly, 'You've just been dyin' for an excuse to use it, haven't you, Molly?'

'Well now,' said Molly self-righteously, 'I can't think of a better one, can you?' Leaning past Mary Rose, she placed a canary-yellow teapot at the centre of the table and slipped a rainbow tea cosy over it.

Mary Rose stared at the teapot and began to giggle.

'What's so funny?' Molly asked.

After laughing out loud, Mary Rose said, 'I'm sorry, but the teapot...it looks like a Rastafarian.'

'Give over, the cheek of you...' Molly said with mock reproach, '...makin' a feck of Maisie's tea cosy after she goin' to the trouble of knittin' it an' all.'

But very soon she was shaking with laughter herself and holding on to the table for support.

'Don't, Jesus, don't,' she said imploringly, 'if she hears us there'll be waaaar. God forgive me for laughing.'

Conway sat looking on, a bemused smile on his face. The two of them seemed to him more like wayward schoolgirls than aunt and niece.

After regaining some possession of herself, Molly gave a polite little cough, turned to Conway, and referring to his interest in the photographs, she asked, 'Recognise her? You couldn't mistake that bould puss of hers, now could you? Plaster on her knee, fecken eejit fell off a wall and grazed her fecken knee just two days before her First Communion. A right hopper she got. Look at her, butter wouldn't melt in her mouth.'

Conway looked more closely at the photograph of Mary Rose, and there, sure enough, was the offending plaster. He was charmed and amused.

In an effort to deflect attention from herself, Mary Rose pointed to another photograph, stating casually, 'And there's Nucky...'

Molly rolled her eyes like someone who was about to go unconscious. 'And as for him,' she moaned, 'Nucky? Don't talk to me!'

Looking at Nucky, in his First Holy Communion suit, Conway could not think of a more unstable amalgam of religious decorum and glum, uncooperative wilfulness than what was evident in Nucky's defiant jaw line.

'You couldn't dress him up, shur you couldn't,' lamented Molly, 'you could throw all the clothes in Roches Stores and Todds on him and he'd still look untidy. And such unruly and unmanageable hair! We had to plaster his cowlick with Brylcreem to get it to lie down. Such a young fella, couldn't get him to hold the fecken rosary beads. He was like an antichrist, he was. He had us demented.'

Responding to Mary Rose's laughter, she added jovially, 'Demented we were from him!'

Addressing Conway, Molly said, 'Come on and sit down and have some tea and some cake, or some biscuits if you prefer. Or a ham san'wich if you'd prefer that.'

'You're very kind. Cake will be fine, thank you.'

'You're more than welcome, my love,' said Molly warmly, then, sliding her eyes away in consideration, she inclined her head to one side. 'Listen,' she said, moments later, 'I think her majesty is up.'

After a somewhat charged expectancy, and the agitated turning of its doorknob, the sitting room door finally swung open. A zimmer frame, grasped by two determined, white-knuckled hands, was plonked down inside the threshold. Emerging from behind the door, the intruder shuffled forward into view.

Her majesty indeed. There was something rather haughty about her. So different from her sister, and a good deal older by all appearances. Her hair, cropped short, was almost snow-white. Behind rimless glasses, her eyes were magnified ice blue and her pale round face and delicate features still implied that she had been a beauty in her day. She wore a baggy jumper thrown over a tangerine cotton shirt, baggy tartan trousers and blue, three-stripe Adidas runners. This seemingly odd and mismatched ensemble somehow hung together. This aging beauty still had presence.

'How are you, Maisie?' asked Mary Rose, 'How's the leg?'

Apparently out of breath, Maisie said tetchily, her pearl drop earrings dangling, 'I can't walk and talk...' then, minding her manners, she added, 'fine, grand, I'm draggin' the fecken thing. It'd bring the sweat out through you, so it would...'

'She did her ankle in,' Mary Rose explained to Conway.

'She wasn't looking where she was goin' and tripped over a sweet wrapper,' said Molly.

'Very fecken funny,' Maisie snapped, 'you're full of your fun aren't you,' then, shaking her head in annoyance, she put on a thin-lipped scowl, 'for your information,' she went on, 'it was a cockeyed, crooked fecken flagstone that did for me. The shaggin' thing shouldn't have been where it was.'

'I know, Maisie,' said Molly wearily, 'I will never hear the end of it, will I? You should sue the Corporation.'

'I will not indeed, I'd have no luck for it. Claimin' for this and claimin' for that, they'd sue the Corpo these days for buildin' the ground too close to their backsides, some people would, so they would.'

Nodding towards Conway, Maisie then said, in a not-overly-impressed way, 'Is that the young fella now?'

With economical formality, Mary Rose performed the introductions, 'This is Edward, Maisie. Edward, this is my Aunt Maisie.'

'Pleased to meet you,' said Maisie pleasantly.

'Pleased to meet you, too,' responded Conway and rose to extend his hand.

With agitated regret Maisie said, 'I can't shake hands or I might fall.'

'Ah, of course, best not to,' said Conway, retracting the errant hand and smiling awkwardly.

Molly sighed a long-suffering sigh and Mary Rose stifled a titter.

'That's why I'm in that fecken room at the moment,' Maisie went on, 'I can't go the stairs, I have to stay on the flat. It's a nuisance with the bathroom upstairs and all.'

Manoeuvring herself into position, Maisie let go of the zimmer frame and flopped down onto one of the armchairs. Easing back into it, she said, 'Aaah, that's better now,' then added, eyeing the frame in front of her, 'that fecken thing would kill you, so it would.'

As Mary Rose took the zimmer frame away and placed it beside the dresser, Molly turned to Conway and said, in a low, fierce whisper, 'She don't need that fecken thing, you know.'

'Did you go to the club?' Mary Rose inquired of Maisie.

'Ah, I'm gone off that. They're all fecken old people.'

'She still thinks she's a young one,' said Molly, nodding her head reproachfully.

'Well, I'm not gone eejy yet.' Maisie retorted.

'You're just fecken odd.' Molly pronounced.

'What do I want with an old fogies' club and them fecken prayers they be goin' on with, and their month's mind mass, their holy this and their holy that, and their fecken movin' fecken statues.'

'Ah, you're a pagan. You believe in nothan,' said Molly dismissively, then added, with all the polite etiquette of a genial host, 'will you have something to eat?'

'I don't think I'll bother.'

'Go on, and have something. You'll only be complainin' afterwards that you're famished.'

'All right so.' Maisie conceded, as if it pained her greatly to do so. Looking around the room in a silly, distracted sort of way, she gave Conway a cursory nod of recognition and asked, 'You're not, by any chance, related to the Conways in O'Curry Place, are you? You have the look of them about you, so you have.'

'No, I don't think so,' said Conway after some hesitation.

Maisie put a finger to her right ear and said, 'You have to speak up. I can't hear very well in this ear.'

'He says he's not, Maisie,' shouted Molly on her way to the kitchen, 'speak up, Edward, she won't bite you,' then she added, 'now you know why I'm roarin' all the time.'

Maisie nodded her head shrewdly, then, after staring into the fire a moment or two, she asked, 'Would you know a Phyllis Conway?'

'Ah, Maisie,' said Molly, coming back from the kitchen and raising her voice in scorn, 'will you leave the young fella alone, shur you're goin' back years ago, before he was even born. The boy wouldn't know any of them, and stop pokin' the fire,' she pleaded with Maisie, who had taken a poker in hand and was jabbing the fire with it, 'you'll have the hot coals all over the floor in a minute and the place burnt down around us.'

'I'm trying to put some bit of life into it,' Maisie protested as Molly removed herself to the kitchen once more. Maisie then turned to Conway, and throwing her eyes to heaven to

241

enlist support, she said, with a resigned grin, 'You see what I have to put up with.'

'Come in, Molly, your tea will be gettin' cold.' Mary Rose yelled out to the kitchen.

'I'll be in, in a minute. I'm just gettin' that one something to eat.'

'*That one*, you know,' Maisie repeated indignantly.

Mary Rose sipped her tea and asked, 'Will I put more coal on, Maisie?'

Looking very imperious, Maisie answered, 'No, there's no need for a while,' then turning to Conway again, she said, 'it can get very cold at night.'

With the perspiration beading on his forehead, Conway clacked his cup down on its saucer and said, 'It can. It can.'

Finger tapping on the arm of her chair, Maisie said, 'It's getting dark, I'd nearly say it's time for the lights.'

Taking her cue, Mary Rose was on her feet and closing the curtains. 'Stick on the light there, Edward, would you,' she said, as she made her way to the other window. The fire's glow, now coming into its own, was throwing shadows about the room. In response to his momentary confusion, caused by the lack of light, Mary Rose directed, 'There, by the door. Over your left shoulder.'

Finally finding it, he flicked the switch.

Adjusting to the light, Maisie narrowed her eyes, and then said, nodding at the far window, 'You have that crooked.'

Mary Rose was on her feet again, adjusting the curtains. She turned, looking for Maisie's approval, 'How's that?'

Maisie nodded and said, 'That's better.'

At that very moment there was a knock at the front door that reverberated through the house.

'Who could that be at this hour?' Maisie frowned.

Molly was out of the kitchen in a flash. 'That's probably Vera Cronin for the Christmas Club money.'

Heedless, Maisie asked, 'What does she want?'

'The Christmas Club money, I said!' Molly shouted. So much so, that the room literally rang with her impatience.

'Oh,' Maisie said softly, her face becoming a mask of indifference.

Sipping tea and eating cake, Conway listened to the voices from the hallway, relishing the blast of cold air the open door afforded.

'Who was it?' Maisie asked, when Molly returned.

'Bock the Robber, who do you fecken think?' said Molly, then, as she sauntered past on her way to the kitchen, she added, 'Vera Cronin! Amn't I after already tellin' you. She was askin' for you. Satisfied?'

Sourly, Maisie said, 'It's a wonder she didn't break down the door. I nearly leapt outa the chair with her.'

When Molly returned from her exile in the kitchen, she was wheeling in a serving trolley that had a pronounced and precarious tendency to lean.

'Fecken thing is goin' all bocady,' Molly commented.

'I thought you said you tightened the nuts...' her sister stated accusingly.

'I did but the fecken things keep comin' loose. It's like the leanin' tower of fecken, what's its name, Pisa.'

Mary Rose sprang from the couch, and crouching down beside the trolley began tightening the wing nuts that were keeping the contraption together.

'Do you see you,' Molly said, rounding on Maisie, 'you're never without something to say.'

Ignoring Molly's words entirely, Maisie said, as she eyed the fare set before her on the trolley, 'I'll have a bit of cake. Just a small piece, mind,' then added, 'and give the young fella a bit, can't you...'

'I gave him three slices. He still have two left on his plate,' explained Molly.

'He might want another one,' Maisie persisted.

'Ah no, thank you,' Conway flustered, 'I have more than enough in two...really...'

'He doesn't...want...any...more...' Molly said, stressing her exasperation.

'Well, you should ask, it's only manners,' said Maisie.

'What do you want me to do, Maisie, ram it down his gob? Force it on the boy when he doesn't want it?'

Though flattered, and bewildered, to be at the centre of such a heated debate, Conway had a feeling that he might be a mere pawn in this battle of wills.

'All right, there's no need to be goin' on about it.' Maisie said, impatience rising in her voice.

Taking possession of the other armchair, Molly muttered, 'My fecken tea's gone cowld with you,' then casting a very deliberate look in Mary Rose's direction, she asked, 'and what are you smiling at?'

'Nothing,' said Mary Rose, with slow emphasis as she tried to stifle her laugh.

'You're enjoying this, aren't you?' Molly accused with a wry grin.

'She thinks we're doolally,' added Maisie, eyeing Conway but nodding in Mary Rose's direction.

Molly concurred, 'Off our rockers, that's what she thinks we are and I wouldn't blame her.'

Mary Rose laughed and said unconvincingly, 'I do not, indeed,' then quickly added, 'well, maybe a little...'

Arching her eyebrows at Maisie, Molly said, 'And would you blame her, with your carry on?'

Ignoring Molly as if she no longer existed, Maisie asked, 'So ye went to the filums so?'

'We did.'

'Who was in it?'

'Michael Douglas,' Mary Rose began patiently, 'Danny De Vito and Kathleen Turner and...'

'Now,' said Molly triumphantly, 'and you think she don't be listening. And she's supposed to be fecken deaf.'

Sending her earrings into a tizzy, Maisie went on the offensive, 'I couldn't help overhearing and you roarin' in the hallway, and that big durty laugh of yours, and I couldn't get a wink a sleep with all the kids out on the road with their jumpin' and leapin' and their fecken skippin', and bangin' balls off the walls. They nearly put the winda in around me, and that little scourge Lawrence Halvey, he's the worst of them. He's stone mad...'

'Ah, for feck sake, Maisie, they're only children.' Molly countered, 'We were just like them ourselves, or have you forgotten?'

This rebuke seemed to rekindle a softness in Maisie and her fit of pique soon subsided. A short time later she turned to Molly and asked, 'Wasn't he the fella in Sparktacus? Michael Douglas? I just remembered his name.'

'For heaven's sake, Maisie, that was years ago. It wasn't Michael Douglas. It was his father, Kirk Douglas. I don't think the child was even out of short pants, back then.'

Heedless to all corrections, Maisie went on wistfully, 'It was above in the Lyric Cinema. Remember, Molly?'

Conway had visions of a kid with home-made sword and skateboard, taking on the might of the Roman Empire somewhere on the streets of San Francisco. When Conway came to, the conversation had moved on.

'...shur that's gone years ago, Maisie,' Molly was saying, then turning to Mary Rose, she began listing picture houses of the past, 'there was the Royal, the Lyric, the City Theatre, *they* used to give you a free thrupenny bar of chocolate to entice you in. Then, there was the Savoy, the Carlton, the Grand Central. And the Thomond, all the kids shoutin', *we want our money back, we want our money back.* You know, like, if somethin' went wrong with the filum projector. Stampin' their feet they'd be, *we want our money back, we want our money back,* and then a big cheer would go up when the filum came back on again. Paddy Tohill, he was the poor misfortunate projectionist, his nerves adbe at him over it. Wooden benches, that's all the seats were. Unless you went upstairs, which was very posh, with carpet an' all. Up in the gods you'd be then...'

'You, of course,' Maisie interrupted, 'always insisted on sittin' right up at the front. Blind you'd be from it. Jaysus, I may as well have been in the filum, we were that close. Is it any wonder I'm half-blind today.'

'And there was the Astor,' Molly went on, oblivious to Maisie's input, 'that was out in Kileely...'

'Remember the Dracula filums, Molly?' Mary Rose said, smiling, 'you used to bring me. I used to love them.'

Molly's face lit up as she said, 'We'd spend most of the time lookin' out through the buttonholes of my cardigan. We'd miss half the fecken filum, we would. Scared out of our wits we'd be. Oh, great fun. We used to love the horrors, Christopher Lee and Peter Cushing. And this one,' Molly went on, pointing her thumb in Mary Rose's direction, '...stuffin' her face with marshmallows every two minutes. She'd eat a whole bag for you, she would, that's the truth, and on our way home from the pictures we'd stop off at the Golden Grill and get ourselves a big bag of chips with loads of salt and vinegar. Walkin' down Gerald Griffin Street we'd be, scoffin' our chips and we'd be talkin' about everything and anything under the sun, moon and stars. Ah, them were the days...'

Maisie, rousing herself from her own thoughts, made the bald and irrelevant statement, 'The Mummy were that slow it's a wonder he caught anyone, never mind throttle them. He couldn't catch meself, zimmer frame an' all...'

Molly rolled her eyes to the ceiling, exhaled a sigh, and said, 'I think I'll put on the kettle for the wash up.'

'I'll give you a hand,' said Mary Rose, rising.

'No, indeed you won't, you'll sit down there now and finish your tea and keep Edward company. I'm only out in the back kitchen, you can talk away to me.'

Minutes later, from the kitchen, came the cry,

'The fecken gaz is out!'

Back in again, Molly headed for the gas meter, which, unhappily, was situated behind Maisie's chair.

'I can't get next nor near the fecken gaz with you,' Molly protested, as she tried to squeeze between the armchair and the dresser.

Not budging an inch, Maisie said wilfully, 'Well, what am I supposed to do, go up the fecken chimley?'

'You can go up in my capital A, for all I care.' Molly said pointedly.

'That's lovely, that is,' said Maisie, 'in front of the young fella and all. There isn't room to swing a cat in this house.'

This set Molly off, 'I know, Maisie, you should never have left Engaland and your big fancy house.'

'Well, I'd agree with you there, I shouldn't...'

'Ah give over, Maisie, you're like a broken record. If Engaland was so fecken marvellous, why didn't you fecken well stay there?'

'I wish to god I had, so I do.'

'There's no pleasing you, Maisie, you wouldn't be happy in heaven, so you wouldn't. Now, shift your carcass.'

'Where am I supposed to sit?' Maisie grumbled, 'stupid place to put the gaz anyway, you'd think they'd put it in the fecken hall, or the cubby, and be done with it.'

Off on her own train of thought, Molly said, in bemused tones, 'I wouldn't mind, you know, but I'm only after puttin' money in. It's atin' fifty pees, so it is.' Then holding up a fifty pence piece, she turned to Conway and said, 'Edward, would you ever put that in the meter for me, please, before I lose the will to live?'

Only too willing to oblige, Conway took up the quest, and, having squeezed through the gap between Maisie's armchair and the dresser, he finally faced the object of such defamation and derision. It was an old style, sickly-green gas meter with a coin slot mechanism and he was unfamiliar with the feeding procedure.

'That's an awkward thing for him now, Molly,' Maisie piped up, 'he might not be able to do it.'

'Will you let him alone and give him a chance, he's not a fecken eejit.' Molly protested loudly.

'I never said he was, I'm only sayin' he might not be used to it, that's all.'

'Turn the flange thingy back fully,' Molly directed, 'to the left, stick in the money. That's it, now turn the flange again. To the right, that's it. Now you have it.'

Conway did exactly as he was told and the coin eventually dropped with a dull clink.

'I think it's nearly full, by the sound of it,' said Molly, 'the gasman should be due, he hasn't been around for ages. I'll have to have it emptied.'

'Didn't I tell you that he called but we weren't in?' Maisie said reproachfully, 'Mary Tobin informed me of the fact. She distinctly said that he'd been around.'

Molly was aghast, 'Well jaysus,' said she, 'thanks for tellin' me. After death, the doctor, and after meat, the mustard. If ever he has a notion of callin' again be sure to let me know after the event, so I can't do nothan about it...'

'There's no need to be sarcastic. I hate that. It puts me right off,' Maisie said, looking terribly offended. 'Do it, you?' she asked quaintly of Conway, then turning to face Molly again, she said resignedly, 'I'll tell you no more, that's what I will...'

'Well, won't I be in the dark,' proclaimed Molly, then addressing Conway, she added airily, 'take no notice of us, Edward, we're always fightin' like cat and dog...'

'We are,' said Maisie affably, now nodding and smiling as if all that had gone before was merely pantomime.

The alteration was truly astounding. Mutual disregard and biting sarcasm one minute, the next, all sweetness and light. The bond between them so strong, it seemed, they could play this verbal head-butting to the very precipice of insult as sure-footed as mountain goats. Just as it looked like things would deteriorate to pitched battle, the subject would be changed and they were laughing and joking about something else entirely.

'You have to take us as you find us,' said Molly.

'You do,' said Maisie, 'that's the way we are,' then she asked, her thoughts taking another byroad, 'what time did the picture start?'

'Seven,' said Mary Rose

'What way did ye come?'

'Up Thomas Street, down Wickham Street, crossed over

to Gerald Griffin Street and down Manifold's Hill...'

'Did ye have a look in Kenneally's winda by any chance, while ye were at it?' Molly asked, laughing.

Mary Rose made a face and said, 'Very funny, Molly.'

'What did she mean by that?' Maisie asked of Mary Rose.

But it was Molly who answered her, 'Engagement rings, Maisie,' she shouted, 'jaysus, you're awful slow.'

Maisie smiled. Then, after collecting her thoughts like loose change, she said rather wisely, 'Ye wouldn't want to be rushin' into things. Ye have yere whole lives ahead of ye, so ye have. Ye'd want to be careful. Takin' precautions, for one thing. I hope ye're using protection.'

Outraged, Molly said, 'For god's sake, Maisie, will you give over. There's a thing to be bringin' up. My god, the things you come out with at times.'

'I'm only concerned, that's all,' said Maisie, rising to her own defence, 'you can't be too careful these days, you'd feel sorry for young ones goin' today, so you would. And there's every disease going. That disease, what's it, aids, that, we never had to worry about things like that in our day. I blame them fecken homulsexuals, so I do.'

'Well,' said Conway, 'in fairness, I think you'll find it's as much a heterosexual disease as anything else.'

'They're even worse feckers...' said Maisie sternly.

Conway, with a perplexed look on his face, was about to seek clarification when Mary Rose, nearly inhaling the piece of cake she was eating, began spluttering and coughing.

'Are you all right?' Maisie asked.

'Drink some of your tea,' said Molly.

'I hate when that happens,' said Maisie with a scowl.

Making great efforts to suppress her coughing, and speak at the same time, Mary Rose gasped, 'I'm okay, just went down the wrong way, that's all.'

'Have a drink of milk.' Maisie advised.

'I'm okay now,' Mary Rose assured her.

'You could have choked to death,' said Maisie with a worried look on her face, 'the Considines always had small throats, I remember a friend of mine, her Great Uncle Dan, god be good to him, he choked on an apple and died. He was very good with his hands, he was, he could make up a chair or a table out of his own head...'

She suddenly stopped talking, looked at Molly and asked indignantly, 'What are you laughin' at? Did I say something funny?'

'No, Maisie, go on,' Molly said, stifling her laugh, 'what were you saying?'

'I was telling you, he could make up a whole suite of furniture out of his head. He was that good.'

With her lips drifting to a smile, Molly yelled, 'He was gifted, in other words?'

'Yes, gifted,' said Maisie, nodding her head defiantly.

'Like, he had a big wooden head,' said Molly, roaring with laughter. Mary Rose, unable to contain herself any longer, soon followed. Even Conway, despite not wishing to give any offence, could only stifle his amusement to a maniacal tittering.

'Jaysus, ye're all very funny, so ye are.' Maisie said with some resentment, 'Is it makin' a feck of me ye are?'

'We shouldn't laugh...the misfortune...' Molly managed to say when she caught her breath, but this attempt at self-restraint only served to send herself and Mary Rose into further hysterics.

Seeing the funny side, even Maisie herself was soon infected with the giggles. Taking off her glasses to dry tears of laughter, she said, 'in respects to ye, I nearly peed meself with laughin', I did...'

'Oh, Maisie, you do come out with the quarest,' Molly pronounced, 'for all your time in Engaland, you're innocent out, so you are.'

When the laughing subsided, Maisie turned to Mary Rose and asked, 'How's your mother?'

'Ah, she's fine, grand. She was asking for ye both....'

'Any sign of that brother of yours making a move?' Molly inquired with a grin.

'Nucky? Nah. He was with that one from Kileely all right, for a while.'

Molly felt obliged to censure. 'Mary Rose,' she said, 'that *one*, has a name and a handle that goes with it, I'm sure.'

'Margie or Marjory,' said Mary Rose, 'I remember 'cause Mikey used to call her Margarine.'

'Don't mind that little fecker,' said Molly, 'he's always calling names. Do you know what he calls me? Molly the Golly!'

Mary Rose laughed, 'I know,' she said, 'I checks him over it but it only makes him worse,' then she added, 'oh, Molly, Tubbs came out with a good one the other day. I can say the Angelus, says he. Can you, says I. I can, says he. Go on so, says I, and do you know what he comes out with?'

'What?' Molly and Maisie said in eager unison.

'Bong! Bong! Bong!' Mary Rose said, laughing, 'Delighted with himself, he was. He has himself persuaded that he knows the Angelus off by heart.'

After some fond laughter, her aunts took it in turn to indulge Tubbs' innocence.

'Ah, shur gawhelpus, he's only a child,'

'The misfortune,'

'The cratur, gawblesshim,'

'The poor mite,' said Molly, 'you must bring him in the next time you're coming.'

'Ah do,' said Maisie, 'I haven't seen him in ages.'

'Maisie wants to try out a jumper she's knittin' for him,' Molly added.

'I do,' confirmed Maisie.

'I remember Nucky when he was Tubbs' age,' Molly said, reminiscing, 'oh, he was a mad hatter. I always remember that time with the cuckoo clock. I caught him at it one day. There he was, the little fecker, waiting with a brush in his hands for the poor, misfortunate bird to come out and go *cuckoo*, so he could down him with the sweeping brush. Oh, but he wasn't satisfied for the cuckoo to be comin' out only every half-hour. No! The clever little fecker copped on to the fact that he could control the misfortunate bird's comings and goings by movin' the hands of the clock with the brush handle. After that, the cuckoo didn't stand a chance and his days were numbered. And as for the clock, he had it in bits by the time he was finished...'

Maisie laughed, Conway laughed, and though Mary Rose had heard it many times before, she still laughed at the image it conjured up.

'What age was he?' Maisie asked.

'He was only four years of age,' said Molly, shaking her head, 'the thoughts of it, you know.'

'And he only four years old,' repeated Maisie to herself, her whole face animated by her amusement.

'I never got up to mischief like that,' Mary Rose declared impishly, 'I was a very quiet child.'

'Is it coddin' me you are,' said Molly, her voice awash with incredulity, 'you were a demon. The two of ye were every bit as bad as each other, and ye were always fightin', like cat and dog ye were.' Then, mimicking their sibling rivalry, Molly's voice took on a whinging wail, 'he got moreder than me, and she got moreder than me...'

Mary Rose, finding this seemingly unflattering disclosure extremely funny, began giggling as Molly continued, 'you'd nearly have to cut everything down the middle with a fecken micrascope and a fecken blade so as not to have ye roarin', pullin' and draggin' out of each other. Will you go 'way, ye were always up to divilment, the pair of ye, yourself and Nucky. And your poor mother was always givin' out about the bad example ye were settin' the younger ones.'

Looking to Maisie for confirmation, she asked, 'Isn't that right, Maisie?'

Maisie simply smiled a knowing smile and nodded.

'I wasn't that bad, was I?' Mary Rose asked, rather lamely.

'No, you were a saint,' Molly said with glaring irony, 'a street angel and a house devil. Yes, you were, don't mind givin' me that look.' Then smiling fondly, she added, 'you weren't the worst, you could be very good when you wanted

252

to and for all that, yourself and Nucky were very united all the same, and if anyone tried to blaggard ye or get between ye in any way, ye'd always stick up for each other.'

Turning to Conway, she stated with obvious affection, 'A right gillygooley she was, Edward, when she was small, and such a temper, oh my god, she'd stand out for you she would. Not a word of a lie...'

Chapter Twenty-four

'Do the wan wid the dolly,' said Tubbs.

Mary Rose picked a dandelion and held it in her fist, then singing, *Molly had a dolly and off popped its head*, she sent the yellow dandelion head tumbling through the air with a flick of her thumb.

Tubbs, looking at the headless stem left in her hand, squealed with delight.

'Do again...' he urged, so Mary Rose grabbed another dandelion and performed her little trick for him once more. Tubbs was ecstatic.

'Do again...' he pleaded, this time picking his very own and handing it to her, 'this wan...'

With weary patience, Mary Rose said, 'D'ya see you, you should be called Tubbs Doagain, not Tubbs Mac. Do you know that!'

Sure of her indulgence, Tubbs shouted, 'Do again...' and beamed expectantly.

'All right, all right, but for the last time, mind,' she said and then sang with a tired extravagance that signalled a finale, *Molly had a dolly and...off popped its head...*

After all his giggling had stopped, Tubbs asked, quite seriously, 'Do Molly have a dolly?'

Mary Rose gave him a withering look.

'No,' she said, her words coming with a pronounced sigh, 'that was a different Molly. I told you before,' then looking at Conway, she added, 'he'll have me demented before he's finished.'

Conway smiled, took on the air of an erudite herbalist and duly commented, '...interesting plant, the dandelion, apparently gets its common name from the shape of its leaves, *dent de lion* which is French for...'

'Lion's tooth,' said Mary Rose, with raised eyebrows and fixed grin.

Like an indulgent tutor Conway said, 'Yes, that's right.'

'Also known as *pissy beds*,' she went on, with a mocking haughtiness, 'or, as the French say, *pis-en-lit*. Apparently, it does act as a diuretic.' Then ruffling Tubbs' hair, she added perkily, 'Tubbs will be peeing in his bed tonight...'

Suddenly the child was looking very worried, 'I won't,' he said with a sullen pout, frowning at Mary Rose from under his eyebrows.

'I'm only jokin' you, love,' she said, grabbing him to her and giving him a hug. Then, to humour him further, she picked a nearby buttercup, 'let's see if you likes the butter,' she said, holding the buttercup under his chin, 'oh, you likes the butter, so you do.'

'And jam,' Tubbs informed her.

Conway couldn't help but laugh at the grave expression on Tubbs' face.

'Let's see if Edward likes the butter, will we?' Mary Rose suggested and Tubbs gave an enthusiastic yell of 'Yeaaah!'

'How does this work?' Conway asked, tilting his head back to take the test.

'I simply put the buttercup under your chin, like so,' she said, placing the flower beneath his chin, 'and if your skin reflects yellow,' she went on, speaking in a tone of voice more often used by Montessori teachers, 'then that means you likes the butter.'

'Very scientific,' said Conway dryly, 'what's the verdict?'

'Yes, you're a butter nutter, so you are,' she pronounced solemnly. Tubbs, who thought the whole thing great fun, clapped his fat little hands together in delight and drooled in his laughter, his baby teeth gleaming like pearly grains of rice. Cupping his face in her hand, Mary Rose took a tissue from her pocket, saying, 'Show me ya,' and after a token resistance she managed to wipe his chin.

The sky had the blue wash of faded denim and was perfectly clear except for a few scattered islands of white cloud that drifted by. Tempered by the river-scented breeze, the bright sunshine imparted a mildness to the air. Conway, overdressed as usual, had unbuttoned his overcoat, allowing it to hang open. And he wore his wellies, as usual, as did Tubbs, who was decked out in terracotta dungarees and a yellow T-shirt that had a bewildered-looking E.T. peeking over his bib front.

Conway was informed by Tubbs that his little blue wellies were his 'Pope's rushers'. Bought specially, as Mary Rose explained, because the huge gathering of the faithful and the curious who turned out for Pope John Paul II's visit to Ireland had to be accommodated at the Limerick Racecourse where the 'going' was very soft indeed after some very persistent rain. They had originally been bought for Mikey, but Tubbs was now convinced they had belonged to no less a personage than the Pope himself.

Mary Rose, in comparison, taking full advantage of the weather to cast off as much clothes as possible and get some decent exposure, wore a navy short-sleeved blouse gathered up in front and tied in a knot to display her midriff. White, figure-hugging trousers, buttoned below the knee, showed off shapely calves that ran to open-toed sandals where lilac painted toenails, colour co-ordinated with her fingernails, peeped out.

Around her neck was a string of amber beads and on her slim wrists she wore brightly coloured bangles and a yin and yang watch that had hands but no dial markings. With the finishing touch of sunglasses pushed fashionably up into her blonde hair, she had about her the look of a pirate, and a movie star.

Now beyond the curve of the bank that marked the beginning of the Abbey River, they continued on their walk with the all the whimsical fits and starts that the child took a fancy to. At one stage Tubbs took it into his head to walk in the opposite direction to where they were going. But as soon as they followed him, he would turn about-face and insist on heading in the other direction. It was as if he was testing the magic of choice, along with their patience. But Mary Rose soon cured him of this.

'All right,' she said, 'if you don't want to go where we're going, we'll go home so. If you want to. How does that sound?'

Not taking kindly to the proposal that was laid before him, his little experiment with the exercise of free will, and the manipulation of possibilities, was quickly shelved.

The attention of all three was pleasantly diverted when a rowing boat with a four-man crew came coasting down the river. Set low in the water, and looking for all the world like a giant pond skater, it approached at speed. They listened to the roll and swish of the oars as the blades dipped in and out of water. A man on a bicycle, apparently following the boat's progress and monitoring the performance of the crew from the embankment, shouted occasional words of correction or encouragement.

'Grand day,' said he, as he approached, then casting his attention back to the boat again, he hollered, 'keep your line ...steady...straight...'

With smooth impulsion the boat raced over the surface and quickly passed, sending waves swelling gently to either bank and setting the reeds to nod as if in appreciation of its speed and grace.

In follow-the-leader fashion, a string of horses, on the move to pastures new, came ambling along the bank. As they approached, Mary Rose, Conway and Tubbs stepped onto the raised pathway to allow them to pass unhindered. And as they passed quietly in single file, Tubbs began clapping his hands and yelling, 'giddy up, giddy up...' which had the effect of sending them into a canter with arching necks and swishing tails.

'I'll kill you for doing that, so I will,' said Mary Rose, showing her disapproval. Enthralled by the reaction of the horses, Tubbs took no more notice of her censure than the man in the moon.

In the wake of this 'stampede incident' came a young girl with copper-coloured hair, pushing a baby buggy. Initiating a conversation from a distance of some twenty yards away, she called out cheerily, 'Hi, Mary Rose, you're all out in your pedal pushers. And hallo, Tubbs, how are you?'

The child lowered his head shyly and Mary Rose shouted back, 'Don't mind him, Josephine, he's as odd as two left shoes today. How's the baby?'

Making a face, the girl said, 'A fear of her, all she wants is her bottle. She's just after finishin' one, bawlin' for more she was. I had to stick the dummy in her gob to shut her up...'

As they drew nearer, the children stared at each other as children often do, each curious of the other and instinctively recognizing the common bond of size and eye-level.

'Ah, she's a dote, so she is,' said Mary Rose.

The chubby-faced baby sucked on her soother, her blue eyes, like saucers, taking everything in.

'Oh, she's an angel,' the girl answered without conviction as she pushed the buggy along, 'look, she knows we're talkin' about her. Then, after a cursory glance at Conway, she added briskly, 'I'd better get her home, she's due for a change. Talk to you later...'

After they had passed on, Conway asked, 'Pedal pushers? What did she mean by that?'

'My trousers, that's what they call them, pedal pushers. Haven't you ever heard of them before?'

'No.'

'Well, you learn something new every day...' she said philosophically and laughed.

'Pedal pushers,' Conway repeated to himself as if he still harboured doubts about the term.

Through the sally trees, he caught the bright blue flash of a kingfisher flying downriver. Sand martins, in their brown and white livery, were sweeping the river just inches above the water's surface. As he watched them in their hectic endeavours, he heard the faint puttering sounds of a light aircraft coming out of the Clare Hills behind him. It drew nearer, its single prop engine getting progressively louder.

'Look, Tubbs! An aeroplane!' Conway exclaimed.

The child craned his neck and squinted into the sky, and as it flew almost directly overhead, he shouted excitedly, 'I sees it! I sees it!'

'Wow,' said Mary Rose, shielding her eyes.

'Something else, isn't it?' said Conway, shielding his.

Staring in open-mouthed awe, as the plane banked away to the left and droned off into the distance, Tubbs asked, 'Where's he goin' to?'

'Down to the shops to get milk for his mother,' Mary Rose informed him.

'He isn't...' Tubbs said doubtfully.

'He is, I tell you,' insisted Mary Rose, laughing, and then, for reasons known only to herself, she began to recite, 'Hi diddle diddle, the cow and fiddle, the cat jumped over the spoon...'

'No, he dident,' said Tubbs, outraged, 'the cow jumped over, the, the...moon...'

But his sister continued, regardless, 'and the little dish laughed to see such fun...'

'No, he dident, that's wrong...' said Tubbs, going red in the face and fuming with frustration.

'And the dog ran away with the moon...'

'No, he dident,' he protested, now in a complete tizzy, '...tell her, Edwoord.'

'You say it so, you're so smart,' Mary Rose challenged.

Taking in a big breath, he began, 'Hi diggle diggle, the cat and the figgle, the cow jumped over the moon, the licle dog laughed to see such fun, and the, and the...'

'...dish,' prompted Mary Rose.

'...dish, ran away with the spoon...finished.'

Mary Rose clapped her hands and shouted, 'Hooray! Well done, that's very good. You're the best in the west, the bee's knees, so you are. Isn't he, Edward?'

'Oh, the finest, the finest,' said Conway, applauding.

Despite going all shy, Tubbs could not disguise that he was delighted with himself.

In a whisper, Mary Rose told Conway, 'He's a howl. Oh, he gets very bad. I shouldn't tease him.'

'Let me take a picture of the two of you,' Conway said, extricating a camera from his coat.

'Do you want to have your phosha taken?' Mary Rose asked Tubbs.

He smiled shyly and then nodded his assent. After some fussing and framing with the camera, Conway finally decided to take the picture.

'Say cheese,' said he.

Leaning into Mary Rose and holding onto her knees, Tubbs managed to say 'cheese' without smiling. The camera snapped and automatically wound on.

'Another one,' Conway insisted, 'and this time, a big, big smile, Tubbs.'

Mary Rose crouched low to put her arms around Tubbs, and pulling him closer so their blond heads were touching, she said, 'Say, *whiskey*...'

'Whiskey?' asked Conway, a puzzled look on his face, then said with a shrug, 'Okay, whiskey it is.'

Together, Mary Rose and Tubbs put their hearts into a big 'whiskeeeeeeeey...'

The camera snapped again. 'That's a good one,' Conway announced, then declared, 'now that *was* a whiskey with an e, Irish whiskey. Did you know that Scottish whisky, Scotch, doesn't have an e?'

'Any what?'

'Any e,' Conway stressed, then clarified, 'it doesn't have

the letter e in the word *whisky*, whereas Irish whiskey does.'

Mary Rose pulled a face. 'How fascinating,' she said, then suggested, 'let me take a picture of you and Tubbs together.' And so she did, and following that she persuaded Tubbs, with little difficulty, to take a picture of herself and Conway. After a few false starts, and wasted exposures, they managed to get him to aim the camera in their general direction and at the same time press the shutter button.

Coming to a bench by an old lime tree, they decided to rest and take in the scenery. Agitated by their presence, a highly strung moorhen, with bobbing head and twitching tail, made a right commotion as it sought the sanctuary of the reeds. At the will of restive breezes from the river, the leaves of willow, alder and lime dappled the undergrowth with emeralds of light and shade.

'Isn't it beautiful?' Mary Rose said, arching her back and stretching out her arms.

'Beautiful...' Conway agreed.

'Swing me up in the air, jump me over the wall,' said Tubbs, offering up his fingers.

'D'ya see you, d'ya, you can't sit still for two minutes,' Mary Rose chided, then relenting, she said, 'come on so...'

Each taking hold of a hand, Mary Rose and Conway, after the customary 'one-two-three and ups-a-daisy', swung the child over the low retaining wall that marked the divide between the raised footpath and the lower bridle path. After many 'do agains' from Tubbs, they jumped him back and forth until they finally wore out his enthusiasm.

As they walked in the cooling shade of chestnut trees, Conway imagined warm summer days of long ago when the citizenry of a bygone Limerick, dressed in the fashion of the day, would promenade along this very same walkway. He could see them now with their parasols and bonnets, top hats and cravats and for a moment he was almost convinced he was hearing the ghostly sounds of coach and horses going by. He quickly dismissed it as one of the 'little episodes' he had suffered since his recent illness. These temporal shifts,

261

he assured himself, were merely the echoes of his outlandish dreams. Nothing more.

At a gap in the brambles that covered the slope facing the marsh, they came upon a pool of water. Here, a concrete bulwark enclosed a sluice gate built to accommodate water flow between river and marsh. Fed by dykes that ran parallel and at right angles to the bank, it was a small pool, not much bigger than a double bed and only a few feet deep. Though tidal, it was an oasis of calm, protected from buffeting winds by the high bank and the screen of lush vegetation that encircled it.

Carefully, they made their way down the slope to the pool, Mary Rose keeping a firm hold on Tubbs who had a tendency to race ahead.

'We always come here,' she said, 'he loves the water, you have to watch him though, 'cause he'd nearly dive in he would, head first...'

'We al'ays come here,' Tubbs repeated proudly.

Going right to the edge of the pool, Conway settled on the concrete surround that made for very convenient seating. Tubbs was determined to follow Conway's example, which Mary Rose allowed but insisted, much to Tubbs' annoyance, on keeping a firm grip on his dungarees as his feet dangled over the edge.

'Lemme go,' he whinged, struggling to shake her off.

'No,' she said firmly, 'now you either sit there and let me hold you or you can go right back home.'

Realising he wasn't going to get his way he gave up his struggle and turned his attention to the water.

'Look,' he said excitedly, 'whirlypools!'

The incoming water, flowing through the iron grating, set up tiny whirlpools that formed, disappeared and reformed again at random. Taking a leaf offered to him by Mary Rose, Tubbs dropped it in the water and waited. For a time the leaf floated placidly along but was soon caught in one of the miniature maelstroms where it was spun around in a swirling cone and dragged below the surface, only for it to pop up again elsewhere. Tubbs clapped his hands and squealed his appreciation.

'More,' he said to Mary Rose.

'What do we say, when we ask for something?'

'Please,'

'That's better,' Mary Rose said, and continued to supply him with blades of grass, bits of twigs and anything else that would float.

At the pool's edge, and along the dykes, there was a profusion of plants, from the tall and stately reedmace, to free-floating mats of tiny duckweed. There was watercress, purple-flowered bogbean, water plantain, milfoil, forget-me-nots, yellow flag and the primordial beauty of the non-flowering horsetails. And, like a bejewelled centrepiece, a single white water lily with its large oval leaves resting on the surface.

The place teemed with life. Midges, in haphazard flight. Hoverflies, like technical draughtsmen, carving geometric flight patterns in the air. Patrolling pond skaters, their feet dimpled in surface tension. Whirligigs, circling and spinning like crazy dodgems.

Eavesdropping on the drowsy hum of a bumblebee as it rummaged in a yellow flag for nectar and pollen, Conway gazed at the limpid water, and looking down through it, as his eyes adjusted to the reflected sunlight, he could see pebbles materializing on the silted bottom. Like precious stones they were, made smooth and lustrous by the pool's enchantment. He lowered a hand to scoop some water and felt its chill. As he let the crystal beads trickle through his fingers, the mass bell for twelve o'clock rang out. He listened as the sombre drift came sweeping over the marsh. From an anthology of school memory, he could hear a Welsh voice, saying softly, '...and the sabbath rang slowly in the pebbles of the holy streams...'

Tubbs plopped a stone into the water and the spell was broken. The ephemeral words played across the surface of the pool and, fanning out on the ripples, disappeared into

263

the reeds. Tubbs set about his new diversion with gusto, gathering up pebbles and stones and throwing them into the water to send ripples radiating into ripples.

Sure of his safety, now that he had taken himself off to the shallow end and away from the steep-sided bulwark, Mary Rose brought her sunglasses down over her eyes and lay back on the grassy slope of the bank with hands behind her head. Conway, withdrawing from his perch, decided to join her.

Before them lay the marsh, acres and acres of yellow irises in all their glory, interrupted only by the narrow dykes where sedge and reed prevailed. The display ran from the riverbank to the housing estates of Stella Maris Park, and Sarsfield Park in the distance. Against the ancient backdrop of King John's Castle and the spires of St Mary's Cathedral, it created a wonderful panorama under the mid-June sky.

Imperceptibly, they were joined by swifts, scything the air about them in great curves as they trawled for insects. At times so near, they could hear the whispered sweep of their wings.

'Look, Tubbs! Swifts!' Conway called out.

'Wow!' said Tubbs, 'will I hit wan wid a stone?'

'Don't you dare!' Mary Rose warned.

Stretched out beside her, Conway said, marvelling at the aerial display, 'Isn't it amazing? To think that these creatures have remained on the wing for the best part of a year, and in some cases, two years, and not once, not once, touched down to land. So aerial are they, they would build their nests in the air, if they could. Most of their life is spent in the air, feeding and sleeping on the wing, only coming to earth to nest and raise their young, even their nest material is plucked from the air...'

'They sleep in the air?' Mary Rose said doubtfully.

'Yes, strange as it sounds, they do sleep in the air. From the moment they are fledged, the moment they leave the nest, they will stay in the air and not land, or rest, on anything solid for at least two years.'

'That's incredible,' she said in response, 'they *actually* sleep in the air?'

'Apparently, they catnap. They climb high into the sky, several thousand feet or so, and circle about and catnap.'

'Astonishing, that's astonishing,' she repeated wistfully.

On gossamer wings, a blue damselfly fluttered into view, hovered in reconnaissance above the pool for a moment or two, then swooped away over the marsh.

Chewing on a grass shoot, Mary Rose casually remarked, 'It's lovely here in the winter, like a lake, with swans and everything, it's so beautiful. I remember, sometimes when it was frozen over, we could walk right across to the bank here, the ice would be this thick,' she said, holding her thumb and forefinger inches apart, 'deep too, the water was, and if we heard the ice crack under us, we'd all shout 'scatter' and we'd spread out as quick as we could. Mad we were...'

As Conway's eyes tracked a pair of mallards flying rapidly overhead, he recited dreamily, *...what would the world be, once bereft, of wet and of wildness...let them be left, let them be left, wildness and wet...long live the weeds and the wilderness yet...*

'Hopkins,' Mary Rose responded.

'Yes,'

'We did him for the Leaving,' she said, then looking away to her left, she added, 'Tubbs, be careful.'

'I'm only playin', that's all...' Tubbs proclaimed.

'Don't go too near the water, shur you won't?'

'I won't, I'll be careful,' he said, letting fly another stone.

'Listen,' whispered Conway, pointing to a bird that was swaying on a reed some way off, 'it's a stonechat, listen to it, it sounds like it's gargling marbles, that's what they sound like...'

She leaned in closer to see where he was pointing, and pushing back her sunglasses, said, quietly captivated, 'Oh, I see it now...'

He loved everything about her. Her apple-scented hair that the sunlight had cast in a golden halo. Her perfume, the 4711 that Molly had given her as a present. She had made it her own. Her eyes, her eyelids, her eyelashes, her eyebrows, her eye-shadow, her nearness, her breath, her lips. She was an enchantment and he was powerless to resist. As he was about to surrender and kiss her cheek, she said, suddenly and emphatically, 'Dobbers!'

'Dobbers?' Conway repeated, somewhat confused.

When Mary Rose spoke again, her voice was filled with nostalgia. 'Yeah, dobbers, we'd never call them *marbles*. We always called them *dobbers*. I'd hold them up to the sunlight and all the coloured wispy bits would seem like wonderful galaxies that tapered at both ends. For ages I would look at them, eye to eye with some far away and mysterious world. The things you do as a kid. An old dobber was best because the pitted surface would add to the magic. It was...a window on the universe. A twoer, you know, the large marble, was even better. That was a treat...'

Fumbling through his coat pockets, Conway retrieved a notebook and a stub of a pencil, and began to write.

'Dobbers...' he muttered to himself, 'how do you spell that? Dobbers?'

Mary Rose cast frowning eyes at him and asked, 'What's with the notebook?'

'Just jotting down some notes...'

'Notes?'

'Oh, just the expressions you use. You know, phrases, sayings, you know. The strange thing is,' Conway went on, 'there seems to be quite a variance in speech patterns, even within Limerick itself.'

'Really, is that so?' Mary Rose responded defensively, 'well, I'd never use the words *marsh* or *meadow* in everyday speech. They're middle-class words. Like *marbles*. And if I did, they wouldn't sound right in my mouth, being working class, you understand. We would rarely, if ever, use them...'

'Then, what would you use instead of *marsh*?'

'I dunno, maybe *the field, the leeks,* or maybe *the swamp*...'

'Technically,' Conway said, 'a swamp should have trees.'

'Really?' Mary Rose answered bleakly.

They both looked out on the marsh. There were no trees to speak of, apart from a few pioneering willows that were sparsely scattered.

'So you wouldn't use the word *meadow?*' he continued.

'No,' she said, then, grabbing hold of the notebook, she added playfully, 'give it here to me, let's see what you've been scribbling.'

She read some, squinting to decipher the notes, flicked through some pages, then read some more. The more she read, the more she frowned and it was very soon obvious to Conway that she was not a bit pleased.

'What's wrong?' he felt obliged to inquire.

She threw him an awkward look, took in a bolstering breath and read, *...it is a curious thing but I observed that if one individual swore it would set the others off, the swear words being reciprocated, one expletive borrowing another, as it were. It is interesting to note that this mirroring of vocal language was often accompanied by mirrored body language...*

'And this,' she continued, her eyes wide with disapproval, *...go on, sham, la, you're sly. Stall on, sham, willa. 'willa' is apparently a shortened version of 'will you' and may be shortened even further still to 'la'. 'Stall on', apparently, is a commonly used directive, meaning 'to wait up'.*

'And this,' she went on, *...I will in my aah, ass, arse, backside, behind, daisy, eye, barny. These expressions of disgust or dissatisfaction, incorporating various parts of the anatomy, along with euphemistic alternatives, are often employed, and, as can be seen, there is a curious obsession with the posterior region, a universal predilection, apparently. Indeed, more vulgar expletives such as...*

Mary Rose paused, 'I won't even repeat those,' she said, before skipping on, *...are used to impart vehemence and strength of feeling, the phrase itself being an ironic affirmative, meaning the exact opposite of what it seems to be expressing i.e. an unwillingness to fulfil a request or demand...*

'Why are you offended?' Conway asked with concern.

'Why! Why! You don't get it, do you? That's you, all out. It's like, it's like, you were some kind of anthropologist or something, studying some primitive tribe in Borneo, or some place. It's offensive, that's what it is.'

'It's purely an academic exercise, that's all. I mean, that's the way people speak. It's the same all over Ireland, with regional variations, of course. To pretend otherwise is to ignore a large part of our cultural heritage...'

'Are you for real?' she interrupted, throwing him a side-glance that questioned his sanity.

'Some people,' he said, a tad defensively, 'are interested in language and the way it is used. A language that's alive is always evolving, and that's fascinating. Don't you think?'

A doubtful expression played across her face. 'You think so? Fascinating? Well, I'm not so sure.'

Taking the notebook from her, he leafed through its pages and finding what he thought was a mitigating entry, he read, ...*the language is robust, earthy, has a unselfconscious fluency to it, rarely is offence intended and rarely is it taken, there is much playful exaggeration, bluff and counterbluff, and ritualized confrontation that seldom, if ever, comes to blows...tension and aggression are dissolved by a language that's expressive and accommodating...*

Coming across another *positive* pronouncement, he went on, ...*colloquial speech is the true, natural habitat for words, the dictionary is merely a zoo...*

In response to her silence, he explained, 'I'm thinking of compiling a book, you see, *The Vulgar Language of Ireland*. Vulgar, both in the vernacular and the classical sense, you understand. It's a play on words, kind of a pun.'

'I do know what a pun is,' she responded, giving him a withering look, 'just because we don't all talk posh like you, doesn't mean we're thick, you know, and you are always correcting people. Why don't you try and live a little, split an infinitive, maybe, mix a few metaphors, or go mad altogether and have after dinner mints for breakfast...'

With disdain in her eyes, she went on, 'Maybe you could call your little book, *Conway's Concise Vulgar Vocabulary*, and as a subtitle maybe you could have,' she paused, then added derisively, '*An In-depth Effing Study*...'

'Very droll,' said Conway impassively.

Lying back on the grass, Mary Rose coolly brought her sunglasses down over her eyes. 'I have had elocution lessons, you know,' she said quietly, 'so I could speak in a *proper and correct manner*, like instead of me saying, *tree tousand, tree hundord and turty tree*, I could say, *thhhree thhhousand, thhhree hundred and thhhirty thhhree*, you know, the la-di-dah way of saying it with the *th's* all over the place. And then, of course, we had to pronounce our *ings*, no more *walkin'* or *singin'* or *dancin'* for me, it was *walk-ing* and *sing-ing* and *danc-ing* from then on.'

With a scornful laugh, she added, 'The nun who taught elocution at our school, Sister Projectyourvoice, would have a tape recorder in front of us. We'd have to talk into it and then she'd play it back so we could hear the way we talked. It was like we spoke a foreign language.'

Turning to Conway, and through the inquisition of dark glasses, she said shrewdly, 'Do you ever swear?'

Conway raised his eyebrows and shrugged.

'No?' she queried.

He shook his head.

'Never?'

'I may have said *feck*, on occasion.'

She lowered her voice so Tubbs would not overhear.

'For fuck's sake,' Mary Rose said as Conway cringed, 'for someone who doesn't use swear words, you have no trouble writing them down. Do you?'

After some huffish reflection, she said more agreeably, 'Tubbs came out full with it the other day, right in front of Mam he said it. I nearly died. The lads had put him up to it. You know the way they teach kids the alphabet these days, house begins with Hairy Hat Man, sleepy begins with Sammy Snake and *fuck*, says he, innocent out, begins with Fireman Fred. Mam nearly had a canary over it.'

Putting a hand to her mouth, she laughed, then said, sensually mobilizing her lips, 'Come on, fuck begins with Fireman Fred. It's easy. Stick your lower lip up behind your two front teeth and make the *f* sound, followed by the *uck* sound, couldn't be easier.'

After much coaxing and cajoling, Conway made several attempts, but, his nature getting the better of him each time, he could not bring himself to do it.

Mary Rose squealed with laughter, and tugging on his coat sleeve she informed him, 'You're an awful fecken eejit, do you know that? There's no harm in it, you know. It's only a word, only wind, you wouldn't want to be taking it so seriously. I mean, my mother says she'll down me with a brush or she'll have my guts for garters but she never does, at least not yet. It's all exaggeration, so it is. You said as much yourself, in your *little* notebook...'

'You used the soldier's word,' said Tubbs accusingly, 'I'm tellin' Mamma on you for cursin'...'

'Do and I'll kill ya, anyway I wasn't cursin', I said *bucket*, okay, tell-tale. I thought you were throwin' stones into the water?'

'I fired dem all away. I haven't no more stones left.'

'Look! There's loads of them there, you can fling away to your heart's content.'

'Oh yeah,' said Tubbs, thrilled at the discovery of a new supply, 'loads a dem,' he muttered to himself as he gathered up more stones.

'Round the rugged rocks, the ragged rascal ran...' Mary Rose chanted softly to herself. Then, reaching down to her right, she picked a small oval-shaped leaf and began to chew on it.

'Sour Sally,' she said, pre-empting Conway's curiosity.

'Sour Sally?'

'Sour Sally,' Mary Rose repeated adamantly, 'that's what we call it. It's sorrel, actually, got lots of vitamin C. Want some?'

Conway took the leaf and tentatively chewed, 'God! It is bitter,' he said, as his face crumpled like a prune.

'The French use it in salads,' Mary Rose explained, after her amusement, 'you wouldn't want to overdo it though, because it does contain oxalic acid, which wouldn't do you any good. Do you know how it got its sour taste?'

Conway's blank expression called for elucidation.

'Because frogs piss on it,' she laughed, then said, 'we used to believe that, when we were kids. I suppose it was said to put us off chancin' anything that might be poisonous. Mikey got sick, once, after eatin' something dodgy down the swamp here, or should I say, the *marsh*, and ended up in the Fever Hospital. Bobsy gave some of his toy soldiers for him to play with and he was ragin' because he never got them back when Mikey came out of the hospital. They were contaminated with the fever, my mother said, though I expect they just kept them for the other misfortunate kids that were in there...'

With a look of disgust on his face, Tubbs yelled out, 'there's all spit over here...'

Going to investigate, Conway took one look at the globs of froth on the grass foliage, and said, 'Oh look, it's cuckoo spit, so it is.'

'Yuck,' said Tubbs, not a bit impressed.

'No, look and I'll show you the little fellow that's inside it, that makes it. Don't be afraid, put out your hand and I'll show him to you.'

'Will he bite me?'

'No, he's a harmless poor thing,' Conway said, removing the froth that was lodged in the angle of the side shoot and the stem, and placing it in Tubbs' cupped hand, '...see him?'

'I sees him, I sees him,' said Tubbs excitedly, 'he's all green! Look, Mary Rose, look...'

Mary Rose, who was already standing and looking over his shoulder, said with interest, 'Oh look, I see him, tiny isn't he. You can see his little eyes, look, starin' out at you. Like full stops they are.'

Looking up at Conway, Tubbs asked, 'What do you call him? Do he have a name?'

'We call him a froghopper, but he's still just a baby,'

'Why do you call him a froghopper?'

'Because when he's bigger, he'll be jumping around just like a frog, only better.'

'Why do he do it? Why do he make that stuff?'

'To protect himself, like making a little tent or a house for himself,' Conway said, then, to Mary Rose, he explained, 'it protects it from predators and from drying out. And since it usually coincides with the arrival of the cuckoo, some people used to think it was the cuckoo that was responsible.'

With a big grin on her face, she said, 'Fascinating. You're a right know-all, aren't you?'

He forced a smile, then said with a frown, 'My uncle, Darragh, informs me that my ignorance is encyclopaedic.'

She laughed. 'Nice one.'

After replacing the froghopper safely in his bubble bath, Tubbs resumed his aquatic experiments and Mary Rose and Conway retired to the grassy slope once more.

'Look, Edward, isn't it beautiful,' Mary Rose exclaimed, pointing to an Orange Tip butterfly that came on the scene, 'doesn't it just gladden your heart, it's so beautiful.'

'It is,' said Conway, as it fluttered off over their heads and over the embankment, 'beautiful...'

After a contemplative silence, she asked, 'What do you want to do with your life?'

'I don't rightly know, yet,' he said, taken aback, 'maybe become, I don't know, a scientist or maybe a teacher, or a solicitor. What do you want to do?'

Brushing away a cranefly that had blundered against her face, she said, as if reading from a list, 'Start my own business. Be my own boss. Travel the world. I want to do lots of things.'

She thought a while before saying, 'Edward, why did you leave the university?'

He sighed dismally and said, with some reluctance, 'I got sick. Someone dropped an acid tab, you know, LSD, in my milk. As a joke. I thought I was losing my mind. I reacted very badly to it. After coming out of the hospital I was sent home.'

Behind her dark glasses, Mary Rose closed her eyes and shook her head in disbelief. Exhaling her indignation, she said, 'That is a terrible thing to do to anyone. A very stupid and dangerous thing to do...'

No sooner had the words left her mouth when the resolute tread of a horse could be heard approaching. They could feel the vibration of every hoof through the ground beneath them. When they looked up they found Gypsy's enormous head hanging over them, jangling his bit as he chewed on it, and on board, grinning from ear to ear, was Nucky.

'God bless all here,' said Nucky jovially.

'Nucky! Gypsy!' Tubbs cried out, dropping his pebbles and making his way to the bank.

Acknowledging the child, Gypsy nodded his head and made a rattle of his bridle. Then, after a few snorts, he adjusted his stance and began tugging away at the short grass.

'How's the soldier?' Nucky asked.

Like a babbling brook, Tubbs responded.

'Mary Rose said the soldier's word an' she were lernin' Edward to say it, an' Edward showed me the froghopper in his house, it was all like a spit but it wouldn't bite you, an', an', an' it jumps up the sky like a aeraplane, an', an' I was firen stones in the water an' I made a big, hugey splash but I diden get soken wet or nahan cos I dident...'

'Blabbermouth,' Mary Rose scolded.

Nucky laughed, 'be cripes, Tubbs, you're havin' a whale of a time, so you are,' then looking at Conway, he said, 'you'd want to be careful, Edward, that one will lead you astray, so she will.'

Shielding his eyes, Conway laughed and said, 'Hi, Nucky.'

Mary Rose made a face and commented, 'There's a fear of him, I'm sure.'

'I suppose, Tubbs,' Nucky said, 'you don't want to ride back with me and Gypsy to see the new baby tweeters?'

'Baby tweeters?' Tubbs yelled, his eyes nearly popping

out of his head, 'yeaaah,' he yelled again as he clambered up onto the bank. Reaching down for him, Nucky hauled him aboard as if he had been a bag of feathers. Seated in front of Nucky, Tubbs hugged Gypsy's neck and whispered, 'Hi, Gypsy, we're goin' to see the baby tweeters.'

'No kiss?' Mary Rose said, 'You're a fine one.'

'But I'm up on the horse now.' Tubbs answered, his eyes wide with obvious justification.

'All right, you can blow me one.'

Tubbs noisily smacked the palm of his little hand with his lips and, like someone desperately trying to fog a mirror, he blew Mary Rose a kiss.

Gathering up the reins, Nucky said, 'By the way, thanks for the present and the card.'

'Don't mention it.' Mary Rose said with a grin.

'You'd want to mind the damp grass, Mary Rose,' Nucky added, with a raised eyebrow.

'Will you stop spoutin', Nucky, I'm not a child. You're like the fecken Sermon on the Mount, so you are, will you go away.'

'Time for us to go, Tubbs, I think,' said Nucky, 'what do we say?'

Taking a deep breath, Tubbs puffed himself up before shouting at the top of his voice, 'Hi ho, Silver, and awaayyh!'

With a deep-throated whinny and a swish of his tail, Gypsy lifted his head and stepped into a leisurely stroll.

Mary Rose waved them off, laughed to herself and then sighed, 'Look at them, two rogues...the biggest pair of rogues you're ever likely to see.'

'What's a tweeter?' Conway inquired.

'Canaries, Nucky always calls them that. The eggs must have just hatched.'

'Is it Nucky's birthday today?' he asked.

'No, tomorrow. June the twentieth.'

'The eve of the summer solstice. The eve of the longest day of the year,' said Conway thoughtfully, then added, with a somewhat troubled look, 'what an amazing coincidence?'

'What is?'

'It's my birthday as well...'

'Go 'way. You serious? What age will you be?'

'Twenty-two.'

Mary Rose just laughed, 'Isn't that strange? Yourself and Nucky were born on the very same day. Ye have the very same birthday. Gemini. Ye're fecken twins, well that's a good one, that is.'

Conway furrowed his brow, 'Yes, it is...'

'I'm a goat,' volunteered Mary Rose.

'Sorry?'

'Capricorn? The Goat? The twenty-second of December. The winter solstice, and the darkest evening of the year...'

'So it is,' he said quietly, then, as if to shift his humour, he added, 'Sermon on the Mount, very good, I'd liked that.' As he watched Nucky, Tubbs and Gypsy heading towards the handball alley, Conway decided to test his own wit.

'There he goes, the cowboy of the western world, off on his steed in search of a few dollars more...'

'God, you're very smart, aren't you,' said Mary Rose with hostility in her voice.

Somewhat bewildered, he asked, 'What's the matter?'

'Well, I'll tell you *what's the matter*,' she said, parodying his question, 'I don't like you talking about my brother like that, so I don't...'

Now crestfallen, he said ruefully, 'It was only a joke.'

'Oh, it's all a joke to you,' she went on, 'I'm glad you can find it funny because I don't. It's easy for you to look down your nose at Nucky but when you were sitting on your arse, reading your books, Nucky had to go out to work.'

His eyes pleading, he said, 'Mary Rose, I never meant...'

But Mary Rose, carried along on her anger, ignored his appeal. 'When we had no one, when my father died, Nucky looked after us. If it wasn't for Nucky I don't know what we would have done. The only reason I was able to go to school, was because of him. But you, of course, wouldn't know anything about that, you're so superior...'

She stopped for a moment, untied the knot of her blouse, then vehemently proceeded to tie it up again. Now standing, with hands on hips, and scowling at him through her dark glasses, she went on in a passion, '...even as a kid he had it tough, I've seen him with those bags of coal and he barely able to lift them, his legs buckling under the weight, when my father was sick, and he only a kid. You were an only child, what would you know? I can see you now, a right mama's boy, in your sailor suit, nothing is good enough for my little Edward, while he went around without an arse to his pants and second-hand shoes and always black with the coal and been kilt at school for being late because he had to feed a horse, or catch a horse, or run a message, and been hauled before the class for being a disgrace to the school. They used to make a right skit of him, they used, comin' to school and he all black with the coal. Do you know what they used to call him? Do you? Nucky the golliwog. What are you gettin' for Christmas, Nucky? A bar of soap?'

Stupefied by her anger, an ashen-faced Conway began to mumble, 'I don't know what to say, I'm sorry, I'm sorry. I didn't mean to...'

But Mary Rose wasn't listening. Pulling on clumps of grass, she hauled herself up the slope of the bank. Conway, tripping on his coat, followed after her.

'Do you know something, Edward,' she said, turning to face him as he walked along the bank behind her, 'you're one condescending, supercilious twit.' Then turning away again and marching off in a huff, she added, 'I think you'd better go home...'

His mind in turmoil, he sat down on the low retaining wall and watched her go. With every step she put between them he felt more lost and desolate. All too soon she had reached the curve of the bank and as she disappeared from view behind the houses of Stella Maris Park, his heart sank. A hooded crow, disdainful of his company, flew from its perch above his head. The breeze coming off the river began to chill and turn contrary, flapping the lapels of his overcoat.

Laying hold of his Concise Oxford Dictionary, he began searching for the word 'supercilious'. Though he had a fair idea of what it meant, he allowed for the possibility that maybe, just maybe, he had overlooked a shade of meaning that might put a different complexion on things. But no, it was just as he expected.

supercilious: *adj. disdainfully superior manner* superciliously *adv.* superciliousness *n.* (Latin *supercilium* eyebrow)

A devil for punishment, he then put himself through the torment of the thesaurus, reading with despair:

arrogant, conceited, condescending, disdainful, haughty, patronizing, pompous, scornful, superior...

Was he really all those things? He looked up in anguish into a powder-blue sky and saw the unravelling vapour trail of a high-flying jet. It appeared as an unwavering speck, silent and remote, like a cupid's dart that had hopelessly missed its mark.

Chapter Twenty-five

Seated in her high-backed armchair, Mrs Conway tilted her head to one side as she inserted the darning needle into the fabric that was stretched over the upturned whiskey glass she held in her lap. Using the bottom of the glass as a platform, she pulled the thread through with practiced ease, teasing the fibres into position with light sweeps of her fingers.

'...a very handsome man, your father,' she said, without looking up from her work, and in the measured voice of one engaged in close concentration, she went on, 'had a fine head of jet-black hair, so he had. Something of the Hispanic about him. He used to joke that his people were descended from some misfortune that had washed up on the beach from the Spanish Armada...'

After replacing the silver-framed portrait of his father on the polished sideboard, Conway asked, 'Mum, where was I born?'

'That's a very odd question to be asking,' she answered, holding the needle poised at its zenith, 'why, Limerick, of course...'

'No, I mean, where exactly was I born?'

Momentarily peering over the rim of her bifocals, she said, 'Well, there is, as it happens, a story to that. I was to have had you in Bedford Row, you know, but the taxi driver, the fool, took me instead to the Regional Maternity in the Ennis Road. By the time I realised what had happened, it was too late, you were on your way, deciding to be born at the most inconvenient and most ungodly hour. So, I ended up in a public ward, didn't I, and not the private one I had paid for and had insisted on. But, of course, there were no private ones available. Oh, it was chaos! Such toing and froing, it's a wonder I didn't come home with the wrong baby. I didn't even have my own gynaecologist, but still had to pay him for the privilege of his absence...'

Though overwhelmed by feelings of despair, Conway's downcast features rallied around an ironic smile. The game was up, there were just too many coincidences to be purely coincidental. A critical mass had been reached and he had to face the truth. So it was true, all the evidence pointed to the same awful conclusion.

He was not Edward Conway at all. He was Nicholas McNamara. He *was* Nucky Mac. No doubt about it. Apart from the myriad implications of such a travesty, the one that cut most deeply into his psyche was the fact that he could never see Mary Rose in the same light again. Not that she'd ever want to look at him again after what happened. But now there seemed no chance of reconciliation. What would be the point? They could never be together. They could never marry. She was his sister, after all.

Facing the inevitable, a numbing resignation descended upon him. In a perverse and irretrievable twist of fate, his life had become a Greek tragedy. A surge of feverish laughter welled up within him and wriggled its way to his throat where he just about managed to suppress it before it could escape and betray him.

A gust of wind sent the net curtains billowing, and the sun, streaming through, cast their dancing patterns on the carpet.

'Shut the window, would you, Edward, please. There's a draught.'

The wind died with the closing of the window and the net curtains, like airy columns, settled back into place. From the hallway the phone rang with a disruptive urgency.

Glad of some distraction, Conway said, 'I'll get it.'

'Thank you, dear...'

Closing the parlour door behind him, he went to the phone and lifted the receiver. 'Hello?' he said briskly.

It was Mary Rose, tentative, sweet, and tender.

'Hi, happy birthday...'

Hearing her voice again, his heart convulsed with pain. 'Hi...' he whispered, closing his eyes.

'How are you?' she asked with concern.

'Fine.'

'I didn't mean to be so mean to you. I'm sorry. I was way out of line...'

'Not to worry, I shouldn't have said what I said...'

'No, no, no,' she protested, 'it was all my fault. I was being stupid. Can we meet? I've got a present for you. Just a little something for your birthday.'

'I don't think that's such a good idea, Mary Rose, I...'

'You're still mad at me. I wouldn't blame you.'

'It isn't that, Mary Rose.'

'Then, what is it? Is there something the matter? Look, Edward, I was annoyed with you, that's all. Okay, I went overboard, way overboard, and I'm sorry. I don't know what got into me, I'm sorry...'

After too long a silence, she inquired, 'Hello? Edward, are you there?'

'Yes, I'm here,' he said, wavering, 'I don't...I don't think we should see each other again.'

With misery in her voice, she asked, 'Are you serious?'

'Yes...'

'So it's goodbye, is it? Is that what you're saying?'

Interpreting his silence as an affirmative, she went on,

'It isn't enough that I love you with all my heart. That doesn't matter to you, does it?'

He hesitated, his voice breaking, as his heart was.

'I do care for you, Mary Rose, I do...'

With pain evident in her voice, she cut in, 'You think you're so clever, so educated, such a gentleman. On your knees pleading your love for me and now, it's not love, but it's you *care for me*. Care? What does that mean? What's next? Don't tell me, let me guess. Indifference? And then amnesia, I suppose. And all your sweet nothings, they were just that, weren't they? Nothings, that's all. You just used me, Edward Conway. What was I, part of your precious research? Well, I hope you're proud of yourself.'

'I'm sorry, Mary Rose, but it's impossible, we can never be together, it just wouldn't work. It wouldn't be fair on our families...'

'Don't you *Mary Rose* me,' she said tetchily, 'and what do you mean, it wouldn't be fair on our families? Is your family going to disown you, or something? Or is it that I'm not good enough for you? Is that it?'

'No, it's nothing like that, it's just that I think I may have been switched at birth. In fact, I know I was...'

'Switched at birth,' she said in disbelief, 'and who, may I ask, were you switched with? A March hare?'

Deciding against disclosure, he faltered, 'I don't rightly know. I don't know who I am.'

'No doubt the fairies are mixed up in all of this. Do you take me for a complete fool, Edward Conway? Of all the excuses, couldn't you come up with a better one than that? Something a little more convincing? It's original, I'll give you that, but if you expect me to swallow it, you must think I'm a complete amadán, altogether. Can't you just come out and say it? At least be a man about it and don't insult my intelligence with such, such bullshit. I never heard such a cock-and-bull story in all my life...'

With unease in her voice, Mrs Conway called from the parlour, 'Who is it, dear?'

'Ahhm, no one, Mum. Just a friend...'

When Mary Rose spoke again her voice was resolute. 'Thank you, Edward, you're a real prince, so you are. You're trying to hurt me at every turn, aren't you? Well, if that's the way you want it, I guess it's goodbye...'

And so saying, she slammed the phone down. With the dial tone ringing in his ears, Conway closed his eyes and sighed in pain.

'Edward?'

'Yes, Mum?'

'Would you ever water the flowers for me, like a good boy. They'll be in need of it with the weather we're having.'

Heartsore, he put down the phone and said distractedly, 'Yes, Mum...'

Chapter Twenty-six

'Go out and tell the rent man, says she to the child, I'll give him the double next week, and how much are you paying now, says I to her, and she told me. That's an awful lot, says I, don't I know, says she, but what can you do, it has to be paid and them fecken water charges are on the way as well. So I says to her, says I, can't you ask for a wafer for the water charges. I'm tired of tellin' her what to do but you might as well be talkin' to the fecken wall...'

Maisie paused a moment, sat back in her armchair, and stared sourly at the pioneering flames of the recently lit fire.

'Well, it'll be a grand fire when it lights,' she muttered to herself, 'as the fox said when he pissed on a stone,' then speaking at the top of her voice for Molly's benefit, she went on, '...and their homes, says she, are like fecken shrines to compensation, you know who I'm talkin' about, says she, and they'd be atin' the statues. They have no scruples, says she, them and their fecken movin' statues. Our Lady of Compensation, that's the statue that's on the move today, says she, they should build a fecken shrine to it. Insurance claim after insurance claim, that's what has the country the way it is, such a country, you know yourself now, says she...'

Molly, returning from the kitchen, rounded on her.

'Give over, Maisie, will you,' she said impatiently, 'you're doing my head in, you've been doing nothan but mouthin' and complainin' since you got up, and give over bothren me with that woman. She'd put years on you, so she would. I haven't time to be listnen to the likes of her and her fecken goings on...'

'I was only tellin' you what the woman said...'

'I couldn't give a fiddler's, Maisie.'

'Ooh, that's just lovely that is, you all out,' said Maisie, directing her eyes to what she felt sure was the corroborating disapproval of Pope Pius IX. Then, as Molly went by her, she asked, 'Where you goin' now?'

'I'm gettin' some asprin for *her*, do you mind?'

'Is she in a bad way?'

'She's in bits...'

'Huh,' said Maisie, crossing her legs and nodding her affirmation, 'I could have told her he'd be off. I could tell by the look of him.'

'Will you just shut it, Maisie, she's upset enough as it is, without you puttin' in your tuppenceworth...'

'There's no need to fly off the handle, I was only sayin', that's all...'

'Aaah, you're always only sayin', give it a rest will you. She's upstairs now, bawlin' her eyes out and if you say as much as one word to her about 'I could have told you so', I'll have your life, so help me I'll swing for you, so I will.'

'I won't open me mouth.'

'Don't!'

'I suppose there's no chance of a cup o' tea?'

'Tell me, when did your last servant die? Do you think I've nothan better to do but wait on you hand and foot, morning, noon and night? I'm like Mag Maney over you.'

Disdainfully, Maisie replied, 'I only asked but if it's too much bother, forget it.'

'I'll make you some tea after. Gimme a chance!'

Mary Rose called down the stairs, her bleak voice echoing in the hallway, 'Where is it, Molly? I can't find it.'

'What's she looking for?' Maisie asked.

'A scarf. Her mother's...' Molly answered in a whisper, then shouted up to Mary Rose, 'It's there in the dresser.'

'Where?'

'On the left-hand side, in the bottom drawer.'

'I can't find it.'

'Over in the corner, under the spare curtains.'

'Where?'

'Oh for goodness sake, I'll have to come up to you!'

'I found it.'

'God bless the mark,' said Molly, as she headed into the hall to climb the stairs.

In jumper, jeans and bobby socks, Mary Rose lay curled up on the bed clutching in her hands a paisley patterned scarf.

'Here, take these, sit up,' Molly said, holding out two tablets and a glass of water to her. With the acquiescence of a child, Mary Rose did as she was told. Without a word she handed the glass back to Molly, then threw herself face down on the bed once more.

Her voice muffled in the floral designs of the duvet, Mary Rose said, 'It's all my own stupid fault, I said some horrible things to him. He'll never forgive me.'

Sitting beside her, Molly said soothingly, 'Com'ere to me.'

Mary Rose nestled in closer and rested her head on Molly's lap. Looking forlornly towards the window, she listened to the pattering rain. 'It's awful quiet,' she said at length.

'There isn't a child on the street,' Molly said, 'they're all gone in outa the rain,' then gathering the wayward strands of Mary Rose's hair and sweeping them from her face, she began to sing, *rain, rain, go away, little Johnny wants to play.* Do you remember that?' she said, softly laughing, 'and do you remember the other one, when you wanted to get out of doing something? Like going to confession, or going to the dentist, *rain, rain, come down in buckets, rain, rain, come down in buckets...*'

Mary Rose smiled a fleeting smile, but her little respite was soon swamped by her misery.

'I always come to you, Molly. Mam doesn't understand.'

'Nonsense, she loves the bones of you, so she does. She's your mother.'

'She doesn't listen to me, and she's always givin' out.'

'Whisht, child, whisht. What am I goin' to do with you at all. I remember the time you ran away from home over some silly little thing that happened at school, with your nightdress stuffed into a Roche's Stores bag. Remember? Your mother was worried sick about you. You were always headstrong, you always had a will of your own, so you had.'

In response to an abject sigh, Molly spoke reassuringly.

'Maybe the boy has his reasons, and maybe it's for the best. You'll get over this, so you will.'

Her eyes glistening, her words drained of emotion, Mary Rose said in a low voice, 'He said he was switched at birth and didn't know who he was...'

'Well, I never heard the like,' said Molly, 'I'm afraid it sounds like an excuse. He hasn't the guts to come out and tell you straight. He mustn't be right in the head to be talkin' like that. You're well shot of him, you'll get over him soon enough.'

'No, Molly, never, never. I'll never get over him...'

'Ah, you only think that,' then, as if to clear up any other doubts in her head, Molly asked, 'You do love him?'

Mary Rose nodded, 'I love him so much...' she whispered and burst into tears again.

'Aaah stop your cryin' now. There's a good girl. Your mascara is all runnin', you look like a sad little panda, so you do. Dry your eyes. Here, blow your nose,' she said, handing her a tissue, 'sure, he's not good enough for you. That's what he's not. It's his loss, my darling.'

'It hurts so much...'

'I know, I know,' Molly said, patting her shoulder.

'He said he loved me, Molly, and I believed him. Why has he changed? Why, Molly?'

'I don't know why, Mary Rose, men are a mystery to me at the best of times. They're just like the weather. You never know what's going on in their heads.'

'What will I do?'

'You'll be all right.'

Then, in a paroxysm of pain, Mary Rose cried out, 'I'll just die, Molly, I'll die...'

'No, you won't die, you silly goose. It will pass, I promise you, it will pass.' Upset at the distress caused to her niece, Molly added peevishly, 'I don't know what you saw in that fella anyway. Look at you, child, you're beautiful, any man worth his salt would be proud to call you his own. You can do much better for yourself. I can't say I ever really liked him, he looks a bit dubious, if you ask me, too shifty about the eyes...'

In a tearful outburst, Mary Rose protested, 'You're being horrible, Molly, don't say that, he's none of those things. How could you say such things, and he's so fond of you...'

Molly looked down at the tear-stained face and sighed, 'Oh dear, this is worse than I thought. I don't know what to do with you, child, so I don't...'

After her passion had subsided, Mary Rose spoke softly, gathering the scarf to her face, 'I can still smell her perfume, Molly. Is it possible? After all these years?'

'Yes,' said Molly, as tears welled up in her eyes, 'it's her perfume.'

Chapter Twenty-seven

It was surprising how high off the water the railway bridge really was. Through gaps in the boards he could see the river below and the flashing glimpses of its surface made him light-headed. He imagined, for a moment, that he walked over some menacing abyss where strange creatures lurked.

There were no sleepers on the bridge, the track being laid inside iron girders that ran its length. It was reinforced at regular intervals by broad crossbeams supported on the four mammoth pillars that filed across the river. Cautiously, he made his way down the centre of the track, walking on old weathered boards that were bound together by iron bands. Some of the securing bolts had popped, making the boards loose so that they sagged and twisted under his weight. Up ahead, the parallel lines of quicksilver, having negotiated the river crossing, curved away to the left past the signal pole and were lost in the trees on the other side.

As he moved through the trellised structure, he became more and more aware of his trespass. Fitful gusts of wind seemed to intimate as much, rudely buffeting him as if taking offence at the intrusion. Faint smells of creosote and oil, coming from the cracked and splintered boards beneath his feet, compounded his misgivings. This bleak and austere creation, with patches of rust showing through its grey, flaking paint, seemed built for a race apart. It was no place for puny souls or mere mortals. Even the rivets that held the massive framework together appeared like giant Braille. It was out of bounds and unwelcoming. But graffiti, it seems, knows no bounds, for there it was, scrawled, inscribed and painted across the iron superstructure. The alfresco artists had struck again, displaying their daring, their doodles and their monikers.

There was Angelo, Buckets, Balla, Elbows and Yonker, Feeney, Inglenook, Sunlight, Hackney, Elder, Rab, Munchin, Eeler and Napoleon. And, as if these weren't exotic enough, there were six unhappy souls, called *The Ghastly Crew* and their names were Bite and Scratch and Pinch, and Howl and Shriek and Boo.

Conway was left bewildered as to why, and how on earth, these 'names' had got there. But what particularly caught his eye was the vivid illustration of three crouching monkeys of the see, hear and speak no evil variety. Above this, in the recess of a girder at least ten feet above the track, impeccably scripted in large letters, was the bald declaration of *Gilgul Was Here*. Again, a most improbable place and difficult to get at. The strange thing was, there was not a single mention of Kilroy or any indication as to his whereabouts.

On reaching the middle section of the bridge he stopped to take his bearings. To the north he could see the bend of the river as it swept around to St Thomas's Island. With the wind in his face he looked south-westwards along the grand expanse of the Shannon waterway. Ahead lay the shoulder of the Island, leaning into the great river as if trying to push it aside. Off to the left, almost hidden from view behind the tree-shrouded grove of the Salmon Weir bank, he could see the narrow mouth of the Abbey River signposted by a water level marker that looked for all the world like a giant cherry lollipop.

Stepping over the rail and supporting girder and onto the adjoining boardwalk that ran both sides of the track, he moved to the side of the bridge. Holding on to cross struts that formed an enormous double X, he groped his way to the very edge. Beneath his feet, the boards, laid bare to the elements, were stained with chalk-white bird droppings and powder green lichens. Here, the winds, like mischievous sprites, were particularly wilful and erratic. His grip tightened as he braced himself against them and, with eyes wide with apprehension, he craned his neck forward to peer down to the river below.

Overcome by the dizzying prospect, he promptly drew back, shutting his eyes tightly as he clung to the X for dear life. Breathing as deeply as his nervous state would allow, he decided to relieve his enfeebled legs and take the precaution of sitting down. It was as good a spot as any. With sloth-like movements he loosened his embrace and discreetly lowered himself into position. It was time for a draught of Dopacof to steady his nerves. He soon retrieved the bottle from his overcoat pocket and with shaking hands unscrewed the cap.

From where he sat he could distinguish, on the fading skyline, St Mary's Church and the towering spire of St John's Cathedral, which, by a distortion of perspective, seemed to have changed parishes to come up alongside it. Farther to the right, St Mary's Cathedral was plainly visible as was the Post Office mast with its clutter of dishes.

Dipping below the skyline, King John's Castle remained unseen, while the spires of old St Munchin's were barely visible. Away to the right, looking like the tilted headstocks of enormous stringed instruments, were the unlit floodlights of Thomond Park, the spiritual home of Limerick and of Munster rugby.

The scene dissolved as his gaze shifted to the foreground. Straight ahead, he could see the handball alley, its geometric flank basking in the last rays of sunshine as it cast long shadows. The dying light, striking some windows in Stella Maris Park, turned glass to glinting gold. Moored off the winding ribbon of sandy shoreline exposed by low tide, the river boats bobbed gently in quiet introspection.

Little by little his nerve returned and, to his surprise, not only did he feel at ease with himself and his surroundings, but became positively euphoric. Every muscle fibre that had been frozen and impotent with fear was now on fire. It was as if his entire body had been shot through with reckless endorphins. Perhaps it was the Dopacof. But he favoured the belief that it was the exultant triumph of logic. He reasoned that the worst that could happen was he might fall and meet his end, but since this was the object of the whole exercise, it seemed inordinately silly to be afraid of what was devoutly to be wished.

A man with nothing to live for has no reason to be afraid. Laughing into the wind that blustered all around him, he shouted defiantly, '...death, where is thy sting...death, thou art redundant...'

The wind grew more fitful now as if vexed by his taunts but he drank it in, becoming all the more intoxicated. Now it was his turn to tempt fate, his turn to dictate terms. Kicking out his legs and thrusting his arms into the air, he howled and hollered, and whooped like one demented. He pitched and rolled at the edge of his seat, he swayed to and fro, and clapped his wellies together like an applauding seal, until it seemed that the only thing keeping him from falling was the wind itself.

It was the sharp, cranking call of a heron that finally put an end to his death-defying antics. Spearing his bravado, it pulled him from the brink and reined him in. Slowly, fears and doubts, held like hostages at the back of his mind, were brought to the fore to make him soberly aware of the grim consequences of his cavalier behaviour. He became more and more content to lean back against a supporting strut and even looped an arm around it for insurance. With regret, he acknowledged that self-preservation had forced a temporary injunction. It was only an adjournment, he told himself. That was all. This death wish thing did seem to blow hot and cold and the wind, as if aware that the crisis had past, at least for the present, eased off in sighs of relief. All became calm and still, and the river began to take on the lustre of black, polished granite.

Overhead, the sky was filling with stars as the light seeped away to the west. Through a triangle formed by struts and girders, he could see the sliver of a moon hanging like a comma over Longpavement. Settling into darkness, the trees faded to ghostly silhouettes as Stella Maris Park became an illuminated crossword puzzle. Across and down, clusters of rectangular boxes winked as house lights were switched on. Off his right shoulder, strung out like penny candles across the Clare Hills, scattered dwellings were lighting up, one by one.

Hanging upside down on the girder above his head, a garden snail was on the move. Conway watched patiently as the creature laid a silver trail. He thought of Tubbs chanting his little rhyme, *shady muddy, shady muddy, stick out your horens.* It made him smile, and he was glad of the snail's company. He did not feel so alone.

Turning from the snail's endeavours, he just caught sight of a shooting star that streaked by the Plough. He closed his eyes to make a wish, then, realising what he had done, he said out loud, his voice carrying in the stillness, 'Come on, Conway, what are you thinking? Wishing on a meteor? You are losing it...'

How bizarre and absurd, he thought, to make a wish on a tiny speck of interstellar debris. Perry Como sang soothingly in his inner ear, *catch a falling star and put it in your pocket, save it for a rainy day.* Sure, thought Conway. He knew better. It was only the annual shower of meteors known as the Perseids, regular as clockwork they were during July and August.

A cranefly floated by, trailing its long legs, followed by the scent of wood smoke that appeared to be drifting up from the tree-lined fringes of Longpavement. He thought of Donie and the lads huddled around a blazing pallet. It was unlikely at this hour, he had to admit. Perhaps it was the rekindling smoke of their fire, fanned into life again by gusting winds. The fragrance was not unlike the incense of

Benediction. It put him in mind of his First Communion days and those angelic, unbroken voices from long ago when as a boy he sang, *O sacrament most holy, O sacrament divine, All praise and all thanksgiving, Be every moment thine.*

How haunting that little hymn of praise was, and how plaintive its cadence. For some reason it had always touched his heart and many a time brought tears to his eyes. He remembered sitting below the white marble pulpit, where he would stare with fascination at the carved figures of saints, while the priest's lilting voice weaved in and out of his consciousness. He would trace his fingers over the sacred pageant. How serene the figures seemed, they appeared to speak to him with pitying looks for being part of a blood-warm and profane world. How he longed to give himself up to that cold marble, to join them in that peace.

What was to become of him? Would he leave the world behind? Through the 'sacrament' of suicide, would he return to a state of nothingness? What matter, he had already spent an eternity there without a bother. To return would be like going home. His life a brief interlude, he would kiss the double helix goodbye and the world would continue on its merry way. Without him.

Or maybe, just maybe, the world was all in his head and would end with his ending. In a weird sort of way he was a doomsday device. He was a killer of worlds. He came into the world and his world came into being, and the world grew as he grew, and when he switched off, the world would switch off with him. To all intents and purposes he was the world. Like the opt-out monkeys, if he could no longer see, hear, or speak, if he could no longer think, or feel, then the world would cease to exist for him. That was all he wanted. That was all that mattered. When he died, the world died.

But the world wasn't finished with him yet. It would claw him before it let him go. It came in the form of an intrusive thought that suggested his arguments were nothing more than the flimsy stratagems of self-delusion. His resolve now began to waver as the germ of doubt took hold and, as crazy as it seemed, he was not at all sure that nothingness even existed. He cast his mind back over the past few days. Seeking confirmation of his own identity, he had gone on a walking tour of his dreams, retracing the twists and turns those strange imaginings had produced, only to discover that his worst fears were well-founded. His entire life had been a lie. And he had definitive proof.

He recalled in his mind's eye his visit to the Tudor Inn. It had turned out to be exactly as it appeared in his dream, a place he had never actually seen before. How was that even possible? And his visit to St Jude's, the same, just as it was in his dream. He had made inquiries, only to be told by an offhand registrar with a liking for euphemism that Navilluso had gone 'next door'.

In answer to his confusion, he was informed that 'next door' was Mount St Lawrence. Navilluso was dead. And buried. But the reality of his existence was not in doubt. He was a real person. It could not be denied. His crazy dreams were real.

From an inside pocket he plucked his battered Concise Oxford Dictionary and, with the aid of a flashlight, went in search of a word. His skilled compulsion for definition soon found what he was looking for. There it was at his finger tips, wedged between *suggest* and *suit, suicide n the act of killing oneself intentionally; a person who kills himself or herself intentionally adj suicidal adv suicidally n suicidologist one who studies suicide*

What an odd occupation, thought Conway, he had never even heard of it. He had often harboured the suspicion that certain words spontaneously appeared in dictionaries, that they weren't actually there until you looked at them.

Should he leave a note of explanation? What was the point, no one listens to the dead anyway. The dead are always disenfranchised. What happens to all those suicide notes? Was there a special vault where they keep them all? To take your own life is always viewed as an irrational act. Society will always close ranks and come up with a reassuring explanation. They're never going to say that he was in his right mind. Society, just like the stock market, survives on illusions. It depends on faith, hope and confidence, and does not take kindly to being exposed as a house of cards. Going absent without leave, deliberately letting your membership lapse, cannot be regarded as anything other than a rejection of its values. It strikes at its very roots. You have to be mad to leave voluntarily.

To Conway, suicide appeared to be the only true act of self-will. A rational response to a very irrational world. Die through carelessness or incompetence or victimization? Sad, but these things happen. Die for your country, die for your religion, die in the moronic pursuit of glory, breaking records until you break your neck, and will they stigmatize you? No, they'll sing your praises, at least until they forget about you. Roll up, roll up, roll up, there are thousands of ways to die but no suicide please. Accidental death, no matter how contrived, is regarded as the lesser evil, but don't ever decide to embrace death for logical reasons. That's unforgivable. That's taboo. That's insane. That's not playing the game.

In his mind, the Grim Reaper seemed as big a fraud as a cheap Halloween mask. What was grim about release? What was grim about freedom? To be free of it all. He rode his courage now as he began to build an argument for death. Yes, he could safely say that he looked forward to the certainty of death. To the luxury of its finality. No more keeping up appearances, no more feelings of inadequacy. No more guilt. Out of sight and out of mind. Away from the awful shackles of expectation and the stifling constraints of a presumptuous and self-conscious species.

That was the trouble, of course. He had lost all faith in himself and in humanity. He belonged to a species that called itself Homo sapiens sapiens. So wise they named him twice. What a joke. If the apes had been able to read, they would have burned every copy of Origin of Species and roughed up Darwin for his impertinence, associating their good name with a tribe of barbarous, upright egocentrics. And now, it seemed, that all creation would gladly dump this miscreant hominid, this large-brained aberration that hadn't an ounce of common sense.

His only regret was that 'the authorities' had dispensed with burial at the crossroads. The idea appealed to him. He could not think of a more fitting resting place for a deceased rationalist. But before he would do away with himself, there was something he must do first.

Holding the dictionary in his hand, as if weighing its worth, he considered his great love of words. From the moment he had discovered that the twenty-six letters of the alphabet could be arranged to form any word that had ever been uttered, or ever likely to be uttered, he was hooked. Enthralled by the fact that, through this strange sorcery of language, he could conjure up something as transient and nebulous as thought itself, he had felt like a medium at a séance, communing with the spirit world.

But, it seemed, he had climbed to the top of Babel only to find that words had too many meanings to mean anything anymore. Language had now become an artifice, designed to supplant feeling and conceal thoughts. The real world, the true world, was wordless. He knew that now.

Filling his lungs with air, he held his breath a moment before liberating it in a long sigh. He now began to tear pages from the dictionary, scrunching them up in his fist before tossing them into the river below.

He watched with a morbid fascination as the snowball of words spiralled downwards. Page after page followed until, adrift in the tide, they formed a straggling line like some doomed armada heading downriver towards the city and the estuary beyond. A farewell to words, the high seas and vast oceans of the world could have them. When the ritual was at the end, all that remained was the sooty black cover with its embossed gold lettering. He let it fall from his hands and down it fluttered like a dead bird into the inky darkness.

A fox yelped in the distance as the twinkling lights of a jet moved across the night sky, dragging behind it a low and grumbling thunder. As he looked at the lights making their way to Shannon Airport, he thought of Red Pepper, Green Pepper and Carbon Copy Blue.

What would those three ball hoppers have to say for themselves? He could imagine them now, coming out with all sorts of esoteric nonsense. Exploring the suggestion, he decided to assign their characters to his own thoughts. Some obstinate streak within him had left the stage door open for discourse, compromise or persuasion. He had always prided himself on the fact that his mind was a democracy. A place where freedom of speech would flourish, a place where all sides got a hearing. If anyone could play the role of devil's advocate, they could. If anyone could tease out the pros and cons, they could. There was no physical manifestation, yet it seemed they were truly there, present in his mind like some virtual forum. Like ducks to water, they trod the boards.

ACT ONE : SCENE 1

RED

(biblically) Rejoice with me, for I have found my sheep, which was lost.

GREEN

How changed from him whom we knew.

BLUE

It's come to a pretty pass, Conway. Suicide, of all things! Who'd have thought?

RED

Why are we here? You might well ask. Well, to quote Burke, Edmund, Irish statesman, 1729-1797,

I am convinced that we have a degree of delight, and that no small one, in the real misfortunes and pains of others.

GREEN

But one cannot be too smug, because, to quote Bonar, Horatius, Scottish minister, 1808-1889,

A few more years may roll
A few more seasons come
And we shall be with those that rest
Asleep within the tomb

BLUE

You've been burning the candle at both ends, Conway. You do need Dr Diet, Dr Quiet and Dr Merryman, seek their professional help. Some of them know what they're doing. Especially the ones who've had refresher courses.

RED

Now, me auld segosha, although you're not such a merry old soul, you did call for your fiddlers three and, if you have any gumption, you might see us as amigos. Homines sapientes, in fact, three wise men, no less. The Medici Balls, at your service. And, wouldn't you know, we also give a two-to-one chance of redemption. With stamps.

GREEN

A right shemozzle he's got himself in. But suicide? What a waste. I can hear Clotho, Lachesis and Atropos laughing their heads off.

RED

(derisively) And who would they be now, when they're at home?

GREEN

Why, the cruel Fates of course. Some people do think they arbitrarily control birth, life and death without giving a toss for anyone's feelings.

BLUE

And those people are right.

GREEN

Yes, but it's not like it's personal or anything.

RED

Did you know that most meteors are smaller than a grain of sand? Or the best throw of the dice is to throw them away? Or that the Walls of Limerick are in bloom with wallflowers? Or that dolphins sleep with one eye open?

GREEN

(wearily) Well, ring out your great bells in victory, but what's that got to do with anything?

RED

Just thought you might like to know.

BLUE

(sagely) The future I see, Conway, and I see your obituary.

(There is a short pause as a radio is switched on in Conway's head.)

RED

(speaking in a funereal, broadcasting tone) The death has occurred of Edward Conway, better known as 'Pockets' Conway, late of Riverview, Sycamore Avenue, Corbally. Removal from Lynch's Funeral home on Thursday at seven p.m. to St Mary's Church. Requiem Mass will be held at eleven a.m. the following Friday. Burial afterwards at Mount St Laurence Cemetery. Sadly missed by relatives and friends. House private, please. No flowers.

GREEN

(sounding uncannily like Maisie) Shur that fecken local radio is only good for the desh noshases.

BLUE

(solemnly continuing) He is survived by his family, two cats and a dog, and every other living creature on the planet.

RED

Maybe once a year, you'll get your phosha in the Limerick Universal Remembrance Weekly and, of course, there's the occasional month's mind mass. But you'll always be in the hearts of those who loved you.

GREEN

Of course, Conway thinks he's one of those people only a mother could love. Even then he suspects she never quite liked him.

RED

He doesn't even like himself.

BLUE

You know your problem, Conway? You're too sensitive. You're an emotional haemophiliac. You need to lighten up.

GREEN

As regards your 'explanatory exit notes', we have observed, over the years, that silence is never written down. But you should see some of the suicide notes we do get, I mean, some people today are just so careless. The punctuation and spelling can be atrocious at times, and the presentation? You don't want to know. But I'll tell you anyway. We gets them in ink, in pencil, in crayon, in chalk, in blood, in lipstick, in eyeliner. We gets them in sand, in Lego bricks, in alphabet soup, on fridge doors, on table tops, on paper napkins, on toilet rolls, on prescription pads, on mirrors, on walls, on floors, on ceilings. You name it.

RED

One chap even peed his farewell against a wall. It simply read, *BYE*. Short and sweet. Sugar in the urine. Diabetic, don't you know.

GREEN

I've come across some extraordinary suicide notes in my time. But I can safely say, without fear or favour, that the most extraordinary was also the longest. Took the best part of thirty years to write, over one hundred and eighty-six thousand pages there were. One hundred and eighty-six thousand, two hundred and eighty-two to be precise. The 'suicide' died of old age in the end. Maybe you should try it, Conway. Kick the bucket down the road. Long finger job.

BLUE

You know, Conway, against the backdrop of geological time your life is but the blink of an eye. It's not a long time to stick in there, to stay awake.

RED (biblically)

And he saith unto Peter, what, could ye not watch with me one hour?

GREEN

The world is what you make it.

BLUE

Live every day as if it were a second chance. Imagine the life you could have. You have nothing to lose. You'll be dead long enough. I mean, what are the odds? You know, there's less chance of you being here right now than, than, well, it's like winning the lotto every day for thousands and thousands of years. And that's something we know about because we

have, on more than a few occasions, filled in as lotto balls, as understudies, you understand, and we've had some big wins too. Howsoever, that's neither here nor there. What was I saying? Oh yes. And yet, you are here. Despite all the odds.
GREEN
(forthrightly persuasive)
You are a survivor, you've survived famine, disease, murder, mayhem, drought, flood, war, peace, contraception, poisons, pamphlets, pollutions, bee stings, final solutions, low sperm counts, inquisitions, cultural shifts, invasions, ice ages, envy, radiations, storms, recessions, meteorites, piracy, prohibition, inhibitions, hula hoops, presumptions, asteroids, adenoids, paranoids, commonsense, insanity, eviction, family planning, the feudal system, the pill, comets, books, bills, the rhythm method, the hucklebuck, radio, television, black holes, sun spots, tilted wombs, dark ages, disco, outrages, constipation, supernova, superstitions, eclipses, ellipsis... and a bazillion other shocks that flesh is heir to.

You name it, all doing their damndest to prevent you from coming to life in the first place. You just would not believe all the things that conspire against you being here, at this moment in time, so improbable as to be impossible, but here you are, boy, you made it. Five billion years of evolution has gone into you, five blooming billion years! You come from the heart of a star, you are star dust, you are gold dust, you are a fucking miracle, my boy, you're a winner, you're unique, you're the man!
RED
And now you're throwing in the towel?
GREEN
Bowing out? Cashing in your chips?
BLUE
Signing off? Slipping away? Giving up the ghost?
RED
Why should you? Go when you're called and not before. In the meantime, what do you say you make a go of it? Give it a lash? Wadduyasay, boy? Waddayagorralose? Noffffink!

BLUE

I see the future, Conway, and there is one, despite the fact that you've decided to take the world with you. And I see a white, biconvex, film-coated tablet marked 7.5mg on one side, and with a break line on both sides. It's a sleeping pill, your mother's, one of many Dr Dalton will prescribe for her after you shuffle off your mortal coil. I hate to lay this on you, kid, but when your trouble ends, hers will begin. She will cry herself to sleep for the rest of her life.

GREEN

Heartbroken.

RED

Heartbroken.

BLUE

Heartbroken.

GREEN

Perish the thought, Conway. Perish the thought.

Consumed in a flurry of winds, the voices evaporated as three snow-white swans flew directly overhead. Listening to the chime of their wing beats, he thought he heard, in dying whispers, the words '...live...live...live...'

Chapter Twenty-eight

Mary Rose sat at the kitchen table doing the books. Spread out before her, covering the rolling landscape and country scenes of the tablecloth, was an assortment of notebooks, memo books and ledgers, and several piles of bills, receipts and invoices held down by old horseshoes that served as paperweights.

Chewing the end of her Biro as she mulled over the accounts, she had come to the conclusion that the coal business produced by far the grimiest, grubbiest and most inscrutable sales receipts imaginable. Those that weren't torn were obliterated by stains, or bleached to such an extent that the faint and ghostly transcript was barely legible.

Considering Limerick's propensity for inclement weather, one would think, she reflected, that they'd at least be waterproof. She held one such specimen in her right hand and cast a critical eye over it. It looked more like an impressionist sketch than anything else.

Apart from, *Reidy's Coal Merchants Limited, The Dock Road, Importers and Distributors of Polish Coal, Doubles, Singles, and Smokeless Fuels*, all she could make out was the word *Total*. But as to what the *Total* was, or what amount of coal it referred to, or indeed what date it was, she had no idea.

The details of the transaction, written in blue ink, had run, producing an effect not unlike a Rorschach ink blot. As she looked at it, trying to make sense of it all, she imagined it might well be a camel wielding an umbrella while attempting a Fosbury flop over the high bar of the quantity margin. Or then again, now that she turned it over to her left hand and looked at it from a different angle, perhaps it was more like an ice-skating moose about to execute a triple toe loop. She pondered for a moment on the kind of profiling her weird interpretations might elicit from an investigative shrink.

Bleary-eyed, she took off her reading glasses and placed them back in a clamshell case lined with navy blue velvet. Stretching her arms above her head and arching her back, she gathered up her hair with both hands and wound it into a coil on top of her head, held it there for a moment, then let it free fall into place again.

As she yawned with weariness and frustration, her eyes alighted on the picture of a nursing red setter that hung over the fireplace. With wayward offspring scrambling in and out of their basket, she thought how so alike the comings and goings of their financial affairs those pups were. Keeping track of everything was not easy. From Vat returns to vet bills, from insurance premiums to horse feed. There was this, that and the other, and everything in between.

As usual, there were gaps in the paper trail. The main problem was that Nucky kept everything in his head. His idea of filing something away was to crumple it up and stuff it in his back pocket. There was no doubt about it but he belonged to the slipshod and slapdash school of accounting. Indeed, his Customers' Order Book was a work of fiction. Written up days, or even weeks, after the event, it was amended and re-amended so often that the devil only knew what was what.

She tinkled out an agitated rhythm on her near-empty mug of tea with the pen. It was her favourite mug, decorated with a stylised illustration that she had whimsically titled *white cat with grin on windowsill with bunch of tulips*. She reached for it, took a sip of the unsweetened, tepid liquid and grimaced. Slipping on her glasses again, she reluctantly returned to the never-ending ebb and flow of credit and debit, and plucked a letter from under the horseshoe pile of 'for your immediate attention'. It was a pointed reminder for the TV licence fee, addressed to Patrick McNamara, Iona, Island View Terrace, King's Island.

Her dad would surely laugh at the idea that the powers that be were under the impression he was still watching the box two years after he had gone to his eternal reward. She could see him now, after his dinner of bacon, cabbage and spuds, his slow, jokey voice repeating the name 'Iona' as he took a matchstick from its box and unhurriedly pared it to a point with his pocket knife. He would then proceed to use it as a toothpick. 'Of course ye know why your mother liked the name *Iona* so much?' he'd say, in that self-assured way of his as his tongue probed a tooth. 'It's all because, behind it all, she's an awful show-off...' Then, in a terrible Italian accent he would add, with eyebrows dancing, 'I-own-a-this and I-own-a-that...'

But her mother would always give as good as she got. 'Go away outa that, and rise outa me,' she'd say back to him, and turning to the rest of them around the table, she would smartly add, 'don't mind your father, to him every silver lining has a cloud.'

He'd laugh, of course, then with a big smile on him as he leaned back from the table, he would declare that, 'it should have been called *Iowa*, not *Iona*, because, if the truth be known, it's a case of I-owe-a-this and I-owe-a-that...'

It was a family joke, told many times, and though they'd always groan, they'd always laugh and never seemed to tire of it. Even Mikey, as a toothless baby, would laugh his head off though he hadn't a notion what he was laughing at. 'You'd want to come up with a new one, Paddy, that one's gettin' so stale you could make bread puddin' out of it,' her mother would say, and they'd laugh all the more. Mary Rose smiled at the memory of it.

In referring to her father now, she would never add, as her mother and others would do, *the Lord have mercy on him* or *God be good to him*. To Mary Rose it wasn't necessary. If Patrick McNamara was not in heaven then the place must be near-empty. He was such a good and kind man and she loved him dearly. She looked across at his favourite chair that the cat had now laid claim to. Her dad would never sit on any soft armchair because, as he so often asserted, '...they're fierce bad for the back.'

She remembered how she had 'found' the cat as a kitten when it wandered into the yard one frosty Sunday morning. So tiny and so helpless and so alone. She had plagued her father to keep it. 'You're an oul' softie,' he had said to her but it was he who fussed over the little mite and set out a saucer of milk for it and that was that. The cat stayed. Her heart filled with a fond sadness at the memory. Was it really all of nine years ago? Not wishing to endure the tightening bands of grief rising from the pit of her stomach, she seized on the distraction of addressing the grey tabby stretched out on the chair.

'What are you looking at, Shibs?'

The cat twitched its tail and gave her an imperious look as if to suggest that her efforts at bookkeeping were a complete waste of time. Locked in a trial of will, she stared at the cat and divined an uncanny look of scrutiny in its eyes. It was as if it knew what she was thinking. For reasons known only to itself, it began to purr. Under the table, sprawled at her feet, Rex stirred and snuffled tetchily before calming down again.

The glowing embers of the fire made little crinkling noises as they settled. She had deliberately let the fire go down. These days, with the weather so nice and mild, it was lit more for comfort than heat. The glow of the fire, the tick of the clock and the purring of the cat, all conspired in making her feel quite dopey and she was on the point of nodding off when she heard the patter of little feet across the linoleum floor. Looking up, she found Rex standing at the back door with an expectant look on his face. Mary Rose guessed it was time for him to answer the call of nature. At her approach, the dog yawned audibly, stretched and shook himself as he waited, then, as soon as she had the door ajar he slipped out.

Shortly afterwards she heard the yapping bark of Rex and the hoarse response of Bowser. Even Gypsy and Shamrock got in on the act with a neigh and a whinny. She thought for a moment about going to investigate but, hearing nothing further to worry about, decided they were just exchanging pleasantries. She was on her way to make more tea for herself when the back door rattled as if it had been kicked. The latch was lifted and the door flung open as in swept Mikey with the aura of the great outdoors about him. In wellies, jeans and anorak, and a canvas bag slung across his chest, he entered backwards into the kitchen hauling a bamboo fishing rod.

'Will you look at the state of you,' Mary Rose exclaimed, 'can't you come in the door without tryin' to break it down first?'

'Sorry...' said Mikey with eyes wide, and imparting to the word all the insincerity he could muster.

It wasn't lost on Mary Rose who said, with a steely directness, 'I'll sorry you the right way,' then, responding to the face he made at her, she added, 'I'd watch myself if I were you. And you can leave that outside,' she went on, referring to the fishing rod, 'you're not bringin' that in here.'

'Where'll I put it?' Mikey challenged.

'Do you want me to tell you? Do you?'

Muttering to himself, Mikey went outside and returned moments later, minus the fishing rod.

Hands on hips, her thumbs stuck into the belt loops of her jeans, Mary Rose shot her head forward and asked pointedly, as she eyed the door which was still wide open, 'Were you born in a stable? Close the door.'

'I'm goin' out agin, I only came in for a cush a bread.'

'Do you know what time it is?'

'No,'

'Time for you to be in.'

'I'm just goin' out for a while.'

To underline her opinion on the matter she pitched her voice to a higher note, 'You're no such thing. You're not goin' out again at this hour of the night.'

In a rapid-fire whinge Mikey protested, 'Mam said I could go down to Paulie's house for a while as long as I wasn't too late.'

'Well, Mam isn't here, is she?' stressed Mary Rose, then seeing the perplexed expression on Mikey's face, she felt some explanation was called for, 'she's gone down around the corner. Marie Moore is home from the hospital and she wanted to see the new baby.'

'Where's Tubbs?' Mikey asked suspiciously.

'She took him with her.'

'Why couldn't I have gone with her? It's not fair, she's al'ays takin' Tubbs.'

'You weren't here for one, and for two, you just want to go because Tubbs goes, you have no more interest now...' Then, as if astonished with herself for even entertaining that Mikey would listen to reason, she added, 'go away from me.'

Thwarted by her accurate appraisal, he folded his arms, stuck out his lower lip and took on an expression of utter disregard.

'Did I tell you close the door, or was I talkin' to myself? There's a draught, and you'll have the rats in on top of us.'

'But Paulie's outside.'

'Well, why didn't you say? Tell him to come in, will you, and don't have him standin' outside like a fool.'

As if he had been calling Lazarus forth, Mikey shouted to the doorway, 'Come in, Paulie...'

As unobtrusive as a shadow, as quiet as a mouse, Paulie edged into the kitchen with Bowser and Rex in tow. He was Mikey's height and build, if a little pale and undernourished. Unsure of what to do, he remained by the doorway, his arms hanging self-consciously from his shoulders.

'Out, out, the pair of ye,' Mary Rose shouted to the dogs, 'what do ye think this is, the changing of the guard?'

The two turned tail and skedaddled as Mary Rose closed the door. Turning to Paulie, she added affably, 'Come in, Paulie, don't be a stranger, nobody's goin' to bite you.'

Paulie took two steps to the left of the doorway where he reassembled his self-conscious posture.

Lifting the kettle to see if it had enough water in it, Mary Rose asked Mikey, 'Did you happen to see Bobsy in your travels?'

'He was with Cyril Flynn and Mousie Ryan.'

'When was this?'

'Earlier on.'

'And when was that?'

'A while ago.'

'Do you know, Mikey, gettin' information out of you is like gettin' blood out of a friggin' turnip, do you know that.' After a resigned sigh, she added, in a voice strained with patience, 'Where was he?'

'Down by the shops. I didn't see him no more after that. I told him he was wanted but he started throwin' bull's-eyes at me and Paulie.'

'Bull's-eyes?' said Mary Rose, her eyelids flickering as her face crumpled up in an effort to comprehend.

'Yeah, do you want one?' said Mikey, taking a bull's-eye sweet from his pocket and holding it up to her.

She took one look at the measly object in Mikey's grimy palm and said, with a look of aversion, 'No, thanks!'

'He hopped one off my head,' said Paulie, pointing a finger to the site of impact.

'And he got me in the arm with one,' Mikey added sullenly, compounding the evidence for the prosecution against Bobsy.

'Did he now?' said Mary Rose, narrowing her eyes, 'I'll sort him when I see him. Wait and see. He's always actin' the maggot.' Under her breath, she added, 'He's never around when he's needed.'

Then, as the thought occurred to her, she turned to the pair of them, 'And how did ye get in the back?'

Mikey frowned at the naivety of the question, 'I climbed over the wall like I al'ays do.'

'How many times have you been told not to do that? Can't you come in the front door like any normal, civilised person would do?'

'I al'ays do it,'

'Just because you *al'ays* do it, that doesn't make it right, and the word is *always*, not *al'ays*, by the way...'

Scornfully, he answered, 'I al'ays say al'ays.'

'No, you always say al'ays.'

'So do you...' Mikey retorted accusingly.

Snootily, she replied, 'No, I sometimes say al'ays. I don't always say al'ays. See now, smart alec...'

Not sure of what to say next, Mikey said simply, 'Well?'

'Water!' pronounced Mary Rose, then laughing at how ridiculous the conversation had become, she added, 'there you are now!'

'See if I care,' he grumbled, cultivating a face like thunder.

'Oh you're a howl, Mikey, do you know that,' she said, laughing as she spoke, then after a moment's thought she asked, 'where were you till this hour, anyway?'

'Fishin' off the surage pipe for eels...' Mikey replied, as if it was the most natural thing in the world. 'We nearly cot one. A big huge one, wasn't he, Paulie?'

'Yeah, we nearly had him in an' all when Mikey dropped him,' said Paulie.

'I wouldn't have dropped him only for you shoutin' at me...' Mikey countered resentfully.

Mary Rose rolled her eyes back in her head. 'In the name agawd,' she chided, 'would ye give over,' then addressing Mikey, she added, 'look at the state of you, wash your hands.'

'I don't need to, I'm goin' out agin...'

'Wash your hands!' she snapped.

'All right,' he said sourly, then heading towards the sink, he asked, 'can Paulie have one too?'

'One what?'

'A cush a bread.'

Paulie said nothing but blinked vacantly and cast his eyes down at the floor as if he suddenly found its pattern of irresistible interest.

'Yes, yes,' said Mary Rose, 'help yourself, Paulie, but wash your hands first, mind. There's corned beef there and cheese there, and brawn. Do you want a mug a tea or a mug a milk?'

'Milk, please,' said Paulie, finding his tongue.

'What about you, Mikey?'

'Milk,' said Mikey, going on tiptoe as he leaned over the sink to reach the tap.

'Roll up your sleeves, or you'll get them all wet,' he was advised by Mary Rose as she opened a carton of milk she had taken from the fridge.

Dutifully, Mikey shoved his sleeves back and grabbed the bar of soap. As the soap lathered in his hands, he said, as casually as you like, 'Oh yeah, Mary Rose, do you know da fella, Conway, he's on the Metal Bridge.'

'What? Edward?'

'Yeah, him...'

'What about him?'

'He's on the Metal Bridge,' repeated Mikey.

'What's he doing there?'

'I dunno, but he was shoutin'...'

'Shouting what? What was he shouting?'

'I dunno, he wor shoutin' sumten...' said Mikey, with a shrug of his shoulders.

'You're not having me on, Mikey, are you? Because if you are, you'll be for it.'

Turning to face her with a scowl of resentment, Mikey protested, 'No, I'm tellin' the truth,' he said indignantly. 'I'm sorry I tell you anyting 'cos you never believes me, you, you don't. I was down fishin' with Paulie, that's how I know...'

Delighted that he could truthfully corroborate his pal's story, and be a 'reliable source' of information that was, apparently, of vital interest to Mary Rose, Paulie could barely contain himself, 'Myself and Mikey were fishin', that's when we heard him...'

Putting down the carton of milk, Mary Rose sprang into action and took off out the back door. She returned soon afterwards wheeling a bicycle. After giving the tyres a quick pinch to check their pressure, she made her way out to the hall, saying, to the accompaniment of the ticking freewheel, 'You're to stay put till I get back, okay? Mam'll be back soon, anyway...'

'But,'

'Don't mind your buts, you're to stay here. Is that clear?'

'Can Paulie stay till Mam comes back?'

'All right,'

'Can I do a fry-up?'

'You can, but be careful and turn off the gas after you.'

'Can we watch the telly?'

'Yes, yes,' she yelled impatiently.

'Can I...'

'Mikey,' she growled, 'don't push your luck. I haven't the time to be puttin' up with you, now get the door for me.'

He squeezed passed her and reaching up for the latch of the front door, opened it.

'Out of the way, Rex,' Mary Rose snapped at the dog, who had followed her in and who was spinning around in six states of confusion at the sudden flurry of activity. 'Close the door after me,' she ordered Mikey as she headed out with the bicycle, its back wheel coming down off the doorstep with a rattling bounce.

'Where you off to?' Mikey inquired.

'Never you mind, now close the door.'

Mikey obliged by slamming the door shut.

'Jesus, you nearly took it off the hinges, you little fecker!'

'You asked me to close it,' came Mikey's muffled answer from the hallway.

'Get in,' she hissed impatiently, before moving down the path. After negotiating the gate, she leaned the bike against the hedge and engaged the dynamo mechanism, setting its tiny wheel against the back tyre. Grabbing the handlebar she nudged the pedals into position with her foot and pushed away from the footpath. As she set off up the road the whirr of the dynamo soon had the front light flickering to a steady beam. The ruby glow from the back light told her it was functioning.

In no time she found herself in the narrow confines of the Water Passage that led to the river. On reaching the waterfront at the junction of Verdant Place, she pulled up sharply and skidded to a halt. The breeze off the river swirled in her hair as she looked right and left, but there wasn't a soul to be seen except some bats that flittered about the trees and the street light above her head. Cautiously, she edged herself out onto the road until she had cleared a blind spot made by the curving wall of a garden. Turning right, she caught the faintest scent of Himalayan Balsam that grew on waste ground just beyond the river wall.

On she sped through concrete bollards that stood before the old swimming baths until finally the coarser surface of the Island Bank was beneath her wheels. Shifting the lever on the handlebar, she slipped into higher gear for smoother running. As if in a tunnel, she raced past shadowing trees only vaguely aware of the hazing lights of Kileely across the river and Stella Maris to her right. The night air held the keen smell of weed-covered rocks exposed by low tide. Appearing like eerie patches of snow, seagulls had taken possession of these transient territories. As she listened to their calls, a moth went churring past her ear and her heart began to pound wildly as emotions were thrown into turmoil by the thoughts that now assailed her.

Cycling beneath the star-strewn sky, she felt a terrible apprehension that something dreadful was unfolding and she feared her role in it. Her mind now began to betray her, usurping her own voice to whisper doubts and fears. What's he doing on the bridge this hour of the night? What if he falls? What if he does something silly? He wouldn't! But what if he does?

Not mindful of what she was doing, the front wheel hit a pothole and it almost unseated her. Thrown forward by the impact, the bicycle lamp had angled its beam down onto the wheel. Without stopping, she reached forward to readjust it and managed to set it right.

Like a ghost ship, the weir loomed from the darkness with a sinister bearing. A gallery of gulls flew from its railings as she approached, filing into the air one by one to register their displeasure. As if provoked by their raucous cries, the wind in her face seemed to chill and she began to regret her sleeveless top.

Coming to the curve of the bank, she stopped cycling and applied the brakes. The lights of the bicycle flickered and died as she came to a halt. Throwing the bicycle aside, she made her way down the slope of the embankment. Pressing on through the shadowy screen of willow and alder, she came to a clearing where an upturned gandelow lay supported on wooden trestles. No doubt, it had been brought up on dry land for repairs, but, for some reason, the sight of the boat reminded her of a coffin laid before an altar. Perceiving it as a terrible forewarning, a panic stirred within her breast and seized her heart. Kicking off her sneakers, she ran to where the boats were moored, some ten to fifteen yards off the riverbank. The grass felt cool and damp beneath her feet as if she moved on the back of some great, dew-drenched beast.

Scrambling down through the reeds, she eased herself off the lip of the bank and onto the sandy shoreline. Standing at the river's edge, she surveyed the gandelows and angling cots and quickly decided that her best bet was to head for Clem Hassett's boat. It looked okay and was riding high in the water. Wading in, until the water reached her waist, she plunged forward in a compromised version of breaststroke, forgoing the froglike movement of the legs for the paddle kick of the crawl.

On reaching the boat, she grabbed hold of the gunwale and then, hand over hand, shifted herself towards the stern.

Taking hold of the seat board, she brought her right leg up and over the gunwale and carefully hauled herself on board without shipping too much water. Resting awhile to recover from her exertions, she listened to the lapping of the waves and the muffled thuds as the boat bobbed about like a skittish horse and knocked against its beer keg mooring.

Relieved to find there was little or no water in the bottom of the boat, she roused herself and began searching for the paddle she hoped was stowed under the stern seat. For a few despairing moments she groped about in the darkness. She drew back in fright when her hand alighted on a coil of sodden rope and, after chiding herself for being a scaredy-cat, she continued her search. Finally, with relief, her hand seized on the handle of the paddle.

Clambering over the seats, she made her way to the bow of the boat and set about trying to untie it from the beer keg, only to find that the chain was secured by a hefty padlock. After several attempts to free it, she swore in exasperation and collapsed back onto the bow seat. For a moment she considered requisitioning another boat but, in no mood to be thwarted, she decided on a more drastic approach to the problem.

Using the paddle as a lever, she jammed the handle into the iron ring through which the chain looped then pressed down with all her strength again and again until, squealing like the extraction of a deeply embedded nail, it was finally prised from the wood. With a rattling drum roll the chain slid over the side and into the water.

The angling cot was an easy boat to handle. Based on the brocaun, a boat used by the ancient guild of the Abbey Fishermen, who, with their snap nets, had fished these waters since time immemorial, it had a long and noble lineage. Designed to be versatile, it was a boat of shallow draught, tapered at both ends and so manoeuvrable that one man could direct it with little difficulty. By simply facing about, stern became bow, or bow became stern, as the situation warranted.

Wet, cold and weak at the knees, yet mightily relieved at having freed the boat, Mary Rose sat back on the bow seat and drove the paddle blade deep in the water to bring the boat around. As the boat turned to the desired bearing, she tucked in the paddle once more and with the deftest of touches stopped it dead in the water. Then, holding it steady, she headed out into midstream before steering a course for the bridge.

The boat had been renamed *Sharon* in honour of the birth of Clem Hassett's only daughter, who happened to be a best friend and a schoolmate of Mary Rose. Previously it had been called *The Swamp* after a local watering hole that was prone to flooding and where, at times in the past, people literally waded to the bar for a drink. Sharon had rather mixed feelings about the honour. Hearing her name being mentioned in connection with having to be tarred had given her sleepless nights as a child.

Mary Rose was well used to handling boats, she had been doing so since she was a toddler. She recalled fond memories of long summer days when her dad would borrow a cot from Tom Barry, or a gandelow from Uncle Pat and the whole family would head off up the river to picnic on St Thomas' Island or Plassey. As children, herself and Nucky were always bickering and vying with each other as to who should take the helm.

'If Nucky can do it, then why can't I? Why does he al'ays get a go and I don't? It's not fair.' Protestations that she was too small just would not pacify her. She would whinge and whinge to have a go until, driving everyone to distraction, she eventually got her way.

'She's uncultivated, that's what she is...' she could hear her mother say, 'she wants her own way in everything.'

Indulgent as ever, her father, holding the neck of her cardigan for fear she might tumble in, simply laughed, saying, 'What do you expect from a Viking?'

Her mother narrowed her eyes at her and said with mock severity, 'You're a bould strap, that's what you are.'

'I'm not,' she had answered back as she pouted and paddled defiantly, barely able to hold the paddle that was as big as herself.

Tonight she was grateful for her childish insistence. With little to contend with but the occasional cross-currents, she made steady progress. Keeping her momentum going with well-practiced, rhythmic strokes, the boat moved smoothly over the relatively calm surface. Soaked to the skin, her hair hanging in rat tails, her eyelashes besparkled with water beads, she glanced at her watch and hoped it was waterproof to a depth of more than four inches, as Nucky had jokingly promised when he presented it to her on her birthday.

Looking at the eerie luminosity of the bow waves, she felt as if she was being assimilated, like some cold-blooded creature, into her surroundings. Though her eyes had grown accustomed to the darkness, and the stars sparkled brightly overhead, the water still had the blackest quality about it and she had the oddest fancy that she was travelling on a river of ink through a silhouette landscape. In the distance, on the upper slopes of the Clare Hills, the honeyed glow of gorse fires blazed through the night as if heralding the rebirth of some pagan ritual. Across the river, drifting in from the shadows, she heard the chugging of an outboard motor. She listened to the dying sounds and felt the heightened anguish of her isolation as the cold now seeped into her bones and the reality of her situation began to impose itself.

Suddenly she found herself surrounded by what appeared to be a flotilla of diaphanous jellyfish. After asking herself what jellyfish would ever be doing so far from the sea, she realised, on closer inspection, that what drifted by her boat was none other than the scattered, sodden pages from a book. Picking one up on the blade of the paddle, she could see, after a quick perusal, that it was indeed a page from a dictionary. With renewed vigour she pushed the boat along until her arms ached. Looking up, she was surprised to find that she had passed the handball alley and was leaving it behind. Paddling for all she was worth now, she drifted past the mouth of the Abbey River. Straight ahead lay the bridge, and as she approached she began to scan its length for any sign of activity. But there was none. Nothing. In panic that she might be too late, she cried out, 'Oh god, please don't do this to me! Please, please, please, don't do this to me!'

Drawing closer, she stood up in the boat and called out to the bridge, 'Edward! Edward!'

From the reeds came the cackling sound of a water rail as if to mock her hope. There was an unearthly silence, and then, as her heart began to sink in black despair, there came a tentative, inquiring voice.

'Mary Rose?'

'Edward!' she exclaimed ecstatically. So relieved was she that she almost tipped the boat over. It pitched and rolled violently, forcing her to sit down. After steadying the craft she manoeuvred it alongside one of the beehive buttresses. The current being quite strong, she had to paddle to keep her position. Directly above her she could see a face leaning from the shadows.

'Edward, what in god's name are you up to? Look, get down from that bridge and stop acting the fool. There'll be a train along in a minute. What do you think you're doing?'

Bemused, he asked, 'What are you doing here?'

Exasperated, she gave him his answer, 'I'm here to ask you the same question. What do you think you're playing at?'

After some reflection, he said glumly, 'Everything is such a mess, Mary Rose. There's not much point to it all. I'm an accident of administration. I was switched at birth...'

'Yes, so you said.'

'But I never told you who I was switched with, did I?'

'What are you talking about?'

'Of all people, Nucky,' Conway went on, 'I was switched with Nucky.'

Mary Rose stopped paddling and screamed, 'What?'

'I'm not Edward Conway, I'm Nicholas McNamara. I'm Nucky. You and I, just happen to be...brother and sister. Can you believe that!'

Dipping the paddle blade to retrieve her position, she screamed again, 'Have you lost your mind?'

'Huh, I think I have.' Conway said dejectedly.

'I can't believe I'm hearing this. I just don't know what possesses you to go believing such nonsense.'

'But I *am* Nucky, and Nucky is me...' Conway declared, hopelessly resigned to his fate, 'can you believe it!'

'Well, if that's true, Edward Conway,' Mary Rose began wearily, 'then my poor mother has raised a right nest of cuckoos because I'm not Nucky's real sister. I was adopted.'

It was Conway's turn to scream, 'What?'

'I was adopted,' she repeated matter-of-factly.

'Adopted? You were adopted?' Conway shouted, sending his incredulous words echoing into the night.

'Yes, adopted,' said Mary Rose, answering the echoes, 'my mother told me...'

'Your mother?'

'Yes, my mother, Mam, who raised me. You know what I mean. My other mother, who gave birth to me, she died when I was an infant...'

'Why didn't you say? You never said so before.'

'I had no need to, had I? Because it shouldn't matter, should it?'

He was silent, and taking advantage of his silence, she went on persuasively, 'It's true, it's true. You can ask Nucky. Don't be so foolish, Edward, this is so stupid of you. Don't do this to me...'

'I wouldn't hurt you for the world, Mary Rose.'

'Then what do you call this carry-on? You're hurting me now, Edward.'

'I'm sorry, Mary Rose, but I never...' He began to speak but his words were suddenly engulfed in a deafening and discordant blast.

Seeing the stunned expression on Conway's face, Mary Rose stated an obvious fact, 'There's a train coming,' then being more practical, she shouted, 'stay where you are, stay into the side and hold on tight...'

The heavily laden goods train, having slowed for the crossing, sounded its bellowing horn once more. The air trembled with the warning of its approach and its blinding light, beaming like some menacing Cyclops, probed the latticed darkness of the bridge, casting a web of shadows out onto the river.

He braced himself, pressing his body tightly against a girder, while the bridge shook to its foundations as if it was about to fall apart and topple into the Shannon below. The train came on with a dead-weight, rolling sound and the timbers groaned and creaked as the shock waves vibrated through his entire body until it seemed the whole universe was shaking.

But as he groped about to consolidate his position, he slipped and fell between the struts. Down he plunged, hitting the surface of the water with a great splash. The shock of the water took what breath he had left and it seemed to his semiconscious and confused mind that some dreadful, cold and elemental creature was dragging him under.

Down he sank for what seemed forever, but instead of his life flashing before him, he felt light-headed and serenely complacent about his predicament. Spread-eagled in free fall he exhaled slowly and surrendered to his fate. Down and down he went, until, like a depth charge, something at the very core of his being protested at the annihilation that was at hand and his lungs began to burn with an excruciating need to breathe. Driven by a sudden panic he clawed his way upwards until, at last, he broke the surface flailing about and gulping air.

The current, being quite strong, had taken him off and he was now some distance from Mary Rose and the bridge. He heard her call his name and tried desperately to remain afloat but his clothes clung like a leaden shroud and he began to fall prey to exhaustion. As he slowly sank for the second time, going down through the muffling water, he was plucked back to the surface by a powerful force. In his panic he tried to resist but the force was too strong. A large hand had fastened on his chin and he was being hauled backwards through the water.

'Don't fight, I have you, easy now...'

Even in his frenzied state he recognised Nucky's voice, it broke through his fear and he obeyed, trusting himself to relinquish his own efforts.

'That's it, lie back. Don't fight me...'

Without knowing quite how he had got there, Conway found himself lying in the sandy shallows of the riverbank.

On his knees, and dripping like a water spaniel, Nucky inquired, 'Are you all right?'

Panting like a bull, Conway could only nod.

'You were nearly drownded...' Nucky said, out of breath.

After a good deal of spluttering and gasping, Conway crawled to where Nucky lay recovering.

'Did you, did you...say...drownded?' he asked pointedly.

Catching his breath Nucky answered, 'Yes, drownded...'

'Drowned,' Conway corrected, spluttering out the word as he raised himself up on one elbow, 'I was...I was, nearly drowned...not drownded...'

With more than a bewildered look, Nucky asked, 'Are you sure you're all right?'

Conway answered with a rhetorical question.

'You do mean drowned and not drownded? One syllable, not two. You make it sound like 'drowned dead', which is, to say the least, somewhat...somewhat...tautological...'

His brow furrowed, his mouth fallen open, Nucky said, with eyes staring, 'What?'

'Repetitive...' Conway kindly explained.

'You're some mad fucker, do you know that, Conway, you're a mad bastard...and no mistake...'

Far from being offended, Conway was now hysterical with laughter. '...I could have drownded...' he repeated to himself, as if it were the hilarious punch line of a joke.

Grabbing hold of Conway's sodden lapels and vigorously shaking him, Nucky said vehemently, 'Hah, is that all that's worryin' you, is it? Drowned or drownded, take your pick, but you couldn't swim to save your life. You're somethin' else, do you know that, Conway, somethin' else...'

This reproach only served to make Conway even worse. Unable to control himself he was now giggling like a maniac.

Nucky went on, his voice fraying at the edges, 'I should have politely let you drown, that's what I should, you mad fucker...'

Then, as if the whole thing suddenly struck him as being completely ludicrous, he broke into a fit of laughing.

'With the amount of shite in your pockets, it's a wonder you didn't sink like a stone and go straight to the bottom.'

Now convulsed with laughter, Nucky let go and Conway collapsed backwards. On the flat of his back and staring up at the stars, Conway heaved a sigh of elation and asked himself a question. How stupid could one person be? He had almost lost his life and all that the peculiarity of his mind could latch onto was the pronunciation of a word that described his near departure from the world. Maybe it was the euphoria of survival. Maybe he *was* mad.

The earth beneath him moved like a slowly revolving disc, the stars streaked overhead and from out of Cassiopeia Mary Rose appeared. He looked up at her and smiled as a wayward breeze ruffled her hair.

'Ye're mad, the pair of ye,' she said, then dropping to her knees and hugging him, she added softly, 'and you, Edward Conway, you're such a fool.'

Clinging to her, he said, 'I thought I'd lost you...'

'You look like a drowned rat,' she said, caressing his face.

'...a drownded rat,' he whispered, then quietly added, 'I wished upon a star tonight, Mary Rose.'

'What did you wish for?' she asked tenderly.

'A life.'

'A life, is that all?'

'No, I wished for a life with you.'

'That's not a lot to ask for.'

'Is that a yes?'

Kissing him on the forehead, she said, 'You *are* quick.'

As they clung to each other, Nucky, who had peeled off his vest and was wringing the water out of it, said, 'Well, if god made ye, the devil matched ye. Ye deserve each other, that's all I'll say.' Then, responding to their preoccupation with each other, he added, '...I'd better go and sort out Clem's boat before it ends up in the Blasket Islands.'

Chapter Twenty-nine

Three gates guarded the entrance to Mount Saint Lawrence. A wide central gate facilitated funeral processions and was a decorative affair, embellished with fleur-de-lys and shamrock motifs. Recent coats of silver paint had not quite obliterated traces of rust that leached like tea stains to its surface. On either side, two narrower gates, again of similar design and condition, were framed with stout pillars and arches crowned with plain stone crosses.

Pushing through the gate on his left, which squealed in complaint on its hinges, he turned right, along a fine gravel path that trailed beneath dappling canopies of oak, elm and beech. It followed the line of a perimeter wall, which, for stretches of its length, was covered with a flourishing mantle of ivy. Though wide enough for two, the path appeared narrowed and confined by the graves that encroached upon it from either side. Leaves and brushwood, brought down by the strong winds of the previous night, lay strewn about its surface.

All about him were headstones of every description. The area to his left was dominated, for the most part, by the older graves where row after row of massive Celtic crosses radiated out as far as the eye could see. More contemporary headstones, modest and understated by comparison, tended to occupy the margins. The shift of time could be charted by the progress and pattern of interment. Funereal fashions had graduated from elaborate to discreet but this had led, as if in compensation, to a greater variety in stone.

He had walked the highways and byways of Limerick, immersed in the colour and pageantry of its mirroring shop fronts. In his memory he saw himself as a ghost traveller amid the hustle and bustle. And in waiting to cross to the other side of the street, he would scan the retail outlets and observe the meeting of old and new. He remembered the sign writer, perched upon a stepladder, intent on giving the illusion of depth to letters of an old name while all around him the easy option of brash plastic and logos abounded.

Distracted by the rattle of a jackhammer as roadworks recommenced, his gaze had shifted from the autumn sales pitch of slashed prices and back-to-school bargains and rose towards another, older Limerick. Georgian facades loomed above the traffic, their oblong windows reflecting streetscape and sky. Many buildings were occupied now by upmarket offices and flats. Those empty and in the *yet to be developed* category were sprouting sprays of buddleia and other plant life as if heralding a resurgence of forest that might one day engulf the business centre and return it to wilderness like some doomed Mayan temple.

With the soft focus of hindsight, he had sifted through the images looking for a sign. But there was nothing to report. He could see no more clearly now than when those moments had first swirled around him. The droves and drifts of people, the busy shoppers, the traffic wardens, the road sweepers, the straggling bus queues, all seemed to be a part of where they were. While he, like some inept method actor, had never quite mastered the art of fitting in. He was just passing through, as always. Trying to find answers. Trying to crack the code.

But what, and where, were all the signs? The boutique manikins that looked like posturing crash dummies out on the town? The ephemeral whitewash scrawl on the butcher's shop window that proclaimed lamb's liver at 33p a pound? The thirteen empty beer kegs chained up outside the *Saints and Scholars* mock antique pub? The bookie office with its euphemistic title of *Turf Accountant*, already offering odds on a white Christmas?

If there was any significance in anything, it was lost on him. Though the more prosaic side of his nature would say that there was significance in everything, if you looked hard enough. A good candidate for a subtle messenger might be the grizzled old man, and his grizzled old dog, sitting by the automatic teller machine of Allied Irish Bank, on the corner of Upper William Street and Lower Gerald Griffin Street. His begging cap open for business on the pavement and, alongside it, a cheeky sign that read, *Deposits Only*.

Self-consciously he had tossed a florin into the grimy tartan lining. The old man fished it out and, after scrutinizing it, chuckled to himself before shouting, '...the Salmon of Knowledge, boy, the Salmon of Knowledge...'

Without so much as a backward glance, Conway strode purposefully on, not at all sure that the declaration was intended for him or the dog. Maybe there was something in it. Maybe he was clutching at straws.

Now within the confines of the cemetery, that world outside seemed very remote. With every step and with every heartbeat it became more distant. It was as if he had entered a twilight jurisdiction where everything lay under the hand of a resigned and overwhelming finality. Here lay the citizens of times past who had travelled those very same highways and byways. All trade, industry and commerce laid to rest. All hopes, fears and foibles of the great and the small, all silent now. What would they make of their city? What would they make of the new miracles and wonders? What would they make of this brave new world?

As if to reassure himself that he was not losing his bearings and slipping into some indefinite state of no return, he stopped and turned to look back along the path he had travelled. To the left he could see, propped high over the cemetery wall, the upper storey of the *Munster Fair Tavern* with its terracotta livery. Across the road it stood, directly opposite the graveyard entrance. Its gable end, which carried a large advertising hoarding for Murphy's Stout, was a great wedge, like the bow of a ship, Conway fancied, dividing the oncoming Blackboy Road in two and sending it left, to Ballysimon and the Tipperary Roundabout and right, to the Kilmallock and Fermoy Road.

It was a peculiar location. A Y-junction, caught between this world and the next. A coming together of tradition and change, a meeting and a parting of the ways. The giant glass of black stout, with its frothy head, seemed faintly ridiculous in the circumstances but he was very glad of it. There was something cheering and familiar about it that supposed all was well. The parting glass that comforted, 'a pint of plain is your only man'. Even if it did have a Cork accent.

Disturbed by his approach, a blackbird flew off in a fit of pique only to alight on a gravestone farther on. As he drew nearer it froze momentarily with tail cocked and orange bill tilted for flight. Flying in a low arc it fluttered noisily to the cover of the ivy before disappearing over the wall.

Hemmed in by the rank and file of the dead, he walked on, the headstones drifting by, as black as ink, as white as snow, as grey as overcast skies. Narrow strips of real estate separated by an assortment of grave surrounds, of stone and iron, wherein final respects were paid with flowerpots of geraniums and cellophane-wrapped bouquets of carnations, lilies and roses. The maintenance of hope and the trappings of grief all jumbled together in miniature statues, nightlights and extinguished eternal flames.

There was the heaped-up earth of recent burials, piled high with floral tributes in the shape of hearts, crosses and domes where trapped vapour condensed like tears inside their plastic casings. Wreaths and ribbons were rain-stained and dishevelled, their handwritten dedications blurring to inkblots above a heavy, indifferent clay. On some headstones were draped the outsized sets of wooden rosary beads. On others, the living portraits of the deceased looked out from glazed roundels.

Conway's eyes began to focus, trying to eke out indistinct letters. Some were indecipherable, others barely legible. At length, names gave up their syllables. Floating up, they came and went like dying whispers that sighed in his memory. And some of the names, how quaint they were, like a saints' registry: *Agnes, Theodore, Jerome, Juliana, Aloysius, Veronica, Martha, Ignatius, Bartholomew, Monica, Ambrose, Benedict...*

And here, a succinct inscription on an elaborate stone: *Sylvester O'Halloran, 1845, His wife Winifred.* Within this same plot, a grave within a grave, was a white marble memorial in the form of an open book inscribed with telegram brevity, *Daughters Mary and Fidelis.*

Interspersed here and there were numbered, black iron crosses. He assumed them to be temporary grave markers, though many, it seemed, had become permanent. And graves there were that were plainly neglected, or forgotten, where sow thistle, dandelion or groundsel took hold. Only nature's homage now for the dead who had slipped beyond living memory, or whom posterity, for whatever reasons, had left abandoned. Instead of gravel or marble chippings, leaves, pine needles and beechmast covered their graves.

What at first sight appeared to be a bay tree, turned out, on closer inspection, to be a holly oak with glossy evergreen leaves. An examination of its distinctive acorn confirmed the identity. Overhead, the cooing of a collared dove seemed to concur. As luck would have it, the Bard of Thomond was nearby. His last resting place marked by a headstone that was both discreet and impressive. The dignified face of the poet was carved in half profile.

Michael Hogan
Bard of Thomond
1832 – 1899
Oh twere a shame to let his name
Like other names decay

And at the very foot of this grave, like an afterthought, a small stone rectangle stated simply:

His wife
Anne
Died 1903
R.I.P.

In order to avoid a pool of water that gathered where the path had dipped and eroded, he was forced to walk over a grave. White marble chippings crunched beneath his feet as if to remind him of his trespass. He excused himself with a mental apology to the deceased. And directly after doing so, a perverse voice in his head sang a snatch of Gilbert and Sullivan making him fleetingly aware of what a *foot in the grave young man* he was, before his sense of propriety silenced the comic opera.

The tetchy drone of a bumblebee drew his attention and he turned to observe the creature tilting the miniature flower head of a red carnation as it eagerly took advantage of an unseasonable bonanza of flowers. Conway found himself confronted with the heartbreaking scene of untimely death. Teddy bears, plastic rattles and other children's toys told the tragic story. A little yellow windmill whirled fitfully with the gentlest breeze in a moving testimony of grief, mourning and incomprehension. Below the names of his grandparents was recently engraved:

Their grandson
Patrick Colbert aged 4
R.I.P.
Erected by their family

With eyes closed and head bowed, he contemplated the reality behind the names and the dates. For some time after, he was left with the sobering thought that the child had lived for as long as it takes to do a degree course. Without quite knowing how he had got there, he found himself travelling past large communal graves so characteristic of the religious orders. He stopped to read an italic inscription at the base of a stone cross.

Erected by the
Third Order of St Francis
To the memory of
Their deceased members
1905
Pax et Bonum
Requiescant In Pace

Looking up, he found the path was taking him towards the disused mortuary chapel. An island of derelict hope, it stood against an ever-changing sky as it had done for over a hundred years. Despite the ravages of time and its state of disrepair, its dressed stone, battlemented tower and fine tracery windows still combined beauty and strength in stout defiance. A silvered weather vane in the form of a fish, a salmon by the look of it, stood at the apex of its spire.

Clockwise, he went on a tour of the building, gazing in admiration at architectural niceties and the craftsmanship of a bygone age. As he walked, craning his neck at a dizzying angle to take in its bell tower, a shaft of sunlight highlighted a monument grave close by. He approached the memorial through strands of drifting gossamer that caught the sun.

After being suitably impressed by its substantial kerbing and its ornate railing surround with rope twist design, he investigated an elaborately carved coat of arms. Below the head of a fire-breathing dragon was the dictum: *Quae sursum volo videre: I long to see what is beyond.* And below that again, the quaintly phrased entreaty:

Of your charity pray that into the company of the saints
may be admitted the soul of Michael Quin Esquire j.p.
for the county of Limerick
who died 6th of March 1866 aged 88 years
R.I.P.

But perhaps the most surprising feature of this memorial to Michael Quin Esquire was the two life-sized angels who knelt in prayer on either side of his tomb. A harvestman clambered tentatively over marble fingers joined in devout entreaty. Before long, Conway was again trawling through his memory. *Harvestman: its legs seem an encumbrance to it. These creatures appear around harvest time, hence the name.* Indeed, the title of daddy-longlegs is often shared with the cranefly. He watched the creature intently, intrigued by its antics until the spell was broken by the sudden disappearance of the slanting pillar of illumination.

Presently, he heard the metal ferrule of a walking stick tap a cold rhythm on the pathway up ahead. An old man, who, by the look of him, had already used up his biblical allowance of threescore and ten, was walking slowly towards him. The walking stick was no ornament for he leaned on it to accommodate a conspicuous limp.

He was a small and portly man, wrapped up in a dark overcoat and wine-coloured neck scarf. A flat cap covered his downcast head. His right hand held a bouquet of dead flowers. Conway stood aside to let him pass. But the old man stopped.

'Good day to you,' said he, his blue eyes sparkling with divination. Conway, who was good with faces, recognized him immediately for who he was. And who he was, was none other than that dedicated lepidopterist and walking encyclopaedia, Tom Madigan himself. Madigan, for his part, had recognized him too but seemed strangely unsurprised at their meeting.

'My dear Edward, so we meet again,' he said in that unmistakable voice of his. 'How fortunate...'

In direct contrast to his halting gait, his speech was brisk and forthright, and had a clipped intonation that made it impervious to indifference or circumspection.

'The last time we met was on the Island Bank. Swinging from a sycamore I was, if I'm not mistaken. Or was it a chestnut? But anyhow, no more climbing trees for me, I'm afraid, young man's game. Had a bit of a fall, don't you know. Came a cropper. Did a right job of my hip. Sore thing. There's talk of a replacement,' then he sighed, and in a mixture of regret and admiration, added, '...the things they can do today. Wonderful. Wonderful.'

Placing the flowers in the crook of his left arm, he shot out a gloved hand and, despite Conway's hesitant response, shook hands with some gusto. Retrieving the flowers, he then inquired with a cajoling enthusiasm, 'and how's that thesis of yours coming along?' But seeing the albatross of unfinished work in Conway's eyes, he went on graciously, 'Aaah, a work in progress, as they say. But stick with it, my boy. Difficult to capture the Island. It has eluded so many. By the by, Maurice Lenihan, the great historian? Buried over there, you know...'

He arched an eyebrow and pouted his lips as a prelude to saying, 'But you've come looking for a Mr O'Sullivan, have you not?' Then, with a meaningful look, he added, dropping his voice to an undertone, 'or is it, Mr Navilluso?'

Conway hesitated before conceding, 'Both, I think.'

'Thought as much,' Madigan declared, 'don't bother to inquire as to how I know,' he advised, holding up a hand of censure, 'unfortunately, I'm not at liberty to say, long story.'

After disposing of the flowers in a nearby waste basket, he pointed to the weather vane with his walking stick and said jauntily, 'Let's follow the signs, shall we?'

'Did you know,' he said, having gone a distance, 'that some believe that the origin of the word *news* comes from the four cardinal points of the compass, North, East, West and South? It's an interesting premise.' Then he added, with resolute conviction, '...utter nonsense, of course.'

The chapel spire fell in shadow across their path as the early-September sun was uncovered by cloud once more. It appeared to be a cue for Madigan. 'What you seek is set square in the middle of the south wall that backs onto the railway line. Am I correct?'

'Yes,' said Conway, surprised and greatly puzzled as to how Madigan could repeat, word for word, the directions *he* had been given by the registrar of St Judes less than an hour before.

Madigan smiled benevolently. 'Ginkgo, no less,' said he, brandishing his walking stick at a tree as if challenging it to a duel, 'also known as the maidenhair, unusual and interesting, thought to be extinct until it was rediscovered in China. A living fossil you might say, rather like myself.'

The path they followed was now bisecting the oldest section of the cemetery. On either side, table tombs and massive limestone crosses stood in derelict commemoration. Cherubim and seraphim heralded the resurrection among elder and ivy and lichen-encrusted headstones leaned askew and forgot their symmetry. Though it was scarcely mid-afternoon, a ghostly shell of a moon could be seen quite plainly above a line of poplars.

'These are strange places...' Madigan was saying, then nodding in the direction of some elaborate statuary, he went on, 'our monuments seem to vie with one another for the attentions of a discriminating god. Or do they proclaim love in proportion to their size. What do you think?'

But true to his nature he didn't wait for an answer.

'It seems to me the greater our monuments, the more pitiful our mortality. But then, these are not monuments of the dead,' he said, rounding his mouth to exhale a plain and self-evident fact, 'no, these are monuments of the living.'

An avenue of yew trees stood like silent witnesses to form a guard of honour. Some offered scarlet fruit on dark, evergreen foliage. As they passed, the plaintive warbling of a robin could be heard above their heads. With a quivering throb of wings it remained unseen, leaving behind no more evidence than a swaying bough and the memory of its song.

'That's the thing about graveyards...' Madigan declared with a nod of conviction, 'time has stopped for so many, it's as if there's a critical mass here that makes it drag its heels. I have walked, for what seems an eternity, among the dead. So many dead, I begin to think that maybe I'm dead myself. Like some misplaced soul I continue to follow a route that is traced in the memory. Most of my people are here, my dear wife...'

His voice trailed off with a sigh and for what seemed an age his walking stick marked time in the silence. At length, he turned to Conway with a preoccupied expression, as if accommodating some great insight.

'It has been said that there are no dead. You stand and you wait for some sign, some affirmation. But there is none, no fanfare, you see, no reply from the other side or the powers that be. Nothing, only silence. But you must listen to the silence. It speaks volumes. Affirmed or not, one must learn that faith rarely gets a pat on the back.' Shaking his head as he shuffled on, he added, 'Over twenty years I've been coming here, looking for an answer, and to paraphrase that dear and celebrated bear, Winnie the Pooh, the more I looked, the more it wasn't there. Or so it seemed...'

As if to draw a line under his philosophical deliberations he forced a smile and recovered brightly.

'But butterflies, wonderful place for butterflies! Common Blue, Meadow Brown, Small Heath, Ringlet, Speckled Wood, Small Copper, Orange Tip, Tortoiseshell, Peacocks and Red Admirals. Moths, too, Hawk, Garden Tiger, Ermine, Burnet, Cinnabar, Little Emerald, White Plume...'

Prodding the air as he aimed his walking stick at a nettle patch that grew nearby, he said, with enthusiastic approval, 'You know, it is truly amazing how nature will respond to a little prudent neglect...'

A freshening wind blustered through the poplars that lined the south wall, setting their leaves quivering until it seemed that the whole cemetery was drawing breath. The moon, too, had changed in its aspect and now hung like a strange, pale fruit on the verge of disappearing.

Drinking in the breeze, Madigan closed his eyes and smiled. 'They're never truly gone,' he said, speaking in such a low voice that it could only have been for his own benefit. Over the sounds of shunting trains that floated vicariously on the air, he added, this time for Conway's benefit, 'Well, here we are...'

There before them, beneath a plain granite headstone, was a recently dug grave. The disturbed soil was cracked and had sunk several inches. A lone dandelion grew at its verge, its full and perfect seed head waiting for the breeze to cast its seeds adrift. Conway read the formal words that were newly inscribed.

In Memory of
Stephen Navilluso
1919 to 1989

Below this was a Latin legend, but before Conway had managed to tease out a translation, Madigan saved him the bother. *The river remains faithful to its source by running to the sea.*

After a silence, Conway pronounced sheepishly, 'I'm not quite sure what it means...'

'All in good time...' said Madigan, then added, 'the true ambition of any civilised man is to understand, and, if he is fortunate, he may even have the luxury of being understood. The pursuit of knowledge is an admirable thing, Edward, but always remember you have the inalienable right not to know everything. The most stupid people on this planet of ours are the so-called intelligent people who should know better. Try and remember that kindness is the greatest intelligence of all and you won't go far wrong.'

Responding to the perplexed look on Conway's face, he inquired, 'Is something amiss?'

'The date of birth,' Conway answered, 'it's wrong, I think, it's four years out.' Then genuinely seeking confirmation, he asked, 'Isn't it?'

'I'll just take the weight off my feet,' said Madigan, as he eased himself down onto the stone kerbing. Settling himself as comfortably as he could, he gave his answer.

'No, it's not wrong,' he said, tapping his gloved fingers on the handle of his walking stick, 'Stephen O'Sullivan was born in 1915, that is true, but Stephen Navilluso was born the day he fell from the Strand Wall.'

With outstretched hand, Madigan then leaned forward and delicately plucked the dandelion. Like a child, in a world of his own, he puffed away the downy seeds of the fragile halo and began to count the hours.

Chapter Thirty

'That man there,' Maisie droned, nodding her head in the direction of the Sacred Heart image in the corner, 'he knows what I have to put up with.'

Conway's attention duly shifted to the 'man' in question and he was a little unnerved by the long-suffering expression of the portrait, which, indeed, seemed to endorse Maisie's feelings.

'Oh the carry-on of her,' Maisie went on, her eyes now fixed and staring into the fire, its flames reflected in the rimless crystal of her spectacles.

From where he sat on the green three-seater couch, his fingers toying with the antimacassar, she appeared to him like some fanatical soothsayer, or pyromaniac, with her head held in rigid fascination while her mouth, as mobile as ever, poured forth a stream of verbiage towards the open doorway of the kitchen.

'...how old did you say he was, says she, six in October, says the other one, go 'way, six, says she, goblesses, very big for his age, goblesshim and the child standin' there and I lookin' on like a fool and she ignorin' me the whole time, with not so much as a how-are-you, or a by-your-leave or anything. I'm due again, says Reesha, and the other one says, well the blessens agod on ya, aren't you awful foolish so soon and all. This'll be my sixth, says the other one, you'd never feel it shur you wouldn't, would you now, goblesses an' save us, you'd want to give that oul' fella of yours a rest, says she, you know the way she goes on, pishy aboush him, it's all right as long as they're not havin' them themselves. Well, I was fit to be tied at this stage, so says I to her, are we goin' to be here all day, the child is perished with the cowld, and didn't she completely ignore me and wouldn't take the hint. It's true for ya, says the other one, goin' on as if I wasn't there and my feet like two blocks of ice. Is that the time, says she, come're I'll have to fly before the chemist closes on me, the youngest fella is dying with a cough, I'm demented from him, so I am, I didn't get a wink a sleep over him last night, the eyes are fallen out of my head, shur that's nothin', says she, Majella, you know Majella, she'd be the eldest, she have the mumps, once one starts they all start. I'm driven up the walls with them and then himself thinks I've nothin' to do but to traipse all over town to get his dinner for him...'

Conway's mind slipped away from Maisie's exposition and indolently sought distraction in the fire. The burr of dancing flames grew louder as if responding to his gaze and the ticking of the clock on the mantelpiece seemed to rouse itself to a new consciousness. Resting his head against the back of the couch, his attention drifted to the moorland scene above the fireplace, then on to the ceiling, where he observed a housefly patrolling the lampshade. Making neat turns, it was describing perfect geometric designs in the air. The aerial skills of the creature, Conway considered, were nothing short of miraculous.

Shuffling in from the back kitchen, where she had been pottering about, Molly raised her voice to a pitch of censure.

'Will you give over and don't be ignorin' the young fella!'

'I'm not ignorin' him at all, I'm talkin' aren't I?' Maisie retorted, and then, turning to Conway, she asked pointedly, 'Am I ignorin' you?'

'No, no,' said Conway, regaining possession of himself, then frowning politely and shaking his head, he added, 'not at all...'

For Molly's benefit, Maisie put on her most challenging face and, looking over her glasses, said emphatically, 'Now, are you satisfied?'

After a half-hearted attempt to swat the fly that had left its lampshade post to enter her airspace, Molly slung the tea towel she carried in her hand over her shoulder, then rolling her eyes she said with a sigh of exasperation, 'I give up,' and departed to the kitchen.

Maisie, still huffed at the interruption, stared after her with an indignant look before continuing seamlessly.

'...but as I was sayin' anyway, pishy aboush him, says she, and the other one comes out with, it's true for ya, there's a fear of him, he won't starve. Go on, says she, you'll be late for the chemist, I'd better go now so, says the other one, I thought, Jesus be praised, give my regards to himself, says Reesha, and she was just on the points of movin' when she says, oh by the way how's your mother, just when I thought we'd be gettin' away from her an' all, ah she don't be well lately says the other on, after the doublenumonia an' all, the misfortune, she's got very drawn in herself, she was always a lovely woman, my mother used always be talkin' about her, I'll tell her you were askin' for her, do says the other one and tell her I hope she gets better soon. I'd better let you go so, and I'll head off. I'll talk again to you, bye so, bye, says she and look after yourself. I'd be there yet with all the shaggin' bye byes...'

After shaking her jowls and her pearl drop earrings at the memory of it all, Maisie, gripping the armrests of her chair, eased herself forward and shouted triumphantly out to the kitchen, '...and that's how come I was late!'

'Such a rigmarole,' Molly howled back in a tired voice.

'I'm only tellin' you what happened.' Maisie said tetchily.

There came a loud denunciation.

'You'd be late for your own funeral.'

'Well, it wasn't my fault. But I knew you'd blame me,' Maisie fumed. Then, looking to Conway, she added with a self-righteous calm, 'See now, I knew she'd blame me.'

As if to distract herself from her annoyance, she suddenly asked, obviously addressing Molly in the kitchen, 'I thought Mary Rose was supposed to be here.'

'She said she'd meet him here,' Molly informed her.

'And the lad is more than welcome, so he is,' said Maisie, rather graciously.

Conway found himself feeling inordinately privileged by Maisie's hospitality. He had never before known anyone so immersed in their own life as Maisie appeared to be. Her single-minded dedication to her own train of thought he found strangely alluring. Indeed, he was somewhat envious of her sense of self. A sense of self that seemed decidedly devoid of self-doubt. That was the thing about such people, when they threw you any crumb of appreciation, you felt blessed that they had taken the time to acknowledge your existence.

'Did you get *The Messenger*, at all?' Maisie shouted to the kitchen.

'It's in the drawer there, behind you,' came Molly's loud directive.

'I just want to know where it is,' said Maisie coolly, 'I'll have a read of it later on.'

Conway was well acquainted with *The Messenger*. A Jesuit publication, it was a monthly magazine full of uplifting articles, measured musings and reflective meditations of days gone by. A spiritual and secular compass with soft-spoken guidelines for today, tomorrow and the hereafter, it had something for all the family with interesting titbits to whet even a cerebral appetite.

He had often browsed through its pages, more to find fault than anything else, but, as often as not, remained to read with interest. Unsettling, it has to be said, for someone who considered the Reformation not an entirely bad thing. Though it would never stray too far from Catholic dogma, it did appear to deal openly with different points of view.

His mother was not only a reader, but also a passionate disperser of the Jesuits' little red book. Not to mention the *Saint Martin Magazine*, *The Catholic Standard*, *The Universe*, and *The Irish Catholic*. She had, it seemed, taken it upon herself to save every soul in Ireland.

'What time did Mary Rose say she'd be in?' Maisie asked.

'Four o'clock, I already said,' shouted Molly, her reply full of rising impatience.

'Shur, it's ten past now.'

'Well, she was probably delayed!'

There was a clatter and a clang from the kitchen.

'What are you after breaking now?' Maisie inquired with little sympathy.

In stressed staccato Molly roared back, 'Would you ever go blow up, would you? I just dropped a fecken fork, okay!'

'A fork to the floor, and a lady to the door...' said Maisie, sagely invoking the old superstition. Eyeing Conway, she added in a whisper, 'she's forever droppin' things, she is...'

'I'm droppin' everything lately,' confessed Molly ruefully, seemingly oblivious to Maisie's disclosure, 'but would you blame me with the carry-on of some people,' she continued, her voice trailing off as she resorted to talking to herself.

With consummate indifference to the mutterings from the kitchen, Maisie turned to Conway like a presiding judge and asked pointedly, 'Well, what do you intend doing with yourself?'

It was a bolt from the blue. He was beginning to get to grips with Maisie's impulsive dialogue but it still could take him by surprise. As he was about to formulate an answer, Molly came to his rescue.

'Leave the boy alone, that's his own business.'

'I was only askin', for heaven's sake. What harm can it do to take an interest?'

Maisie now changed tack and set off on another tangent.

'How's your mother?' she asked kindly.

'She's fine, thanks,' said Conway.

'Mary Rose was very taken with her, said she was a lovely woman. She was all about her, she was. She was tellin' me that your father died when you were a child...'

After blinking at the candour of the statement, Conway crossed his legs and responded cautiously, 'That's right...'

Maisie nodded benignly, 'Still, you have your mother and that's a blessing. Family is very important.' After a moment's consideration, she added, 'I never married, myself...'

'Jaysus, who'd have you?' Molly called from the kitchen.

'I heard that,' replied Maisie sourly, 'that's lovely, that is...'

Then, to Conway as much as to Molly, she said, 'Oh, I've had my offers. But it wasn't to be, between one thing and the other. Noreen was the only one mad anuff to marry...'

Responding to Conway's puzzlement, she said, almost reproachfully, 'Noreen, that's Mrs Mac to you. Didn't you know she was called Noreen? Of course you wouldn't, how would you, unless someone said it to you. That's her name, now. After my grandmother she was called, on my father's side. As I said, Noreen was the only one to marry. Apart from Jimmy and Martin. Jimmy lives in London and Martin's in Dublin. Ah yes,' she sighed wistfully, looking into the fire as if reviewing the past. After a silence and some adjustment to her spectacles she proceeded to ask, 'You do know, of course, that Mary Rose was adopted?'

'Of course he does,' Molly said impatiently, arriving in from the kitchen and drying her hands on a towel, 'wasn't the whole thing explained to him.'

'Any sign of the tea?' Maisie inquired, as if addressing a meddlesome subordinate.

Molly took possession of her armchair to face Maisie and put on a most indignant look. 'I'll have it for you now, Maisie, give me a chance. Will you wait while Mary Rose comes in? I have the kettle on.' After heaving a sigh of restraint Molly continued, 'Mary Rose showed him the birth certificate an' all, she did, and her baptismal, even down to her silver christening plate, and all the photographs, the whole lot. Isn't that right, Edward?'

'That's right,' said Conway awkwardly, somewhat anxious that they might be of the opinion that Mary Rose had to be endorsed or justified for his benefit.

'I'd have raised her myself, you know, only for Noreen insisted,' Molly continued, 'and only for I was looking after my mother at the time, she was very poorly...'

'Bedridden she was,' said Maisie.

With downcast eyes, Molly said sadly, 'She was,' then rousing herself from the ensuing silence, she went on, 'In fairness to Noreen, she raised her as one of her own. A little thing she was, oh she was tiny, five pounds four ounces, that's all she was. I'd say she put more into her now, not being her own and being in need. And she always wanted a little girl, she had lost a little girl. Miscarried, the poor mite. God be good to her, though nothing can replace the loss, I'm not saying that, but she was delighted to have the child. Nucky was only a toddler at the time. I thought his nose would be out of joint but no, there wasn't a bother on him...'

Molly's beautiful brown eyes softened with a smile as she continued, 'Anyway, Noreen was delighted with Mary Rose though she must have been a handful. Her mother's name was Carmichael, as you probably know, Theresa Carmichael. She was Noreen's best friend, oh they had been friends for years, they were very close, she made her promise her faithfully that if anything happened to her that she'd look after the child. I think the woman had a premonition. She knew she wasn't long for this world...'

With an edge to her voice, Maisie then decided she had something to contribute. 'Got pregnant by this fella, she worshipped the ground he walked on, but he fecked off to America and left poor Theresa to fend for herself. She couldn't manage, she had no one to turn to as her family disowned her. She died not long after havin' the child...'

'Now,' said Molly with a nod of affirmation, 'you have the whole story.'

Glancing at the clock, Maisie asked, 'What way would she be comin' in. Mary Rose, I mean?'

'Be the Long Can,' said Molly.

'I don't like her comin' in that way.'

'She always comes that way.'

'I never liked it,' Maisie declared, putting on a face, 'it gives me the willies. It's fecken haunted so it is. She'd be better off comin' up Broad Street.'

Catching Conway's curious look, Molly explained, 'The Long Can, that's what they call it. It was always called that, after some school or other, I don't know the full story behind it. Quakers were involved in it in some way. So I heard tell anyway.'

'Funny oul' name,' said Maisie disapprovingly.

It just so happened that Conway had come across an explanation of its origins on one of his research forays. Unlikely as it seemed, *Long Can* was merely a contraction and a corruption of the name Lancaster. The Lancaster school system, a non-sectarian school, was set up in Limerick by one Joseph Lancaster, a London-born Quaker, as far back as 1806 or thereabouts. But not wishing to seem an imperious know-all, Conway decided to curb his impulse to expound and just smiled stupidly instead.

Maisie interpreted this as pure ignorance, and deemed it necessary to put him in the picture as to its whereabouts.

'It's there, as you go past the Good Shepherd Convent.' Eyeing Conway over her glasses, she added with more than a hint of admonition, 'The Good Shepherd was for those poor misfortunes who found themselves put in the family way, for girls who got into trouble. *He* had a name of being an awful womanizer...'

'Who you talkin' about, Maisie?' Molly inquired.

'The fella what did the dirt on poor Theresa.'

'Ah give over about it, Maisie, that's all in the past now. It does no good goin' on about it. Let it lie.'

But Maisie, stuck in a rut of obstinacy, persisted. 'Throw a stone over the Good Shepherd wall and you'd hit one of his. That's what they used to say.'

'That's all gone now,' said Molly, 'what's past is past...'

'No harm, so it is,' said Maisie peevishly, 'the Laundry's still there, that place is haunted...'

At a loss, Molly exclaimed, 'What is?'

'The fecken Good Shepherd Laundry, of course!' Maisie said impatiently, 'I've heard it said they used to use it as a place of execution.'

'For heaven's sake, whatever do you mean?' asked Molly, entirely unconvinced.

'They used to put people to death there, what do you think I mean. They used to hang people there...'

'The Good Shepherd Laundry? Will you go 'way, Maisie, is it losin' the run of yourself you are?'

In answer to Molly's dismissive comments, Maisie loudly protested, 'Yes. On that very site, where the Laundry is now. I'm talkin' about years ago, long before the Good Shepherd was even there, and you needn't look at me like that.'

'I never heard tell of that,' Molly quietly countered, 'and there's no need to get high over it.'

Maisie was unrepentant, 'Well, that's what I heard now. Just because you haven't heard of it doesn't mean it didn't happen.' Drawing breath a number of times, she pronounced more affably, 'shur the whole of Limerick is haunted.'

Molly responded in kind and said jovially, 'Well, if Saint Patrick got rid of all the snakes, the ESB got rid of all the ghosts.' Noting Conway's blank expression she went on to explain, 'when the Electrification Scheme came in, all the ghosts in Ireland disappeared overnight.'

Seeing Molly's expectant smile, Conway forced a polite if feeble laugh, then the penny dropped and, released from pretence, he allowed himself the luxury of a hearty outburst.

Maisie chuckled away to herself like a grizzling infant while Molly, after snorting delight from a belly laugh, roared, 'God said, let there be light, and the ESB said, let them pay for it!'

The room reverberated with laughter once more, though Conway's was subdued by an eerie conviction that he had heard the words before, somewhere.

All this conviviality brought about such a transformation in Maisie that she began to drop her detached airs, and said animatedly, 'Oh remember the old oil lamps, Molly, and the shadows they used to throw on the walls?'

'God, yes,' said Molly, as if reviewing them in her mind's eye, 'like dancing demons they were, give you the heebie-jeebies they would. And they were awful bad for the chest, those old paraffin lamps. Choked you'd be from the fumes. I wouldn't be surprised if they were responsible for half the sore throats and chest infections that were goin' around back then. The mother was forever runnin' up to the Dispensary for cough bottles...'

'And it was always pink,' Maisie commented, 'the cough medicine was, remember that?'

'Indeed I do,' said Molly, 'strawberry flavour, if I'm not mistaken, horrible stuff it was. You'd want to be bad now to be takin' it.'

All this talk of cough bottles put Conway in mind of his old friend Dopacof, and he was puzzled as to why the elixir held little or no charm for him these days. He had come to the conclusion, with mixed feelings, that his 'addiction' may have been more obsessive compulsion than any real physical dependence. For whatever reason, it seemed he no longer had a need of the sweet placebo.

'You'd be forever trimmin' the wick,' Maisie recollected, 'and the whiff of the paraffin would turn your stomach at times. I much preferred the candles...'

'Whisht...' said Molly, cutting in, 'did I hear the gate go?'

With the assurance of a psychic, Maisie said knowingly, 'That'll be Mary Rose.'

'That'll be her,' Molly confirmed, looking past Maisie to the window, 'here she's in now,' she added, 'I'll get the door.'

Chapter Thirty-one

After tugging down on her blouse to straighten herself out, Molly, walking in her sedate ballerina manner, went out to the hallway and before a knock could be registered opened the front door with a muted salutation.

'Well, you arrived?'

'I did,' came Mary Rose's unmistakable voice in a gasp of laughter.

'Well, God bless the mark,' said Molly, 'were your ears burning? We were just talkin' about you.'

'I hope ye weren't sayin' anything too bad,'

'Now, would we do that?' Molly answered mischievously.

'Is Edward here?' Mary Rose inquired.

Molly's reply was drowned out by the sounds of children playing. In through the hall their voices swelled:

My mother and your mother were hanging out the clothes
My mother gave your mother a dig in the nose
Did she mean it or did she not?
What colour blood came from her nose?
Red, blue, purple, yellow, brown, green...

Conway was fondly remembering how Mary Rose had explained the protocol behind this rather belligerent skipping rhyme, '...you'd have to list all the colours you could think of and you were out if you couldn't think of any more...'

As soon as Molly shut the front door, the hue and cry faded to a background murmur.

All light, bright and breezy, Mary Rose popped her head in the doorway of the sitting room and gave Conway a meaningful look, 'Hi,' she said, all smiles, then untying her ponytail, she shook out her golden hair. To Conway, there was always an aura of the exotic about Mary Rose, but now the air seemed to bristle with ions. The whole room seemed invigorated by her presence. Like being near a waterfall, or a refreshing sea breeze. His heart had leapt on hearing her voice at the door. Now it did cartwheels. Was it possible that this windblown, elemental creature had eyes only for him?

'Hi,' he answered with a smile. Only he knew that this seemingly casual response, this two-lettered, monosyllabic greeting was uttered more as a fervent prayer that it would always be so.

Turning to Maisie, Mary Rose cheerily asked, 'Hi, Maisie, and how are you?'

'Not too bad,' said Maisie, giving the impression that she was cautiously optimistic.

'She's off the zimmer now an' all,' Molly confided.

'I am,' said Maisie, then changing the subject, she said quaintly, 'well, you came. Did you bring your bike at all?'

'It's outside under the window,' Mary Rose informed her.

'Why don't you bring it into the hall for fear it be taken.'

'There's no fear of it. There's a lock on it anyway.'

'I was thinkin' you came be shank's mare, you being late an' all,' said Maisie, then tucking in her chin, she remarked, 'God, you're all decked out in your gear. Give us a look at you. Turn around there...'

'Do,' said Molly.

Like a recalcitrant child Mary Rose said, 'Stop, will ye!'

'Aaah go on, can't you,' Molly coaxed, 'turn around there a minute and give us a look at you.'

With a sigh of reluctance, Mary Rose did a quick turn to show off her outfit.

After shrewdly reviewing the cream blouse with its puff sleeves, the ruby-red bolero jacket, the medium faded jeans and the impractical, open toe sandals, Maisie declared, 'You look like a bullfighter in that getup.'

'Thanks a lot,' said Mary Rose, with an indignant laugh.

'Why haven't you on a proper coat?' Molly admonished, 'that bit of a waistcoat wouldn't cover your navel. You must be perished with the cowld on that bike of yours.' Then, taking hold of Mary Rose's arms, she exclaimed, 'mother agawd almighty, your poor arms are freezing...'

'Nah,' Mary Rose reassured, 'it's lovely out, so it is.'

'Young ones today,' Molly continued, 'ye're forever goin' around half-dressed, so ye are.'

'You're lookin' for your end, mind,' said Maisie, with a reproachful frown.

'Stop goin' on, will ye?' Mary Rose protested, 'ye're like two mother hens, I swear.'

'All right,' Molly warned, 'but if you get your death out of it, don't say you weren't told.'

Pointing the finger at Conway, Mary Rose said, 'Look at him, and he in his shirtsleeves, why don't ye give out to him?'

It was true that since his inauspicious dip in the Shannon, Conway had relaxed his dress regime to some extent, now preferring to travel light. Within reason of course.

'Never mind him, he's a man,' said Maisie.

Wide-eyed with indignation, Mary Rose asked, 'What's that got to do with anything?'

'He had a decent coat on him, for one thing,' Molly argued, 'and he didn't come be bike.' Then, deciding she was wasting her breath, she asked, 'What kept you anyway?'

'I had to do a message for Mam.'

'How is she?'

'Grand.'

Observing the interaction between Mary Rose and her aunts, Conway was left in no doubt as to the great fondness they had for each other. That she loved them was obvious.

That they were proud of her, and that they loved her, was also obvious. Maybe that was why he felt so at home in their company, for when someone loves the someone you love, there is bound to be affiliation.

'How's all the lads?' Maisie asked.

'There's a fear of them.'

'How's Tubbs? Did he get his booster vaccination yet?'

'He did,' said Mary Rose, 'he had the life frightened out of him by Bobsy, telling him he was goin' to get a big hot injection. Who's been frightening the child, Mam said. I was only jokin' him, said Bobsy. You didn't find it so funny yourself, said Mam, we needed a bucket and mop for you with all the crying you did.'

Molly laughed, 'It's true for her,' then, addressing Mary Rose, she added, 'come on, we'll go and get the tea.'

After offering his help, Conway was informed nicely but firmly that he was to sit where he was and relax for himself while Molly and Mary Rose sorted things out. He could keep Maisie company while they set about bringing in the tea.

After declaring, 'Do you think the young fella has nothan better to do than to be talkin' to an oul' one like me and keepin' me in conversation,' Maisie proceeded to ramble on in her own peculiar way while Conway played his part of stoker with appropriate hums and haws, nods of affirmation and the odd word or two. But he very soon lost track of Maisie's convoluted tales. With their twists and turns, asides and overlaps, it was impossible to gauge where one began or one ended. He listened with incomprehension, and a certain amount of awe, to Maisie's astonishing facility for language.

'...they came in on top of me, says she, and I in the middle of the wash, they're always rubbin' me up the wrong way, and he wasn't sittin' down two minutes when he was lookin' at his watch. Men, they have no patience. Anyway, she was tellin' me that Fiona met her outside Tylers, standin' over a basket of shoes. Are you buyin', says Fiona. I haven't a notion, says she. I have more shoes than Imelda what's-her-name. Standin' in ousha the rain she was. Anyway, didn't she call into the sister on the way and dragged me along with her. This was a Tuesday. The last time I was there, there was pandemonium. We were no sooner in the door when she started givin' out to the kids. The sister. The five of them and they like steps of stairs. Only playin' with the fire irons they were. Gimme that, she said, takin' the shovel off the youngest fella. Do you know what it is but ye'd wear the patience of a saint. I won't have a thing in the house left with ye. Carry on like that now and ye'll get what's comin' to ye. They weren't payin' her one blind bish a notice. Next thing, anyway, didn't himself arrive on the scene given out oul' guff out of him...'

'Who?' asked Molly, who to Conway's amazement had, seemingly, been following every word that Maisie had said while still in conversation with Mary Rose.

'Who,' Maisie continued, 'only Jimmy, of course, looking for his supper. I have enough to do for, says she, and look after the house, and Una is above in St John's in intensive care. Then she was tellin' us that Fiona had been in Guiney's the day before. Givin' out over the vests, she was, they had them in every size goin' but they were out of them be the time she got there and all they had left were the small sizes, they wouldn't cover your belly button...'

'When was this?' Molly inquired from the kitchen.

'This was a Wednesday comin' from John's,' said Maisie, not missing a beat, '...goin' like hot cakes they were, and didn't she bring up about the phooshagraf. I'll have that blown up for you, Jimmy told her. How many times have she been told not to be givin' that fella anything. Anyway, he couldn't find it in the heel of the hunt, done away with it I expect. Or lost it. I was sorry I ever mentioned it, and I only said it for the want of makin' conversation. Then she was tellin' me she bought a bit a beef for the dinner and she could be cookin' it yet, it wor that tough. She'd left it in a pot of boilin' water while she popped out to go to confession, and when she returned wasn't the place full a steam. Are there no windows in the house, she said to the young one

350

and she lookin' at her, you fecken eejit, says she, do I have to drum everything into you...'

While Maisie continued with her saga, the table was set with the finest bone china, and the yellow teapot, brought in ceremoniously by Mary Rose, took its place at the centre of the spread. A fine spread it was too, with bread and butter and lettuce and tomatoes and cheese and ham and potato salad. As if crowning some important dignitary, Molly made a great show of placing the rainbow coloured cosy over the teapot.

Exchanging knowing looks with Mary Rose, she said, 'I'll bring in yours now, Maisie.'

Monitoring the wheeling in of the serving trolley, Maisie suddenly stopped speaking for a moment to ask, '...is that thing gone all scaways again?'

'It's not, it's just your imagination.'

'Well, it looks scaways to me.'

'It can't be, I've tightened up all the nuts. It's solid out. Like the Rock of Gibraltar on wheels, so it is.'

'If you say so,' said Maisie doubtfully, then casting a wary look down at her plate, she asked, 'What's that?'

'What's what?'

'That,' said Maisie, pointing an accusing finger.

'Potato salad...' Molly stressed, '...what does it look like, what's your gripe now?'

'I'm gone off it. It repeats on me.'

'Since when?'

'Since the last time. The other day, if you remember. I had to leave it. It doesn't agree with me.'

'I don't remember you ever saying anything of the sort, but never mind...' said Molly, then she added, 'now is there anything else you don't like, or doesn't agree with you?'

'No.'

'Well, that makes a change, thanks be to God and all his saints for small mercies.'

'Shur, can't you give it to the young fella there,' Maisie suggested magnanimously.

Before Conway could say he had enough on his plate, Molly had transferred the unwanted potato salad to it with a deft stroke of a knife and he found himself saying, 'Thanks,' and Molly saying, 'You're welcome, love,' and Maisie saying, 'He's more than welcome.'

Finding it all highly amusing, Mary Rose took her place alongside Conway and teased, 'Is everything satisfactory and to your liking, Edward?'

'Everything is just fine, Mary Rose,' he said with a grin.

Mary Rose then shouted to the kitchen, 'Will you come in, Molly, and sit down and have your tea.'

'I'll be in now in a minute.'

'She's forever on the go,' Maisie said loudly, without a trace of self-consciousness.

'I'd be waitin' a long time for you to get off your behind to do anything,' Molly roared.

'You know I can't go at the minute,' Maisie roared back.

'You're never without an arse or an elbow,' came Molly's ready reply.

Dismissing this indictment, Maisie said, as cool as you like, 'You won't have to put up with me for long more. I'm not long for this world, so I'm not.'

'Will you listen to the creaking door,' said Molly, on her return, then announced, as pleasantly as ever, 'there's cake for afters.'

Now that they were all seated, and settled down to the meal, the conversation ebbed and flowed between mouthfuls of food and sips of tea. The fire burbled brightly as the Angelus rang out from the Cathedral, and Molly, after a quick glance at the mantelpiece, stated, 'that clock is nearly five minutes slow.'

'What date is today?' asked Maisie.

'Today is the seventh,' said Molly, 'it's hard to credit that the lads are back at school already.'

'It is,' said Maisie, then after she swallowed a morsel, she asked of Mary Rose, 'when are you back?'

'The twentieth...'

Her fork chasing a wedge of tomato to the edge of her plate, Molly said, 'between their uniforms now and their books and everything, it must cost a fortune. I don't know how people keep goin' today, so I don't, with the cost of everything, not sayin' that we had much in our day...' She stopped, the skewered tomato held poised before her, then went on, 'in fact we had very little, but do you know, we were just as happy...'

Maisie pursed her lips in preparation, and in a voice full of reminiscence, she began, 'One pound of mixed biscuits on Sunday for the four o'clock tea, Mikado, Kimberley and Coconut Creams. And Marietta. And Ginger Nuts...'

What on earth was Maisie talking about? Conway asked himself, sure that this flibbertigibbet way of saying out loud whatever popped into her head would at least incur some disapproving comment. Instead Molly picked up on Maisie's theme.

'I remember when I was small,' said she, 'the sugar used to be sold loose, in a willow pattern paper bag. We used to go to Barry's shop for it. I used to sing that song, you know the one, ...*sugar in the mornin', sugar in the evenin', sugar at suppertime*. I thought it was specially written for me...'

'You were an awful eejit,' Maisie said with a disparaging fondness.

'I was,' Molly admitted, laughing.

'That was a lovely song,' said Maisie, 'Vera Cronin used to sing it. Oooh, she had a lovely voice, so she had. Out on her own she was.'

Incredibly, Molly now began to sing, and, even more incredibly, Maisie joined in.

Sugar in the mornin', sugar in the evenin', sugar at suppertime, be my little sugar and love me all the time, put your arms around me and swear by stars above, you'll be mine forever in a heaven of love, oh sugar in the mornin', sugar in the evenin', sugar at suppertime...

Her whole face alight and her eyes smiling, Mary Rose said, 'Ye're stone mad the pair of ye, so ye are...'

'Mad as hatters,' said Molly.

'Cracked we are,' said Maisie, laughing.

It was one of those magical and spontaneous moments. Conway had to admit that he was reminded of the madcap tea party in *Alice's Adventures in Wonderland*. He wondered which daft character he might be. The Dormouse sprung to mind. He would not have been surprised if he ended up in the teapot.

After the laughter settled down, Molly said, 'Talkin' of, Barry's shop put me in mind of it. Do you remember the shopping list? Ah 'tis all changed now but when I worked in the shop people would be comin' in for small things. Back then, it was two eggs, three Sweet Afton, or a Woodbine, two slices of corned beef, brawn or sliced ham, small tin of peas, quarter pound of butter...'

'A quarter pound of butter?' Mary Rose was incredulous.

'Yessss,' said Molly, with a triumphant *you don't know the half of it* reproach in her voice, 'people didn't have the money then, they couldn't afford it. There were no supermarkets back then in them days. Nearly everybody was on tick. You'd settle up at the end of the week or next payday, if you could. Making do from one week to the next you were, trying to stretch your money. People don't know they're born today.'

'And you'd have kids comin' in chancin' their arm,' said Maisie, then putting on a childish voice, she went on, 'my mudder said I could have sweets and to put them on the book,' she laughed, then added, 'but there was no sweets on the book...'

Molly took a clip from her hair and placed it between her lips. Then gathering up a strand of hair that had come loose, she clipped it back into place and, as she settled it with a pat of her hand, she began laughing to herself.

'What are you laughing at?' said Mary Rose.

'I was just thinkin' of Nucky when he was small, in the shop. Give him three carmels, says I, and Nucky, with an oul' puss on him says, *don't want them*. Well, what do you want, says I, *cleevtopee*, he says, the misfortune, he couldn't pronounce the word, he couldn't say *Cleeves Toffee*. Give him a square of that so, says I, that'll do him, that might stop his gob for a while.'

Molly laughed again, then shaking a thumb in Mary Rose's direction, she said, 'And this one here had to have ice cream after havin' all her teeth out, under gas, if you don't mind. And fine straight teeth she have now, god bless her. Gummy she was. I can tell you, the tooth fairy was robbed from her, he nearly went bankrupt so he did...'

'Remember the ice cream wafers?' said Mary Rose, 'You used always get me one.'

'Oh god I do, thrupenny wafer, sixpenny wafer, shillingy wafer, and the roller with sections marked off on it. And then there was the lucky bags, remember them?'

'There was nothin' in them, they were a waste of money,' said Maisie sourly, 'lucky bags me arse.'

A roll call of consumer items and icons from the past now followed, prompting a random auction of memories.

'Golf Ball bubble gum, two for a penny,'

'Black Jack, Macaroon Bars and Trigger Bars,'

'Cough No More Bars,'

'Andrews Liver Salts,'

'Rot your guts drinkin' that,' Maisie informed everyone.

'Mrs Cullen's Powders,'

'Seidlitz Powders,'

'Beechams Powders,'

'Slabs of rib, with the salt caked all over it,'

'Eyebones, breastbones, backbones,'

'Skirts and kidneys,'

'Fish of a Friday,'

'Crubeens,'

'Packet and tripe,'

'You'd go over to Treacy's for that,'

'I'd almost forgotten,' said Molly wistfully.

With an air of regret, Maisie said, 'it's all la-di-dah now, people are gone too grand and sophisticated...'

Molly was in agreement, 'It's true for you,' she said, 'the kids today would look at you if you served them up eyebones or backbones or breastbones. But faith, we were only too glad, we were, to get them...'

As the flickering remains of nostalgia faded into thin air, Maisie turned to Molly and said, 'I meant to say it to you, you'd never guess who I bumped into the other day, only Lizzie Lipton, above in Cathedral Place. I was tryin' to duck her but she spotted me, she came runnin' up the road, she did, she'd wither you, she would, delayin' me and I hadn't time to cross myself, I was pepperin', so I was, that I'd be late again for the doctor's appointment, and didn't she have a prescription from the doctor but she couldn't make head nor tail of it. I can't even read what's on that, says she to me, now I don't know what the effin jaysus is wrong with me, she says, it could be anything. He gives you the prescription, says she, and doesn't even look up. And she laughs out loud like a hyena. The way she do...'

'She nuroshic, that one,' Molly pronounced, 'he'd want to be givin' her billiard balls, the poor misfortune. I don't think she was ever the full shilling.'

Maisie continued, 'what ones are you on now, she says to me. The red and grey ones, says I. I'm on them as well, she says and Roche 5...'

'Come're to me,' Molly interrupted, 'wasn't she due to have her gall bladder out?'

'She was,' Maisie said with a nod, 'and she was hopin' that she'd get Dr Belling.'

'Never mind that Dr Belling,' commented Molly, 'he's an alarmist. Too fond of the knife, so he is.'

This last reference to the knife seemed to remind Molly of her 'afters' for she immediately asked, 'Who's for cake?'

'I wouldn't say no,' said Mary Rose.

'Will you have some, Edward?' asked Molly, then added, in response to his non-committal smile, 'of course you will.'

Turning to Maisie, she then inquired, 'And how about you, Maisie?'

Casually and enigmatically, Maisie answered, 'Ah, I don't know should I...'

'Do you or don't you, Maisie?' said Molly tersely, 'I can't stand here all day waitin' for you to make up your fecken mind. Jesus, but you'd wear the patience of a saint. Do you know that?'

Not to be rushed, Maisie made a face as if considering her options.

Fit to explode, Molly asked, 'Well?'

'I'll have a half slice so, if it's not too much trouble.'

And so the cake was brought in, with Molly and Mary Rose doing the honours. Several cups of tea and several slices of cake later, they had a visitor. From out of nowhere came the menacing and investigative hum of a wasp. With designs on Conway's cake, it made several tilts before he managed to shoo it away. Its persistence gone, it swooned off towards the window.

'There's a lot of them around lately,' said Maisie.

'I betchu anything,' said Molly, 'that's the fella that was plaguing me in the kitchen,' then, with a plea in her voice, she said, 'Edward, would you ever be a dote and open that window and let him out?'

'I will of course,' said Conway, charmed at the idea that he had even the potential of being a dote to anyone, 'no problem,' he added, laying down his cake and rising to the challenge.

'Mind he doesn't sting you,' warned Molly.

'Well, he'll only do it the once,' Maisie piped up, 'they die after they stingin' you, you know.'

How comforting, thought Conway, apart from the pain, there was always the outside chance they'd be seeing him on the floor with anaphylactic shock. Putting his thoughts aside, he said, almost apologetically, 'Actually, that's not strictly true. Wasps can sting repeatedly...'

Forgetting himself, Conway now slipped into a cosy declaration, 'You have to feel sorry for them,' said he, 'the drones and the workers will all die. Only the queen will survive to start a nest again next year. This one would be a worker, now out of a job since the nest has broken up. They like sweet things, they're vegetarian, though they feed their grubs with flies and caterpillars and things...'

'Edward, puleese!' Molly shrieked, 'You're putting me right off me cake!'

'Jaysus, I'm gone right off mine, so I am,' said Maisie.

His face a map of apology, Conway mumbled, 'Sorry...'

'Yes, Edward,' said Mary Rose, shaking with laughter, 'thanks for sharing your knowledge of wasp cuisine.'

'Don't mind her, Edward,' said Molly, 'she's always feck actin', so she is.'

'It's not polite to snigger,' chided Maisie.

Still laughing, but endeavouring to control herself, Mary Rose protested weakly, 'I'm not sniggering, honest.'

'No, only half,' said Molly.

Reaching in behind the net curtain, Conway undid the latch and pulled down on the upper window frame.

'It's a bit stiff sometimes,' said Molly, and indeed it was, but eventually it slid down with a rumble, and, as soon as it did, the noise of the road came rushing in, along with a grand breeze that Conway was very grateful for. Gathering up the folds of the curtain on which the wasp had settled, he gently lifted the creature towards the gap and, after a few shakes of encouragement, the wasp took flight.

In response to the barrel organ rendition of *Popeye the Sailor Man* that was coming in the window loud and clear, Maisie said with annoyance, 'Mr Whippy, what's he doing sellin' ice cream this hour of the night? Has he lost the run of himself?'

'Maybe he's had a row with Mrs Whippy,' Mary Rose suggested with a giggling laugh.

'You're full of your fun, aren't you,' Molly answered with a wry smile.

'Him and his ice-cream van,' Maisie added, as Conway reluctantly shut the window, 'he have all the fecken dogs in the scheme howlin' with his plinky plonky music.' Then, as if to justify her point of view, she stressed, 'the racket he's making...'

Wiping crumbs from her blouse, Molly intoned, 'Ah leave the poor man alone, he's only tryin' to earn a living.'

'I suppose so,' Maisie conceded, then added, 'that fecken wasp will have a field day.'

Not displeased with the stir of amusement she evoked, Maisie continued in a more serious vein, 'Remember I was tellin' you, Molly, that Mr Kernan died, god be good to him, well, Nora Newsom was tellin' me she was looking out the window, she was, and she said to herself, there must be a big funeral going on, be the size of the mourning cars gone up the road. Wasn't it poor Mr Kernan. He was very low for a few days before, and Sister Anastasia was tellin' her that the nurse found it very hard to get a pulse that mornin', the poor misfortunate man was dyin' all the time...'

'When was she tellin' you this?'

'Only the other day, she was on her way to the chemist. She had just been there gettin' her antibioshics and sleepin' tablets but she was handed out the wrong ones and she was bringin' them back. That's when I met her...'

'What age was he, Maisie?' Molly inquired.

'Who?'

'Mr Kernan, of course, who do you think?'

'Well, she's seventy-six anyway,' said Maisie, 'he must have been touchin' eighty, at least.' Then she added, as the thought occurred to her, 'In England now, they go in a lot for crimination...'

'Don't mind what they be doin' in Engaland,' said Molly loudly, 'they do all sorts in that godless country.'

'They're runnin' oush of space, sure they have to,' Maisie pointed out indignantly.

'Well, I don't agree with that now at all,' Molly persisted, 'it's no way for a Christian to be buried.'

'His poor wife have the diabeetees, you know...' Maisie informed her.

'Who?' Molly asked.

'Johnny Kernan's wife...the man what's dead. Ah jaysus, aren't you listening to me at all. Or his widow, I should say, and Nora Newsom was tellin' me she knew a woman next door who had it as well, and she was scourged from it. It'd be an aise to her, she said, if she kicked the bucket.'

'Don't be talkin' to me about that woman,' said Molly derisively, 'she doesn't know what she be talkin' about half the time.'

After some quiet nurturing of her own thoughts, Maisie suddenly came out with, 'Wasn't her daughter married to the fella in the Carasmashics, or whatever the fecken hell they calls it these days?'

'Charismatics,' Mary Rose helpfully prompted.

'All that fecken singin' and dancin' and clappin' hands,' Maisie said, 'a holy show they're makin' of themselves, that's what they are.'

'That's all the go now,' Molly confessed, 'I can't fathom it myself. I suppose it takes all kinds.'

'Half of them are round the twist, so they are,' Maisie concluded.

'What did I want to say to ye now,' said Molly, putting fingers to her lips, 'it's after goin' out of me head...' After some drumming of her fingers and some thoughtful pouting, she went on, 'what was it at all, I'm forever forgettin' things. Ah, now I remember, there's a bike out there in the shed. I was thinkin' it might be an idea if Edward was to have the use of it. The two of ye could go off cyclin' together. It belonged to my father, the Lord have mercy on him. You're welcome to it, Edward. It's only gathering dust where it is, it's out in the shed doin' nothing. A sup of oil and a bit of a clean is all it needs and you'll be flying it.'

'That bocady ould thing?' said Maisie sceptically, taking on an expression that might have suggested she had a bad taste in her mouth.

'What's it to you?' Molly asked.

'I have no objection to the boy havin' it,' said Maisie, 'he's more than welcome to it. That old bicycle has been in and out of Pashie Dolan's more often than the man himself.'

'Who?' asked Mary Rose.

'Pashie Dolan,' Maisie explained, 'the fella with the three balls. The pawn shop below in Broad Street. Ah, it's long gone now.'

Not making a great job of disguising her amusement, Molly said, laughing, 'Maisie, the things you come out with. In front of the young fella an' all. Is it tryin' to embarrass the misfortunate boy you are?'

With a haughty pretence, Maisie answered, 'I didn't say anything out of the way. It's only your durty mind that's workin' overtime.'

In response to Molly's laughter, Maisie decided to carry on mischievously, 'he had three balls, over his shop they were. I don't know how many times the father went down to redeem that bike...'

'What do you mean, *redeem*?' asked Mary Rose.

'That's what they called it,' explained Molly, 'when you paid in the money to get back whatever it was you pawned in the first place.'

Conway was not embarrassed. In normal circumstances such ribald remarks by such company, and in such company, might well elicit an anaemic blush, but the mention of the three balls drew his particular attention. For the briefest of moments he thought Maisie was in some way privy to the comatose escapades he had endured with the Medici spheres and was about to disclose some obscure secret. But nothing of the sort was forthcoming and the moment passed.

'I wonder what ever happened to them,' Molly asked, then added, for the sake of clarification, 'the balls I mean...'

'Maybe they were redeemed,' Conway suggested with a smile, 'maybe someone redeemed them...'

Molly and Mary Rose gave him a very old-fashioned look.

'You never know,' said Maisie cheerfully, 'stranger things have happened.'

Chapter Thirty-two

Nucky stood square, his legs spread for balance as he held the reins lightly. With the cart lightened of its load, Gypsy strolled leisurely across Thomond Bridge. Overhead, a heron was making its way upriver. Its flight remained ponderous until, becoming wary of the bridge, it swished the air with sudden downbeats of its wings and hitched itself higher and away from prying eyes. Down below, the tide was in full and would soon be on the turn.

'Any luck, Joe?' Nucky shouted to a lone angler who sat perched on the parapet of the bridge with legs dangling over the side.

'Not a blessed thing,' came the reply from Joe, a ruddy complexioned man who was kitted out in fishing regalia and mirrored sunglasses.

'Maybe your licence is ourra date,' Nucky suggested.

Elbowing aside his shoulder bag, Joe laughed and said, 'You might be right, Nucky. Never thought of that. But if anyone asks, I'm fishing for glass eels and periwinkles.'

Joe's words were met with a nod and a wink.

On approaching the turn-off for Verdant Place, Nucky brought the cart out in a wide arc to take the turn, forcing oncoming traffic to stop in the process.

'Hold on,' he shouted to Mikey, who lay sprawled against the three remaining bags of blocks at the back of the cart.

With a shake of his head Gypsy rattled his bridle and pricked up his ears, as if to say he had everything under control. He could do it blindfold, never mind the blinkers. After all, he had done the manoeuvre hundreds of times.

As engines were revved for imminent departure, King John's Castle towered above the scene like some dark and disapproving authority. Imperturbable, Gypsy pulled the cart neatly through the narrow breach that separated Pain's Folly from the bridge. They were on the downslope now as the road fell away and they began to pick up speed. With a coaxing reminder of 'hike' from Nucky, Gypsy slowed to a more comfortable pace.

Elevated high above the strand wall, Nucky looked out over the river. In the far distance the Clare hills appeared to be fading behind the veil of evening as mists drifted over wooded regions. Off to the west, the distant clouds, floating high and vaporous, appeared like violet blue sandbars. Below them, a rose-coloured sky blushed with the afterglow of the setting sun.

From out of Thomondgate, a dark undulating ribbon of starlings flew high and wide about the sky. Sweeping over the distillery, the flock headed across the river and out over the weir. Above the Island Bank and the shrine they trailed, before veering to the right, where, after hovering wraithlike, they descended en masse on the warren of chimney pots that adorned the Villiers Homes. All atwitter, they then began the process of settling down for the night.

To his right, Nucky could see the Gothic spires of old St Munchin's. Wallflowers and valerian sprouted from crevices in the stonework of its high boundary wall. Above the rim, casting their shadows, the taller headstones and table tombs could be seen.

Mikey, who had remained curiously quiet, now found his voice. '...one hundard and turty-five, one hundard and turty-six, one hundard and turty-seven, one hundard and turty-eight, one hundard and turty-nine, one hundard and forty, one hundard and forty-one...'

'What the fuck are you doin' back there?' Nucky inquired over his shoulder.

Scrutinizing a block of wood he held between his knees, and tracing an index finger slowly across its surface, Mikey stopped momentarily and, without looking up, said casually,

'Countin' rings...'

'What?'

Frowning, as he tried to hold his concentration, Mikey continued his calculations in silence. Finally, he announced in triumph, '...one hundard and forty-seven!'

'You can tell,' he went on eagerly, 'how old the tree was by countin' the rings. Conway wor tellin' Bobsy and he wor tellin' me. It's cinchy to do. One hundard and forty-seven years old this one is. I counted them all. And he wor sayin' you could tell what the weather wor like back then by lookin' at the rings and how big they wor...'

'One hundard and forty-seven?' Nucky said doubtfully, 'that can't be right, where did you get that from? Shur, that was only a branch...'

'I counted them all, shur,' said Mikey confidently, then asked, 'where did this one come from, Nucky?'

'What?'

'The tree,' said Mikey, 'where did it come from?'

'St Munchin's College. That came down in the storm. A big shaggin' thing. Fell right across the Red Path. Made shit of the wall. You'd want to see the roots that was on that tree, big as a fucken house they were. That was some tree, boy...'

'How much did it cost you?'

'Not a bob,' said Nucky, yawning, 'they paid us to take it away. Never pay for anything, Mikey, when you don't havta. Speshally if it's free.'

Hearing the crunching bite of an apple, Nucky asked with hopeful suspicion, 'Have you apples back there?'

'Yes, I have one apple, delicious too,' said Mikey, 'I will leave you the heart...'

Nucky was less than impressed, 'You're a generous soul, Mikey, do you know that? I wouldn't want to put you out.'

Mikey answered with another crunch.

Passing a line of ancient trees enclosed by ornate railings, they drew level with the entrance to the Water Passage. The air, funnelled through the narrow confines of the passage, created a freshening breeze and leaves rustled overhead like innumerable whispers. A flock of homing pigeons wheeled about the sky in a tight formation. The smell of cooking was in the air and a dog barked half-heartedly in the distance.

Heading towards the old swimming baths, Nucky looked up at the swallows that were arrayed on the telephone wires like pegs on a clothesline.

'I love to see those fuckers go,' he said casually.

'Go where, Nucky?' asked Mikey.

'Are you fucken tick?' Nucky asked jovially.

Mikey considered the question. 'No,' he said simply.

'Well, you must be, those fuckers are off to Afraca...'

'How ju know?' challenged Mikey.

Nucky rolled his shoulders and said, 'never mind how I know, I just know.' Then, after some hesitation, he added, '...I read it in a book, all right? I love to see 'em go because it means the summer is over, and winter's not far off.'

His disgruntled features begging to differ, Mikey said, 'I like the summer...'

'Well, I prefer the winter.'

'Why?' asked Mikey.

'Because, people buy more coal. That's why.'

'Oh yeah,' said Mikey, his eyes narrowing to slits as he considered the implications, 'I think I prefer the winter too.'

8182922R00217

Printed in Great Britain
by Amazon.co.uk, Ltd.,
Marston Gate.